Betrayal of Blood

by
LESLIE SWARTZ

Copyright © 2024 by Leslie Swartz

ISBN: 9798322136279

Design & Formatting by LunaCco Design

All rights reserved.

No part of this book may be reproduced or used in any manner without the written consent of the copyright owner.

This is a work of fiction. Names, characters, places, and incidents are either the product of the author's imagination or are used fictitiously. Any resemblance to actual persons, living or dead, businesses, companies, or events or locales is entirely coincidental.

Playlist		VII
Trigger Warning		VIII
Part One - Violet		
1.	Chapter 1	3
2.	Chapter 2	13
3.	Chapter 3	17
4.	Chapter 4	20
5.	Chapter 5	26
6.	Chapter 6	32
7.	Chapter 7	37
8.	Chapter 8	43
9.	Chapter 9	48
10.	Chapter 10	51
11.	Chapter 11	58
12.	Chapter 12	65
13.	Chapter 13	73
14.	Chapter 14	78
15.	Chapter 15	83
16.	Chapter 16	89

17. Chapter 17   95
18. Chapter 18   96
19. Chapter 19   101
20. Chapter 20   107
21. Chapter 21   116
22. Chapter 22   123
23. Chapter 23   132
24. Chapter 24   138
25. Chapter 25   146
26. Chapter 26   154
27. Chapter 27   158
28. Chapter 28   162
29. Chapter 29   167

Part 2 - Rue

30. Chapter 30   172
31. Chapter 31   186
32. Chapter 32   193
33. Chapter 33   202
34. Chapter 34   207
35. Chapter 35   218
36. Chapter 36   223
37. Chapter 37   227
38. Chapter 38   230
39. Chapter 39   233
40. Chapter 40   238

41.	Chapter 41	242
42.	Chapter 42	244
43.	Chapter 43	246
44.	Chapter 44	251
45.	Chapter 45	258
46.	Chapter 46	264
47.	Chapter 47	271
48.	Chapter 48	277
49.	Chapter 49	279
50.	Chapter 50	280
51.	Chapter 51	286
52.	Chapter 52	289
53.	Chapter 53	293
54.	Chapter 54	297
55.	Chapter 55	305
56.	Chapter 56	308
57.	Chapter 57	312

Part 3 - Ophelia

58.	Chapter 58	316
59.	Chapter 59	321
60.	Chapter 60	327
61.	Chapter 61	339
62.	Chapter 62	345
63.	Chapter 63	348
64.	Chapter 64	354

65. Chapter 65	361
66. Chapter 66	366
67. Chapter 67	371
68. Chapter 68	379
69. Chapter 69	387
70. Chapter 70	393
71. Chapter 71	398
72. Chapter 72	402
73. Chapter 73	406
74. Chapter 74	415
75. Chapter 75	422
76. Chapter 76	428
77. Chapter 77	434
78. Chapter 78	437
79. Chapter 79	443
80. Chapter 80	450
81. Chapter 81	456
82. Chapter 82	465
About Author	472
Also By	473

Playlist

All Mine - Portishead
Mouth - Bush
Sonnet 18 - David Gilmour
Extraordinary - Liz Phair
There She Goes - Sixpence None The Richer
Love It When You Hate Me - Avril Lavigne featuring blackbear
She Knows It - Maggie Lindemann
Where Is My Mind - Pixies
Only Love Can Hurt Like This - Paloma Faith
Uninvited - Alanis Morissette
Until I Found You - Stephen Sanchez
Alone - Heart
Work - Pop Evil
Don't Wait - Dashboard Confessional
Everybody Talks - Neon Trees
Enjoy The Silence - Depeche Mode

Trigger Warning

WARNING | The following book contains topics and scenes of:
Domestic Violence
Murder
Mentions of SA
Religious Abuse
Drug & Alcohol Use
And Graphic Sex Scenes

If you have sensitivities to these topics please proceed with caution!

Part 1
Violet

Chapter 1

Flames licked the vampire's back as he clawed his way up the wall, his fingertips aching as they broke through the stone. His ears were ringing from the thunderous boom of the initial explosion but he could still make out the muffled screams of the others, dozens of vampires desperate to escape the fiery hell they'd found themselves confined to. With the windows and door blocked by flame-thrower-wielding madmen, there was only one way out.

Kenton climbed to the ceiling, the room now filled with so much smoke, he couldn't see his fist in front of him as he punched through the clay-tiled roof. When he'd made a hole big enough, he squeezed through it, crawling across to the edge of the over three-hundred-year-old building. Lying on his stomach, he coughed, hacking up pitch-dark phlegm onto the terracotta tile. He rubbed his stinging eyes, his vision adjusting to the moonlight.

In the distance, he saw a white van with blacked-out windows parked near the edge of the forest. Below, one of the firestarters lowered his weapon. "Damn!" he shouted. "I'm out of petrol!"

From the other side of the building, Kenton heard another man call back, "Me, too! You got any of them HG 85s?"

"In the van!"

Kenton flattened himself against the roof to not be seen as the first man marched toward the vehicle several yards away. From behind, he heard someone climb out of the hole he'd created, coughing as they grabbed his leg. He looked back, relieved to see his friend and owner of the now-destroyed club army crawling his way next to him.

"Alexander," Kenton whispered. "It's good to see you alive."

"You, as well."

Kenton put his finger to his lips, instructing his friend to remain quiet. He then pointed to the van where the first man was opening the sliding door to retrieve his grenades. Alexander nodded in understanding.

"There's one more on the back door." Kenton's irises went dark, his fangs descending. "Take him out as stealthily as you can and when this one gets close, I'll--"

He was cut off by the high-pitched screams of victims, their burning bodies racing through the unattended door. They ran in all directions, some escaping into the woods, others falling to the ground, succumbing to the flames.

"Oi!" the man at the back door shouted. The vampires watched as he came around the building, chasing down the injured as they fled. The first man pulled the pin of a grenade and tossed it at two vampires that had made it to the treeline. It blew, littering the grass with blood and charred body parts. "Nice one," the second man said as he neared the van. More vampires staggered from the building, the men hurling grenades in their direction as fast as they could pull the pins.

"We can't just hide up here like cowards," Alexander said, his nails scraping the tile.

"No," Kenton agreed, scanning the area. "I count fourteen vampires between us and them. Plenty to distract from our plan."

"We have a plan?"

"Yes. I'll go left, you'll go right. We'll then dash for the trees and meet at center, just behind the van. You'll then take the bearded one while I interrogate the other. Are you ready?"

He bared his fangs, the moonlight twinkling in his forest-green eyes as they went black. "Absolutely."

They nodded to one another and broke away, disappearing from the roof in a flash. Their blurs went unnoticed by the preoccupied men who continued to assault the fleeing vampires. None were spared as grenades flew and bodies exploded. By the time Kenton and Alexander made it to the van, the rest were lost, nothing but flaming piles of limbs and ash where they once stood.

The two again nodded to each other before leaping over the van, knocking the men to the ground. Alexander wasted no time in tearing the second man's throat out with his teeth and guzzling the blood that flowed from the gaping wound.

CHAPTER 1

Kenton, meanwhile, gripped the first by his collar and slammed him into the side of the van, disarming him at supernatural speed.

Alexander dropped the man's body and wiped his mouth on his sleeve. "I'll check for survivors."

"Do be careful," Kenton told him, his eyes never leaving the man's defiant face. "What *do* we have here?"

"Let go of me, monster!"

"You call *me* monster? *I'm* not the one slaughtering innocent people in the middle of the night, am I?"

"Innocent?" the man scoffed. "I know what you are, strigoi rubbish. None of your kind are innocent. Far from it. Kill me if you like but there's more where I came from."

He squeezed the man's throat, sneering as he watched his face turn red then purple. "You have no idea what we're like, how safe you are from most of us. Safe, that is until you--" He gasped, looking down to see a knife plunged in his gut. He dropped the man who let go of the blade and scurried into the van, climbing to the front seat, and starting it up.

Kenton grunted as he removed the weapon, taking note of the license plate as the vehicle sped away. Blood seeped through his fingers as he covered his wound, sitting on the ground while he waited for it to heal. After a few minutes, Alexander returned, two vampires staggering behind him, their skin covered in slow-healing burns.

He pushed his sandy hair away from his eyes as he looked his friend over. "Are you all right?"

"I will be in a moment," Kenton answered, getting to his feet.

"He got away, then?"

He smirked. "He thinks he did."

"Stop gawking at my singer," Rue teased, wiping down the bar as her sister sat opposite her, eyes fixed on the man on stage.

"I'm trying but you see him, right?" Violet said, amber eyes glued to the man as he sang a soulful ballad, lips just touching the microphone. "I love when he does the slow songs. Feels so," She lifted her glass. "Intimate." She took a sip of whiskey and placed the cup on the napkin.

Rue sighed, glancing in the singer's direction before putting her towel under the bar. She had to admit, he *was* handsome. Sharp features and a strong jawline, his face covered in about a week's-worth of stubble. His curly, sable hair fell to just past his ears and as he gripped the mic stand, emotion furrowing his thick brows, the tattoos covering his bronze skin popped, the spotlights showing them off as if they were the star of the show.

"He's got like, nineties vibes."

Rue scoffed. "Like you remember the nineties. You were one."

"I can appreciate the past, can't I? Especially when the men looked like *that*."

"Fine, but can you please unfixate for five minutes? Dad called tonight. *Again*."

"Fuck." She took another drink. "What now?"

"He wants you to 'stop flittering about and come work with him'. His words."

"Clearly."

"I know you want to. You didn't major in art history because you wanted to wait tables in a bar for the rest of your life. The museum is your dream job. What's the holdup?"

"I like it here," Violet said, her gaze returning to the singer.

"He's got a point. You're wasting that degree."

She let out an exasperated sigh, tossing her chestnut locks over her shoulder. "At least I have a degree to waste. We *both* work at a bar, don't forget."

CHAPTER 1

Rue's cheeks went red. "Bitch, I *own* this bar, and the building, including the apartment you live in *for free*. I worked my ass off for the money to get my business going instead of spending Dad's on a degree I'd never use, unlike *others*. Keep being a dick and I'll fire you, kick you out, and ship you off to Dad's myself. In a fucking box."

"Okay, sorry, geez." She finished her whiskey and tapped the bar, indicating that she wanted more. Rue grabbed the bottle and poured, her expression still angry. "I'm just sick of everyone wanting me to move on, grow up, blah, blah, blah. I have this small window of time where I can do whatever the fuck I want. I just want it to last a little while longer. The museum is my forever job and forever is a long-ass time when you're," She looked around to make sure none of the patrons would overhear. "What we are."

The room bustled behind her, dozens of people watching the band from booths that lined the wall opposite the bar while others stood directly in front of the stage. Two couples danced in the center of the room, half-drunk and clearly in love. A twinge of jealousy pulled at Violet as she watched them but she ignored it.

"Mm. Speaking of 'forever', Dad mentioned something else."

She reached for her glass. "What?"

"Another gift came from you-know-who."

"Ugh, Kenton?"

"Mm-hmm. He sent a book of poetry for Saint George's Day. Dad said you can pick it up whenever."

"Saint George's Day? He knows we don't celebrate that, right?"

"He's British."

"So's Dad but I'd never even heard of it until…"

She cast her a knowing look. "Last year?"

"The wall of roses. *A wall*. Who sends something like that for an antiquated holiday most people don't even know exists?"

"Rich people."

Violet chugged the whisky and put it back on its spot on the napkin.

"How many of those have you had?"

"Not enough."

She took the glass away.

"Hey! I didn't say I was done."

"I did."

She folded her arms. "Rude, but okay."

"Kenton's older and lives in Sussex. It makes sense that he'd still buy you presents for Saint George's Day. Besides, I think it's sweet that he sends you things."

"Is it, though? Or is he just showing off his money? Seriously, he's so pretentious. It drives me crazy."

"Well, he's been rich for like, four hundred years. What do you expect?"

She shrugged.

"Is he gonna want you to move to his castle and shit?"

"No, just," She made quotes in the air and rolled her eyes. "Summer there."

They both laughed. Rue shook her head. "Yeah, that's pretentious as fuck."

"Right? So, can you please not give me shit about stuff I'm putting off? He's agreed to give me space."

"For now. But, you've been out of school for a year. He won't wait forever."

"No, he won't. But, in the meantime..." She eyed the singer again.

Rue chuckled. "Whatever, just not in the bathroom again. People could hear you."

Her lips turned up in a sly grin. "I promise."

Iman guzzled half a bottle of water and wiped the sweat from his brow, the cheers from the crowd on the other side of the curtain beginning to die down. The backstage area was dusty, dimly lit, and cramped with barely enough room for a mini fridge, a couple of amps, and a chair. He sat, taking a few deep breaths but it was no use. He was too pumped to relax. Adrenaline flowed through his veins like electricity, the buzz from performing like a B12 shot. He tapped his foot, putting the bottle on top of the fridge. He rubbed his hands on his thighs, the smooth leather of his pants warming at his touch. He stared ahead, the scarlet curtain only a few

CHAPTER 1

feet away. The audience had quieted, going back to their drinks and conversations. He blew out another breath, his shoulders relaxing.

"Hot performance," he heard the woman say. He jolted up, turning to his left to face her. She giggled. "You're jumpy."

"Violet." He put his hands on his hips and shook his head, laughing at himself. "I didn't hear you coming."

"Oh?" She slinked toward him, a mischievous grin spreading across her face. "That's okay. I'm sure you will next time." She ran her hands down his arms as he moved his hands from his hips to hers.

"I have another set in twenty minutes."

"Plenty of time." She stood on her tiptoes to brush her lips along his Adam's apple and up to his chin. His skin tingled as her fingertips crept up to his shoulders and down his chest. "On second thought, I'll try to be quiet. Rue gave me a lecture about being loud."

"Did she?" he asked, lowering his voice.

"You know Rue," She dragged her teeth along his right cheek before finishing her thought. "Always complaining." She unfastened his belt, looking down to admire the chrome skull buckle as she loosened the buttons of his pants.

"I don't know how I feel about your sister hearing us."

"You want me to stop?" She slid her hand down the front of his pants, finding him already throbbing.

"I didn't say *that* but if we can avoid upsetting her…"

She yanked her hand away and sighed. "Fine. You're right. No one needs an angry Rue on the loose. We can play later." She ran a finger from his full lips down his stubble-covered chin and over his Adam's apple. "In the meantime, I'm awfully hungry."

"I have another set."

"So?"

He re-buttoned his pants, casting her a knowing smirk.

"I'll be careful. Promise."

"Fine, but--"

She clutched the back of his head, her incisors extending, not letting him finish his sentence before pulling his head to the side and clamping down on his neck, piercing his skin and sucking the hot, salty fluid from his veins.

He didn't struggle. He knew better. He let the euphoria wash over him, the venom from her bite like an opiate. As he drifted, the room went dark. Soon, he was weightless, floating on a cloud of indifference.

"*Shit!*" Violet whispered, pushing him away from her. He fell, unconscious on the dirty floor. She hopped down and knelt next to him. "I'm so sorry." She nicked her finger on the edge of her fang and smeared the blood over his wounds, sealing them. "Iman," She tapped his cheek. "Iman, are you all right?"

He groaned, tilting his head to the side.

"Oh, thank fuck. Come on. Let's get you home." She stood, yanking him up and throwing him over her shoulder. "My sister's gonna kill me."

"You *what?!*" Rue snapped.

"Shh. People will hear." Violet looked around from behind the bar. No one had seemed to notice.

"He's supposed to go on in," she checked the time on her phone. "Seven minutes ago."

"I'm sorry. I got carried away. He'll be fine for tomorrow night, I swear."

"That doesn't help me *now*, does it? These people are expecting to hear the house band. I have three guys up there waiting to play, but they can't without a singer. What am I supposed to do now?"

"You need a singer?" a woman asked, sitting at the bar.

"Yes," Rue answered, hope replacing anger in her voice.

"I can do it. I mean, I'm not a professional or anything, but I do great at karaoke night."

She looked her over. "Oh, yeah. Marley, right?"

CHAPTER 1

She nodded.

"Great!" Violet said. "Problem solved. See you later." She bolted from the room, going through the door that led to the office and kitchen.

Rue sighed, stifling the urge to chase after her and wring her irresponsible neck. Instead, she turned her focus back to Marley. "It would just be for the night. Our singer got, um, sick. Just tell the band what you want to sing. They can play just about anything. You'll need seven songs, I think. It's just a half-hour set. Can you handle that?"

"Sure."

"Awesome."

"Boss," a man shouted from the kitchen door.

"Yeah, Lou?"

"Violet took off. I need hands back here."

"Are you fucking kidding me?"

He shook his head and disappeared behind the door.

"Looks like I'm waiting tables on top of everything else." Rue grabbed a waist apron. "Thanks for helping me out. I'll pay you before close. A hundred good?"

"Yeah," Marley said, flashing a toothy grin. "That's great."

She nodded and rushed to the back. Marley looked toward the stage, the agitation on the band members' faces giving her butterflies. "It's okay," she told herself. "You got this."

Chapter 2

Marley took her place at the mic, her breathing shaky as she noticed the confused stares from the crowd. Her hands trembled as she adjusted the stand, the usual singer being much taller than her. It stuck and as she struggled, someone in the back shouted, "Where's the dude?" She shrugged as the mic finally cooperated.

"Don't be nervous," the guitar player said. "You'll do great."

"You think so?" She swallowed hard, wishing she'd gotten some water before stepping on stage.

"I've heard you sing. You'll be fine."

She nodded, closing her eyes and gripping the mic.

"You ready?"

Again, she nodded. The guitar player raised his hand, quieting the crowd. Her mind cleared in the silence, her confidence returning. Her ocean-blue eyes flew open as she belted out the first line of "Only Happy When It Rains". The band joined her, the thunderous guitar and drums whipping the audience into a frenzy. All of her anxiety melted away, the cheers from the crowd spurring her on. When the song was over, the band went directly into a punk version of "As It Was". The crowd loved it and as she sang, whisps of forest green hair sticking with sweat to her forehead, she couldn't help but smile. The weight of her responsibilities floated away on a cloud of music and the audience's adoration.

The band closed the show with a cover of "Heat Above", the song showcasing Marley's range beautifully. She paced the stage, leaning against the guitar player's back as she belted the last few drawn-out notes. With the crash of a symbol, the set was done, applause erupting from the crowd.

"Thank you," she panted, placing the mic back in its stand and backing away.

"Told ya," the guitar player said, patting her on the back.

She laughed, her hand on her chest as she caught her breath.

At the bar, Rue filled glass after glass, more than double the drink orders on a typical Wednesday night. She took a quick headcount. There weren't any more customers than usual. They were just drinking more, by a lot. They were also tipping more as evidenced by her apron being stuffed with bills. *Violet missed out*, she thought. *Serves her right*.

"What did you think?" Marley asked, bouncing up to the counter.

Rue got a glass and filled it with soda water. "You were great," she said, sliding the glass to her.

Marley drank greedily, water dribbling from the corners of her mouth. She set the glass down and wiped her lips on the back of her hand. "Thanks. I was really nervous at first but then it just clicked."

"You want to maybe do it again? Tomorrow night, same time?"

"Really?" she beamed.

"Yeah, you saw these people. They love you."

"I'd love to, thank you!"

She reached into her apron and pulled out five twenty-dollar bills. "As promised." She handed them to her.

"Thank you so much! I'll see you tomorrow."

She waved as the girl scurried off, the back of her blue tank top drenched in sweat. She looked young, barely old enough to be in a place like this. Rue would have to look out for her, make sure the guys didn't do anything creepy. She wasn't too worried about it, though. Ever since the first drummer "disappeared", the band had been sure to mind their manners.

Upstairs, Violet tucked Iman in and sat on the edge of his bed, holding his hand as he slept. "Sorry, big guy," she whispered, glancing around his room. His was the smallest of the four bedrooms in the loft apartment with only one window overlooking the street. It was stark with a bed, chair, two guitars, and not much else. The closet held five pairs of pants, some leather, the rest torn-up jeans, and a few tee shirts and belts. His biker jacket hung over the back of the chair and his only pair of boots lay where Violet had dropped them after taking them off before throwing his blanket over him. She smiled to herself, remembering the story he'd told her about how he'd stolen it from a motel three years before. He'd been on tour with his last band. They had four gigs left in four different cities and were out of money. They'd have to sleep in the base player's van the rest of the trip and it was the dead of winter. She quietly laughed thinking about him and his bandmates snuggled together under this blanket. Had that tour gone better, maybe she never would have met him. She tucked her hair behind her ear and stood to leave. "Get some rest."

"Everything okay?" Ophelia asked from the kitchen as Violet closed the door.

"Fine." She joined her at the round, black-lacquered table, grimacing at the sight of her lover eating a bowl of grapes.

She giggled. "You want me to put them away?"

"I would never tell you you can't eat."

"No, but you make sure to let me know how grossed out it makes you every time I do."

She raised her eyebrows. "Sorry, I didn't realize."

"It's okay. I understand." She returned the bowl to the fridge and sat back down. "You know, if you made me a--"

"Please, not this again right now."

"Fine," She put her hands up as if in surrender.

"Is Lennon in bed already?"

"Yeah," Ophelia took a swig of water from a bottle. "They tried to wait up but you know how they get when they've been on a bender. Tons of energy drinks all night and then crash."

"I like how you call playing video games 'a bender'."

"If it lasts fourteen hours, that's what it is."

She laughed. "I guess that's true."

"They're addicted. It's a problem."

"How is it a problem?"

"It's *all* the time. I know we don't pay rent, but *damn*. They still need a job."

"They make money. Sponsors or ads or something. Believe me, they pay their bills."

"It's not a real job."

"It pays their bills and doesn't make them miserable so I'd say it's job enough. And, I mean, you see how much they love it. They're happy."

She shrugged. "I guess."

She put her hand on her thigh. "What about you, baby? Are you happy at your job?"

Ophelia chewed on her bottom lip. "I started dancing with a fake ID when I was sixteen. It's been nine years. I don't know how to do anything else. Besides, Black goth chicks are in high demand. I'm a hot commodity." She winked.

Violet laughed. "Yes, you are." She kissed her and got up. "Just remember, no matter who's gawking at you, that ass is mine."

"You," She twirled her curly hair between her fingers. "Feeling frisky?"

"Not right now. I need a shower and then I'm going to bed."

She looked at the clock on the microwave. "You sure? It's only four."

"Yeah, I'm sleepy. Oh, I got some of that fancy soap you like. I put it in the shower for you."

She smiled up at her. "Thank you."

"You're welcome, sweetie. Get some rest. Remember to drink enough water." She kissed her forehead. "Night."

"Okay, night." When she'd gone to her room and closed the door, Ophelia went back to the fridge and retrieved her bowl of grapes. "Mildly disappointing, but that's okay," she muttered to herself. "I'm starving."

Chapter 3

Rue hurried the last group of patrons from the bar, following them out and locking up. She'd called a cab for the girls, three blondes, all wasted, oblivious to the world around them. As they waited, laughing and incoherently scream-talking to one another, Rue held back, leaning against the building and enjoying the cool night air. She cracked her neck and rubbed her shoulder, another hard night's work at an end.

Or so she thought.

To her left, she saw two men, both wearing black caps and standing awkwardly still in the middle of the sidewalk. She listened as they whispered, the four hundred feet between her and them no problem for her enhanced hearing.

"Whichever one you can," the man closest to the street said.

"But, there's three of 'em," the other one responded.

"Dude, look at them. They're in no condition to fight back."

He laughed. "Yeah, you're right. I'm just not in the mood to get scratched up again."

Three? Rue realized she must be shadowed by the darkened sign above. They couldn't see her.

The first man took a drag from his cigarette and dropped it to the ground. He blew out the smoke and began walking toward the girls. Rue sped past him, too fast for him to see, coming to a stop behind the man that hadn't yet taken a step. She leaned in close to his ear and whispered, "Sup?"

He spun around. "What the--"

She snatched him up by the throat and carried him to the alley, pinning him to the wall.

"What the fuck?" he shrieked.

"Shh." She peeked her head around the corner to see how close the first man was to the girls. "Too close," she complained. "No time to play." She pulled him away from the wall and then slammed him back against it, knocking him out and letting him fall as she flew out of the alley. She rushed to place herself between the predator and the group.

"Whoa," he said, stumbling back. "Hey, honey. Where'd you come from?"

"Depends on who you ask, I guess. Religious people say Hell but that's an oversimplification. See, there was a witch whose soulmate died and she wanted him back, right? So, she made a deal with a demon like, thousands of years ago who said he'd re-alive him to repay her for setting him free or whatever but he warned her not to have kids with him because they'd be fucked up. She didn't listen, obvs."

He tilted his head "Huh?"

She sighed. The cab pulled up and she turned her head to see the girls get in before returning her attention to the man. "I usually just say, 'Connecticut'." She grasped his collar and hurried him to the alley where his friend was still slumped on the ground. She threw him up against the wall and tore into his throat, ripping flesh away with her teeth, her fangs sharp and her mood self-righteous. As he bled out, she slapped the other man awake.

"What the fuck?" he muttered, his eyes opening wide at the sight of his friend, now a lifeless heap on the cement. He looked up at his assailant, blood covering her lips and chin, a twisted grin on her crimson-stained face. "*What the fuck?!*" He tried to stand but she knocked him back on his ass with one hand to his shoulder.

She knelt in front of him, allowing him to see the blackness of her eyes. "You're not going anywhere, Sport." She glanced at the corpse and back at him. "I was a smidge hasty with your friend. I should know better by now. My dad drilled it into my head growing up. 'Remember, darling, we don't waste food.' Stupid." She took his jaw in her hand. "I guess it's just you for dinner, then."

"*What?* Wait! Please!"

She ignored him, bending his head to the side and clamping down on his carotid. She drank him dry, feeding until she felt his pulse weaken then stop. "Blech," she complained, wiping her face clean on his shirt. "No sweetness at all. Would it have killed you to eat some fruit once in a while?" She stood, kicking the body and looking around. As far as she could tell, no one had seen anything. She looked back

CHAPTER 3

down at the mess she'd made, hands on her hips, brows scrunched. "Too far?" she asked herself. She lifted her head to see the moon peeking out between the clouds. "Ugh, probably." She bent to hoist one of the bodies over her shoulder. "You had it coming, though. Dick."

After disposing of the bodies in the incinerator in her bar's basement, she went upstairs to her apartment. Across the hall from her sister's, her place was smaller; two bedrooms instead of four. She didn't need the space her sister did. She didn't keep lovers like pets and on-demand food sources. She liked the quiet that came with living alone. Most of the time, anyway.

She flopped onto the red velvet sofa and kicked off her boots, the events of the night swirling in her mind as she attempted to relax. "Those guys were trash," she told herself, pushing the small bit of guilt she felt from her thoughts. She sat up, brushing her dark, wavy hair over her shoulder and taking off her choker. She set the necklace on the coffee table, taking a second to admire the charred wood and epoxy top. She ran her fingers over the sapphire streak winding through the center, a river of brilliance in an otherwise dark landscape.

She wondered if she'd ever find *her* streak of brilliance or if she'd be forever condemned to live her life in darkness, cold and alone. Her sister had been lucky to find Kenton, though she didn't feel that way. For as much as Rue valued her solitude most days, her freedom, she did get lonely. Maybe she'd take up dating the way humans did. It seemed to work out fine for them at least half of the time. It'd be nice to have someone to share things with, spend time with. Love.

She dismissed the idea, glancing around her apartment at the slate-gray walls, concrete countertops, and kitchen cabinets she'd painted blood-red. She liked the darkness, in her aesthetic and in her mood. Besides, if she was going to be in a relationship that lasted more than a weekend, she wanted it to mean something. If it wasn't forever, she didn't want it.

Chapter 4

Kenton sleuthed around the semi-detached brick home, the Oxford Road residence smelling of cheap whiskey even from the outside. Peering in through the bow window, he could see the man that had attacked him the night before. He sat in a tattered recliner, remote in one hand, half-empty glass in the other, button-down untucked, and trousers unzipped. His forlorn face was covered in a patchy five o'clock shadow and as he turned off the television and set the remote on an end table, he finished his drink, his disconnected stare giving Kenton pause. What was the look on the man's face? Guilt? Regret? It was hard to tell in the dim light of the small lamp in the corner of the room but ultimately, it didn't matter. His emotions were of no importance. Kenton was there for two reasons: information and revenge.

He took the four steps to the front door and kicked it in causing the man to jump from his seat. He dropped the glass to the hickory floor, the sound of it shattering startling him again. His cheeks flushed as he stumbled to put the chair between himself and the intruder.

"Strigoi," the man said through clenched teeth.

Kenton didn't bother closing the door, instead inching toward him. "This is the second time you've used that word as an insult. Admittedly, my Romanian is quite rusty but if memory serves, it's not inherently offensive. Am I meant to be offended?" He closed the space between them, allowing his eyes to go black. "Tell me, Brian, would it hurt your feelings if I were to describe you as human?"

He stiffened his upper lip in an attempt to hide his fear. "How did you find me, then? Sniff me out like a dog?"

He snorted. "Don't be ridiculous." He glanced around the room, noticing several photographs of a woman with dark, graying hair. He listened but detected no other

CHAPTER 4

heartbeats in the home. For a second, he wondered if she was just out or if she'd left him. It would explain the sadness in the man's eyes. Though, that could also be attributed to seeing his murderous companion's throat ripped out the night before.

"How, then?"

"An old friend matched your number plate to this address. Well, an ex-lover but that's irrelevant. She looked you up. Said you have no criminal record so either you're very good at covering your tracks or the only people you attack are," He flashed a devious grin, showing his elongated canines. "Like me."

He spat on his shoes.

"That's not very hospitable, now is it, Brian?"

"How'd you get in here? I didn't invite you. Don't have so much as a welcome mat."

He stifled a laugh. "You believe I need an invitation? This isn't the movies, Brian."

"Stop saying my name!" His heart beat faster as he tried to move away.

He matched his movements, the two now circling one another like boxers at the start of a match. "So, a new crop of hunters. I haven't tussled with your lot since the late 18th century. It was in Blandford, I believe."

"You've never seen *my* kind, strigoi." He edged toward the opened door of a bedroom, the vampire following.

"Of course, I have. The weapons have changed but the intent is the same. You have grenades and flamethrowers where your forefathers had pitchforks and torches but you want the same thing they did. You wish to drive us from your lands and if we do not flee, you kill us. But, we're not the isolated creatures we once were. We are not afraid of a handful of self-righteous men." He coughed. "We--" He coughed again and then, again. His brows furrowed in confusion as he clutched his throat, his esophagus and lungs burning as if on fire. "What?" He fell to his knees, spitting blood on the rug in front of the bed. He listened in between coughs, finally hearing the low hum of some sort of machine.

Brian backed away, the fear on his face replaced with a smug smirk. He moved to the nightstand, touching the top of the running humidifier.

"Holy water," Kenton choked, his eyes red and watering.

"Yeah." He opened a drawer and took out a sharpened piece of wood. "I might've been wrong about you needing an invite but I know from experience that monsters like you can be killed with a stake to the heart. And, Holy water, well, that hasn't let me down, yet, either."

He hacked up more blood and bits of tissue, his skin the color of a day-old bruise. Hunched over the rug, he managed to get out the words. "How," He spit the blood from his mouth. "How many?"

"How many what?"

"Of you." He sat up on his knees, the blood vessels in his sclera breaking, causing tears of blood to run down his cheeks. "How many more of *you*?"

Brian again smirked, standing over him, chest puffed in victory. "We are Legion." He lifted the stake and brought it down but just as it was about to strike, Kenton batted it away, grabbing the hunter's leg and pulling it out from under him. He fell, hitting his head on the bloodied rug with a thud.

The vampire snatched the stake from where it landed and plunged it into the man's chest. "Seems these work on humans, as well." He watched as the life drained from Brian's body, spitting more blood and lung tissue onto the corpse's still face. "Legion," he mocked as he crawled to the door.

The fresh night air began healing him before he reached the porch. Once outside, he lay in the grass, waiting for his body to fully heal. He knew he'd have to go back in to retrieve the body. He couldn't risk it being found the way it was. He kicked himself for not unplugging the humidifier before leaving the house but there had been no time. He was sure he would've died had he stayed much longer.

He looked up at the stars, the ground under his head like a firm pillow. "All right," he whispered to himself. "I'll run in, take him out, and dump him in the woods." He closed his eyes for a moment, feeling his body rejuvenate. He sighed, getting to his feet and standing straight. He readied himself, covering his nose and mouth. "Fucking Legion," he again mocked, shaking his head in derision and bolting inside.

CHAPTER 4

"Kenton, old boy," Alexander greeted, shoving his hands in his pockets and kicking a discarded wine bottle to the other side of the room. "I trust you've been well since our last encounter."

"Well enough." He entered the burned-out club, stepping over broken glass and avoiding toppled-over chairs.

"I've already buried what was left of our fallen but if you'd like to pay your respects, I can take you to their resting place in the forest."

He nodded and the two headed out through the same door Kenton had come in through. They walked slowly, neither in a hurry to dwell on the loss of their friends nor on the incident that had claimed their lives.

"How many made it out alive?"

Alexander looked up at the stars, cracking his neck before answering. "Genevieve, Bradley, and Emily got away. Oscar and Ionna, as well. They've checked in, made sure I hadn't perished. I saw a few more escape into the woods but I couldn't identify them. I assume they're in hiding until this new threat passes. Hunters. Can you believe it? Like the old days and not the good ones."

They got to the burial site and stopped, a pile of smooth, gray stones the only marker. "Murderous creatures, them." Kenton dropped his chin. "And they call *us* evil."

For a few moments, they allowed themselves to feel the loss of their friends, the still night air like a blanket around their shoulders. They stood in reverence, quiet and holding back tears. In the distance, the coo of an owl broke the silence.

Alexander cleared his throat. "Were you able to track the last one?"

"Yes, but--"

"Tell me you made him suffer before killing him." His face had tightened, no longer dropped in grief but hard. His rage shone even in the darkness of the forest.

"Sadly, I had to end things quickly as I was tricked into inhaling Holy water."

He tilted his head in confusion.

"He had it in a humidifier."

His eyes widened and he let out a surprised laugh. "These new hunters are innovative, I'll give them that."

"Also, unfortunately, he claims there are more."

His eyebrows raised. "More?"

"Yes. He used the word *legion*. Ridiculous. I wonder if he was being glib or if there really are five thousand hunters running amok."

"I imagine a handful are still milling about Crawley proper. Best we find and extinguish them before any more of us are attacked."

"Yes. This has already taken too much of my time. I'd like to nip this nuisance in the bud and get back to my life as soon as possible."

"Your life?" Alexander snickered.

He lifted an eyebrow. "My existence amuses you?"

"Only slightly."

He crossed his arms and furrowed his brow.

"Oh, don't be insulted," he teased. "The way you live just seems a bit...shallow."

"*Shallow?*"

"Perhaps that's not the right word. Lonely may be more fitting."

"I'm not--"

"Don't get so defensive, Kenton. I'm only pointing out the obvious. You waste your nights on wine and women, none of whom are the one you truly desire. You hole up in your estate away from everyone except to occasionally grace us with your presence at an orgy or party as if those count as healthy socialization."

"Orgies and parties *you* facilitate, need I remind you?"

He grinned. "You do not. But, do you think this is what Florin had in mind for you? What he'd approve of?"

"I think if Florin had an opinion, he would have bothered to show himself at some point in the last two hundred years, don't you?"

"I wouldn't dream of trying to decipher what goes through that man's head. But, I do remember him making it clear last we spoke that you were meant to be a leader in our community. Someone the rest of us could turn to when--"

"Buildings get torched?"

"Among other things."

Kenton sighed. "You know I'm here, ready and able to fight any battles that need to be fought."

He considered it. "I do."

"So, is there anything you remember that might help me track the rest of these bastards down? Anything the psychotics with the grenades said? Did they mention any names?"

"I don't think so but it was difficult to hear with eardrums blown out. That first bomb exploded not three feet from me. I was only shielded from the blast because I was underneath a table at the time." Sadness returned to his eyes as he remembered. "I'll miss Aaron most of all." He blinked away tears before they could fall. "It should have been me in that chair. If I hadn't just finished with Rebecca, it would have been."

He pat his friend's shoulder. "I'm glad it wasn't you."

"I'm not sure that *I* am. Had it been, I'd at least have my honor. You've no idea the humiliation of fleeing your own property in fear of *humans*."

He squeezed his shoulder and lowered his head to make sure his friend was looking him in the eye. "Better embarrassment and self-loathing than death, I'd say."

Chapter 5

By the time Violet woke up, she was already beginning to climax, Ophelia having taken initiative, her expert tongue acting as an erotic alarm. She gripped the headboard, the holes in the geometric design just big enough for her fingers to poke through. The sweet scent of vanilla filled her nose as waves of pleasure washed over her, her quiet moans a signal to Ophelia to speed things up. She swirled her tongue over Violet's clit, applying more pressure, and sending the vampire into a frenzy of ecstasy. As she reached the peak of her orgasm, she lost control, pulling bits of wood from the headboard with a loud snap.

"What was that?" Ophelia asked, throwing the covers off of her head.

Violet showed her the white-lacquered pieces still in her hands. They both laughed.

"How many is that now?"

"Five, I think. I should probably get something padded next time. Something I can't hold on to."

"Should I stop waking you up like this?"

"Don't you dare."

Ophelia smiled as she climbed out of bed.

"You're dressed?"

"Have to get to work."

"At," she took the phone from the nightstand and checked the time. "Six?"

"Unfortunately." Ophelia slid on her boots, zipping them up the sides. "A conference is in town and some business guys rented out the club for two hours. Requested *all* the girls be there. Should be good money. Lennon's up if you're hungry." She bent down to kiss her cheek. "I'll be back around three."

"Have fun," she called after her as she disappeared out the bedroom door.

CHAPTER 5

"I probably won't," she called back, leaving the apartment and closing the front door behind her.

Violet sat up in bed, checking her phone for messages. There was only one from her sister. *Tell Iman to rest tonight. No way he's fully recovered. And, don't fuck him up like that again. I need him here.* She rolled her eyes and got out of bed wrapping herself in a silk robe before going to check on Iman. She peeked into his room where he still slept, color returned to his face.

"Hey," Lennon greeted, not altering their gaze. They were glued to the television, tapping buttons on their controller, their pale brows furrowed in concentration.

"Hey." She sat next to them, feigning interest in the game playing on the screen. "Are you winning?"

"Always." They pressed the A key several times, causing their character to kill their opponent in a flurry of moves Violent couldn't force herself to follow.

"Almost done?"

"Just need to get to a save point." A map popped up and the gruff-looking cowboy on the screen walked to a dirt road.

She tapped her foot. "I'm very hungry."

"Just a second," they said, still not looking at her.

"You know I don't like waiting."

"I know."

She looked around the room and folded her arms. "I'm getting impatient."

"Getting? I thought you were born that way."

"You think you're funny?"

"I *know* I'm funny *and* delicious so hold tight for *one* second."

She sighed, watching as the cowboy approached a barn. Soon, the screen changed, a menu popping up. After a few clicks, Lennon put the controller down and turned to face her, brushing a few stray wisps of bleached hair away from their emerald eyes.

"See? Took no time at all."

"Mm."

"Do I want to know why Iman's still in bed? He's usually up way earlier than this."

"You probably don't."

"He's all right though, right?"

"He's fine."

"You sure?"

"Remind me, is it your place to question me?"

"I doubt it, but somebodies got to."

She held back a smile. "Is that so?"

They shrugged.

"I may have overindulged last night but he'll be fine. Just needs a little rest."

"Uh, huh. Don't over-indulge in *me* today, okay? I have a big mission I need to get through and I need to be firing on all cylinders."

"When have I ever?"

"Let's see, Christmas after you drank that pink concoction O made."

"She called it a Bubble Gum Colada. I was *so* sick. So much rum."

"Pretty sure it was the coconut milk. You know better than to have real food."

"Okay, but you can't blame me for that. I was wasted and needed to feel better."

"Well, I needed to not be a useless heap for three days, but,"

"Fine. *One* time."

"Hardly. Remember last July when you went to some festival and didn't feed all weekend? You came home looking like death warmed over twice and nearly *killed* me."

"That's dramatic."

"That's *true*. And, when I came back from a con and--"

"I was just happy to see you."

"So happy you almost broke my neck yanking my head to the side so hard."

"Since when is being a smidge overzealous a crime?"

"Pretty sure murder has been illegal for like, ever."

She laughed. "You know I would never."

"Not on purpose."

"Okay, all right." She giggled, holding her hands up. "I'll be careful."

"You fuckin' better." They flashed a teasing grin, holding out their wrist. Violet took it, pulling it to her lips, breathing in the intoxicating aroma of the fluid just under the freckled skin. Lennon looked away as she bit down, flinching for just a moment before relaxing, the euphoria of her bite soothing them.

CHAPTER 5

Ophelia worked the pole, Ride or Die blaring as she spun, upside down, her legs wrapped around the chrome. She came down in a split, turning her ass to the men at the end of the stage, twerking as they placed bills in her g-string. One of the men, balding and tipsy, pulled the string far enough out that her cleft was exposed. She twirled around, kicking his hand away with her gladiator stilettos. "Uh, uh," she said, waving her finger, a seductive smile creeping across her face. "You want to see more, you gotta buy a private dance."

He nodded enthusiastically, taking a wad of bills from his jacket pocket and showing it to her. She took it, winking and hopping down from the stage, giving a nod to another girl to take her place. As the next dancer took the stage, Ophelia led the man by the hand to a room at the back of the club. Once inside, she gently pushed him onto a purple sofa, its gold trim glistening in the dim, red light. She placed the money on a table and looked up at the security camera to make sure its light was on. She waved to it, indicating to the watcher to turn on the music. Teenage Fever began to play through the speaker mounted to the wall, not loud enough to drown out the base from the club beyond the closed door, but it would do.

"H-how does this work?" the man asked, loosening his tie.

"You just sit right there," she told him, her voice husky. "I'll do everything." She straddled him, holding on to the back of the couch for leverage as she started to grind.

"Can I touch you?" he asked, his hands already climbing up her thighs.

"No higher than here," she said, pointing to a spot on her leg less than an inch above his fingers. He nodded. She straightened her back, moving her hands from the sofa to the hooks of her bra. She unhooked it, letting the straps fall and sliding them down her arms. His fingertips dug into her skin as she dropped the lingerie to the floor. "Gentle," she warned.

"Oh," he stammered, taking his hands away. She stood and turned around, lacing her fingers through the waist of the thong and shimmying it down, keeping her legs as straight as she could as she bent over, giving him a full view of her ass and pussy. He let out a breath as he took off his jacket, tossing it aside and unbuttoning his silver cufflinks. He pushed his sleeves up as she retook her place in his lap, grinding against him as she shoved her small breasts in his face. He ran his hands up her legs again, this time on the back side. He grabbed her, spreading her legs apart, causing her to lose her balance. She again held onto the back of the couch.

"Easy, baby," she said, continuing to grind against his raging boner. She tried to keep low, only making contact with the balls and bottom of the shaft through his thin slacks, but he was moving with her now, sliding himself along her exposed vulva. He grabbed her ass hard and kissed her neck. She should have stopped it right then and there. That kind of touching was against policy. But, as she rubbed her clit against the stranger's erection, memories of Violet from earlier that night flooded her mind. The feel of her pussy in her mouth. Her taste. She wished she'd had more time. Wished she'd have let her lover reciprocate. But, she hadn't. Now, she was horny as all hell and there was free dick literally up for grabs.

She unbuckled his belt, unbuttoned and unzipped his pants, and pulled out his cock. Without a word, she shoved it into her, a gasp of shock emanating from the customer. He threw his head back, his eyes like saucers as he watched her ride him. She squeezed her eyes shut, Violet's face the only one she wanted to see. She imagined her fingers inside of her, her tongue licking her. She covered her mouth to quiet her cries as she came but it didn't matter. The watcher had seen and was already at the door.

He burst in, lifting her off the man and throwing a robe at her. "What did I tell you about this?" he shouted.

"I'm sorry." She put on the robe and picked up her lingerie and money.

"This is the third time this month!"

"I know, I'm sorry. It won't happen again."

"It better fuckin' not. If it does, you're done." He turned his attention to the client who was trying to button his pants with shaky hands. "And, you. Get the fuck out of here. And keep your mouth shut." He nodded, picked up his jacket,

CHAPTER 5

and scurried out. The watcher closed the door behind him and continued to scold her. "The fuck's wrong with you? You know that shit isn't allowed here."

"I know."

"You wanna do that shit on your own time, that's up to you. But, I'm not trying to get fired because I let you get away with it here."

"I get it."

"Do you? Because you keep fuckin' customers. We're not a brothel. People are gonna start talking and get this place shut down. If you need more money--"

"They don't pay me extra," she told him. "It's not like that. I just get...urges."

"Sex addict?"

"No, I just get--"

"I don't want to hear it. Just keep that shit *out* of the club. You hear me?"

She nodded.

"Go home for the night."

"What?! You can't--"

"I don't give a fuck about the convention guys or how much money you might be losing. You need to get it through your head. Besides," He opened the door to see a group of men talking, the man from the couch at the center. "The rest of them are gonna expect that shit from you now. No matter what I say, they *never* keep their mouths shut."

Chapter 6

"He needs another day," Violet said, helping Iman onto a stool at the bar.

"No shit." Rue tossed an apron to her sister and got a clean glass from under the counter. "You should really learn to control yourself with your humans if you're gonna insist on keeping them alive."

"I second that motion," Iman said, resting his elbows on the bar.

She rolled her eyes. "Noted. You want some food?"

He nodded.

"Be right back." Violet disappeared into the kitchen while Rue filled the glass with water from the tap and slid it over.

"Thank you," Iman said, holding it to his lips and taking a sip.

She gave him a knowing look.

"I'm fine," he insisted.

"Mm-hmm."

"*I'm fine*...mostly."

She chuckled. "I tried to warn you."

"Yeah, well," he sat his cup down, teasing her with a smile. "Maybe if you hadn't shut me down..."

"I told you, humans aren't my thing."

"And, I told *you*, I'm fine." He finished his water, placing the glass back on the counter.

"All right. Just don't come crying to me when she accidentally fucking kills you." She winked and took the glass, refilling it and placing it back in front of him.

"I promise I won't haunt you unprovoked but if you summon me with a spirit board or some shit, I'm showing up."

They both laughed.

CHAPTER 6

"Order up," Violet said, holding her nose and placing a plate of sliders and fries on the bar.

"For fuck's sake," Rue sighed. "How are you still this precious about the smell of food?"

"It's fucking gross."

"You know I'm running a business here, right? Maybe don't make my goods look like trash."

"It's not personal. It's *all* food."

She gestured to the room. "They don't know that."

"Fine. I'll try harder to ignore it." She turned her attention to Iman. "When you're done eating, go upstairs and get some rest. I'll be needing that D later." She gave him a peck on the lips and walked off to begin her shift.

"Speaking of gross," Rue muttered.

"Don't knock it 'til you've tried it." Iman smirked, taking a bite of a fry. He glanced at the stage where Marley was singing "Where Is My Mind". "She's pretty good." The singer glared back at him, her eyes like daggers. "Hates me, though, it looks like."

"She's probably gunning for your job."

"You think?"

"That'd be my guess."

"Do I have anything to worry about?"

"Course not. But, how would you feel about an opener? I was thinking about putting her on a few nights a week. Three songs just before you go on."

"Hmm." He watched the singer who no longer stared at him.

"Don't be jealous. She'd be *in addition* to you, not instead of. Besides, look at the crowd. They love her. What kind of entrepreneur would I be if I didn't cash in on that? She's like catnip to these people."

"I'm not jealous." he insisted.

"So, you'll play nice?"

"Of course." He ate as Marley finished the Pixies cover and thought to himself, *As long as everyone knows who the headliner is.*

Upstairs, Ophelia rushed to get her clothes in the washer, stripping naked in the hall in front of the machine. She set it to hot and when it kicked on, she made a mad dash for the bathroom.

"Girl," Lennon complained from the sofa as she passed. "This is not the club. Put something on."

"Don't like the show?" she called as she turned the doorknob.

"Ace, remember?"

"Yeah, yeah." She went inside, locking the door behind her. She turned the shower on and as she waited for the water to get warm, she put on her shower cap, looking herself over in the mirror. "The fuck's wrong with you?"

She stepped into the shower and pulled the glass door closed. She scrubbed herself down, using more than enough vanilla scented shower gel to wash away the scent of the man from the club. If Violet smelled him on her, that would be it. She'd be kicked out of the loft and more importantly, out of her life. Thankfully, the watcher had interrupted before he'd finished. Had he come inside her, she would have had a lot more work to do to get clean including douching, which she hated. As it was, a twenty minute shower would do.

"You have to stop doing this," she told herself as she rinsed. "Hooking up with outsiders is against the rules. You know this." *Maybe I should quit dancing*, she thought. *It's too tempting and I do not want to get put out.*

As she ran her hands over her body, she again imagined Violet's face. She closed her eyes, imagining her watching her. She pictured her leaning against the door on the other side of the room, unzipping her jeans and slipping her hand inside, massaging herself in a curtain of steam. She let one hand wander to her freshly cleaned pussy while the other glided over her wet nipples as she imagined Violet using her free hand to unbutton her shirt and pull it open, revealing her perfect breasts.

CHAPTER 6

Maybe I am a sex addict, she thought, taking the shower head down and holding it between her legs. *Or, maybe I'm just way too into this bitch.* The hot water pulsed against her clit, her knees beginning to go weak. She smacked a hand against the shower wall, bending slightly to steady herself. She knew as she came that both things could be true. She could be a sex addict *and* she could like this girl way too much. The truth was, she was in love with Violet and just like hooking up with randoms, that was also against the rules.

Back at the bar, Violet waited impatiently for an order of wings for a table of not-so-friendly business types. Not only did she have to deal with the nauseating stench of human food, but she also had to pretend the unfiltered stink of toxic masculinity wafting off of them wasn't enough to make her gag.

"Rough night?" Marley asked, taking a swig of water from a bottle she had hidden behind the bar.

"That obvious?" She relaxed her face, realizing she'd been sporting a grimace since she walked away from the men's table.

"Kind of." She giggled, putting the bottle back and taking a seat next to her.

She looked up at the empty stage. "You guys on a break?"

"Just for a minute. One of the guys had to," she paused. "I think he ate something he shouldn't have."

"Ah." She laughed.

"Can I ask you something?"

"Sure."

"Do you think I'm any good?"

"Yeah."

"Really? Because I haven't seen you look at the stage once. It's okay. I can take it. Do I suck?"

"No, you're great," she told her, knowing that's what she wanted to hear. In all honesty, she hadn't been paying attention. Between drink orders coming so fast, checking on Iman, and fighting back the urge to vomit from the foul scent of cooked meat and fried everything, she hadn't noticed the band at all. She couldn't say that, though. No singer wants to hear that their performance isn't so good it makes people stop what they're doing and listen. So, in the interest of not shattering this girl's confidence, she lied. "I've been listening all night. You're amazing. But, you know that. I mean, look at all the people that came out to see you."

Marley glanced around the room. "I guess you're right. I just get nervous."

"Well, don't. You're doing great."

"Yo, V," the cook barked from the kitchen. "You gonna come get these or am *I* the server now?"

She shot him a look. "I didn't know they were done."

"That's why you're supposed to wait for 'em back here, not out there where you can't hear shit." He let the door swing closed as he went back to work.

"This dude right here."

Marley smiled. "Kind of a hard-ass, huh?"

"Hard-ass, giant dick, tomato, tomahto."

Marley laughed.

"Break a leg or whatever." She moved past her in the direction of the kitchen.

"Thanks but, um, are you working tomorrow?"

"Tomorrow, the next night, every night."

"Oh, good. I mean, maybe I'll see you later, then."

"You probably will."

"Right." She bit her bottom lip as she watched the waitress walk to the kitchen. "Damn," she whispered, her eyes fixed on her backside.

At the other end of the bar, Rue and Iman waited for the singer to retake her place on stage. "Oh," Rue said, stifling a laugh.

"Yeah, I saw," Iman sighed. "At least it's not my job she's after."

Chapter 7

While Marley opened the show, Iman drank a cup of warm tea with honey at the bar. He found it helpful to keep his throat relaxed and his voice from becoming scratchy.

"You sure you're feeling good enough for this?" Violet asked, sitting next to him.

"It's sweet of you to worry, but like I told your sister, I'm fine."

"Okay, then." She hopped up. "I better get back to work." She bent to kiss him then turned her back to him. She stood there for a few seconds, tapping her foot.

"What are you doing?"

She scoffed. "I'm waiting."

"For what?"

"Um, duh, this ass isn't gonna slap itself."

He laughed. "My mistake." He smacked her on the butt.

"That the best you can do?"

"You're crazy." He slapped her again, harder this time.

"Thank you," she sang as she walked off.

He shook his head, taking his last sip of tea. From the stage, Marley began singing "She Knows It". He nearly choked, hiding his smile behind the cup, not wanting her to see him laughing at her. *So thirsty*, he thought.

"Subtle," Rue said from behind the bar.

"Yeah, you might want to get her some water. She looks *parched*."

She laughed. "Hey, can you get a box of nuts down for me? I'm out up here."

"Don't you have super-strength?"

"Yes. If only I weren't also super short."

He snickered and got up from his stool, following her to the kitchen.

"Five minutes, guys," Marley whispered to the band. They nodded and she hurried from the stage to the bar where Violet had just sat down for a break. "Another bad night?"

"Not terrible. Just long."

"Ah." Marley looked back to the kitchen door as she took a bottle of whiskey from behind the bar.

"Don't let my sister see you doing that. She'll kill you a little."

"Just a little?" she smirked. "Maybe I should hide." She ducked down, out of sight.

She giggled. "I'm serious. You should get out of there."

She popped back up, a full shot glass replacing the bottle in her hand. She held it out to her. "I won't tell if you don't."

She took it, knocking it back and shaking her head. She winced. "Strong."

"I better get back up there before boss lady catches me. I'll talk to you later." She hurried back to the stage just as Rue and Iman emerged from the kitchen, jars of peanuts in hand.

"Drinking instead of working *again?*" Rue scolded.

"No," Violet said, getting up and adjusting her apron. "Just resting my feet for a minute."

"Uh, huh."

"I'm working, see?" She picked up a towel and began wiping the counter.

"Whatever." Rue opened the jars Iman set in front of her and began filling bowls.

"Gotta go," the singer said, slapping Violet's ass again and heading backstage.

"If you're going to fake clean, you may as well wipe down the bar stools while they're empty."

"On it, boss." she mocked, taking her towel to a red, patent-leather seat. Focused on something sticky on one of the stools, she didn't notice "Extraordinary" start

CHAPTER 7

to play. But, at about twenty-five seconds, her ears pricked up. She turned to look at the stage, Marley's voice floating above all other noise and flooding her ears. It was the most beautiful thing she'd ever heard. By fifty seconds, she was completely transfixed. Not only was her voice captivating, but the girl was stunning.

"Earth to Violet," Rue said, but she couldn't hear her. She was lost in the music and Marley's beauty. How had she not noticed her until now?

Ophelia spread the woman's legs wide, running her hands up her thighs as she climbed onto the sofa. "You know, you shouldn't wear jeans." She turned around, the red light from the camera warning her not to let things go too far. She sat between the client's legs and ground her naked ass against her pussy. "You really don't get your money's worth."

"I'll have to remember that for next time," the woman said, brushing a strand of her short, blond hair from her eyes.

She leaned back, reaching up to put a hand on the back of the woman's neck. She could feel her breath on her cheek as she closed her eyes, the movement of her hips getting her wet.

"I'm having a really hard time keeping my hands to myself," the client admitted.

"Try," she breathed, cupping her own breast.

"Fuck, you're gorgeous."

"Thank you."

"Are you sure I can't..." She traced her fingers up Ophelia's right thigh.

She let out a breath as she continued to move her hips. "Just...stay outside."

"Whatever you say." She pulled her fingertips up both thighs now, sending shivers up her spine. She kept her hands moving, from her legs up her torso and settling on her breasts. She kissed her neck as Ophelia reached up to hold onto the back of the couch.

Don't do it, she warned herself. *Don't you fucking do it.*

"When you say, 'outside', how outside are we taking?" She slid her fingers between Ophelia's legs and gently pulled them apart.

"*Fuck*," she whispered.

She ran her hands up her body again, teasing her nipples before slowly moving back down. "If your legs are still open by the time I get to where I'm going, I'll take it as an invitation." Her hands were sliding down her abdomen now, almost at her belly button. "If you close them, I'll stop touching you. Okay?"

She nodded, so turned on, she could barely think straight. The woman's left hand rested on her stomach while the right kept going. *Close your legs*, she thought. *It's not hard. Just close them.* But, she didn't. She widened them further, sliding herself down to allow the woman full access to her pussy.

She nibbled on her earlobe as she slipped her fingers over her clit, massaging it as it swelled. She plunged deeper, penetrating her with two fingers, stroking her G-spot in a come-hither motion.

"*Oh, fuck*," she moaned as the woman again worked her clit. Just as she was about to come, the door flew open.

"For real?!" the watcher barked.

"Oh, shit," the woman muttered. They both jumped up, the client wasting no time in fleeing the room.

The watcher slammed the door behind her. "What the fuck did I say?" he asked. "What did I fucking say?"

"I know." Ophelia sat back down and began touching herself.

"What the fuck are you doin'?!"

"I get that I'm probably fired, but I was like, ten seconds from a hard O so..." She continued to masturbate in front of him.

"Girl, that's," he wiped his mouth. "I'm not gonna lie, that's sexy as fuck."

"You know, it's not really the same when you do it yourself."

He raised his eyebrows. "You serious?"

She heard the words come out of her mouth but couldn't stop them. "Lock the door."

He looked up at the camera to make sure he'd turned it off and sure enough, the light was off. "*Shit*." He locked the door and pulled off his shirt, kneeling in front of her and gobbling her pussy like a ripe peach.

CHAPTER 7

She gripped the back of the sofa, biting her arm to keep from screaming as she came. *Last time*, she promised herself. *Never again*.

While he went down on her, the watcher took down his pants and underwear, stroking himself a few times. He got up on his knees, pulled her to the edge of the sofa, and shoved himself into her.

"Oh, fuck!" she yelped in surprise.

"Good, 'oh, fuck', or bad, 'oh, fuck'?" he asked, thrusting hard.

As he continued, his balls slapping against her ass as he pounded her, she couldn't help but start to come again. "Good," she said, her voice husky. "Fuck, it's so good."

Iman took the stage, starting his set with Call Me Little Sunshine. As he sang with his signature rasp, Marley took a seat at the bar where Violet placed a shot of whiskey in front of her. She smiled. "To return the favor."

"Thanks," she said, gulping it down. "Did you like the show?"

"I did." She let her eyes fall to her lips as she licked her own. "The singing was good, too."

A wide grin spread across her face as she leaned in. "Can I tell you a secret?"

She, too, leaned closer. "I love secrets."

"I have a little crush on you."

Violet twirled a bit of Marley's hair between her fingers. "You don't say."

"Maybe something we can talk more about when I get back from the restroom?"

"Definitely a topic I'd like to discuss further."

Still smiling, she got up from the stool and made her way through the crowd to stand in line at the unisex bathroom door. Violet took the empty shot glass and placed it in the "to be washed" bus tub.

"Another one?" Rue asked, standing next to her behind the bar.

"No," she said, her tone defensive.

"Are you sure?"

"I don't know. We'll see. What's it to you?"

"Oh, I couldn't care less but Iman's *right there*. Consider his feelings, maybe."

She scoffed. "He doesn't care. Besides, he knows the rules."

"A smidge one-sided, aren't they, your rules?"

She shrugged. "Yeah."

She chuckled. "At least you *know* you're an asshole."

She too laughed. "Oh, I'm well aware."

Chapter 8

"Yo!" Rue's voice boomed over the rowdy crowd. She stood on the bar, clapping her hands to get their attention. The room quieted. "Last call!" She got down and wiped the counter where her boots had been. A handful of people rushed the bar, ordering one final drink while most began filing out. On the opposite side of the room, Violet and Marley sat at a booth, giggling and flirting.

"They're still talking?" Iman asked, stepping behind the bar and getting himself a glass of water.

"Looks like. You jealous?"

He drank his water, his eyes fixed on the women across the bar. "A little."

"Just a little?"

"Yeah." He set the glass down and picked up his guitar case. "I knew what I was getting into with your sister. We're not in love or anything. She can do what she wants. Now, if *you* were seeing someone, that would be a different story."

She laughed, rolling her eyes. "Yeah, yeah. Get the hell out of here."

"You mind if I grab some dinner before heading home?"

"Go ahead. I'll see you tomorrow."

He winked, waving as he headed to the kitchen.

"Oh, no," the cook said.

"What?"

"I've already shut the fryer down. Don't ask me to make you shit. It's closing time."

"Come on, please?"

The man sighed. "Only if it's fast."

"I'll take anything."

"Mm," He took a plate from the line. "Someone canceled an order of wings after I got them ready. They've been under the light for about twenty minutes."

"I'll take them." He took the plate and walked toward the stairs.

"Hey, where you goin' with my plate?"

"I'll bring it back."

"You better. I know where you live."

He snickered. "See you tomorrow."

"Yeah, see ya."

Ophelia stumbled into the bar, plopping herself down on a bar stool and tapping the corner.

"One," Rue told her, pouring a shot. "I'm closing soon."

She knocked it back and put the glass upside down on the counter.

"Girl, you smell like a brewery. I thought you didn't drink at work."

"I don't."

"You're wasted."

"I'm not *wasted*, just buzzed."

"If you say so."

"And, I don't *work* anymore. I quit."

"For reasons?"

"Several."

"Okay."

She turned to see Violet talking to someone she didn't recognize." "Who's that girl?"

"A new you, I suspect."

She looked back at her. "Huh?"

"In case you haven't noticed, my sister's kind of a ho-bag."

She lifted her eyebrows. "Kind of a cunty thing to say about your own blood, isn't it?"

"No judgment. As long as you're all good with your arrangement, I say have fun. But, your heart rate sped up the second you saw her with Marley. I know you like her more than you let on."

"*Marley?*" she mocked. "Is that her name?"

"Mm-hmm. She's my new singer. And your new...I don't know. What do you all call yourselves?"

"Our names," she said, glaring at her.

"All right, don't get defensive. I know it's not my business, I'm just saying, be careful. I don't want you two making a scene in my bar when this blows up. Keep your relationship drama upstairs, k?"

She smacked her lips and again turned to stare at the two in the booth, her leg shaking as she crossed it over the other. "No drama here."

"Fuck," Ophelia whispered, tripping over the curb and catching herself on a lamppost. She opened the door to the diner a few blocks from the bar and sat at a table. While she waited, she tried to push the memory of what happened at the club from her mind. Quitting was the right thing to do. It was too tempting. Maybe at her next job, she'd insist on no private dances.

"You know what you want, sugar?" the server asked, setting a menu in front of her.

"Carbs," she told her. "And coffee. *Lots* of coffee."

"Rough night?"

"Something like that."

She poured her a cup of steaming hot coffee. "I got just the thing. Comfort food at its finest." She turned her head to call to the kitchen. "I need a jack benny with frog sticks in the alley!"

"Heard!" a man behind the counter called back.

"You want me to leave the pot?" the waitress asked.

"Please," Ophelia said, taking three sugar packets from the dish on the window side of the table and tearing them open.

"Well, I guess my nickname for you was accurate." She winked, setting the pot down and shuffling off.

She dumped the sugar in her coffee and stirred it with the spoon she'd taken from the folded napkin. Her head was already pounding, filled with the image of Violet with that girl. *Marley*, she thought. *Her parents are probably hippies. Feels like cultural appropriation but whatever.* She sipped her coffee and checked the time on her phone. It was still a couple of hours before sunrise and she wanted to stay out until Violet was asleep. She knew she'd say something dumb in her current state and didn't want to make any waves if she didn't have to. *Just need to clear my head.*

"Here we are," the server said, reappearing with a plate of food. "This should fix you right up."

"Thank you."

"You're welcome, sweetie." She placed the check on the table and walked off.

Ophelia ate a handful of fries and took another sip of coffee before diving into the sandwich, its melty cheese and crisp bacon doing little to ease her mind. *Don't be jealous.* She finished her coffee and poured another cup. *At least, don't show it.*

She got home just before seven a.m., relieved to see Violet's bedroom door closed for the day.

"You're just getting back?" Iman asked, not looking up from his notebook.

"Yeah. Working on a new song?"

"An old one. I think after some polishing, this one will be ready for its debut."

"That's nice." She sat across from him at the dining table.

He put his pen down. "What's with you? You sound upset."

CHAPTER 8

"A lot of things. Quit my job."

"Dudes start getting handsy?"

"You could say that."

"I wouldn't sweat it. You'll find another club to dance at. Black goth chicks are always in demand."

"That's what I said!" She leaned back in her chair and crossed her arms. "That's not my real problem, though."

He raised an eyebrow.

"Did you see Violet with that girl tonight? Marley?"

"Oh, yeah. I saw." He took a sip of water from his bottle.

"And?"

"And, what?"

She threw her hands up and let them fall to her lap. "Of course, you don't care."

"What's that supposed to mean? I care," he defended.

"Please. It's *obvious* you have a crush on Rue."

"I do not."

"Bullshit," Lennon said from the sofa, eyes glued to the television screen.

"Hey!"

"See?" Ophelia said. "Obvious."

"*Anyway*, yes, I saw Violet with Marley and yes, it bothered me. A little. But, we all agreed she can fuck who she wants. What's the point of getting worked up?"

"This wasn't just a sex thing. The way she was looking at her was different."

"Different than what?"

"Than how she looks at us."

"And, how does she look at us?" he asked.

She got up to head to bed. "Like food."

Chapter 9

From the shadows, the vampire stalked his prey, his eyes shining in the dimness of the pub's neon sign like a cat's. The woman, a pretty redhead draped in fuchsia chiffon stumbled toward him, her stilettos more of an obstacle than a fashion statement. He waited, letting her come to him, hidden in the dark next to the pub's entrance. He watched her, her curves moving beneath her dress inciting in him a twinge of arousal. Today, she would be described as "thick" but when he was alive, she would have simply been considered healthy, the gold standard of femininity.

As she got closer, he revealed himself, blocking her path. "Excuse me, love," he said, stopping her in her tracks. Her eyes widened, her hand flying to her chest. He could hear her heart beating faster as she clutched her purse, moving her hand from her ample cleavage to the zipper. "I'm wondering if you could help me. I've seemed to have gotten lost."

"Lost?" she asked, taking a step back.

"Yes. I'm meant to be at the Arora but I've somehow gotten myself turned round. Would you happen to know how I might get there?"

"Oh, um, yes." She took one hand away from her bag and pointed to the street. "You'll take Peglar south to Brighton then turn left on East Park. The building's huge. Can't miss it."

"Thank you." He stepped closer, buttoning his suit jacket, his smokey eyes dancing over her body. "Tell me, are you here with friends?"

"No, why?"

"Well, I don't actually know anyone in Crawley. I live in the country and spend most of my time there. I thought you might help me," He closed the space between them, a charming grin curling his lips. "Kill some time."

CHAPTER 9

She flashed a smile, her button nose crinkling as her muscles relaxed. "Really? What did you have in mind?"

"I don't know. What is there to do around here?"

"We're at a pub. Why don't I buy you a drink?"

"I thought you'd never ask." He scooped her up and sped to the alley next to the pub, pinning her between the wall and him. He ran his fingertips down her cheek to her neck, resting his palm against her clavicle as he looked her over.

"What are you doing?" she asked, her heart racing.

He moved his hand up her throat to her chin and tilted her head to the right. She trembled as he breathed her in, her too-sweet perfume mingling with the blood pumping through her veins. His pupils dilated, the black of them replacing the blue-gray of his irises. As his fangs descended, he whispered his answer, "Taking you up on your offer."

He bit down, his teeth sinking into her pale skin with ease. She gasped, her eyes going wide before rolling back, her heart rate returning to normal as the effect of his bite washed over her. He drank, ignoring her hands that now pawed at him, running up his thighs to grab his backside. She wrapped a leg around his, quiet moans escaping her strawberry lips.

When her heart began to slow and her arms dropped to her sides, he withdrew, holding her against the wall with one hand while slashing open the index finger of the other. When his own blood rose to the surface, he smeared it over the puncture wounds in the girl's neck, healing them. He licked the blood clean from her skin and gave her cheek a light tap.

"Wake up, love," he said, his voice gentle.

"What?" Her eyes flickered open. "What happened?"

"You seem to have overindulged. Would you like me to call a car for you?"

She nodded, holding onto his shoulder as she attempted to stand on her own. "What, what did you--"

"You're perfectly safe, love. Just a little drunk. I'll get you home, don't worry. No harm will come to you."

"Oh, okay." She looked into his eyes, her own barely able to focus. "What's your name, again?"

"Kenton," he told her. "You rest here, now. I'll fetch you that car."

The black cab drove off, carrying the cute redhead safely to her flat. When it disappeared around a corner, Kenton turned to begin the long walk home. He could run, making it back to his estate in Bramber in just a few minutes. But, the air was crisp and the moon full and all that waited for him at home were stone walls and an empty bed, not exactly things he was in a hurry to get back to. No, he'd spend more time in the night, letting the spring breeze tousle his hair and prickle his skin.

He took his phone from his pocket and, against his better judgment, clicked on the social media app he knew his beloved posted on most frequently. Immediately, he was bombarded by pictures of her snuggled up with a woman in black lipstick and a man covered in tattoos. It hurt more than he could bear and he wondered why he continued to look at them. Punishing himself, he supposed. It was his fault, after all, that she continued to torture him. He should have expected it. He *had* expected it. Still, the images pained him and he wondered how much longer he could endure this agonizing separation.

Chapter 10

"Luna Park?"

"I hope that's okay," Marley said. "I promised myself when I moved to the city I'd check it out and what better excuse than our first real date?"

"*Date?*" Violet teased, slinking her arm around hers as they walked through the crowded amusement park.

"Call it what you want but *I'm* calling it a date."

"Date's good." She smiled as they strolled, making their way to a roller coaster.

"Good. You're not mad it's not dinner, are you? I ate early."

"No, I'm not hungry. This'll be fun." Violet adjusted her wristband and showed it to the ticket-taker. Marley did the same and they sat in the ride.

After they were strapped in, Marley bounced in her seat. "The Cyclone. Sounds ominous."

"It's pretty tame. It doesn't go upside-down or anything."

"You've ridden it before?"

"Years ago. My dad brought us, me and my sister. He knew the guy that designed it."

She cast her a bewildered stare. "How old is your dad?"

She swallowed hard, realizing her mistake. "Old." Just then, the ride started, sending their cart forward on the track. She closed her eyes for a moment, relaxing as she thought, *Saved by the freakin' bell.*

Marley screamed with the first drop, her face lit up like an excited child's, laughing with every turn and holding her breath with every climb. Violet watched her, admiring the pink of her cheeks and the way her tiny nose scrunched when she closed her eyes. Her lips were the color of cherry blossoms and the freckles that dotted her skin were so light, even she could barely make them out in the dark.

Violet stared, ignoring the ups and downs of the coaster, her sole focus on the beauty sitting next to her.

The coaster slowed with a screech, drawing Violet's attention back to the world around her. It was over. By lusting after her date, she'd missed the entire ride. "You wanna go again?" she asked when the ride came to a stop.

"No," She got out, her steps wobbly as they walked away. "I'm a little dizzy but that was awesome! Games?"

"Sure." She pointed to a stand a few feet away. "Pyramid Smash?"

"Let's do it."

"Knock all six cans off the ledge, win a prize," the man at the stand said, his voice less than enthusiastic. He handed them each two balls and stepped aside.

Marley tossed her balls, knocking the top three cans off.

"Not bad," Violet said as she took her place.

"Not great, either." She folded her arms and pretended to pout.

She laughed. "You want a prize?"

She pursed her lips. "Kinda."

"Say no more, fam." She threw the balls hard, knocking all six down so fast, the man in charge did a double-take. "Pick your prize."

She pointed to an eighteen-inch stuffed dinosaur, her face beaming. The man took it down and handed it to her, his eyes still wide in disbelief.

Marley hugged the toy to her chest. "That was amazing! Thank you!"

"You're welcome," Violet said, taking her hand and leading her to the next game. They played Whac A Mole, then Three-Point Challenge, Violet winning both easily.

"Are you sure you haven't been here in years?" Marley asked, her arms full with the dinosaur and a giant teddy bear. "You're so good at everything."

She moved the plush bunny from one arm to the other as they walked to Tube Dash Splash. "Just luck, I guess." *Tone it down, stupid.* She thought. *She thinks you're human.*

"You think if I rub you, some of that luck will transfer to me?"

She lifted her brows and smirked as they got in line. "One way to find out."

"I want to ride the Ferris wheel but after that, we could maybe go back to your place and test the theory."

CHAPTER 10

"In the name of science."

"Step right up," the worker said. They did as he instructed, placing their prizes on the ground and taking the water guns in their hands.

"You're going down, sister," Marley jokingly threatened.

Violet snickered. "If you play your cards right."

They pulled their triggers, the streams of water blasting out and hitting their targets. After a few seconds, Violet faked a hand cramp, releasing the trigger. She started again, shooting just past the target.

"I win!" Marley yelped, putting down the gun and jumping up and down.

"Seems we're both lucky." She watched her as she picked her final prize of the night, a giant, pink elephant. *Fuck me, she's hot.*

They left their toys with the attendant and climbed into a basket. As the Ferris wheel lifted them into the air, the noise of the park getting quieter the higher they went, Violet couldn't help but notice how small everything looked. She wondered how small she looked to the people below. How insignificant. *My whole life is insignificant.*

"Where'd you go?" Marley asked.

"Huh? Sorry. I got lost in my stupid thoughts for a second."

"Oh. I do that sometimes. A lot of the time, actually." She stared. "Jesus, your eyes."

"What?" She panicked. Had she lost control? Were her pupils dilated?

"I guess I never really noticed before. They're the color of amber. In the moonlight, they almost glow. They're beautiful."

"Oh," she said releasing the tension in her shoulders. "Thanks. I kind of hate them, though."

"What? Why?"

"They remind me of my mother."

"You don't get along?"

"We *did*." She shifted in her seat. "She took off pretty early on."

"Oh, I'm sorry. That sucks."

"Yeah, no note or anything. One night she went for a walk and just never came back. My dad looked for her for years but she didn't want to be found, I guess. He thinks she went back to Egypt but who knows?"

"You're Egyptian? That's cool."

"Half. My dad's British. Like, full Giles vibes."

"Is that where you get your sass?" she teased, her tone lightening the mood.

Violet laughed. "*Yes*, actually. He's very dry, though. Calls himself 'witty'."

"He sounds nice."

"He is. A little sick of my bullshit but nice."

She laughed again, pushing her dark hair behind her ear. "Whatever your bullshit is, I'm here for it." She leaned in, ever so softly touching her lips to Violet's. They both closed their eyes as the kiss deepened, Marley brushing her fingertips along Violet's cheek, their tongues dancing in each other's mouths.

Insignificant, Violet thought. *But fun*.

Now in Violet's bedroom, the two couldn't keep their hands off each other, pawing at one another's breasts and backsides as they kissed. They rolled on the bed, legs entwined, the friction of their jeans warming their skin.

"Let's get these pants off," Violet whispered, her fingers finding Marley's zipper.

"Wait," she said, pushing away. "Wait, I think we should stop."

"Too fast?"

"Probably." She slid off the bed and zipped up her pants. "First date and everything."

"Okay." She too stood. "No problem. Second date, then?"

"*Maybe*." Her lips turned up in a smile. "I should go, though. It's late."

"I'll walk you out." They left the room, finding Ophelia perched on the bar.

"Whose this?" she accused.

"This is Marley," Violet answered, flashing her a warning glare. "Marley, this is my roommate, Ophelia."

Ophelia scoffed.

"Nice to meet you," Marley said, waving as she walked to the door.

CHAPTER 10

"Mm, hmm."

Violet shot her another look before opening the door for her date. "Talk tomorrow?"

"Count on it." Marley kissed her again and turned to go. Violet closed and locked the door before addressing Ophelia.

"What the fuck was that?"

"Does she know what you are?"

"No, not that it's any of your business."

"So, you haven't bitten her, yet?"

"Of course not. Again, not your business."

"But, you like her."

"Chill out. We've been on *one* date."

"Plus all the time you've been spending making googly eyes at her at the bar."

She sighed. "What's your point?"

"She feels very 'girlfriend'. I'm just wondering if that's what's going on, what does it mean for us?" She gestured to Iman standing in the doorway of his bedroom, his bare arms crossed in front of the Farvahar tattoo on his chest.

"Nothing," Violet told her. "Nothing's changed between us. We are what we've always been."

"Really?" She hopped down and pulled off her top. "Prove it. Take off your clothes."

She arched an eyebrow and laughed, slipping out of her own shirt. "You're giving *me* orders now?"

She pulled down her skirt and kicked it away. "You're doing what you're told, so I guess I am."

She took off her pants, stepping out of them and leaving them on the floor as she unhooked her bra.

Ophelia finished undressing and walked over, grabbing her by the back of the neck, their faces now only inches apart. "Maybe it's time *you* go down on *me* for a change."

She bit her bottom lip. "I think I like this side of you."

She slapped her ass and turned her to face Iman, guiding her toward him. The two walked past him, climbing onto his bed as he followed, unbuttoned his jeans, and kicked the door closed.

Violet flicked her tongue over Ophelia's swollen clit, slipping two fingers inside of her as she moaned, gripping the headboard and writhing on the mattress. Iman stood behind the vampire, pushing her legs apart and entering her, one hand on her breast, the other fondling her drenched pussy.

She went through the motions, allowing her body to respond to every touch and sensation, but it wasn't her lovers that ignited her arousal. Thoughts of Marley swept through her mind like a hurricane, the memory of the taste of her lips and the smell of her skin doing more to spur her toward climax than the man railing her from behind.

As Ophelia's groans grew louder as she finished, it was Marley's voice Violet heard. When she looked up at her, it was Marley's face she saw twisted in pleasure. And, when she, herself began to come, it was Marley, not Iman, who she imagined pulling her up on her knees.

He pressed her back to his chest as he continued to thrust, his right hand still tickling her clit while the left wandered her body. She reached up, throwing an arm over his shoulder and cradling the back of his neck as he kissed her ear.

Her eyes flew open, the pupils completely dilated and her fangs growing. Ophelia crawled toward her, getting up on her knees. She moved her hair away from her neck and tilted her head in offering. The vampire bit down, holding her by the shoulders, keeping a few inches between their bodies as Iman railed her from behind.

While Violet was distracted by feeding, Ophelia looked Iman in the eyes. He returned her gaze, squinting in bewilderment. She took the hand he'd been using to tease the vampire's nipple and glided it down her own body. His eyes grew wide as she plunged his fingers inside of her.

CHAPTER 10

Now with two hands knuckle deep in pussy, Iman massaged both in unison. Ophelia reached forward, grabbing his ass and urging him to pump harder. He obliged, quickening his hands' movements as well. All three came, their cries so loud it was hard to tell whose was whose.

Iman backed away, catching his breath. Violet stopped, dropping Ophelia, limp on the bed. She used the tip of a fang to cut her finger and used the blood to heal the wounds on her lover's neck.

"Still think there's a problem?" she asked, heading toward the door. But, as she retrieved her clothes and went to her own room, thoughts of Marley lingered.

"I know there is," Ophelia whispered, struggling to stand. Iman helped her to her room, getting her into bed to rest.

"I'll get you some water," he told her.

She grabbed his hand, not letting him leave. "I'm right. I know I am. This Marley girl is trouble for us. I can feel it."

Chapter 11

Ophelia knocked back her fourth shot of the night, half-listening to Iman's band play and ignoring the middle-aged man on the stool next to her. His drunken stares went unnoticed by *her* but not by the vampire directly across who'd had more than her fill of creepers for one night.

"Yo," Rue snapped, getting the man's attention. Ophelia too blinked out of the bubble she'd been in to see what was happening. "Time to go."

He squinted as if trying to decide if she was being serious.

"For real, get the fuck out."

He leaned over the bar, the stench of whisky and arrogance wafting off him making her stomach turn. "I'm not going anywhere, young lady."

She met his stare with her own, stone-faced and unflinching. "I beg to differ."

He smirked. "Get me the manager."

She too offered a cocky grin. "Okay." She spun around, doing a complete three-sixty and facing him again. "Hi. I'm the manager. Get the fuck out."

His cheeks went red as he sat straight. "You can't kick me out. I haven't done anything wrong! What's your problem?"

"Call it a vibe."

"This is a public place! You can't just--"

"Wrong, my guy. It's a private place. Privately owned. By me. And, I say it's time for you to get your windowless van-having ass out of my building before I have you arrested."

He scoffed. "Arrested? For what? I was just sitting here."

"Seems pretty drunk and disorderly to me," Ophelia chimed in, recognizing the entitlement of a predator. She'd dealt with guys like this a million times and was in no mood to do it again. If Rue was willing to handle it, the least she could do

CHAPTER 11

was help out. "And, since you told him to leave and he refused, I'd say he's also trespassing."

"No one was talking to you, slut."

Rue's eyes began to dilate, her lips pursing. "I'm very close to giving up on this whole asking nicely thing."

Ophelia noticed her eyes and hopped off her seat, scurrying around to the other side of the bar. She'd only seen Rue angry a few times before but that was enough for her to know better than to be in her way once her pupils start to change.

Rue clenched her fists as she held herself back. "I'm gonna count to three."

"Go ahead," the man taunted. "Count. Call the cops. I'm not leaving." He threw back the last of his drink and folded his arms in defiance.

"You fucking better."

He rolled his eyes. "Bitch, make me."

She relaxed her hands, her pupils returning to normal. She turned her gaze to Ophelia standing a few feet to the right of her. "You heard that, right?"

She nodded.

"Not my fault, right? No one can blame me."

"*I* sure can't."

"What are you skanks blabbing about?" the man asked.

Rue shifted her focus back to him. "I tried to let you walk out of here. I really did. But, remember," She leaped over the bar, landing next to him and gripping his thinning hair, pulling his head back and speaking into his ear. "You were asking for it."

She dragged him across the bar to the entrance, his kicks and shouts of, "Let go!" going unnoticed by the crowd whose attention was held by the band. Once outside, she quickened her pace, skidding the man along the pavement in a blur to the alley around the corner.

She threw him against the wall, holding him there with one hand, amused by the terror in his eyes. "Normally, I'd mutilate you somehow, torture you a bit. Luckily for you, I have to get back to work so this'll be quick."

"What the hell?" he whimpered.

"Not super lucky, though." She opened her mouth wide, letting her incisors descend and clamping down hard on his neck. She swallowed fast, not wanting to make a mess. She let him go, his limp body hitting the ground with a thud.

"I'm on it," she heard a voice in the distance. She recognized it as Marley's and peeked around the corner. She saw her with an older woman wearing a long, flowing dress and several bracelets made of various stones standing next to a cab, its door open.

Her mother? Rue guessed, their similar features clear in the light of the streetlamp. Their body language was stiff and their expressions tight. Not quite arguing, but she could tell the conversation was tense. She knew she shouldn't eavesdrop, but she also couldn't let her sister's latest conquest find her with a dead body. *Guess I'm staying put.*

"You should have been home days ago," the older woman complained. "You know how important this weekend is for your sister."

"*Sister*," Marley said, making quotes in the air.

"Adia *is* your sister." Her features hardened, her eyes like daggers, her thin lips pressed together so tightly, they all but disappeared.

"Yes, ma'am," Marley sighed.

"Blood isn't the only thing that makes a family. Your sister may be adopted but she's my baby as much as you are. She didn't come from me but she's been mine since I watched her come into this world."

"I remember." Marley shuddered as if cold but Rue didn't feel a breeze. She kept listening, glancing around to make sure no one could see the body slumped in the shadows.

"Be kind to your sister," the older woman said, her voice softening as she touched her daughter's cheek. "Eighteen is a big deal. She needs you now."

"I know," Marley said, looking down at her shoes. "I'll be nice."

She smiled. "Good. Now, wrap things up here and come home. And, remember dinner tomorrow. Everyone will be there."

"Everyone?"

"Your cousins are done with their thing upstate. They'll be expecting you."

She nodded.

She sat in the cab. "I'll see you tomorrow. Love you."

CHAPTER 11

"Love you, too." She closed the door and waved as the cab pulled away.

Rue could see her body relax as she turned and headed inside. "About time," she whispered to herself. With the women gone and no one else close enough to hear, she dragged the body over broken bottles and discarded cans to the side entrance of the bar. "It's oven time for you, dude."

Inside, Ophelia retook her place on her bar stool, resting her elbow on the counter and her cheek on her fist. She listened to Iman and the band, their cover of Crazy Bitch hitting a little too close to home. She waited for Rue's return, her mind again drifting to thoughts of Violet with Marley, the way she'd introduced her like a knife to the heart. *Roommate*. She winced at the word repeating in her mind. Bitch, skank, slut, and the myriad of other derogatory words men used to belittle or mistreat her over the years she could handle. She was used to them, but *roommate*? Roommate was the most insulting of all.

She looked up to see the kitchen door fly open, Violet rushing through it and into the bar. A smile began to form on Ophelia's lips but was quickly halted when the vampire sped right by her, seeming not to notice her sitting there and running into Marley's awaiting arms near the entrance. The two shared a brief kiss before swiftly exiting, leaving Ophelia to stew in solitary anguish.

She bolted up, slamming her hands on the kitchen door and heading up the stairs to the apartment, her stomach in knots and her cheeks hot. The music faded, but her anger only grew.

Iman watched Ophelia leave the bar as he sang, doing his best to keep his head in the performance but knowing he was doing a mediocre job at best. His thoughts bounced between the night before, the memory of Violet and Ophelia's wet pussies in his hands arousing him to the point that he was grateful for the guitar he held in front of him, and the twinge of jealousy he hated to admit he felt when he watched Violet leave with Marley.

He'd always known the arrangement he had with Violet was temporary and purely physical. She wasn't in love with him and he didn't love her, either. Still, seeing her with Marley did feel strange. Ophelia was right. She did seem different with her.

He pushed his emotions from his mind and finished the song, the cheers from the crowd reassuring him that even at his worst, he was still an amazing frontman.

"Did you see that shit?" Ophelia said, not waiting for Iman to close the door before hurling complaints in his direction. "The way she ran over and hugged that bitch? Went right past me. I bet she didn't even notice I was there."

"Yeah, I saw," he said, taking a sip of beer, the third bottle he'd taken from behind the bar after his show, putting his guitar case on the dining table, and sitting to take off his boots.

"And introducing me as her roommate? What the fuck was that?" She paced the floor, hands on her hips and rage in her steps. "You know what that means, right? She hasn't told her about us. I don't think she plans to, either. She's *hiding us* like

CHAPTER 11

some dirty secret." She got a bottle of water from the fridge and placed it in front of him.

He twisted off the cap and took a sip. "Thanks."

She crossed her arms and continued ranting. "She has no respect for us. We're *pets* to her. Mistreated pets, even, that she leaves in a crate while she gallivants around with her new girlfriend."

"The apartment being the crate?"

"I'm serious. You saw how she looked at her, how she kissed her. Our time with her is coming to an end, I know it. That girl has her wrapped around her finger and pretty soon, we're gonna be out on our asses, homeless and alone."

"Is that what you're worried about? Being on the streets again?"

Her shoulders slumped as she hugged her arms. "It's not the main thing I'm worried about but it's on the list."

"You won't be homeless. I have money saved. Worst comes to worst, we'll get a place together. Lennon, too, if they want."

"Really?" She sat across him, her demeanor softening.

"Yeah, we'll be like that show from the nineties. Three friends hanging out all day, working on a rare occasion, drinking coffee and shit."

She giggled but as soon as the noise escaped her throat, her face fell. "She's gonna leave us behind."

"Probably," he agreed. "I just always thought it'd be that British guy Rue's always mentioning that ended our arrangement, not some random girl from the bar."

"Right? I *wish* it was that guy. I can compete with a guy. I can *share* with a guy. But, this girl..." Her voice trailed off and Iman rested a comforting hand on hers.

"I guess we just have to enjoy the ride while it lasts."

She nodded, her eyes moving from their hands to his face. She looked him over, her eyes filling with lust. "We've never fucked, have we?"

His eyebrows shot up and he sat back in his seat. "No."

"It's against the rules, isn't it?"

"I think so."

"The rules only *we* have to follow."

He swallowed hard.

"But you've thought about it, right?" she purred. "Thought about me?"

He looked around the room, half expecting Violet to pop out of a corner and slash their throats for even having this conversation.

"I know you have." She stood, unzipping her jeans and pulling them down along with her panties.

"Ophelia,"

"Last night," she continued, stripping off her shirt. "When you touched me."

"*You* did that," he said. "I never would've taken that risk."

"But, you did." She unhooked her bra and slid it down her shoulders, dropping it to the floor. "I started it but you finished it, remember?"

He grew hard as she stepped closer, the memory of her coming in his hand and her naked form in front of him arousing him fully. "You know we can't." His voice strained as he fought to control himself.

"Okay," she said, bending to unbuckle his belt. She unbuttoned and unzipped his leather pants. "If you want me to stop," She tugged on the pants, moving them down his legs with his boxer briefs, revealing his rock-hard erection. She swung her leg over him and sat, her pussy just touching his balls. She slid herself up and down his shaft, his cock twitching in anticipation. "Tell me no." She hovered, circling her clit on the head of his dick, trembling as her pussy tingled.

"This could get us killed," he all but whispered, gliding his hands up her thighs and grabbing her ass.

She used her hand to help guide him into her, licking his earlobe as she began to buck, his gasps of pleasure spurring her on. "Maybe," she breathed, closing her eyes. "But, at least we'll die coming."

Chapter 12

Alexander sat alone in the dark club, its only working source of light three sconces along the far wall opposite his table. He'd finished clearing out the debris and took a moment to rest which turned into several moments which turned into hours. He took a sip of rum straight from the bottle, his eyes taking in the gutted remains of his life's work. The club had been everything to him. A sanctuary of sorts for not only himself but for all vampires. He'd managed to keep its whereabouts and patronage secret for hundreds of years and in one night, the blink of an eye, really, it was gone. The shell remained and he'd rebuild, of course but it would never be the same. It would never again be the safe harbor it once was.

He chugged the remainder of the bottle's contents and threw it hard against the wall, breaking the middle sconce in a shower of sparks and broken glass. He covered his lightly-freckled face, weeping into his palms. It had been so long since he'd felt grief, he'd forgotten what it was like. The emptiness. The cold. The unending pain of death's grip around one's heart. He'd thought he'd escaped it as most vampires do by not keeping human acquaintances. He'd been fooling himself, he decided. He wasn't truly immortal. None of them were. Just harder to kill.

From outside, he heard the slamming of a car door. He jumped to his feet and skidded across the ashen floor to peer out the broken window. There, he spied the hunters' van, two men already out of it and another four leaping from the open sliding door. They carried what looked like children's high-pressure water guns spray-painted black. "Filled to the brim with Holy water, no doubt," he whispered to himself, taking his phone from his back pocket and sending a text. "Too many to take on alone." He scanned the room for weapons but found none. The place was barren, wiped clean with fire and broom.

He planted himself against the wall next to the door, the muscles in his face twitching as he tensed, the fury in his chest building with every step he heard his would-be attackers take. The green of his irises went dark and his fangs slid down, his fists balled tight as he prepared himself. But, instead of a half-dozen men storming through the door, balloons came shooting in through the window. Dozens of Holy water-filled balloons were thrown in, a few hitting Alexander in the chest and legs as he tried to dodge them. He cringed, his skin sizzling underneath his wet clothes. He scurried to a corner until the borage subsided, black and white bits of latex floating in puddles in front of him.

"Here, monster, monster, monster," one of the men called. One by one they entered, guns drawn, headlamps lighting their path. Alexander moved to another corner of the room, closer to the back door. "What was that?" the man asked, holding up his fist. The others stopped. He made a swirling motion and the men spread out, their lights all pointing in different directions. Alexander took a step toward the door, the floor creaking under his boot.

"Got him!" A second man announced, his light shining in the vampire's eyes.

He squinted, shielding his vision as he bolted for the door. He'd gotten a few steps from freedom when the first man yelled, "Fire!" Suddenly, he was drenched in the Holy water of six guns, his skin burning as if doused in acid. He tried to run but it was no use. The searing pain was too great. All he could do now was drop to his knees, cover his face, and curl into a ball to protect his heart.

"Move your hands!" the first man barked. He didn't. "I said, *move your hands!*" He made a fist in the air, again signaling for the others to stop. They holstered their weapons as he walked toward him, his own gun still pointed but not firing. He kicked him in the ribs causing Alexander to wince. "Move them, *now!*"

Still, he refused, every nerve in his body screaming so loudly, he could barely hear the order.

"goddamn it," the man huffed, dropping his weapon and kneeling in front of him. "Help me out, Johnny."

The second man rushed to his side and the two pried the vampire's hands away from his face.

"Is this the one?" the first asked.

"Nah, it's not him," Johnny answered.

"I bet you know who it was, though, don't ya, strigoi?" a third man chimed in.

"Is that true, vampire?" the first asked. "Do you know who offed our friend the other night?"

Alexander snapped his wrists free and focused his eyes on the man in front of him. "Wha, what?"

Johnny stood up and kicked him in the gut. He gasped, clutching his stomach and quickly moving his hands away when they touched the wet cloth of his shirt. "Don't play stupid!" Johnny said. "We know Brian didn't just up and leave without sayin' nothin'. You think we don't hide surveillance cameras in our homes for just this sort of thing? We do. I watched the footage myself. Could see your mate's face, clear as fuckin' day."

"So," the first man said. "You're gonna tell us where we can find him, right now."

Alexander scoffed. "Or what?"

"Or, we get what we need out of ya the hard way, drag you along, make sure your mate knows you betrayed him, then make you watch us kill him before takin' your sorry ass out as well."

"Fuck off."

The man's lips curled in a vicious grin. "Have it your way." He picked his gun up off the floor and pointed it at him. "This'll be fun."

***

With his belly full and his senses heightened, Kenton walked to a secluded garden that, though open to the public twenty-four hours, was empty this time of night. He admired the trees and flowers for a time, imagining bringing his beloved to see them one day. He wondered if she'd find it as beautiful as he did or if she didn't care for such things. There was still so much he didn't know about her, and she him. He let his mind drift, lost in memories of the last time they'd been together. The softness of her hair, the sweetness of her skin. He wondered if he'd given her enough time or perhaps, far *too much* time. Could the wounds of separation be mended by closing the distance? Could what he'd done be easily forgiven or would she make things difficult? Of course, she would. Their time together had been brief but there was one thing he was sure of after years of stalking her social media and sending her gifts with no reply, if he knew nothing else was that Violet doesn't make *anything* easy for him.

He was startled from his thoughts by the screech of tires, the hunters' van squealing to a stop a few feet behind him. He spun in time to see the band of hunters jump out, two of them dragging his friend between them. Alexander was bound in iron chains, paler than usual, clothes damp, and head bobbing as if his neck could no longer support it. Then men pushed down on his shoulders, forcing him to his knees, and in the light of the moon, Kenton could see the slow-healing Holy-water burns covering his cheeks and forehead.

"This the one?" the man to Alexander's right said.

"Yeah, that's him," the one on the other side replied.

"Good." He kicked Alexander in the lower back. The vampire grunted. "Would've hated havin' to torture this one longer to get the real answer." He looked to the rest of the men with a sleazy smile plastered on his face. "Who am I kiddin'? I wouldn't have minded a tick."

The others laughed.

"So," he said, turning his attention to Kenton. "What'd you do with him, then?"

He flashed a sly smile while feigning innocence. "With who?"

The four behind them raised their weapons as the first man responded. "You know very well with who. We've got ya on film stakin' him, draggin' him from his flat. So, before we join our mates in celebratin' the end of your kind here in Crawley, we're gonna give him a proper burial, after cuttin' his head off, that is. Just in case."

"And, after we dispose of you strigoi pieces of shit," the second man seethed.

"One thing at a time, Johnny." The first man held the barrel of his gun to the back of Alexander's head. "Tell me what you've done with him, where you buried him."

"Why should I do that?" Kenton asked, folding his arms and shifting his weight from one foot to the other.

"Because, I reckon if I start squirtin' in one spot and keep goin' in that spot, eventually the Holy water here will burn straight through to your friend's brain. Am I right?"

He shrugged. "Don't know. It's a definite possibility."

His lips pulled back, his cheeks going red. "*Where is he*?!"

He sighed. "You mean Brian? I dumped him in the woods not far from here. From the looks of things, I'd venture to say I did him a favor. I only caught a brief glimpse of the sad sod's life but from what I could tell, it was pretty grim. The man reeked of whiskey and loneliness."

Alexander let out a quiet snicker.

Johnny kicked him in the outer thigh. "What are *you* laughin' at?"

"You absolute charlie's." His eyes lifted to meet Kenton's, smirks on both of their faces.

"Now, Alexander," Kenton mock-scolded. "No need to be smug."

Johnny scrunched his brow. "The fuck are you two on about?"

Alexander cracked his neck. "There were six of you wielding Holy water and who knows what else. I could have taken two, maybe three of you down before the rest killed or subdued me. But, this one," He tilted his head toward Kenton. "He's built for brawling. Raised in it since he was a neophyte. Trained. Taking you on alone would have been suicide. I knew my best chance was to play along."

"Play...along?"

His irises went black, fangs protruding as he spoke. "I brought you right to him."

"He sent me a text," Kenton told them. "You're not the only ones who can adapt to the times." He glanced at the water gun held to Alexander's head. "Those toys look ridiculous, by the way." He altered his gaze to his friend, a twinge of excitement running through him as he heard the men's heartbeats quickening. "Those chains look terribly cumbersome. I'll relieve you of them, shall I?" He winked as his own eyes blackened.

"FIRE!" the first man shouted, but before he could pull his trigger, Kenton had him by the arm. He swung him away, then flung him forward, hurling him into two others. He swooped around behind Alexander, kicking Johnny in the chest, sending him careening backward while he made quick work of breaking the chains. The two men still standing sprayed acid-like water in their direction as Kenton whisked Alexander out of sight behind an exceptionally wide champion tree.

"Here," Kenton unbuttoned the cuff of his left sleeve and rolled it to his elbow. "Just enough to get your strength up."

Alexander took the wrist to his lips and sank his fangs into the cool flesh. He drank for a few moments, his wounds healing and his energy returning. He pulled away, licking his lips. "Thank you, old friend."

"Of course." He slapped him on the shoulder and rolled up his other sleeve.

He peeked around the tree, spying all six men headed toward them, weapons raised. "What's the play?"

Kenton too took a glimpse at their opponents. "Standard disarm and dismember?"

He nodded with an upside-down grin. "An oldie but a goodie."

"You ready?"

"As ever."

"On go, then."

They moved to just outside the tree's protection, arms wide and lips pursed.

In a low voice, Kenton gave the command. "Go."

Faster than human eyes can see, the two launched themselves toward the hunters, swiping away four of their guns and snapping the necks of the last two to remain armed. The four scrambled to retrieve their weapons, turning on their headlamps to see better in the dark. The vampires could hear their pulses pounding and smell the sweat clinging to their fragile bodies as they stalked forward, the gentle hiss of the wind through the grass drowned out by the men's frantic breathing.

"You look rather famished," Kenton said. "Perhaps you should stop for a bite while I finish up here?"

Alexander flashed a fangy grin. "How very kind of you."

They descended on the men, Alexander chomping into Johnny's neck, gripping his arms until he stopped struggling. He pulled away. "I hate this one the most." He went back to it, drinking him dry as his eyes glazed over.

Kenton couldn't help but have a snack, himself, snatching the man that had first spoken to him by the hair and biting him from behind. As he drank, another man barreled toward him, fists raised. Not breaking his bite, he thrust one arm out to his side, plunging his fingers into the attacker's abdomen, gathering a handful of intestines, and yanking them from the man's body. He let the two go and chuckled at the sight of his friend still sucking on Johnny's throat, eyes fixed in determination.

CHAPTER 12

"And then, there was one." Kenton stepped to the final hunter who stopped crawling in front of him, tears pooling in his bloodshot eyes.

"Get away from me, demon!" He sat up on his knees and shoved a hand into his jacket pocket. "I said, get back!" He pulled out a small, white and gold cross and held it up.

Kenton scoffed. "Again, you people show your ignorance." He knelt down, plucking the object from his grip.

Terror filled his eyes. "But...but, the Holy water."

"Hurts us because the man that blessed it believes. He has faith. This," He spun the trinket in his palm and tossed it aside. "Was made in a factory by machines. It's plastic, for God's sake. Perhaps, if you had faith in it. If you truly believed. But, you don't, do you? Tell me, hunter. Do you believe in anything?"

Again, he reached into his pocket, bottom lip quivering but eyes like steel. "One thing." In his fist, he held a grenade and in the blink of an eye, he pulled the pin, a single tear dripping down his cheek. "Moarte la strigoi."

Kenton's eyes went wide, the grayish blue replacing the black as his pupils adjusted. He leaped up, flinging himself as far as he could. The grenade exploded, bits of charred hunter scattering in a plume of smoke and flame.

"Bloody hell," Alexander gasped, dropping Johnny's depleted body. "Kenton?!"

"I'm here!" he called back, dusting off his slacks. They met in front of the burning remnants of the exploded man.

"What do you think? Bury or burn?"

Kenton considered it, looking down at the flaming mess. "He was kind enough to start a fire for us. Be a shame to squander it."

Alexander nodded in agreement, taking a flask from his back pocket.

Kenton piled the other bodies around the flaming corpse and Alexander sprinkled them with rum.

"By the way, that celebration they were talking about,"

"Mm?"

"I found out where they're having it."

Kenton raised a brow. "How'd you manage that?"

"Snooped through Johnny's phone between gulps."

He laughed. "I guess there's more fun to be had, then."

He nodded, holding his palms open to the fire that rose from the hunter's corpses. "Chilly night."

Kenton joined him in warming his hands. "Indeed."

Chapter 13

"So," Violet said, taking in her surroundings, her lips turned up in a condescending grin. "This is your place."

Marley closed the door and giggled. "I know it's a little sparse."

"Sparse?" She glanced around at the bare, white walls, tiny kitchenette, and pink curtain that offered little privacy for the wall-less bathroom. The only furniture was a futon along one wall with a blanket draped over the back and a crate on one side that held a laptop and box of tissues. Clothes were in a pile on top of a suitcase with a small makeup bag on the floor next to it. "Girl, I've seen dungeons with more of a personal touch."

"Have you?"

She pulled her close and moved the hunter-green hair off her shoulder. "Are you on the run?" she teased. "Hiding from the law? I promise I won't tell."

"It's temporary," she said allowing her hands to wander to Violet's backside.

She laughed. "Clearly."

"Are we gonna keep talking about my sad studio or are you gonna put that mouth to better use?"

She smiled, her eyes twinkling under brows lifted in surprise. "Okay, I see you." She kissed her, her hands running up her arms to her shoulders, neck, and head, her fingers like claws in her hair.

Marley led her to the futon, still in its sofa position, and lay her down, kissing her harder as Violet's head rested on the stiff, black fabric. Their legs intertwined as they pawed at each other, Marley's tongue dancing in her girlfriend's mouth as the heat between them grew. She slid a hand down her pants, finding the smooth skin of her pussy completely drenched.

Violet moaned as Marley's kisses moved from her mouth to her neck, her warm breath against her skin sending shivers down her spine. She grabbed her ass with one hand and held on to her arm with the other, begging with the movement of her hips for her not to stop the swirling motions she made on her clit.

More moans escaped Violet's throat as she neared orgasm but before she could get there, she felt the ache of her teeth descending from her gums. She held the back of Marley's head and turned her face away, hoping to conceal her showing fangs. She tried to keep them tucked in her mouth, but as they cut through her bottom lip, she yelped in pain, realizing that had been a mistake. The pain overrode the pleasure she'd been feeling, allowing her to force her teeth back to their normal size.

"Are you okay?" Marley asked, popping her head up. "Oh, God! You're hurt. What happened?" She reached over Violet to pluck a tissue from its box. She dabbed the blood away and sat up. "Did I bite you?"

"No," Violet assured her, feigning embarrassment. "I did. I guess I got too excited. I should go."

"Now? Are you sure?"

"Yeah." She jumped up and made a beeline for the door, sure if she let anything else happen, she wouldn't be able to control herself. "I'll see you tomorrow?"

"I can't tomorrow," she said, a twinge of disappointment in her voice. "I have a family thing. The day after?"

"Okay, I'll see you then." She scurried out of the apartment, closing the door and leaning against it, her hand over her heart as she whispered to herself, "That was close."

Violet walked into the loft and was greeted by Iman and Ophelia sitting on opposite sides of the kitchen table. Iman's leg shook, his foot tapping on the floor and his gaze averted. Ophelia sneered, her expression smug but her eyes flashing with anger.

CHAPTER 13

"What's up?" Violet asked, dropping her purse on the table. "No, tell me tomorrow. I need to get some sleep. It's been a long, frustrating night."

"Why?" Ophelia stood, her hand on the back of her chair. "That bitch couldn't get you off like we can?"

Violet sighed. "I'm not in the mood for your theatrics right now. I'm going to bed."

"I'm right, aren't I? You were with *her*. Again." She pulled the chair out and threw it aside, knocking it over.

"Ophelia!" Iman warned.

"No." She took a step toward Violet. "I'm sick of this shit. You treat us like trash. Three can play that game, though. While you were off with your new flavor of the month, me and our boy were fucking. Right here at the table. It was good, too." She got closer. "Can you smell him on me?"

Iman let out a shaky breath as he waited for the impending punishment, rubbing his arms, his throat so dry, he couldn't swallow.

"I can, actually." Violet sniffed the air and took a step back. "Huh."

"What?" Ophelia asked.

"I just," She crossed her arms and pressed her lips together. "I don't care."

"What?" Ophelia snapped.

"Yeah, what?" Iman asked, his leg going still.

Violet shrugged. "I don't give a shit. Do what you want. Each other, other people. Whatever. I know it's against the rules but I just can't bring myself to give a fuck."

Heartbreak mixed with rage in Ophelia's eyes. She gritted her teeth, taking a step forward. Before she could stop herself, blinded by her emotions, she raised her hand, letting it fly through the air between them and slapping the vampire hard across the face.

Iman gasped, jumping in his seat.

"Oh, God," Ophelia whispered, terror covering her face as Violet's expression went dark. "I'm sorry. I didn't mean to--"

Violet's eyes went black as she grasped her by the throat, walking her across the room, kicking the fallen chair out of her way, and pinning her to the fridge. Ophelia grabbed the vampire's wrist, unable to speak as she tried to breathe. Iman stood but Violet shot him a look that planted him back in his seat.

She looked back to Ophelia who continued to squirm. "You seem to be confused, so I'll clear things up for you. We are not in a polyamorous relationship. We aren't together. You're my *entertainment*. Why do you think that no matter how many times you've begged, I haven't made you like me? We only turn people we love." She paused, letting the words sink in. "You're only here for as long as you please me and you're very close to wearing out your welcome. Like I said before, Marley is none of your business. Do whatever you need to do to deal with your jealousy but don't bother me with it again. Do you hear me?"

Tears pooled in Ophelia's eyes, the sound of her choking growing fainter as she nodded.

"We fuck and I feed. The end. Cool?"

She nodded again.

She turned back to Iman, still holding Ophelia against the stainless steel appliance. "Are we cool?"

"Yes," he blurted. "We're cool."

"Good." She let go, storming off alone to her bedroom.

Ophelia coughed as she labored to breathe, rubbing her throat and leaning on the table.

Iman got up and helped her sit. He got her a bottle of water and tilted her chin up to look at her eyes. "You have a broken blood vessel," he said examining the streak of red in her left sclera. "You'll be okay, though."

She took a few small sips, her throat burning when she swallowed the cool liquid. "I shouldn't have hit her."

"No, you shouldn't have."

"I've never seen her like that."

"Me, neither."

"I knew Rue was violent but I thought she just had anger issues. I guess it's a vampire thing."

He picked up the toppled chair and sat next to her. "Rue isn't like that."

"She is."

"She's not."

"That girl kills bar creeps *for fun*. I mean, I don't blame her but--"

CHAPTER 13

"Rapists and would-be rapists, sure," he conceded. "She's gotta eat *something* and they kind of have it coming. But, what Violet just did," He shook his head. "There's no excuse."

She lowered her head. "I hit her."

"Yeah, and you shouldn't have done that but she could have *killed* you. She knows her strength. She didn't even lose control like with me the other night. She was just proving a point. Listen, I think we should--"

"No."

"Ophelia,"

"No." She looked up at him, new tears threatening to fall. "I won't leave. Not while there's still a chance."

"A chance for what?"

A tear tumbled down her cheek as she grabbed the water bottle, refusing to look him in the eye. In a voice so small he could barely hear she responded, "For her to love me."

Chapter 14

"Where the hell have you been?" Ophelia barked from her seat in the kitchen as Lennon entered the apartment, pharmacy bag in hand.

"Hello to you, too," they said, locking the door behind them.

"Where?" She stood as Iman rubbed his temples.

Lennon cast her an annoyed glare. "Contrary to what you think, I do actually have a life outside of this loft."

"Convenient time for you to discover outside."

"Okay, you're in a mood. What'd I miss?"

Iman slouched in his seat and answered, "Argument about Violet's girlfriend."

"Ah," Lennon said, setting their bag down, getting an apple from the counter, and taking a bite.

"That's all you have to say?" Ophelia snapped. "It doesn't bother you that she has a full girlfriend that I'm pretty sure she's in love with?"

"Why would it bother me? We all agreed a long time ago to her rules." She took another bite. "It's called respecting boundaries."

"Ugh! Just zip it. Your opinion doesn't matter, anyway."

They scrunched their brows. "The fuck's that supposed to mean?"

Iman let out an exasperated sigh. "Ophelia, please stop talking."

"No," Lennon said, setting the half-eaten fruit on the counter and folding their arms. "I want to know exactly why my opinion doesn't matter."

"You know why," Ophelia told her. "You don't care about her like we do. You aren't interested in her. You don't even fuck her."

Lennon tilted their head, eyes widening. "Wow."

"She didn't mean it," Iman interjected.

"Yes the fuck I did. You don't have a *relationship* with her. You're just dinner."

CHAPTER 14

Iman stood to look her in the eye. "You're out of line."

"I'm right and they know it."

Lennon pushed Iman out of the way, closing the space between them and Ophelia. They looked her dead in the eye, anger covering their features for the first time since moving into the loft. "You think because I'm Ace I don't mean as much as you to her? You think I'm somehow less than when it's *you* going around begging for scraps of her attention?" They shook their head. "I'd feel sorry for you if you weren't such a bitch. I might not have the kind of physical relationship with her that you do but I guaran-fucking-tee I'm closer to her than you are." Lennon turned, retrieving their apple and bag, and stormed off to their room, slamming the door.

Iman leaned against the fridge, shooting a disapproving glare in Ophelia's direction.

"What?" she said.

He stared.

"Fine," she sighed. "I'll apologize later. Right now, I need a walk."

"Hey!" Rue shouted, locking the bar's entrance and turning toward the noise she heard behind the counter. "Bar's closed!"

"Sorry," she heard as she made her way across the room. She walked around the counter to find Ophelia sitting on the floor, knees pulled to her chest with a bottle of whisky in her hand. "I didn't know where else to go."

Rue relaxed her posture, sighing as she lowered herself to sit next to her. "Maybe you've had enough," she said, taking the bottle.

"Maybe you should mind your business."

She smiled, holding the bottle to her lips. "In case you forgot, this *is* my business." She took a swig and set the bottle on the floor.

"Oh." She wiped her nose on her sleeve. "Right."

"What's the haps, Drunky McDrunk-Face?"

She held back tears as she answered, "I think it's over."

"With Violet?"

She dropped her head and nodded.

"Because of Marley?"

"Fucking Christmas tree-looking bitch," she mumbled.

Rue laughed. "Hey, I like her hair."

"Not as much as your sister likes her pussy, apparently."

"Not a visual I need, fam."

"What's the deal? Why does she like her so much? I don't get it. She's not even that hot. And, why is she bored of me? I'm awesome. I do anything she wants. I mean, *anything*."

"Girl, I'm begging you to stop."

"For real, it doesn't make sense. That bitch has been in here a million times, V doesn't even notice. Then, one day, BAM, obsessed."

"My sister's a fickle bitch," Rue said, picking up the bottle and taking another sip. "Always has been. Hyper-fixates then gets over it. Best to not get attached."

"Too late."

"I know it won't make you feel better, but this girl is just another distraction. Pretty soon, she'll be off with her dude and once that happens, the days of her boning whoever are over, anyway."

"You mean that British guy? The old-ass vampire?"

"Yeah."

"You're right. That does *not* make me feel better." She wiped away a stray tear.

Rue held out the bottle. "Fine, drink what you want."

"Thanks," Ophelia said, taking it and guzzling the remainder of its contents. When she was done, she tossed the bottle toward the trash can directly across from her. It bounced off the side, shattering on the floor.

Rue closed her eyes in aggravation. "Motherfu--"

"I'm sorry. I'll clean it up." Ophelia got to her knees, then her feet, stumbling into the counter.

"I'll get it," Rue said, getting up and leading the drunk woman through the kitchen to the stairs but once at the base of the staircase, Ophelia stopped.

She shook her head. "I don't want to go home. Not until I'm sure Violet's asleep. I don't want to risk another fight."

"Fight?"

"It's not a big deal," she said, rubbing her throat. "I was yelling and then--"

Rue snatched her hand away, revealing the marks on her skin now visible in the brighter light of the kitchen. Rue's eyes darkened as she examined the bruises and the red line in the white of her left eye. "My sister did this?"

"I'm fine."

"Mm-hmm."

"I slapped her first. It's not just her fault."

She pulled a key from her back pocket and handed it to her. "You can stay at my place tonight."

"Rue, don't--"

"I'm just gonna talk to her."

"I appreciate all the times you've looked out for me but you don't have to--"

"Go to bed, Ophelia. Nothing's gonna happen."

Rue threw the door open to Violet's apartment, storming in without bothering to close it behind her.

"Oh, shit," Iman whispered from the kitchen, watching her stomp to Violet's room, the determination on her face giving him chills.

She kicked open the bedroom door, startling her sister who'd just gotten into bed for the day.

"What the hell, Rue?" she said, pushing back her covers and swinging her feet over the side of the bed.

"I told you," she said through gritted teeth. "Didn't I? I told you when you got with my singer that keeping live-in human lovers was too dangerous but did you listen? Of course not. Violet does whatever the fuck she wants, no matter who gets hurt."

She rolled her eyes. "You're just jealous I got to him before you did."

Rue ignored her jab. "And then you brought in Ophelia, knowing her self-esteem is shit because you, what did you say? 'Needed variety'?"

"I'm bi. Sue me."

"You're an entitled, self-absorbed piece of shit and if you were anyone else, I would have killed you already."

"What is your problem?!" She stood, taking a step toward her.

"You left bruises on that poor girl's neck! Do I have to remind you what I do to humans that do that shit?"

"Don't look at me like I'm some kind of wife-beater. She smacked me *first* after insulting the woman I love."

"Love?" she scoffed. "You've been on what, three dates? The fuck's wrong with you?"

"I can't have feelings?"

"Not when they don't make sense. And, *not* when you use them to justify hurting people."

"Look who's talking!" she shot back. "You straight *murder* people every goddamn day."

She folded her arms. "Not *every* day."

"But, that's fine because they're *bad* people."

"Pretty much."

"But, I get a little out of control in an argument and suddenly *I'm* a monster."

Rue stepped closer, letting her pupils dilate. "We were born monsters. Nothing sudden about that. But, it's no excuse for getting people to care about you and treating them like garbage." She leaned in, speaking quietly in her ear. "I love you, but if you hurt that girl again I'll make you wish you hadn't."

She scoffed. "What are you gonna do?"

She shot her a knowing look.

"You think because you're older you can take me?"

"I think it'd be dumb as shit for you to give me an excuse to find out."

Chapter 15

Kenton and Alexander slunk around the side of the country house, listening through the stone wall. There were seven heartbeats muffled under the sounds of cheers and laughter. Their voices were loud as was the snapping of can lids. The vampires could smell the stench of cheap beer from outside, its repugnant bitterness making their stomachs turn.

Inside, the men drank, downing can after can in celebration. "All right, boys, all right," one of them said, motioning for them to be quiet. "Let's all settle." The room went silent but for a few slurping noises as the men finished their beverages. "Now, I know we've all been down since the girls were killed in Worthing and we've had a hard go of it without them but," he opened another can. "Well, boys, we avenged them, didn't we?"

"Yeah!" they shouted, slapping each other on the back and clinking cans.

"We've done well here but now it's time to move on."

"Move on?" another man asked. "Where are we going?"

"Brighton. Word has it, there's a blood-sucker there that tosses his victims in the sea when he's done with them. Authorities say they drown but do drowning victims lose all of their blood when their lungs fill with water?"

The men shook their heads, mutterings of, "no" and "I don't think so" passing their lips.

"Course not. So, drink up, boys." He lifted his can in a toast and the others did the same. "We've done real good here but the work's not over. These monsters are everywhere so we have to be, too. Tomorrow, we fight again. But tonight, we celebrate."

Alexander positioned himself on the roof where he could watch for anyone that might try to escape while Kenton readied himself near the front entrance. Before he could make a move inside, however, a man stumbled out, thick fingers fumbling with his belt buckle. Kenton snatched him by the collar and dragged him around to the side of the building out of earshot of the hunters inside.

"What the fuck?!" he yelped.

"A bit drunk, are we?" Kenton pinned him to the wall, his eyes shifting. "Seems you've all celebrated prematurely as I am, as you can see, very much alive."

"But," He grabbed his wrist but it didn't budge. "We were told--"

"You were lied to, clearly. Someone jumped the gun."

He took a sharp breath, ready to scream but the vampire covered his mouth.

"So many different ways I could kill you. Disembowelment, beheading, tearing you apart with my bare hands. Plucking your eyes from their sockets, pulling your scalp from your head. Prying your jaw apart and sticking my hand down your throat so I might yank your lungs from your over-fed body and watch happily as you suffocate. I still haven't actually made up my mind. Shall I ask your opinion?" He took his hand away, allowing the man to speak.

"Fuck you, vampire."

"Not my type, sadly."

"Piss off!"

"Come now. We don't all get the chance to choose how we come to our end. Seems you're wasting a perfectly good opportunity." He leaned in, his fangs glinting in the light of the stars blanketing the sky. "You must have a preference."

CHAPTER 15

Inside, the men continued to celebrate, the leader chugging his third beer of the night. "Oi," he called to a man a few feet away. "You called Johnny, yeah?"

"I did," he answered.

"Well, what's keeping him? You'd think he'd want to be here."

"Why should he be here? He wasn't there the other night, was he?"

"Nigel, you can't blame a man for making a living."

"And, I suppose he won't be joining us in Brighton, either?"

"That's for him to say, innit?"

"Since when do we put things like jobs above the mission?"

"He's doing his best. You know--"

"Yeah, I know," Nigel said, setting his can down. "I feel for him, I do. Sarah was a good woman. But, Johnny hasn't been right since."

"Have any of us? You forget it wasn't just Johnny who lost someone. Harold and Devon also lost wives. Andrew lost a sister. And, we all lost Kate."

"Kate," Nigel leaned against the wall. "That was tough."

"Yeah, it was. So, cut Johnny some slack, yeah? If he needs to drown his sorrows in the mundane for a tick, who are we to whinge?"

"Maybe you're right."

"Course I am." He slapped Nigel's back. "We all grieve differently. Johnny takes a job where he can drink all day and no one notices. He still finds blood-suckers for us to go after, though, with his gadgets, doesn't he?"

He nodded.

"Right. Some people cry. Some eat their weight in sweets. And, we take revenge, don't we?"

"That's right!" He picked up his can, clinking it to the other's. They both drank. "Speakin' of missing lads, didn't Jasper go for a piss ten minutes ago? Where the hell is he, now?"

The door burst open, a severed leg, shoe still laced on the foot, flying into the room. "There," Kenton said from the entrance. "Scattered in the field, some pieces in the trees on the other side of the property. A little in my teeth."

The men jolted to attention, scurrying around the room looking for weapons.

"You know, I gave him the chance to choose a less painful death but he'd have none of it. Told me to do my worst. I think he underestimated my resolve." He rushed in, grabbing one of the men before disappearing out the door. When he returned, he was alone, his chin covered in fresh blood.

Nigel raced toward him, balling his fists. Kenton laughed, speeding to meet him and dragging him by the hair to the field outside. There, he thrust his hand into his chest, pulling out his heart and taking a bite of it as the man's body fell.

Inside, the leader threw wooden stakes to his friends before arming himself with a crossbow he took from a black bag under the table. Kenton flew in again, taking another man outside. After a few seconds, the man's corpse broke through the window, landing in front of the leader in a spray of broken glass.

Their eyes couldn't keep up as another man was taken. The final three stood, backs to one another, as they listened. "What's that noise?" one of them whispered.

"It's coming from the roof," the leader said. They looked up, weapons drawn as the footsteps from above stopped.

"You think he's up there?"

The leader nodded, pointing his arrow to the ceiling. But, before he could get a shot off, the roof caved in, the missing man's body falling through, crushing one of the last men standing.

"Holy shit," the leader said, backing away, pulling the other man with him.

"We've got to get out of here." He jerked away from the leader and made a break for it. He'd gotten to the doorway when he was stopped in his tracks by Kenton stepping in front of him.

"Where are you off to?" the vampire asked.

The man raised his stake but Kenton snatched it, spinning him around and driving the wood into his heart.

"Jesus, Mary, and Joseph," the leader said.

"I assure you, they won't be joining us."

He pointed his weapon. "You stay right there, you evil son of a bitch!"

CHAPTER 15

"Now, why would you go and insult my mother? She was actually a very lovely woman."

"I mean it, freak!"

He stepped closer. "Or what?"

He released an arrow. It whizzed through the air on a direct course with the vampire's heart. He caught it, holding it in front of him and snapping it in two.

"So, you boys travel about, hunting vampires in your spare time for what, amusement?"

"Get the fuck out of here!" He reloaded, again pointing the crossbow in Kenton's direction.

"Or, is this more of a holy mission you think you're a part of?"

"Not one step closer!"

He kept coming. "No one's been caught hunting my kind in centuries. I was sure people like you no longer existed."

"You don't know what *kind* I am." He squeezed the trigger, another arrow releasing. Kenton swatted it away like a fly as he moved closer.

"Enlighten me."

"I'd rather die."

He smirked, closing the space between them, tossing the crossbow aside, and hooking his fingers through the man's hair. "As you wish." He jerked the leader's head to the side and sank his fangs into his neck, drinking until he heard his heart stop. He dropped the body, retching on the foul taste of sour beer that defiled the man's blood.

He took a handkerchief from his pocket and wiped his face, listening carefully for sounds of life. There were none. He surveyed the damage he'd done, considering the best ways to dispose of the corpses that littered the floor. As he pondered, a strange rustling came from outside. He looked to the hole Alexander had put in the roof and saw what looked like flickering in the sky. The noise grew louder and was soon accompanied by odd shrieks.

"You about done in there?" Alexander called from above.

"Finished."

He jumped down in front of the doorway. "Good, because it's getting rather strange out here."

He left the building, looking to the skies. Hundreds of crows flew overhead, descending onto the roof, their cawing so piercing, he had to cover his ears. They filled every inch of the roof while still more came, landing in the trees on the edges of the property. They were all around him, wings flapping and voices loud; pained even. If he didn't know any better, he'd swear they were in mourning.

"What in the bloody hell is this?" Alexander asked, covering his ears, as well.

"I've no idea."

Chapter 16

After a few hours of restless sleep on Rue's sofa, Ophelia went home. While her roommates slumbered late into the afternoon, she crept into Violet's bedroom, her tip-toed footsteps soft as to not allow her heeled boots to click on the hardwood. As she got close to the nightstand, she kept her eyes trained on the sleeping vampire, her throat going dry. She lifted the phone from its charging station and quickly opened the contacts menu. When she found Marley's number, she silently repeated it to herself and put the cell back where she'd found it. She took her own phone from her pocket and typed the number into a tracking app. Once she had the location, she shoved her phone back into her pocket. Before leaving, she took a moment to watch Violet sleep. Her muscles remained tense, her jaw tight and her eyes slits as she stood there staring, unsure of everything that mattered. She took a breath and left the room.

"Watcha doin'?" Lennon asked from the kitchen, shoveling a spoonful of sugary cereal into their mouth.

Ophelia jumped, her hand flying to her heart. "Jesus, you scared me." She joined them at the table. "I was just--"

"Stalking?"

She shot them a look before lying. "I just wanted to talk to her but obviously, she's not up, yet. I didn't realize how early it was."

"Mm-hmm." They took another bite, skepticism coloring their pale features.

She quickly changed the subject. "I like your hair. You do that this morning?"

They nodded.

She bit the inside of her cheek. "Listen, I want to apologize for last night. I--"

They held a hand up to stop her. "Don't worry about it. It's fine."

"No, it's not. I was a dick. This whole Marley thing has me feeling--"

"Insecure?"

She glared at them. "I was gonna say twitchy but whatever. Anyway, I shouldn't have taken my frustrations out on you. I'm sorry."

They shrugged. "Yeah, well, I shouldn't have called you a pathetic bitch so I guess we're square."

She raised her eyebrows. "I don't remember you calling me pathetic."

"It was implied."

"Rude, but apology accepted." She stood and made her way to the front door.

From their seat, Lennon called after her, "I didn't actually apologize."

She opened the door and laughed before calling back, "It was implied."

"Fuck," Ophelia whispered, realizing she'd left her bag at Rue's. She crossed the hall and used the key Rue had given her to sneak back into the apartment. She retrieved her bag and as she turned to go, she heard the bedroom door close.

"Where are you hurrying off to?" Rue asked, her tone suspicious.

"Just out for breakfast." She squeezed her eyes shut, mentally crossing her fingers.

"Try again."

"What do you mean?"

"Your heart's beating faster than a teenage boy home alone. You're nervous and lying. Come on, spill."

She turned to face her, her shoulders slumping. "Fine. I'm going to do some digging into this Marley bitch, okay? I don't like her, I don't trust her, and if I can find something proving she's bad news, maybe Violet will dump her ass and things can go back to normal."

She cleared her throat, folding her arms, one eyebrow raised.

"You're judging me? I don't care. Call me what you want; impulsive, crazy, jealous, *pathetic*. Maybe I *am* those things. But, something is *off* with that girl and I want to prove it."

CHAPTER 16

Rue let her arms fall and puffed her lips.

"You think I'm ridiculous?" Ophelia accused.

"I didn't say that."

"But you're over there making faces."

"I'm just," she thought for a moment.

"Are you gonna stop me?"

She looked her over. "No. No, I don't think I will. I *could,* obvs but I think you might be on to something. I don't know *what* but V *has* been acting out of character lately."

"Right?!" Ophelia said, hope filling her eyes.

"Yeah. I mean, she's been banging you and Iman for years without catching feelings. All this has just been her blowing off steam until--"

She rolled her eyes. "Yeah, yeah until she goes back to her man."

"I'm not trying to hurt your feelings, I'm just saying she doesn't get attached like that but a week or two of hanging out with this girl and she's *in love*?" She shook her head. "Doesn't add up. Not to mention that bullshit last night."

"I know, right? This bitch has her brainwashed." She took her phone from her pocket and pulled up the tracking app, flipping the screen to show her. "I'm gonna go see what she's hiding."

She peered at the screen. "Is that where she is right now?"

"Yep." She turned it to face her and read the location. "Openaki Road, Denville, New Jersey."

"That's about an hour from here. Go. The sun'll be down in a little while. I'll check the address she gave me when I hired her. Be careful."

She nodded and turned on her heel.

"And, Ophelia,"

"Yeah?"

"Don't get caught."

Rue knocked on the door, ignoring the bark of a dog coming from the apartment next door. "Marley," she called. No answer. She knocked again, making sure no one was home before turning the knob, breaking the lock, and letting herself in. She flicked the overhead light on and closed the door behind her. "Marley, are you here?" She knew she wasn't but didn't want to take any chances. Getting caught snooping through her employee's stuff wasn't exactly a good look.

Her boots squeaked on the cheap flooring as she walked around the small studio apartment. The place was nearly empty, the futon the only thing that wasn't permanent to the building. "Does she even live here?" she wondered, opening the kitchenette's solitary cabinet to find it empty. The dorm-sized fridge was also bare. Just when she thought she had the wrong place, a draft blew through carrying the scent of something foul. "The fuck is that?"

She followed the scent to the window and tugged on the string of the mini blind. It lifted, revealing a small, white satchel sitting on the window ledge. Her eyes widened, her mouth hanging open as she stared, the putrid stench of too-many herbs wafting up from the tiny bag. She let go of the blind's toggle and took a step back. "Fuck me."

"Am I the asshole?" Violet asked, fiddling with a napkin, the smell of Lennon's lunch mixed with other foods in the restaurant making her stomach turn.

"Usually," they said, taking a bite of steak.

She cast an exasperated glare.

CHAPTER 16

They scoffed. "What? Like you don't know."

"I'm being serious."

"So am I. You're selfish, self-absorbed, lack impulse control, and generally give zero fucks about how your behavior affects anyone else. Everything's your way or get the fuck out."

"Please, don't hold back."

"Do I ever?"

"I guess not."

"Listen, V, I love you but you're kind of a dick. We all put up with it, though because usually, you're also pretty sweet. Thoughtful, you know? You get us little gifts here and there for no reason, you talk to us about our days. You give a shit. Lately, though..."

"Lately," she sighed, rolling her eyes and crossing her arms. "You mean since I started seeing Marley."

"I'm not saying it's her fault, or yours, or anybody's. I'm just saying, you used to treat Ophelia and Iman with more respect. I mean, not a *ton* more, but still."

"They've been getting on my nerves lately," she admitted. "Ophelia especially. She's jealous and clingy and--"

"It's because she's in love with you, dumbass."

She shook her head. "She knows better."

"Right, because she's known for being logical."

"She keeps pushing me and testing me--"

"So you freaked out on her? You think what you did was okay?"

"You don't know what happened. You weren't there."

"No," they said, dropping their fork to the plate, the sharp clang making Violet flinch. "I wasn't there. But, I was there earlier today when Ophelia came home with fucking bruises on her neck. I was there last night when your sister broke the goddamn door down and screamed at you. I could hear her lecturing you all the way from my room and that bitch *never* yells at you like that. It's usually just condescending looks and not-what-I-would-do-but-whatever-*idiot* speeches. So, no, I don't know exactly what happened but I can say with one hundred percent confidence that in this instance, you are *definitely* the asshole."

"Fine," she said, again playing with her napkin, looking down at it in her lap. "I was wrong. I went too far."

"*Way* too far."

"Yes, way too far."

"And, taking *me* out to a fancy restaurant is *not* a way to make up for it. I'm not the one that needs an apology, not that an apology is anywhere near good enough."

She threw her napkin in her lap and put her elbows on the table, leaning in and lowering her voice. "I know what I did was fucked up. I feel guilty and I feel ashamed. But,"

"*But?*"

"The idea of apologizing to her, or even just seeing her makes me want," Her phone buzzed on the table. She picked it up, saw a text notification, and put it down. "It makes me," The phone buzzed again. "For fuck's sake." She turned it off and slammed it down so hard, the screen cracked.

Lennon sat back, fear in their eyes.

"Sorry," Violet said. "I just can't with people right now."

"What does it make you?"

"What?"

"You didn't finish your sentence. The idea of seeing Ophelia right now. What does it make you?"

"Oh, right." Her pupils dilated as she lowered her head, still holding eye contact with the human she trusted most. "I'll never admit it to them, especially to Rue but I'm starting to scare myself."

Their voice trembled. "Why?"

"Because what it makes me is angry. Not just annoyed or pissed off. Like, rage-y. I don't want Ophelia to stop being jealous or to accept Marley. I don't want her to forgive me." She stared, her hands beginning to shake as Lennon's stomach dropped. "I want to *hurt* her."

Chapter 17

The aroma of stale blood lingered in the air as Kenton untangled himself from the limbs of the two women he'd finished feasting on. He hadn't killed them; only left them exhausted by draining them just enough to satiate himself and gifting them with hours of spirited sex.

He'd treated himself to drink and debauchery after a long night of slaughtering hunters but now, after a good day's rest, he was once again bored. Perhaps Alexander was right. His life *was* lonely and shallow.

As the two rested, he draped himself in a paisley-print satin robe, not bothering to close it before picking up a book of poetry from the nightstand and walking out onto the veranda. The night air was crisp against his exposed skin, the breeze a welcome relief from the heat of the bedroom. He gazed down upon the gardens, admiring the wild, purple flowers he'd had planted along the periphery. He hoped, in the future, they would be appreciated by his beloved.

He tied his robe and sat in the hand-carved Mughal swing, the wood less comfortable than his bed, but the ambiance more conducive to relaxation at the moment. He opened the book, the moonlight enough to allow him to see the words on the page. He sighed, wondering if *she* was reading the copy he'd sent to her at that very moment. But, of course, she wasn't. She didn't care much for poetry, gifts, or romantic gestures of any kind, it seemed. He'd done everything he could think to do to endear himself to her whilst giving her the space she continued to demand but he was growing impatient. It was becoming painfully clear that if he was to have what he wanted, he would have to take it.

Chapter 18

"Is it done, yet?" Adia asked, watching Marley grind the ingredients together with a mortar and pestle, the impatience in her voice grating on the older sister's nerves.

"Not yet," she told her, adding a little grass to the basil and pepper concoction.

"How much longer?"

She grunted, adding a splash of water to the mixture.

"Leave your sister alone to work," their mother said, entering the room.

"This is taking too long," Adia griped. "She'll never be done in time. She should put her stuff off until after--"

Marley slammed her hand on the kitchen counter. "I might've been done by now if not for your incessant badgering."

"Adia, go help your aunt with preparations," their mother instructed.

"But,"

"Now."

The girl pouted, fists balled at her sides. "Fine." She spun around and stomped off, leaving the two alone.

"Yeah," Marley scoffed. "*She's* ready."

"There's that tone again."

"Well, excuse me, Mother but being right is a touch irritating when no one will listen to you."

"Stop it now. That girl has worked harder than anyone to get here. You know what she's--"

"Kind of my point. It shouldn't be that hard. And, it *isn't* when you're--"

"That's enough. Now, I expect you to be back here by midnight, whether you're done in the city or not."

CHAPTER 18

"I'll be done."

"Good, because you know how important the Initiation is and how important it is for you to be there."

"It's not *actually* that important for me to--"

"*You will be here.*"

"I'll be here, geez. Can you give me a little space so I can do this, please?"

She took a step back and waited.

Marley arranged blue, purple, and white candles around the now-finished potion and lit them, taking a deep breath and closing her eyes before speaking. "May the truth I seek be revealed to me. May the hidden come to light, so mote it be."

"Huh."

"What?" Marley snapped, opening her eyes and flashing a cold glare at her mother.

"Nothing, nothing. I just usually use a lapis lazuli crystal for that incantation but whatever works."

She rolled her eyes, taking the bloodied tissue from her pocket and dipping it into the potion, careful to avoid the flames.

"Finally get what you needed?"

"Yep," she said, holding up the tissue that now glowed in the spots Violet's blood once was. A satisfied grin crept across her face, the low light dancing in her eyes. "Proof."

A cool, spring breeze sent chills up Ophelia's bare arms, her studded black tank top doing nothing to protect her from the elements. She'd left in such a hurry, she hadn't thought to bring a jacket on her spy mission. She had no idea what she was looking for, skulking around the old two-story house in the middle of nowhere like a burglar. Worse, a burglar without a getaway car. She'd gotten a ride via an app on her phone and now that she was there, alone in the dark of night, surrounded by trees and not much else, the house the only one on the block, no street lights in sight, the main road a good ten minute walk away, and her phone's battery at fifteen percent, she was starting to regret all of her life's decisions.

"The fuck am I doing here?" she whispered to herself, leaning against the home's white siding. She knew Violet didn't love her. She knew she never would and with the events of the night before replaying in her mind, she wondered if she even wanted her to. She'd hurt her, treated her as bad if not worse than some of her previous abusers. She knew she should stand up for herself; leave the loft, get a place with Iman away from the vampire that could kill her in a second if she felt like it. She knew it was the right thing to do. Still, her obsession wouldn't allow it. Not yet, anyway. She had to fight for Violet; for the way things were before this girl disrupted everything. She had to exhaust every possibility of making things work. She had to so if it ended, at least she'd know she tried. *I need therapy*, she thought, blowing out a breath before edging closer to a window. She peeked inside, the lacy curtains obscuring most of her view.

It looked to be a living room with several women walking around, a teenage girl seeming to be the center of everyone's attention. She smiled as she mingled, talking to a few of the women before skipping to a table and picking up a bunch of white unlit candles. She had long, dark hair and her skin tone reminded Ophelia of Violet's. *For fuck's sake, bitch, not everyone looks like her. Get a grip.* But, she couldn't help but stare, her addiction bringing her back to thoughts of her lover with every reminder. From the girl's skin to the sound of women laughing to the scent of flowers somewhere out of sight, it all took her back to times she'd spent with Violet. She closed her eyes, reminiscing about a particular night a few months before when the vampire had come home particularly hungry for more than just blood. They'd fucked for hours, Ophelia coming so many times, she'd lost count. When Violet had bitten her, the world went away. It was then that she realized she loved her. When she knew she was fucked.

The sound of the back door snapping shut jolted her from her memory. She crouched underneath the window, holding her breath, hoping no one could see her. She popped her head around the corner of the house to see the girl carrying a box through the yard and into the woods beyond it. Soon, an older woman joined her carrying her own box, this time propping the door open. *The fuck are they doing?* she wondered.

"Stop worrying," a voice said from inside. "I'll be back in plenty of time. The city's only an hour away. I have four."

The voice belonged to Marley, she was sure of it by the way it grated on her nerves. *Back?* she thought. *From the city? Bitch, you're not going anywhere.* Before she could stop herself and not thinking her actions through in the slightest, she bolted to the line of cars in the driveway. She crouched next to the first one, took her pocket knife from her pocket, and jammed it into the front passenger-side tire. She pulled it out and moved on to the next one, repeating the process for all six cars before darting into the treeline to the left of the house, hiding behind a red oak until she was sure no one had seen her. "Well, that was disappointing," she whispered to herself, her body relaxing as she looked back at the house, seeing no one outside that would've spotted her. "Just a midnight party in the woods for the kid. Probably her birthday."

She pulled up the ride-share app on her phone and made her request. A driver would be there in twenty minutes. As she waited, she kept an eye on the house, hoping she'd see *something* she could use. *Anything* to make Violet suspicious or angry with her new girlfriend. *Girlfriend.* The word made her sick.

"I'm hurrying!" she heard Marley call as she rushed out the front door. She ran to the vehicle nearest the street, a VW bus, not seeming to notice the now-flat tire as she went around to the driver's side and hopped in.

"Oh, shit," Ophelia whispered as the headlights came on. She made herself as small as she could against the back of the tree as she heard the engine turn over. "Fuck." She hadn't expected her to not see the flat. She meant to keep her there, unable to get back to the city. Unable to get back to Violet, at least for a little while. "It's fine. She won't get far on that tire. She'll get to the street and turn right around." But, she didn't. Instead, she peeled out, barreling onto the road, passing the trees Ophelia ducked behind. "That crazy bitch."

She watched as she made it about a block before losing control, swerving then over-correcting, causing the van to tip over, sparks flying and glass shattering. The sound of metal grinding against the pavement shrieked in Ophelia's ears as her heart raced. She ran as fast as she could through the trees next to the road, arguing with herself as she went. Should she try to help, or should she let the bitch suffer? She stopped, directly across from the crash, windshield cracked and facing her. By the light of the full moon, she could see her, her enemy's blood-soaked face, her eyes rolled back and unmoving. "Jesus Christ," Ophelia muttered. "I fucking killed her."

"Marley!" a woman shouted in the distance. "Baby!"

Ophelia sank back further into the dark of the woods as the woman and two others sped toward the wreck. When they made it to the van, the first woman screamed.

"Settle," the second woman told her, holding her hand out. The first nodded and all three joined hands before saying in unison, "Movere." As if on command, the van lifted up and righted itself, squeaking into place as Marley slumped inside. The first woman opened the crushed door and pulled the girl out onto the street.

"Do you have--" she began to ask but the second one cut her off.

"Always." She took something from her pocket and handed it to the woman. Ophelia couldn't see in the dark what the object was but it looked as if the woman opened it and took something out. She rubbed a dark substance on Marley's head and held her hand there, nodding up to the others. The three held hands again and together said, "Sana." With that, Marley's eyes began to flutter and she gasped, still limp but alive.

"Let's get her home," the third woman said, bending to help pick the girl up.

"Wha," Marley mumbled. "What happened?"

"You're okay," the first woman said, her voice cracking. "You'll be okay."

"But, I have to--"

"It can wait."

The women walked back to the house leaving Ophelia in a state of shock. She was numb, her hands going cold and her throat feeling like she'd just eaten ten crackers. "What the fuck did I just watch?"

Chapter 19

"I thought I locked this," Rue said as Ophelia blew past her. She closed the door to the bar and turned the lock.

"You did. I have a key, remember."

"Yeah, but," she paused. "Excuse you."

Ophelia was already behind the bar, pouring herself a glass of the first alcohol she could find.

"You're gonna have to pay for that."

She shrugged, lifting the full glass and chugging the contents before gagging. "The fuck is that? Gin? Gross."

"What happened?"

She sat on a stool, pouring another glass and shaking her head. "I have no idea. You're closed?"

"Yeah, I need the night off. I need to talk to Violet. Like, *now*. Have you seen her?"

She shook her head again and downed the clear liquid. "Fuck, it tastes like floor cleaner."

"What did you see?"

"I don't know." She set the glass down, her hands trembling. "I don't know what the fuck I just saw. It doesn't," She wrung her hands and looked at Rue for the first time since she got there. "It doesn't make sense."

"What doesn't make sense?"

She covered her mouth, tears forming in her frantic eyes.

"Hey," Rue said, sitting next to her and putting a hand on her shoulder. "It's all right. I know what she is."

She slowly uncovered her mouth, her stunned expression clear in the dim bar lights. "You do?"

She nodded. "I'm handling it. Just tell me what you saw at Marley's."

"At whose now?" Violet said, charging in with Lennon not far behind.

"Your girlfriend's," Rue confirmed, turning to face her sister. "Which is not, in fact, the bullshit apartment she claimed to live in. Now, lock that door behind you and pull the cage down while you're at it."

"You two are *spying* on Marley?" She stomped toward them, fists clenched, rage in her eyes.

"I'll get it," Lennon offered, locking the door and standing on tiptoes to grab the fence.

Rue stood, blocking her sister from getting to Ophelia and daring her to raise a hand to her. "You need to hear what she has to say."

"The fuck I do!" Violet shouted. "What's wrong with you? Since when do you have your buddies go snooping around people's personal spaces?"

"Since *you* started acting like a complete psycho. I had probable cause. You know I'm right."

"Oh, of *course*. Rue the all-knowing. Rue the perfect. Rue the--"

"Shut the fuck up and listen to the girl." She grabbed her arm and walked her to the bar, stopping so close to Ophelia that their legs almost touched.

"I don't want to hear her bullshit," Violet snapped.

"You'll listen and you'll keep your mouth shut until she's done. You hear me?"

She grimaced, prying her arm away. "Fine. But, make it quick. I haven't fed, yet and I'd hate to *accidentally* take too much."

Ophelia recoiled and Violet smirked.

"You want me to get rowdy?" Rue asked. "Because I'm already in a mood. If you want to tussle..."

"I'm kidding. Let's hear her story."

The woman took another sip of gin, holding onto the glass like a safety net as she began. "It was nothing, at first. Just a bunch of chicks. Looked like they were planning a party. There was one girl, seventeen or eighteen, maybe. She looked like--"

"Skip ahead," Violet huffed. "I'm sure there's a point in here somewhere."

She nodded, still shaking. "I was hiding behind some trees and I saw Marley get into a van. She drove off but," She thought about how much of the truth she should tell and how much she should omit. On one hand, Rue deserved the truth. On the other hand, if Violet knew what she'd done to Marley's tire, she'd kill her for sure. She decided to keep her mouth shut on the finer details. "Something was wrong with the van. Like, she couldn't control it or something. It swerved around for a few seconds and then,"

"Then, what?!"

"It, it fell over on its side. I could see through the windshield. She was..."

"She was what?! Is she hurt?!"

She shook her head. "I don't," Her hands shook harder as she held back tears. "I don't know. Now, I mean. I don't know if she's...I can't--"

"Bitch, spit it out!"

"The girl was dead!" she yelped. "She was fucking dead, or at least close to it. There was so much blood and her eyes," She put the glass down and wiped away a tear. "I can't get how her eyes looked out of my head."

Violet nearly collapsed, leaning into her sister for support. "This is your fault." She stood on her own, pushing her sister away.

"What?"

"Somehow. It has to be. You did something. You--" She lunged for her but was quickly yanked back.

"What did I say?" Rue warned. "I swear to fuck, if you don't keep your hands to yourself,"

"She's not dead now," Ophelia said, unable to believe it herself. "I don't think. These women, three of them, they came and they did, I don't know, *something*. They picked up the van without touching it."

"What?" Violet asked, still poised to pounce, Rue holding her back.

"They took her out and smeared some kind of goop on her head and held hands and said something in some other language and--"

"What the fuck are you talking about?"

"I know how it sounds but they said the word and she woke up. The dead bitch *woke up*!"

"Holy fucking shit," Lennon said from the other side of the bar.

"What the fuck is wrong with you?!" Violet shouted. "Why would you make that up?"

"I didn't make it up, I swear."

Lennon sat down. "I think she's telling the truth."

She spun around to look at them. "She's *obviously* lying."

"She's not," Rue said, gently pushing her away so she could step between her and Ophelia.

"How could you possibly believe that bullshit?"

"Because I found a protection bag in the window of her apartment."

Violet's eyes became saucers. She took a step back, her face falling. "You're lying."

"I'm not."

Lennon raised their hand. "Sorry, a protection bag? What does that mean?"

Rue took her sister by the shoulders and sat her on a stool. "It means, children, that Marley is a goddamn witch."

"A witch?" Ophelia asked. "That's real?"

Rue scoffed. "You've been living with a vampire for years but witches are crazy-talk?"

"So, I haven't lost my mind?"

"I didn't say *that*, but--"

"I don't believe you," Violet muttered.

Rue sighed. "Yes, you do. You just don't want to."

Violet burst into the apartment, pulling Lennon behind her and ignoring Iman sitting on the sofa. The two went into Violet's bedroom and slammed the door. Iman got up to close the front door, still barely on its hinges after the night before's commotion, only to be confronted by Rue and Ophelia.

He sighed. "Something I should know about?"

"I'd say." Rue moved past him while Ophelia closed and locked the door. The women sat on the couch, leaving room between them for Iman to sit. Rue patted the cushion. "We need to talk."

CHAPTER 19

In Violet's room, the vampire cried, her anger being replaced by despair. "You don't understand," she wept. "Witches *hate* us. It goes back centuries. We're like, mortal enemies. They avoid us at all costs. If she finds out what I am, I'll never see her again." She put her head in their lap and sobbed as they pet her hair, offering what comfort they could.

"I'm sorry you're upset."

"You're sorry I'm upset? That's all you got?"

Lennon shrugged. "I don't know what else to say. This crying-like-a-baby stuff isn't exactly in character for you. I don't know how to deal with it."

"Right. Everything I do lately is 'out of character'. I forgot I'm not allowed feelings."

"I didn't say you couldn't have feelings. I just said it's not really your normal thing. Feel all you want. Emote away. I just--"

"Maybe she never has to know."

"Um, kind of a hard secret to keep but sure."

"No, not really. Lots of people don't know. Ninety-nine point nine nine percent of people don't know." She sat up. "I can just, you know, *never* tell her."

"That's a plan, I guess."

"You look skeptical."

"Only because it's ludicrous."

"Come on! I could pull it off." She grabbed the end of their oversized tee shirt and wiped away her tears with it.

"Dude."

"It's worth a shot, right?"

"I don't know."

"If she starts getting suspicious, I can break things off. It's not like this whole thing isn't temporary, anyway. Eventually, I'll have to go to England. Unless," Her eyes lit up. "Do you think Kenton will mind if I bring in a third?"

"See, now I *know* you're off your chain. From what you've told me--"

"It doesn't hurt to ask." She threw her arms around their neck and hugged them tightly. "I'll just keep the vamp stuff a secret. This could work."

"You're choking me a little."

"Oh, sorry. Hey, when did you dye your hair?"

"This morning. Where have you been?"

She laughed. "Distracted, I guess. I like it, though. Purple suits you."

"Uh, huh." They looked at her, wild-eyed with an exaggerated grin plastered on her face. "Yeah, you're not right, I feel."

"I'm just hungry. May I?"

"Sure, just don't have any *accidents*."

She held up three fingers. "Scouts honor."

They pulled their shirt away from their neck and leaned their head to the side. "Go ahead."

"Thanks." Her pupils dilated and her fangs descended. "You're my best friend. You know that right?" She placed a hand on the back of their head and opened her mouth, clamping down and beginning to drink.

"Yeah," they grunted as the room started to spin. "I know."

Chapter 20

"A witch?" Iman asked. "Are you sure?"

Rue rolled her eyes. "I don't know why that's so hard for you two to believe."

"It's just," He shook his head. "Nah, what the fuck? A *witch*? That came back from the *dead*?"

"I swear to God," Ophelia said, her hands wringing in her lap.

Rue brushed her hair away from her eyes and rested her elbow on the arm of the sofa. "Yeah, and I'm a thousand percent sure she did something to Violet. You see how she's been acting lately. It's not normal. She's always been a little careless but she's never been...*this*."

"Abusive." Ophelia declared, turning her head to meet Rue's gaze. "Call it what it is."

Iman gave her knee a comforting squeeze before again addressing the vampire. "You think she put a spell on her? To what? Make her violent? Why would she want to do that?"

"I don't know," the vampire sighed. "I don't know *what* she did, I'm just *positive* she did *something*."

"It's over now, though, right?" Ophelia asked. "Violet will have to dump her now, won't she? Or, if she doesn't and that witch bitch finds out what she is, *she'll* dump *her*, right?"

She chewed the inside of her lip, her serious expression getting Iman's attention.

"Hey," he said, pushing her hair behind her ear. "Is there something else? Why do you look so worried?"

She looked into his eyes, emotion building in her chest. "What if she knows?"

"What do you mean?"

"What if Marley already knows what we are? Think about it. There's no way those two have spent all this time together, kissing and whatever else without her figuring it out. Our skin is cooler. We don't go out in daylight. And, there's no way she hasn't noticed Violet's lack of food intake. Witches have hated us for-god-damn-ever. They're terrified of us. They're taught the signs, what to check for. And, when they figure out what we are, they run, and I don't just mean like, crossing the street when they see us coming. I mean, they leave town. What if she knows what we are and she's done some spell to make her, I don't know, like, a weapon or something? A super-soldier type of thing she and her coven can control like a homicidal puppet?"

His eyebrows lifted. "Do you think that's possible?"

"Dude, I don't know what's possible at this point but I know she did *something* to my sister and we have to figure out what before--"

"Before what?" Ophelia interrupted. "Before someone gets hurt?" She lifted her chin to show her bruises. "Too late."

"I meant--"

"I know what you meant, I just..." She wiped a tear from her cheek. "I can't keep doing this."

Suddenly, a loud thud came on the door, breaking its already weak hinges and toppling it to the floor. On the other side, a wide-eyed Marley stood, hand still raised as if in mid-knock. "Kind of thought that was gonna take more effort."

Rue leaped from her seat and rushed to meet the witch. "What do you want?"

She peeked her head inside, noticing the two on the couch. "Just looking for Violet. She here?"

"I feel like you should go."

She tilted her head. "So, she's not here?"

"Oh, she's here." She looked her up and down, crossing her arms. "I just don't think she should see you right now."

"Um, what?"

"Call it sisterly intuition. You have," She waved her hand in front of her. "a vibe."

She squinted at her, moving closer as if studying her face.

Rue's brow furrowed. "Girl, back up, maybe."

"Are you one of them, too?"

CHAPTER 20

"One of--"

"A vampire." She flashed a knowing grin. "Of course you are. I should've seen it sooner. She made you, didn't she? What was her excuse? Couldn't imagine living forever without her sister? Didn't want to watch as her sister got old and died? Hated the thought of losing the closest thing she's had to a mother since yours took off? Sweet of her, in theory. Too bad all she ended up doing was putting a target on your back. Now, I have to kill you both. Iactus." With the word, the vampire went flying, hurtling across the room and crashing into the wall next to the hallway.

Rue was quick to stand, laughing as the shock wore off and turned to anger at the mention of her mother. "You think my sister turned me?" She brushed off her leather pants and cracked her neck. "You don't know the difference between born and bitten? What kind of dumbass witch are you?" She stepped closer, motioning for the others to go down the hall. They complied. "Did no one teach you *anything* about our history?"

"I know all I need to. Confractus."

Her femur snapped, sending her crashing to the floor.

She moved closer, her arm raised as if winding up a pitch.

"You should have studied harder," Rue quipped, getting to her feet. "Looks like you missed the chapter on self-healing." She lunged, throwing her body into hers, knocking her to the ground, and climbing on top of her. She punched her, first in the jaw, then in the eye. She hit her again and again, her features twisted in rage. "You fucked with the wrong family, bitch."

"Stop!" Violet called from behind, exiting the bedroom and speeding past the humans to pull her sister off of a bleeding Marley. She tossed her back toward the others who yelled at her to wait. She could hear their pleas but ignored them, her only concern being her badly beaten girlfriend lying helpless on the floor. "Are you okay, baby?" she cooed, taking her face in her hands.

Rue rushed back, grabbing Violet by the arm and yanking her away.

"Get off me!" she snapped, pushing her sister away. "What the fuck is wrong with you?! How could you--"

"Iactare," Marley shouted, throwing Rue up off the ground, sending her slamming into the ceiling and back down to the floor, her head cracking on the hardwood.

"Rue!" Iman yelled, hurrying toward her only to be hurled back by a wave of the witch's hand.

"What the fuck?" Violet said, watching as Iman got to his knees and crawled to her sister. She looked back at Marley who now stood, waving a hand over her own face.

"Sana." Her skin healed as the broken bones underneath mended. Blood still stained her cheeks and teeth as she smiled the devious grin of a sociopath.

"What are you doing?" Tears formed in Violet's eyes as her heart began to break. "I thought--'

"You thought what I wanted you to think."

"I don't understand."

"It's simple. Just a few drops of a potion. A beginner's potion, even. Just some rose, jasmine, vanilla, and," She held up her index finger. "A bit of powdered fingernail. I put it in your drink, activated it with a few song lyrics, and *boom*, you're hooked."

"Hooked?"

"In love. Not real love, of course. More like obsessed. It was the only way to get close enough. Nasty side effects, though."

"Side effects?"

"Just one, really. It causes the spelled to absolutely *hate* anyone with genuine feelings for them. Like, violently." She altered her gaze to the man trying desperately to revive the vampire lying motionless on the floor. "Her being what she is, I'm surprised you're still alive."

Ophelia, huddled next to Lennon in the hall, addressed the witch through a flood of tears. "He's not the one that loves her."

She arched an eyebrow. "Oh. I guess that explains the bruises on your neck. Sorry about that. It's nothing personal. I was hoping to avoid any human, you know, collateral damage. It was just the only way to get close enough, get her guard down. I wanted to get proof it was her before I," She made a line with her finger across her throat.

"Made sure what was me?" Violet asked, holding back tears.

"The vampire that's been killing people around here, duh. For years, men have been going missing from this neighborhood. Real assholes from what I could tell.

CHAPTER 20

Most with records for domestic violence. A few had accusations of sexual assault but no convictions. I'm guessing you thought you were doing the world a favor but still."

"That wasn't her," Ophelia said.

She looked at Violet then down at Rue. "Oh."

"Did you like me at all?" Violet whimpered.

"Sure. It wasn't *all* fake. You're hot and pretty fun to hang out with if I don't think about what an abomination you are. But, I have a job to do."

"A *job*?" She let the tears fall as she trembled in despair. "Killing people is a job to you?" She stepped closer. "What the fuck kind of psychotic shit is that?"

"Not *people*," Marley condescended. "*Vampires*. Your kind shouldn't exist. You have to know how fucked up you things are. You *eat people*. So, we hunt you. All of you. For generations, my family has been--"

"You hunt them?!" Iman asked.

"Like the animals they are. We used to try to cure them but that never worked so now we just--" She looked back to Violet who stared daggers, nearly shaking as more tears slipped down her blazing cheeks. "You can't do it, can you?" The witch smirked. "You're telling yourself to hit me, push me down, punch me the way your sister did. But, you can't do it. You can't hurt me. No matter what I do, you won't lift a finger against me because thanks to my spell, you still love me." She waved her hand, tossing Violet to the side and stepping toward Rue. "I don't want to hurt a human," she told Iman. "Get out of my way and let me finish what I started."

He stood, planting himself between the women.

She shrugged. "Have it your way." She waved her hand again, this time flinging the man across the room, sending him crashing into the television screen, his arm getting stuck, sparks flying as he shook, his body filling with electricity.

"Oh, my God!" Ophelia shouted, rushing to unplug the set. "Iman! "Iman!" His body went limp, his eyes rolled back. She knelt, slapping his face and shaking his shoulders. "Iman, wake up!"

Marley walked toward the unconscious vampire, a ball of energy forming in her hand. As she approached, Violet stepped in front of her.

"I may be heartbroken right now thanks to your parlor tricks," the vampire seethed. "I might be confused, still wanting you, not able to think straight. But, no matter what, there is always one thing I know for goddamn sure. No matter what she's done, no matter how big of a pain in the ass she might be, I would rather fucking die than let someone fuck with my sister."

Marley let out an exasperated sigh. "So, you first then?"

Ophelia and Lennon ran to push themselves between the two.

"Oh, come on, guys."

"No," Ophelia said.

"Move."

Lennon shook their head. "That's not happening."

"Seriously?"

Ophelia put her hands on her hips.

"Guys, for real. Why are you trying to protect her? She's a *monster*."

"Yeah," Lennon said, looking over their shoulder and giving Violet a wink before turning back to face the witch. "But, she's *our* monster."

"Whatever. I don't have time for this. Motus." The two went flying in opposite directions, Ophelia falling into the sofa and Lennon slamming into the dining table.

Violet ran to them, listening for breathing sounds. Their eyes fluttered open and they whispered, "I'm fine." The vampire turned back to the witch, her irises going black, fangs descending as she hissed, speeding toward her former lover so quickly, she was little more than a blur. But, before she could reach her destination, the witch put up a hand as if to say stop. She didn't. Instead, she was hurled by an unseen force across the room and out the window, the shattered glass, cutting tiny scratches into her face and arms. She barreled toward the ground, slamming onto the pavement several stories below. In an instant, she was numb, unable to hear the shouting of bystanders that fled the scene. Her vision was blurry at first, then shrouded in flickering lights. She could just make out a pair of men's dress shoes walking toward her and the muffled sound of a male voice. Soon, those things, too disappeared, the cold setting in as the world went dark.

CHAPTER 20

She rolled onto her back, her head throbbing as she opened her eyes.

"You didn't have to hurry down on my account," the man said.

She stood, wobbly at first. She shuffled to the building and leaned against it, her vision clearing. "Dad? What are you doing here?"

"Your sister called. She was worried. Now, you know I have no problem with you keeping playmates but really, Violet. A witch? Have I not told you time and again to vet your lovers?"

She rolled her eyes. "Yes, Dad. We had the talk when you caught me with Andrea O'Toole in ninth grade and again when I brought Sam whats-his-name home when I was sixteen and--"

"Well, clearly you didn't take notes."

"Okay, this lecture is gonna have to wait. I have to witch to murder." She turned to face the building, digging her fingers into the side of it and clawing her way up.

"That's good dear," he called. "Make Daddy proud."

She scaled the building, cutting her hands on broken glass as she climbed back into the loft. She was relieved to find Rue up and fighting, again throwing punches, cracking Marley's ribs causing her to cough up blood. The witch fell, clutching her abdomen.

"Nice of you to join," Rue said, looking her sister over. "You okay?"

She nodded.

"You want to finish this or should I?"

Violet looked down at the bleeding witch, her mind racing. "I, I don't know."

"Oh, God! He's not breathing!" Ophelia shouted, crouched next to Iman. "I got his arm out but he's not..." She covered her mouth.

"Move!" Rue said, racing to his side. Ophelia stood, backing away, tears streaming down her face. "Iman," the vampire said, her voice soft. "Iman, sweetie, can you hear me?" She put her ear to his chest, the faint sound of his heart beating slow and weak.

Her eyes pooled as she lifted her head. "It's okay," she said, shaking as she placed a hand on his cheek. "You're okay."

Ophelia sobbed into her hand, the crazed look in Rue's eyes frightening her as she mourned the impending loss of her friend. "He's not," she whispered as Lennon put an arm around her shoulders. "He's,"

In a flash, Rue bared her fangs, turning Iman's head to the side and biting down on his neck. She drank, just a little.

Just enough.

She pulled away and used her sharp teeth to tear open her wrist, using her opposite hand to open the man's mouth. She pressed her wrist to his lips, letting her blood pour in and fill his throat. Soon, she felt him swallow the life-giving fluid, his tongue gliding over her skin, his mouth suctioning, pulling more and more from her. His eyes flew open, the irises completely black as he grabbed her arm with both hands, keeping her close as he drank. She bent to kiss his forehead, fresh tears dropping from her eyes, her pupils returning to normal. She pushed the hair away from his eyes, making sure he could see her. He stared, still drinking, the color returning to his once-pale face.

"What the…" Lennon muttered.

Ophelia watched, mouth agape. "What…I don't understand. Violet said you guys only turn people you love."

Rue shot her a look, part warning, part confirmation.

Her eyes widened. "Oh."

"Did she just," Violet started, seeing what was going on across the room.

"I think she did," Marley said, clearing her throat. "Just another one of you things I have to put down."

Violet looked down at her. "You're not really in a position to make threats."

"Of course I am." She struggled to get to her feet, her hand still holding her ribs. "Your sister's distracted and you won't hurt me."

"Wanna bet?"

"You won't. You can't. If you could, you would've by now. Face it. No matter what I do, you won't stop me. You love me too much."

"Well, *I* fucking don't," Ophelia said, popping up behind her and hitting her over the head with a lamp.

"Nice one," Lennon said, grabbing a chair from the dining room and breaking it against the witch's back. Again she fell, catching herself with her hands, blood dripping from her head wound onto the hardwood.

"I tried," Marley choked. "I tried to spare you. I didn't want to hurt human beings. The *point* is to *protect people*."

"We're people and we're fine," Lennon said. "You, on the other hand--"

"I," she said, raising her hands at her sides, her body floating up from the floor and hovering in front of them. "Am done playing nice with you people." They backed away, their eyes like saucers as the room began to shake. "You take the side of the vampires, you deserve to burn with them. Ardeat." Flames erupted from every surface. The couch and curtains were instantly engulfed. Smoke filled the room, slowly escaping through the broken window.

Rue covered Iman's head, not able to move him until he drank his fill. Lennon and Ophelia pulled Violet toward the door but Marley waved her hand, flinging them back. She blocked their exit, an evil grin curling her lips as she cast the final spell. "Cor confractus." Violet fell, her hand flying to her chest as she felt her heart begin to tear itself apart. Blood poured from her mouth as the others screamed, kneeling beside her and sobbing. Marley lowered herself, her sandalled feet hitting the floor with a click. She backed toward the door, keeping her eyes on the dying vampire, a proud smile on her blood-covered face. "And, with just enough time to get home to the--" Faster than their eyes could see, the witch's head spun one hundred and eighty degrees, her neck snapping like a pencil.

As her body fell, Violet was restored. Her heart muscle mended and any feelings she had for Marley vanished, replaced with rage and relief. The flames seemed to extinguish themselves and as the smoke cleared, the figure of a man leaning against the door frame appeared.

Violet stood, stepping forward to get a better look. The last of the smoke dissipated revealing his face; the sharp, stubble-covered jaw, high cheekbones, and thick, dark brows over eyes the color of the sea after a storm. Her legs nearly gave out at the sight of him, her newly-healed heart pounding like base in her chest. "Kenton?"

His eyes met hers, a sly grin crossing his lips as he greeted her. "Hello, love."

Chapter 21

"What are you doing here?" she asked, frozen where she stood, afraid of the pull she felt between them.

"You were in danger. Where else would I be?"

"Um, England? How'd you get here so fast?"

"I flew."

"It's an eight-hour flight."

"Maybe on a plane. I can actually move faster without one, or did you forget how old I am?"

She closed her eyes for a moment, resisting the urge to roll them. "I did not." She looked at him again, holding her arms as she fought the urge to run to him. To comb her fingers through his cocoa-brown hair. To kiss his full lips. To tear his clothes off right there in front of everyone. "How did you know I was in trouble?"

"*I* called him," her father said. Kenton stepped in, sliding to the left to allow him entrance. "You may be too stubborn to ask for his help but given the stakes, I think I was justified in intervening on your behalf."

"I'm sorry," Ophelia interjected. "Who are you?"

"Apologies," he said, stepping closer and taking her hand. He held it to his lips for a second then pat it gently before letting go. "Booth Witcomb, Rue and Violet's father."

"Oh." She glanced at Kenton. "So, he must be the *other* British dude. The soulmate or whatever."

Kenton laughed. "I'm much more than that, love."

"And, what's this?" Booth moved to stand over Iman, the new vampire's head in Rue's lap, his body drenched in sweat and seizing.

CHAPTER 21

Rue locked eyes with her father, covering Iman's chest with one hand like a shield as she pet his hair with the other.

"Very well, then." He turned his attention to the two remaining humans. "You two should go before this one wakes. He'll be quite parched and as the nearest food source, you won't make it out of the building alive. As grim as it sounds, I must warn you. I've seen it happen. Neophytes are...unstable, to put it kindly."

"Neophytes?" Lennon asked.

"Baby vampires," Rue clarified. "He's right. It won't be safe for you here. Go across the hall. There's a credit card in the pizza box in the freezer I keep for emergencies. Take it and go to a hotel. I'll call you in a few days when things are settled."

Lennon looked to Violet who nodded in agreement. "Okay," they said, taking Ophelia's hand and leading her to the doorway.

"Wait," Violet said, touching Ophelia's arm as she passed. "I'm so sorry. I wasn't--"

"I know," she said, stopping for a second and looking her in the eye, her expression stoic. "I get it." She turned away and kept walking. The two left, disappearing into the dark hall.

Violet dropped her head, whispering to herself, "Fuck."

"The rest of you should go, as well." He looked down at Marley's corpse. "I'll clean this up."

Kenton sauntered to where Violet stood, placing his hand on the small of her back and leading her to the hall. Her muscles relaxed at his touch, the need to follow him too strong to resist.

Rue got up, lifting Iman and throwing his arm around her shoulders. She half-carried him toward the door and as she moved to pass her father, he gave her a look that stopped her in her tracks.

"I don't have to remind you of your responsibilities," he said, his tone stern.

She swallowed hard. "No."

He nodded, looking back down at the body as she left. He waited until he heard the door to his oldest daughter's apartment close, kneeling next to the witch's lifeless body and unbuttoning his suit jacket.

"I'm fine," Violet lied, waving at Kenton to back off as he tried to help her down the stairs. She held onto the railing but her grip was weak, her legs wobbling more and more with every step.

"You're not," he said, placing one hand on the small of her back and the other on her shoulder. "You were nearly killed. Now that the adrenaline is wearing off, you're feeling the effects of the witch's brutality."

"I can make it down a flight of stairs on my own." But, just when she'd finished the sentence, her knees buckled. She felt something like a cool breeze hit her chest as her vision went dark and she began to fall.

Kenton caught her, scooping her up and carrying her the rest of the way down the steps. "Come on, darling." He took her through the kitchen, and to the bar where he lay her on the counter, careful to rest her head gently on the wood. He listened to her heartbeat, its rhythm slower than he'd like. "Violet, darling, can you hear me?"

"Mm." Her head tilted to one side but her eyes remained closed.

"It's all right," He moved a few stray hairs away from her cheek. "You just need to feed." He looked up, the shadows of people walking by on the other side of the glass door visible in the lights of the busy street. "I'll fetch you something." In a flash, he was gone, leaving the fence that covered the door broken and the door itself hanging open. Within a few seconds, he was back, an unconscious man slung over his shoulder. He dropped the man onto a bar stool, placed his head on the counter next to Violet's, and walked around to the other side of the bar. "Violet, sweetheart," he said, his voice soft. "You should drink." He lightly tapped her cheek until her eyes fluttered open.

"Kenton?" she whispered.

"Yes, darling." He motioned to the sleeping man. "Drink." She turned her head to see her dinner and slowly rolled to her side, scooting herself close enough that her lips hovered over the man's exposed neck. She bit down, drinking greedily, her eyes widening as her heart rate increased. She let him go, not wanting to take too much, and lay back on the bar top.

Kenton pricked a finger with his teeth and covered the puncture marks on the man's neck with his blood, closing the wounds. He then found a clean cloth behind the counter and got it wet before holding it to Violet's chin, wiping dried and fresh blood from her flushed skin.

"I can do it," she said, taking the cloth and cleaning her own face.

"Ah, still pretending you hate me?"

She flashed a condescending glare.

"That's all right, love. I hate *myself* a little for what I did, even if it *was* the right thing."

"You sure about that?"

"The self-loathing or the validity of my decision?"

She sighed. "The validity."

"Oh, yes. I've never questioned that. Though I do, at times, regret it."

She sat up, her face now inches from his, the heat between them threatening her resolve. "At what times?"

His jaw twitched as he held himself back, his pupils dilating and returning to normal as he looked her over. "Most times, actually." They stared into each other's eyes for a few moments, both fighting their impulses with every bit of strength they had. He cleared his throat, taking a step back. "Come now, love." He held his hand out for her to take. She did, hopping down. He put his arm around her and led her to the door. "I'm taking you away from this place."

"Aren't you forgetting something?"

He looked back to the man at the bar. "Yes, of course. One moment." He sped away, dragging the man outside and dumping him in the alley. He returned within seconds, again helping Violet to the exit. "Now, let's get you somewhere safe."

Contempt flashed in Booth's eyes as he took the dagger from his jacket, the inside pocket just deep enough for it to fit. He set it on the floor and reached into the outer pocket, removing an empty vial and popping off its cap. Again, he took the knife in his hand, staring at the dead woman's face as he jabbed it into her carotid. Blood spewed as if from a faucet, pouring into the vial he held in the stream. When it was full, he pulled the container away and replaced its cap, wiping it and the blade on the witch's sleeve before putting them back in his pockets.

He got to his feet, reaching down to grab the body by the hair. He dragged it across the floor, out the door, and down the two flights of stairs to the basement, the thud of it hitting each step behind him doing nothing to alter his intense expression. Once in the room, he made his way to the incinerator, ignoring the pain as the hot handle seared the flesh of his palm as he grasped it. Once the door was opened, he hoisted Marley's limp body up and shoved it inside, careful to avoid the flames himself. He slammed it shut, holding his hand up in front of him as the skin healed itself, his jaw muscles twitching as he clenched his teeth, his eyes glued to the contraption.

After a few moments, he turned, buttoning his jacket and adjusting the lapels, walking to the staircase, his face finally relaxing as he took the first step.

"Where are we going?" Violet asked, Kenton driving the rented black sports car entirely too fast up I-95.

"Your father's. No doubt the rest of the witch's coven will notice she's gone missing and come looking for her. You'll be safe there until we know more."

"What's there to know? *They hunt us*. We should kill them all before they figure out what happened."

"As much as I love a good slaughter, it would be unwise to go in without knowing what we're up against. How many witches, how powerful they are. How much they know about us. About you. I don't think this was an isolated incident. I too was attacked by a group of hunters. I thought they were just vigilante types, men with too much time on their hands and not enough attention from the fairer sex. However, when I'd finished them off, something strange happened. I can't explain it but I think they were more than they seemed. Perhaps another coven. And, if that's the case, then it stands to reason that perhaps the covens are working together. "

"That's impossible. Covens never work together for anything. They don't trust each other. Always worried their magic will be stolen."

"That's been true but what if it's no longer the case? Think about it, love. When was the last time a witch had the courage to be anywhere near one of us, let alone seek us out and try to kill us?"

She bit her lip and shrugged.

"I don't think this is a coincidence and until we know just how insidious this whole thing is, I want you as far away from it as you can be."

She shifted in her seat. "Fine. I'll hide. For now. You can drop me off and be on your way."

He scoffed. "I'm not going anywhere, pet. As long as you're in danger, I'm here."

"Listen, I appreciate the save and everything, really. But, I've got it from here. I don't need you."

His voice lowered, his eyes meeting hers for a split second before again focusing on the road. "That's not what you said last time we were together. It was the summer before you went to university, do you remember?"

Butterflies flooded her stomach as he reached for her, running his hand up her thigh.

"Remember my hands on your body, my breath against your cheek. Do you remember pulling me to you, begging me to fuck you just once before I left?"

She swallowed, closing her eyes and shaking the memory from her mind. "But, you wouldn't."

"No."

"For reasons?"

"You were a child."

"I was eighteen."

"That's what I said."

"Right," She rolled her eyes. "You didn't want to *groom* me or take advantage or whatever. But, the second I graduated you started with the letters and the gifts and--"

"Twenty-two is a world away from eighteen if I'm remembering correctly. As you know, I was twenty-five when I was turned. Seems appropriate enough."

"You haven't been twenty-five since you partied with Shakespeare."

"I never 'partied' with Shakespeare. I only knew him in passing. We barely spoke. And, you know as well as I do, once you've turned you're perpetually--"

"Yeah, yeah. You'll be twenty-five forever, physically and mentally. I know."

"And, when this threat has passed, I'll give you the bite and you'll be twenty-three forever."

"You…" Her heart pounded in her ears, her throat dry and her pussy wet.

He tightened his grip on her inner thigh. "I've grown tired of waiting for you. We will crush the witches under our boots like the vermin they are and once it's done, I will take what's mine."

She touched his hand, part of her wanting to move it away, the other part desperately wanting it to inch higher. With a shaky but defiant voice, she told him, "I'm not your property."

He grunted, whipping the car to the right and pulling onto the shoulder. She jostled in her seat, hanging onto the door handle for balance. He turned his body to face her, his stormy eyes glowing in the dim streetlight. He pressed his hand to her cheek, his thumb cupping her chin. His touch was firm but not painful. He stared into her as she trembled, his tone determined as he spoke. "You are my wife. By blood and by law, we are bound. You are mine," He looked down at her parted lips and back up to her wide eyes. "As *I* am *yours*."

Chapter 22

Five years before, Violet had been interning at her father's museum in Connecticut. It was the month of the Frederic Church exhibit and while she loved the history and art, she was itching to get out of the stuffy old building and have some fun. She'd be off at school soon; another four years of doing what she was "supposed to". She yearned for a bit of excitement. Something to break up the monotony of her life before settling into the role of schoolgirl and full-time tour guide.

"Good turnout," her father said, standing next to her near the opening of the hall that led to the office. He held a brochure out for her to take, which she did.

"Yeah, people love that Hudson River shit."

He clicked his tongue. "Language, Violet, please."

"Sorry."

"Speak as you wish in your personal life but at work--"

"I know. I said sorry, geez."

"Fine." They watched the people examining paintings and glass-covered letters, shuffling around the crowded space and talking amongst themselves. "I am quite proud of you, you know?"

She raised her brows and looked up at him.

"Oh, don't look so surprised."

She chuckled. "But, I'm the wild one. I'm *uncontrollable*. Isn't that what you told Rue?"

"Yes, well, you have given me cause to worry over the years, as has your sister. That's the burden of parenthood, I suppose. But, for all your misadventures, you've always been very smart. And, you follow your dreams. That's an important quality. I remember when you were a child, sitting in the corner of the storeroom while I'd unpack new pieces. You were transfixed, so interested in every item. You'd spend hours marveling at them, reading about them. I could hardly tear you away."

She smiled as she remembered.

"Once your education is complete, I think I'll make you a curator here."

"Really?"

"Of course. Who knows? Maybe one day, this entire place will be yours."

"Unlikely."

"Why not? I could retire. Travel the world. Relax on a beach somewhere sipping overly-sweet cocktails and pondering my existence."

She laughed out loud. "That doesn't sound like something you'd enjoy."

His nose scrunched. "No, I hated it as it came out of my mouth. And, I have already traveled the world, multiple times."

"Face it, Dad. You love this place. You'll run it 'til the wheels fall off."

"There are no whee--ah. Figure of speech. Yes, well, I will still give you more responsibilities. More interesting things to look forward to than telling people where we keep the Revolutionary War relics."

She noticed his jaw twitch and laughed. "Still stings, huh?"

"Only a little."

"Excuse me," a woman said as she approached. "I was told you have an Italian Baroque exhibit?"

"Ah, yes," Booth said, gesturing to the staircase across the room. "It's in our European Art room. I'd be happy to show you."

"Thank you." The two disappeared into the crowd leaving Violet to stand alone, her excitement about her future renewed by her father's promise, but still bored in her current predicament.

Her eyes drifted to the entrance where a man stood staring at her. He looked flushed, his cheeks blushed and his chest heaving as if he'd been running but he was motionless, not even blinking when strands of his dark hair fell over his right eye. Her instincts told her he was like her, a vampire but there was something else; a pull, like a tether dragging her attention to him. Her heart leaped to her throat as the realization hit her, who he was and what it meant. The connection. The undeniable understanding that he felt like home.

CHAPTER 22

Finally, he stepped forward, slowly as if in disbelief, pushing up the sleeves of his jet-black button-down. Her mind clouded as he got closer, her legs nearly giving out. She squeezed her eyes shut and tried to think, the noise of the crowd suddenly too loud in her ears. She dropped the brochure as she backed away, down the hall, and through the open door of her father's office. The man followed, never taking his eyes off her as he closed and locked the door behind him. She kept backing away until there was nowhere to go, her ass bumping into the desk. Emotion flooded every part of her, overwhelming her senses as he closed the space between them, trapping her between him and the mahogany.

Her eyes again met his as he took her cheek in his hand, running his thumb over her parted lips. A strange combination of awe, confusion, and hope colored his expression as his gaze bore into her, her feelings now so intense she had to grip the desk with both hands to keep herself upright.

"Do you know who I am?" he asked, her heart melting at the sound of his voice.

She nodded, remembering the stories her parents had told her of their first meeting in Egypt. Her father had been there acquiring a rare artifact from the Archaic Period. She'd never understood just how strong the connection was. Her voice trembled as she uttered the word, "Soulmate."

"Yes." He looked her over, studying her face, letting his hand slide down to her neck.

"How did you find me?"

"I didn't. I had assumed you didn't exist. I just felt compelled to come to this place. I told myself it was for the art but I knew better. I knew there was something else here. Something important. I was drawn to it like--"

"Fate," she whispered, breaking eye contact and lowering her gaze to his full lips.

His hand slid up and around to the back of her neck, his thumb brushing her earlobe as he leaned in. "I've waited centuries for you." He kissed her, his lips soft against hers, their eyes closing as waves of emotion overtook them. She felt weak, her arms beginning to shake as she fought to stay standing. As the kiss deepened, he lifted her onto the desk, pushing her legs apart and standing between them. His hands ran up her bare thighs, underneath her plaid flare skirt to her hips. His fingers dug into her skin, his touch electric as she felt him stiffen against her. She pulled him closer, wrapping her arms around his shoulders as he wrapped his around her waist.

She ran her hand up and into his hair, her kisses hungrier as their tongues gently danced. She'd never felt anything like this before. The intensity, the heat between them. Her responsibilities drifted away, the only thoughts in her head those of pure, unbridled lust.

She jumped at the sound of the phone ringing, the old rotary phone her father refused to throw out shrill, the abrupt shrieking of it like a demand. She pulled away, sliding back and hopping down on the other side of the desk. Now, with the wood separating them, her mind began to clear. She took a breath, smiling at him as he watched her, hands on the desk and leaning forward, looking as though he might pounce at any moment.

She picked up the receiver, fully intending to answer it, but as their eyes locked, she put it down, her smile turning mischievous. "You feel like doing something crazy?"

The sky was a sea of fire as the sun set over Violet's father's backyard. There were no guests. Only the Justice of the Peace and Booth as their witness. No rings were exchanged. Instead, they bit their own tongues, discreetly so as not to reveal their true nature to the human performing the ceremony, and took one another's blood into themselves with their first kiss as a married couple. They'd only known each other a few hours but time meant nothing as far as they were concerned. After all, what does time matter when your forever is staring you in the face?

CHAPTER 22

That night, the couple retreated to Kenton's room at the Delamar. He carried her in, setting her on her feet and locking the door.

"Any regrets?" she asked, a twinkle in her eye.

"Never." He took her face in his hands and kissed her softly. "Would you like some champagne?"

"Maybe later. You like my dress?"

"It's beautiful, as are you."

"Really?" She did a turn, the glitter covering the Prussian blue fabric sparkling in the light like tiny stars. "It was my prom dress, been in the back of my closet forever. But, no time for wedding dress shopping when you're in as big of a hurry as we were."

"I find your impulsivity endearing."

"And, I find this dress binding." She turned her back to him, looking over her shoulder. "Help me out of it?"

"I would like nothing more." He stood behind her, kissing her neck, his fingertips brushing down her shoulders and back until they found the zipper. Ever so slowly, he pulled the bit of metal down the length of the bodice, revealing her bare skin underneath. The dress fell to the floor and she stepped out of it, kicking off her shoes and turning to face him.

Her tone turned vulnerable as she stood before her new husband, her gaze lifting to meet his. "Are you sure you don't have any regrets?"

Again, he cupped her face in his hands, his eyes like burning pools of intensity. "There will never be a second of my life that I'll regret spending with you. I'd marry you again and every day if you told me it would please you. I will devote my life to your happiness." He kissed her again, firmer this time, the taste of blood still lingering on his tongue as hers slid over it. He guided her to the bed and she sat, scooting back to lay her head on the pillow while he crawled to meet her. They kissed again, her fingers in his hair as he ran one hand up her thigh, over her hip and torso, and around to rest behind her shoulder. She spread her legs wide, dying for him to enter her.

He kissed her neck then down her chest, getting to his knees and unbuttoning his shirt. He peeled it off and flung it to the floor, bending down and gripping her thighs. He looked up into her eyes. "I'll spend all of eternity worshiping you."

"Oh, shit," she whispered as his tongue went to work in long, slow strokes. Her back arched as she squeezed her breasts, ripples of pleasure spreading over her body. She moaned as he focused his attention on her clit, his tongue swirling over it as it swelled. He continued, plunging his middle finger into her and massaging her G-spot. "*Fuck*," she panted, grabbing him by the hair. She writhed, using her free hand to grip the pillow. "Wait," She let go of his hair. "Wait, stop."

"Stop?" he asked, getting up on his knees. "But, you were--"

"Yeah, I know." She sat up, sweeping her hands over his broad chest. "But, not yet. I want to come with you. I want to feel you in me. All of you."

He licked his lips, sliding off the bed and stepping out of his shoes. "Then lie back, darling."

She did as she was told, his low tone giving the instruction the feeling of a command. She bit her bottom lip as she watched with anticipation as he unbuckled his belt. He whipped it off, discarding it and going for the button of his slacks. But, before he could get it through the loop, three loud bangs came on the door.

"Leave us!" Kenton barked.

The door knob jiggled, then snapped, the chrome ball dropping to the carpet. The door flew open.

"What the fuck?" Violet shouted, throwing the comforter over her and sitting up as her sister burst into the room. "Way to clam jam, Rue."

"You got married without telling me?!" she shouted, closing the door.

She sighed. "Kenton, my sister, Rue."

"Ah," he said, his face relaxing. "Pleasure to--"

Rue held her hand up, eyes still trained on her sister. "Yeah, we'll meet and greet another time. Seriously, Violet? *Married*?"

"I called to invite you."

"It was day. You know I don't keep human hours anymore. You couldn't have waited like, forty-five minutes?"

"Sorry, we just," She looked over at Kenton and smiled. "Got caught up."

"Yeah, Dad told me. Soulmates. I get it." Her features softened. "But, it would've been nice to have been there, seeing my baby sister do the whole vows thing."

"Okay, you're right, *as usual*. You mad at me now?"

"I'm not *not* mad." She crossed her arms in feigned irritation.

She laughed. "How will you ever forgive me?"

"Well, I *could* use a waitress on the weekends."

She gasped. "You got the license?"

"I did. Rue's will be up and running as of next week."

"Congrats! And, I *guess* I could find time to help you out, as long as it doesn't interfere with class."

"Fordham has classes on Saturdays?"

"I haven't gotten my schedule, yet but I doubt it."

"Good because I expect to be *very* busy." She turned her attention to Kenton. "Sorry about busting in like that. Didn't mean to freak you out."

"Don't mind her," Violet told him, noticing the anxious look on his face. "She's just a little snippy sometimes."

"You say snippy, I say justified. Anyway, I'll leave you two alone to consummate."

"Gross!," she laughed. "Can you not say things like consummate in front of my husband?"

"Husband," Rue snickered. "That's gonna take getting used to. See you later." She opened the door to leave and tried to close it once she was in the hall, but with the knob broken off, it wouldn't stay. Violet laughed as she watched the door open just a little and close again, over and over until Kenton pushed a chair against it. "K, bye!" Rue called, walking to the elevator.

"Sorry about her. Since our mom left, she thinks she's in charge of me or something."

"Fordham?" he said, standing at the foot of the bed. "The college?"

"Yeah, I start next month."

"Start? Violet, darling, exactly how old are you?"

"Eighteen."

"For how long?"

"Since March. Didn't you see my birthday on the marriage license?"

"Yes, but I assumed that was..." His voice trailed off as he realized. "You were born a vampire."

"Duh. Did you think someone turned my whole family? You okay? You look a little green."

He picked his shirt up off the floor and put it on.

"What are you doing?"

He found her dress and tossed it on the bed. "Put your clothes on."

"What? Why?"

"I should get you home."

"What are you talking about? This is our honeymoon."

"Not anymore. One day, yes, but--"

"Was it my sister? She won't be back. She was just--"

"No, no, your sister isn't a problem. Her interruption was actually quite fortunate. Get dressed."

"Oh," she said, pulling the blanket tighter around her and fighting back tears. "You *do* have regrets."

"No."

"It's me. Something about me or something," she looked down. "I did something wrong."

"No, love," He hurried to the side of the bed, kneeling and taking her hands in his. "You did nothing wrong. You're perfect."

"What, then?"

He kissed her hands and held them to his chest. "One day soon you will be the great love of my life. Of all my lives. But, you aren't ready for this."

"I'm not a virgin if that's what you're worried about."

"It's not. Violet, once we're together, once you receive my bite, you'll stop aging. Stop growing as an individual. We will be as one. Forever."

She touched his cheek. "I know that. My parents were soulmates. I get what happens."

"Then, you understand why I must leave you now."

She yanked her hand away. "What do you mean, leave? We're married!"

"And, married we shall remain. You here, having experiences, making memories. Living your life, coming into who you are. Maturing."

"And, you?"

"Across the Atlantic. Home, in England."

"Are you kidding me?"

He stood. "When you're a little older, wiser, I'll return to you and I will never leave your side again. Not for a moment."

She got up on her knees grabbing his arm as he turned away. She pulled him to her, kissing him once more. She put her forehead to his, tears now spilling down her cheeks. "Don't go."

His eyes squeezed shut. "As much as it pains me, I must."

"But, how can you? We're *meant*."

He put her hands to his lips again. "I've been waiting for you for four hundred years. A few more will torture me relentlessly but they will not kill me."

"Fine," she whimpered. "Go. But, not before we--"

"Violet,"

"Just once. No biting. Just be with me, one time. I need you."

"And, I you. Believe me, I've never wanted anything more. But, I have no delusion that I'll be able to control my passion for you. I *will* bite you, change you. It wouldn't be right. Not yet."

Chapter 23

She'd been so lost in her memories, she hadn't noticed that the car had slowed or that it had started raining. They drove up the long driveway, her family home looking slightly eerie in the drizzly night. Its Colonial style and enormous size were somehow more imposing than the tall buildings she'd grown used to in Manhattan. It occurred to her that, having grown up here, maybe it would always make her feel small.

She got out of the barely-stopped car and slammed the door, harder than she meant to. She made a beeline to the side of the house where she knew her father kept a spare key hidden under a planter. She knelt to retrieve it then stood, stopping for a moment, feeling Kenton only inches behind her. She turned, her eyes lifting to meet his. He stared down at her, licking his lips.

"Why?" she all but whispered.

"Why what, love?"

"Why are you waiting?"

He leaned in, putting his hand on the building over her shoulder. "Because as long as you're under threat, I can afford no distractions. However," He moved closer, his voice husky in her ear. "Truth be told, it's damn near killing me. If this were not your father's house, I imagine I would have taken you already, right here against the cedar planks, the siding as wet as you are now, I think. Am I right?" He brushed her earlobe with his lips as she tried desperately to stifle her desire. "Are you wet for me, pet?"

He jerked away, the sound of another car pulling up snapping them both out of their lust-filled haze. They went around to the front of the house where they saw Booth heading up the walk.

CHAPTER 23

"What are two doing skulking about?" he said, waving them in. "Come now. We have much to discuss."

Once inside, Booth locked the door, peering through the small glass window near the top. When he was sure he hadn't been followed, he gestured for the others to sit on the sofa. He unbuttoned his jacket and sat across them, the antique coffee table separating the couches.

"I'm really sorry, Dad," Violet blurted. "I didn't know--"

He held his hand up and shook his head. "No need to apologize, Violet. Your sister called after her sired fell asleep. She explained everything. I can hardly fault you for falling under a witch's spell. I was once enamored by a witch, myself, in my Oxford days. I can't recall how many lectures I missed by losing track of time in her cottage. She had the loveliest scent. Juniper berries, I believe."

"Dad, gross."

He cleared his throat. "Right. Anyhow, Rue told me what the human girl saw at the witch's compound. We have a vague idea of how many more we could be dealing with and with what we know of Marley, we should assume they're quite powerful. Therefore, until the threat has passed, you will stay here where I can look after you."

"You know I'm not a child, right?"

"I'm well aware of your age but you are, in fact, *my* child." He looked her in the eye, demanding she hear him. "You will remain here until I deem it safe for you to return. Have I made myself clear?"

She sighed, crossing her legs. "For how long?"

"I'm not sure. The coven will surely be suspicious by daybreak. My hope is that, should they come looking for their witch, they'll see your apartment in shambles, assume you both perished in the fire, and move on."

"That doesn't sound super likely, Dad."

"No, it's a bit of a fairy tale, I'd say. That's why I said 'hope'. It's much more probable they won't find any sign of either of you and decide to start looking. As your sister tells it, Marley didn't know *she* was a vampire until tonight which means she didn't have time to inform her coven. I've instructed her to tell whoever comes asking about you or the witch that she saw a girl with green hair enter the apartment around nine. Shortly after, she heard screams and smelled smoke. Upon exiting her apartment, she was confronted by a wall of smoke so dark, she could barely see to make it out of the building alive. By the time the fire department arrived, the blaze was out. She didn't see anyone else leave the building."

"You think they'll buy that?"

"I don't know."

"And, what are they gonna think happened to us? Will they think we went out the fire escape?"

He rubbed his temple. "Violet, I don't know."

"There's no way they'll believe we burned to nothing. If we'd died, there'd be bones, at least. And, how do I go back *ever* without risking them figuring it out? Change my name? Dye my hair? Be looking over my shoulder for the rest of--"

He slammed his hand down on the table between them causing her to jump. "Damn it, Violet, I don't know! I haven't worked it all out, yet. I just," He covered his mouth for a moment before clearing his throat and steadying his tone. "My priority is keeping you safe. Anything else can be thought through later after we've all had a chance to clear our minds." He stood, adjusting his jacket. "I apologize for my outburst. It's after midnight. I must be tired. I should get some rest. Kenton, would you mind staying as well? Safety in numbers and all that."

"Of course," Kenton agreed.

"Tell me, do you walk in the day as I do or are you a traditionalist?"

"I keep to the night as much as I can."

"Then, might I ask that you keep guard, just in case?"

"Your home will be a fortress."

"Good man." He walked over and kissed Violet's cheek. "Your room is as you left it. Goodnight."

"Night," she said as he went up the stairs. When she heard his door close, she turned to her husband. "What the fuck was that?"

"What was what?"

"I've never seen him freak out like that *in my life*. With the hand and the slamming."

"He's just worried about you, darling."

"That's not normal dad worry. You don't get it. When I was six, I fell through a pane-glass door. Slit my own throat. Blood everywhere. He was fine. When I was ten, I was impaled on a fence after I crashed my bike. *Impaled*. The man was cool as ice. But *this* has him yelling and making with the crazy eyes?"

"He knew those things couldn't kill you. Scrapes to things like us. But, a witch intent on homicide, let alone a full coven, that's another thing entirely. He'd be a fool not to be protective."

"I guess. Still," She looked up the staircase. "Feels off."

He brushed the hair off her shoulder, his touch sending shivers down her spine. "And, how does this feel?"

She closed her eyes. "What are you doing?"

He moved closer, kissing her neck the way he had the night of their almost honeymoon. He slid his hands down her arms as she gripped the cushion beneath her.

"Kenton," she whispered.

"Say it again."

"I--I thought you said..."

He squeezed her arms, shutting his eyes, putting his forehead to her shoulder, and grunted. "Yes. I must wait." He shot up, speeding to stand in front of the door. "You should go rest, as well."

"I feel like we should talk."

"There is nothing to say."

She got up and went to him. "I want to talk about what this is. Us."

He held his arms as if holding himself back. "We are what we've always been."

"Except now, you're here and while I've got you in a trying-to-control-yourself kind of mood, I want to tell you that I like my life the way it is. I like my--"

"Freedom," he spat.

"Yes."

He laughed. "You lie to yourself."

"Excuse me?"

"You pretend that you fear losing your freedom as if being free of me is so precious to you. But, you and I both know that what you truly fear isn't loss of freedom. I would never keep you from doing as you wished or from being who you are. You know that. What *you* fear is loss of control." He took her by the shoulders and spun her, pinning her to the door, his eyes like daggers cutting right through her. He slammed his hands against the door over her shoulders, staring down at her like a beast stalking its prey. "You've spent years convincing yourself you value the distance I put between us while still resenting me for it. You distract yourself with your stable of lovers, occasionally posting a photo of you with one of them on social media, knowing it will hurt me. I suspect you treat them with the same level of contempt. It's very obviously your way of asserting dominance, a reaction to my abandonment. You've become dependent on the control, desperate for the fiction that you don't need me. You hate that you were vulnerable with me those years ago and that it caused you pain and what you hate more is that you now know I was right to go." He backed up, stepping aside to let her pass.

Her heart raced, his insights leaving her exposed. No one had ever called her out so accurately and for the first time, she felt like he really saw her. Not who she was to *him*, not her eternal soul that he had forever been bound to. Not her essence. Just her, Violet, as she was in the here and now.

He turned to face her, again hugging his arms and leaning against the door.

She made it to the sixth step of the staircase before turning around, tears pooling in her eyes. "I don't resent you."

He looked up at her, blinking back tears of his own as she turned away and went up the steps. When she was safely in her bedroom, he peered out the door's window, cracking his neck and releasing his breath.

Upstairs, Violet sat on the edge of her childhood bed, the purple flowers on the comforter bright against the mint background. She wiped her tears away and put her hand to her chest, the tapping of the rain on her window soothing as she relaxed her muscles.

Down the hall, Booth paced the floor, tearing off his jacket and tossing it onto the bed. Rage filled his eyes as he flung open the closet door, pulling the chain to turn on the light. He rifled through a few boxes before finally finding what he'd been looking for. He took the old journal from the box and began flipping through its pages. He read the last entry, as he'd done hundreds of times in the past. "Right," he muttered to himself, feeling as defeated as he had the first time he'd read it. He put the book back in its place and stood in front of the bed, picking up his jacket and reaching into its pockets. He took the dagger first, opening the nightstand drawer and placing it inside. He then retrieved the vial, glaring at the witch's blood with a hatred he hadn't felt in decades. "I will find you," he vowed. "I will find *all of you*."

Chapter 24

"I think I'm done," Ophelia said, pulling the covers up around her waist.

"Done what?" Lennon sighed, clicking on the light for the third time since the two decided to go to sleep in the matching twin beds. The hotel room was cold, sterile even but it was safe. At least, they hoped so.

"With Violet and her bullshit."

"Well, who could blame you?"

"I mean, I love her. Like, *love* her. And, I know what happened wasn't really her fault but it's not just lately, you know? Even before, she's always been selfish and greedy. She for sure doesn't love me back so what the fuck am I doing?"

"I couldn't tell you."

"I'm tired of being pushed around. I'm sick to death of--"

"I get it, *shit*. Violet's kind of a bitch. Agree. Can I go back to sleep now?"

"It's not just her. It's me. I need to grow. Heal. I need--"

They covered their head with their pillow. "Fucking therapy, bitch."

"Rude. I was *going* to say I need to take control of my life. Be independent."

"Totes. Bed now?"

"Speaking of people with a take-charge attitude, did you see Mr. Witcomb?"

"Yeah."

"Dude has like, an air of authority about him. You feel that?"

"Well, he's old and Violet's dad, so--"

"Yeah, but how he just took the reins. As soon as he came in, everyone just shut up and did what he said. He's like, *a man*, you know what I mean?"

"Not really."

"His wife left years ago, right? You think he's seeing anyone?"

They sat up and threw their pillow at her.

CHAPTER 24

"What?"

"Girl, how many kinks do you have? *Jesus*. Daddy issues, much?"

"Speaking of daddies, you think Iman's all right?"

They shook their head. "I don't know. He looked every kind of fucked up when we left. I can't believe you two--"

"It didn't mean anything. I was just trying to make Violet jealous. Besides, I think we both know who he's *really* into."

"You think Rue can handle it? His whole transition thing?"

"*Rue*? Of course. That bitch can handle *literally* anything."

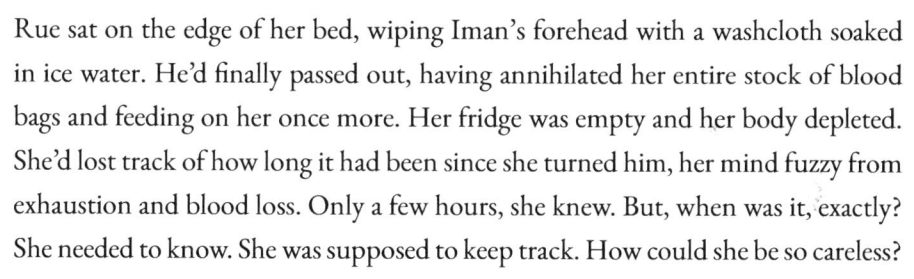

Rue sat on the edge of her bed, wiping Iman's forehead with a washcloth soaked in ice water. He'd finally passed out, having annihilated her entire stock of blood bags and feeding on her once more. Her fridge was empty and her body depleted. She'd lost track of how long it had been since she turned him, her mind fuzzy from exhaustion and blood loss. Only a few hours, she knew. But, when was it, exactly? She needed to know. She was supposed to keep track. How could she be so careless?

Steam wafted from his chest as she rubbed it with the wet cloth, his fever now too high to measure with a thermometer. His arms were raised over his head, his wrists cuffed to the headboard. She couldn't risk him getting out if she fell asleep, not that she'd allow herself rest. She had to stay with him. Had to keep an eye.

Her thoughts were interrupted by the sound of women talking. They were in Violet's apartment. "Witches," she seethed, looking in the direction of the hall. She dunked the cloth in the bowl of cold water and ice cubes, this time laying it out flat on his chest, pulling it up so the edge covered his neck. She checked that the handcuffs were locked tight and got up. "I'll be right back," she whispered. She left the room, quietly closing the door behind her and making her way through the living room to the front door. She opened it to find two women standing in the rubble of the burnt-out loft.

"Can I help you?" she asked, her voice scratchy.

"I hope so," the one on the left said. "What happened here?"

"Not sure," she lied, trying to remember what her father had told her to say through her brain fog. "I saw a girl with green hair go in sometime around nine when I was taking my trash out. I went to bed and got woken up by my smoke alarm. I heard women screaming--"

"Women?" the one on the right asked. "More than one?"

"Two, I think. I'm not a hundred percent because of the alarm noise but I'm pretty sure. I couldn't see through the smoke. It was really dark. I tried to yell, see if anyone needed help but I couldn't stop coughing. I got scared and ran."

"Outside?" the first one said. "Did you see anyone else leave the building?"

She shook her head. "It's weird because when the fire department got here, they said the fire was out. They never even turned on their hoses."

The women exchanged knowing glances.

"Do you know the girl that lives here or are you cops?"

"Actually," the second woman said. "We're family. Not of the occupant but of her friend, the girl with the green hair. Are you sure you didn't see her leave?"

"No."

She stepped closer. "And, does that make sense to you?"

"Nothing about tonight has made sense. If you'll excuse me, I need to get back to bed. It's been a long night."

She grabbed her arm. "And, what about the blood on your clothes?"

Rue looked down at her shirt, just noticing the splatter that must have come from pounding Marley's face in earlier. "I--I don't know," she stammered, yanking her arm away. "I must've gotten hurt hurrying down the stairs."

"It's you, isn't it?"

"Me?"

"Yes. I can see it now. Go ahead, vampire bitch." She grabbed her face, squishing her lips open like a fish. "Show me your fangs."

Out of the dark, Iman barreled toward them, the handcuffs dangling from his left wrist. He threw himself into the woman, knocking her to the ground, sitting on her, and tearing her throat out with his teeth. He snarled, jumping up and kicking the corpse out of his way. Faster than the other witch could see, he flew at her, clamping down on her neck and drinking her dry. Her body fell and he followed it to the floor, continuing to suck even as no more blood came.

Rue inched toward him, eyes wide as she attempted to sound calm. "Iman, sweetie," she said, kneeling next to him. "Iman, we have to go now."

He ignored her, continuing his fruitless efforts at getting more blood.

"Iman," She touched his shoulder. "Iman, let's go."

He whipped his head up, his eyes wild, his pupils covering the irises completely. A low, guttural grown escaped his crimson-stained lips as he slowly shook his head 'no'.

"You need rest, okay? Let's go home." She stood, pulling him up with her. But, as he got to his feet, he broke away, speeding toward the door. "Fuck," she muttered, grabbing him by the hair and slamming his head into the wall next to the doorway. He was knocked out cold. "Sorry, bro," she said, throwing him over her shoulder. "Can't let you out here going on murder sprees."

"Couldn't sleep?" Kenton asked.

"Not a wink," Booth said, joining him in the living room. They again sat opposite each other, both men weary from the events of the evening.

"I've been listening. Nothing but the occasional squirrel dashing through the yard."

"Very good." He leaned back, crossing one leg over the other, his elbow on the sofa arm. "Speaking of hearing things, I couldn't help but catch bits of your conversation with Violet earlier."

He raised an eyebrow.

"I tried to ignore it but," He pointed to his ear. "You know how these things are."

"Yes." He looked down at his hands folded in his lap.

"I know it's not my business and I tend to stay far away from my daughters' personal lives but I feel I should tell you--"

"About her mother?"

He blinked. "Yes."

"Me leaving triggered her abandonment issues. Is that what you want me to know? Because it *had* occurred to me."

"Well, perhaps but I was thinking more about her mother's abandonment of me."

"Oh?"

"You see, Violet has always known that her mother and I were soulmates. We'd told her the story of how we met dozens of times; I was on an expedition to track down rare Ptolemaic artifacts and she was a school teacher in Edfu. I spotted her on a boat of some kind. I was so taken, I jumped off the pier. Swam straight to her." A small smile appeared on his mournful face. "We had a happy life together." His smile faded as he continued. "Until, one day, she left for an appointment, never to return. Violet was crushed. Poor girl was unfortunate to have been the one to find Zarah's goodbye letter."

"That's terrible. I'm sorry that happened to you. To *all* of you but--"

"Violet doesn't trust easily. Hasn't since. And, when you left, it was a reminder to her that even a soulmate can break your heart." He sat forward, looking him dead in the eye. "All you have to do is prove to her that you mean to stay."

"How do I do that?"

"No clue. She's very stubborn, that one."

He laughed. "Oh, you cheeky--" He went silent, the sound of a car pulling into the driveway causing them both to stand. Kenton went to the door and looked out the glass. "Speaking of your stubborn daughters..." He opened the door, stepping out of the way as Rue dragged a chained Iman over the threshold.

"Hey, Dad," she said, fighting to keep the new vampire contained. "I need to borrow your cage."

Booth waved her toward the kitchen. "Of course, dear. Keys are on the hook next to the basement door."

"Thanks." The two disappeared into the kitchen.

Kenton laughed again. "Booth, you old scoundrel. I didn't know you had a *cage*."

"Yes, well, it's seldom needed but you know what they say. Better to have a cage and not use it than to be...cage-less in an emergency. Since I'm up, would you like a spot of tea?"

In the basement, Rue pushed Iman into the cell, waiting until she'd locked the door before reaching her arms through the bars and loosening his chains. He wiggled out of them, throwing them down onto the concrete floor. He paced, hands on his head as he struggled to hold a thought. When he looked up, she was gone, only the iron and cold to keep him company. He banged his temple with his fist, tears in his eyes as his fangs grew and then rescinded. He sat on the ground, rocking back and forth in the pale glow of the light bulb hanging overhead.

"Take this," Rue said, hurrying back down the basement steps and holding a blood bag through the bars. He looked up, tears now rivers down his cheeks. He snatched the offering, puncturing the bag with his teeth and drinking until it was empty. "Dad's got more if you need some. You should sleep now, though. Try, at least."

He dropped the plastic and rushed to stand, gripping the bars that separated them. "I'm sorry," he said, his voice gruff, barely recognizable. "I was confused. I thought they were hurting you."

"If you'd been a second later, I'm sure they would have. I was in no condition to fight. You probably saved my life, so no guilt needed."

"But, you're scared. Of *me*."

"Not so much *of* you as *for* you."

"How long will you keep me here?"

"You'll be out tomorrow. Get some sleep. There are extra blankets under the cot."

"Wait, please."

She headed toward the steps. "Dude, I need to get some blood in me, myself."

"Rue!"

She stopped.

"I would never hurt you, no matter what I become."

"I know that." She looked back at him. "Better than you do."

"Iman's in the cage?" Violet asked.

"Your sister thought it prudent," Booth said, sipping a cup of PG Tips.

"Guess I picked the wrong night to turn in early."

"I'd apologize for the noise but since it wasn't I that made the ruckus, I won't."

"And you wonder where I get my smart-ass attitude."

"Oh, I don't believe I've wondered about that once."

Rue emerged from the basement, closing the door and taking a breath. "This is why I don't do this shit."

"Turn people?" Violet asked.

"Care about people." She opened the fridge and grabbed three blood bags.

"Of course, you may," Booth said. "Be my guest. Take all you need."

She rolled her eyes, putting on her most annoying fake-British accent. "Thank you, Father. You've been oh so helpful in my time of need."

"Don't be an asshole, dear."

Violet laughed. "And, here I was thinking it would be awkward being home again."

He finished his tea and put the dishes in the sink. "I'm sorry, Rue." He kissed her cheek. "It's been a trying evening. Perhaps I'll join Kenton outside. A walk around the grounds could be just what I need to clear my mind." He opened the back door, held his arm out into the rain, brought it back in, and closed the door. "On second thought, perhaps I'll retire to the living room for some light reading."

"Have fun," Rue said as he left, sitting at the island and opening the first bag.

"Hey," Violet said. "Before he comes back, I should probably apologize."

"For what? You didn't know she was a witch."

CHAPTER 24

"No, I mean about Iman. You know, fucking him all those times."

She took a sip from the bag, tilting her head as she swallowed. "Why?"

"I knew you liked him. But, I also knew you'd never do anything about it so it felt like why not, you know what I mean?"

"It's fine."

"Doesn't feel fine."

"Bitch, I'm good. No worries."

"I'm *not* good. Witches trying to kill us aside, it's been pointed out to me that I use sex with others to punish Kenton and make myself feel powerful. In charge."

She slurped the last of the bag and opened a fresh one. "You needed someone to tell you that?"

"Not really but I'm kind of feeling like a dick about it now."

"Well, sure."

Violet's tone turned serious. "Do you think he's gonna make it?"

She shrugged, guzzling the second bag and opening a third. "I guess we'll find out soon enough. By this time tomorrow, I'll either be the proud sire of a fledgling vampire or he'll be a wild, blood-thirsty animal without a shred of humanity left."

"In which case…"

"In which case," she said, her tone like ice. "I'll have to kill him."

Chapter 25

"Just gonna hang out alone?" Violet asked, wandering into the living room.

Booth set his book on the end table. "It seemed favorable to bickering with your sister. How are you feeling?"

"Tired, mostly. A lot of mixed emotions." She glanced around the room. "Where did you put--"

"Kenton's gift is on the mantel."

She cast him a sideways glance and went to retrieve the book of poetry. She fingered the cover, taking it with her as she sat next to her father. She stared down at the pages, flipping through them without reading a word.

"It's a good one," he told her. "I met him once, you know."

"Who?"

He pointed to the author's name on the cover.

"Oh."

"A bit eccentric, Mr. Blake but I found some of his opinions to hold merit."

"That's great, Dad."

"Ah, not in the mood to hear one of my stories? You usually love learning about what you'd call 'historical figures'."

"I'm a little preoccupied with my own historical figure right now."

He laughed. "Yes, I suppose you and your Kenton have some catching up to do."

"Catching up? Dad, we don't know anything about each other. What music does he like? What TV shows? Is he Team Logan or Team Jess?"

"Is he...what?"

"I don't even know what he does for work."

"Oh, of course, you do. He made his money in textiles, I believe."

"That was a million years ago. What does he do *now*?"

"What is it the children say these days? Ah, yes. He's living his best life."

She snickered. "That sounds really ridiculous coming out of your mouth."

"I'd venture to guess it sounds ridiculous coming out of *anyone's* mouth."

She shook her head, her smile fading. "Dad,"

"Yes, dear?"

"Why did you let me get married?"

He burst into laughter. "*Let* you?"

"I'm serious."

"As I recall, you brought Kenton home, signed marriage license in hand, and demanded I throw a ceremony together in, what was it? Two hours time?"

"I was eighteen and dumb as shit."

"Yes, I remember thinking that at the time."

"You should have talked me out of it."

"Would you have listened had I objected?"

She sighed. "I doubt it."

He covered her hand with his. "Oh, sweetheart. Would you honestly have wanted me to stop you?"

She chewed on the inside of her cheek.

"You'd found your soulmate. I remember what that's like. The pull of it. The mist that fills your mind when they're close. When I first laid eyes on your mother, I thought I might die, I loved her so much. How could I deprive you of that joy?"

"Why, though? Why is it like this for us? Other people don't--"

"Other people are human, Violet. Their senses are dull. They don't recognize their other halves when they're staring them in the face most of the time. But things such as us know. Some say it's something to do with the way the first of us was created but I don't know about all of that. I only know that we are somehow lucky enough to feel them, our true mates. To know beyond doubt that they are the ones for us. That's not to say, had it been up to me, I might have chosen someone different for you. Perhaps someone less--"

"Boujee? Ancient?"

He laughed again. "Maybe. But, as it stands, he is your other half, and fighting that fact won't make it any less true."

She flopped her head on the back of the couch. "Ugh. I hate it when you're right."

"Well, then you must be terribly irritated every time we speak."

She giggled. "So sassy for an old man."

"Old? I don't look a day over forty."

"Yeah, getting turned by a drunk Revolutionary War soldier does wonders for the skin."

"I'll have you know, I also moisturize religiously."

She laughed and put her book on the coffee table. "I guess I should talk to him, then."

"Kenton? I'd say so, life being short and whatnot."

"Short? For who?"

"I don't know, dear. It seemed like the right thing to say."

She shook her head as he went back to reading and walked through the kitchen to the back door.

"Take an umbrella," Rue said, shoving her empty blood bags into the trash can. "Rain's getting worse."

She went to the closet and took a black umbrella from inside. She glanced at the back door then looked to her sister. "He's hot, right?"

"Smokin'."

She nodded, opening the door and heading outside.

"You're awake," Kenton said, taking the umbrella as she extended it to him.

"Yeah," Violet said, stepping out onto the deck. "It was pretty loud with all the chatter and you know, the baby vamp losing his shit in the basement."

"I still can't believe your father has a *cage*."

"Oh, yeah. He was pretty kinky back in the day."

"Was he?"

She giggled. "I have no idea. No, he had it put in after the Battle of Ridgefield. Never knew when he might need to hold some poor Patriot hostage."

"He's quite the character, your father."

"He's something, all right. Speaking of cages, does it bother you, Iman being here?"

"No," He scanned the yard. "He's best kept locked away until his transition is complete."

"No, I mean--"

"I know what you meant." He turned to face her. "And, no, it doesn't bother me."

"You're sure?"

"Knowing you had lovers while we were apart is uncomfortable. Painful, even. But, how can I fault you for your indiscretions when I, too had my share of trysts in your absence?"

She raised an eyebrow. "Oh, really?"

"Oh, yes. Dozens, in fact."

"*Dozens?*"

"Yes, each one lasting a handful of days at most. The women offered release, meeting my physical demands with their bodies and their blood. It was a temporary indulgence. Something to fill my time until--"

"Now."

He smiled down at her. "Yes. Until now."

"Listen, I'm glad you're okay. You know, after whatever happened in England with those hunter guys."

"Well, I'm glad you're glad."

A mischievous grin turned up the corner of her lips, her eyes locked on his. She ran her hand over his chest causing his breath to catch. "Do the thing."

"What thing, love?"

She gripped his collar and pulled him along as she backed herself against the house a few feet from the door. "The thing where you pin me to something and look at me like I'm food."

"Violet," he warned.

"Come on. I'm a giant bucket of blood and you're *starving*."

He put his free hand against the siding over her shoulder. "Why are you teasing me so?"

"Because you were right. Everything you said before. I didn't think you really knew me but you do. You see me," She pulled him closer. "In a way no one else can." She slid her hands up to his face. "I'm tired of fighting my fate."

He growled, biting his lip as he restrained himself.

"Say something sexy."

"What would you like to hear, love? How I yearn for you? Pine for you every second we're apart?" He leaned in, his voice low in her ear, his breath warm on her neck. "How my body aches for you? Anguishes in your absence? Or, shall I remind you that I will never again allow myself to endure the unimaginable pain of being without you? That I will never leave your side, not for a moment?" His body pressed against hers as she ran her hands up his back. "I would crawl on broken glass for the promise of your touch."

"Tell me you love me."

He threw the umbrella to the ground and held her face the way he had the day they'd met, his thumb brushing over her lips as he stared into her lust-filled eyes. "I love you more than anyone has loved anything in all of time."

She stared. "Why do I believe you?"

He moved his hand down to her neck and kissed her, deeply and deliberately. He told himself to stop. Even as he wrapped his arm around her waist, his manhood pushing against her, he screamed in his mind to let her go. It was disrespectful to her father not to mention the looming threat of Marley's coven. He knew he should stop this now but he couldn't. His hunger for her was too great.

She threw her arms around his neck as he slid her leggings down. With both hands, he grasped her exposed bottom. Sheets of rain now soaked them as he spread her legs apart, gliding his right hand up her naked thigh. He dove in, two fingers deep, massaging her G-spot while his palm caressed her clit. She moaned into his

CHAPTER 25

mouth as they continued fervently kissing, her legs nearly giving out. He held her up, his left arm around her back, keeping her close.

Her body trembled as a wave of pleasure washed over her. She broke the kiss, taking him by the hair and holding his face to her neck. "Bite me," she whispered.

"I mustn't."

"*Fuck*," she groaned as he sped up his movements.

"That's it," he breathed as he nuzzled her neck. "Come for me."

She shook, clenching around his fingers as spasms of pleasure overtook her. She held tight to his shoulders as she exploded, a rush of fluid spewing forth.

He kissed her neck as she trembled. "Good girl." He pulled her pants back up and kissed her again. "You should get out of this rain. You're positively drenched."

She smiled. "Oh, no." She went for his belt. "Turnabout's fair play."

"Stop," he commanded, grabbing her hands and turning his head to the right.

"What is it?" She tried to listen but couldn't hear anything.

He sniffed the air, his eyes growing wide. "Get inside."

"Why? What's--"

"Get in the bloody house, Violet!" With supernatural speed, he took her by the arm, flung the door open, and shoved her inside, slamming it closed.

"Where are you?" he whispered to the night, turning around to look in all directions. He couldn't see them but he knew they were there, the stench of their foul herbs strong even in the rain. His face twisted in rage as he searched, their tricks no doubt keeping them hidden. "*Witches.*"

He heard faint footsteps from behind so he turned his head. Still unable to see the person approaching, he was only able to move slightly to the right as a wooden stake plunged into his back. It pierced a lung but missed his heart giving him the opportunity to spin on his heel, reach out, and grab the invisible witch by the throat. She showed herself, clawing at his arm in a futile attempt to break free of his grasp.

"You shouldn't be here, witch," he told her, slamming her to the ground and kicking her in the ribs. He reached behind and removed the stake poking out of his back, catching his breath as he healed. He spun it in his hand and raised it, smirking down at the terrified woman. "You come for a vampire as old as I am, you should really have better aim." He brought the stake down, sinking it into the witch's heart. She gurgled in protest, her eyes glazing over. As she let out her final breath, he felt an odd stinging sensation spread over the side of his face and neck. The pain seared, like acid burning away at his skin. He clenched his teeth, fury rising in his chest as he realized what the substance that had been thrown on him was. *"Holy water."*

He turned to his right, spotting the older woman armed with a flask. She doused him again, the fluid reaching his cheek and left eye. He winced, covering his face for a moment while she threw the last of the water at him, scalding his hands. "Ambustum," the witch commanded, causing blue flames to engulf his hands. He pulled them away from his face, shaking them wildly in the rain. They extinguished but his rage did not. He flew at her, shoving his hand through her chest and ripping out her heart, showing it to her as it beat one last time. Her eyes rolled back as she fell, dead before she hit the ground.

"Sisto!" a woman called from the dark. He tried to move toward the voice but he was frozen. "Levare!" At the word, he was lifted, dangling and helpless three feet in the air. He fought against it, grunting, sweat mingling with rain on his forehead. But, it was no use. He was hers.

She appeared before him, long graying hair matted to her head and face in the downpour. There was no fear in her eyes like there had been in the others'. Only anger and determination. In a flash of lightning, he could see a scar over her left eyebrow. "So," she said, looking down at her fallen sisters. "You must be old."

"Must I?" he snarled.

"Experienced enough to kill two armed witches from the most powerful coven on the East Coast. I'd say at least three hundred. How long exactly *have* you been a monster?"

He scoffed. "Since the fifteen-sixties. You know, in the old days, we would've reported you to the town elders, had you burned."

"Too bad it's not the Dark Ages anymore." She waved her hand in his direction, the buttons of his shirt popping off, the material flying off his body.

"It was actually The Renaissance. Honestly, open a book."

She waved her hand again, calling out, "Vulnus!"

He squeezed his eyes shut, wincing as three claw marks appeared on his chest. "Well, that smarts."

"Where is my daughter?" the witch demanded.

CHAPTER 25

He looked down at her, recognizing the resemblance. "The one they called Marley?'

She nodded.

He laughed again. "Dead."

"I know you're lying."

"I wouldn't dream of it."

"I did a blood-to-blood spell. I know she's here. Bring her to me or I will--"

"The bitch is dead, you bohemian plank. I snapped her neck myself."

She screamed, waving frantically in his direction, scratches appearing all over his face and chest. "Propatulus!" On her command, his abdomen tore open, the skin and muscle pulled back, his organs exposed.

He cried out, blood and bile spilling from the cavity as his intestines uncoiled and fell in a steaming pile to the white-washed deck below.

She motioned for him to come down, releasing him from the spell that kept him immobile, his body thudding against the wood planks. Blood filled his throat and spurted from his mouth as she stood over him, her hand outstretched as he convulsed. "We'll kill you, the girl, the other one, and any more that may be inside," she told him through gritted teeth. "But, first," She plunged her hand into the open cavity. "Let's see what happens when a vampire's heart is *removed* instead of just staked."

Chapter 26

Inside, the front door burst open, three women in their forties floating in, the toes of their shoes scraping along the floor. Booth jumped up from his spot on the couch, his book dropping to the brown, leather cushion as he bared his fangs.

"Comminuo!" the three shouted in unison. He fell in a loose heap, every bone in his body completely pulverized.

Violet and Rue raced to the living room but were thrown back, slamming into the coffee table, their backs breaking through the antique wood. Rue bounced up quickly, speeding to bite the neck of the nearest witch. She drained her, tossing her corpse aside and licking her lips.

"Commin--" the second witch started but before she could finish the spell, Violet was on her, reaching inside the redhead's mouth and ripping out her tongue. Rue went for the third witch but was thrown back by a flick of the woman's wrist.

From downstairs, they could hear Iman screaming and bashing his fists into the bars. The blonde witch rushed to the basement door, down the steps, and to the cell.

"No!" Rue yelled, following at lightning speed. She caught up to the witch, shoving her fingers into her back and pulling out her spine. Her body fell, Rue tossing the blood-covered backbone next to it. She caught her breath, looking over the vampire in the cage who finally quieted.

"I heard," he said, his voice shaking as he held onto the bars. "I hear your heart racing. I tried," Tears streamed down his cheeks. "I tried to help but--"

"It's okay," she told him, stepping over the body to get to him. She put her hands over his, her eyes reassuring him.

He shook his head, his eyes squeezed shut as he cried. "I couldn't--"

"I'm fine." She touched his cheek. "I don't need you to protect me. I can watch my own back."

He opened his eyes to look at her but instead saw a woman rushing toward her, blood running down her chin and saturating her shirt, stake raised in her right hand. Before he could get a word out to warn her, Violet ran up behind the witch, snatching the stake and thrusting it into the woman's right kidney. She dropped to her knees, Violet kneeling behind her, grabbing her by the hair, and tilting her head to the side. She bit her, sucking the last of the blood from her veins.

Rue smiled, looking to her sister and back at Iman. "And, when I can't..."

"Bitch had a fucking *stake*," Violet said standing up and walking to meet them. "What is this, medieval times?"

From upstairs, they heard their father screaming in pain. The sisters bolted up the steps and to the living room where they found their father on the floor, at the mercy of another witch, her hands hovering over his chest as white light seemed to float up from him to her. "Where the fuck did you come from?" Rue snapped.

"Run," Booth told them, his voice scratchy and barely audible.

They ignored him, sprinting toward the woman who shouted, "Iactare!" They were thrown back, breaking through the railings of the staircase.

"Go," Booth whispered. "It's *my* fault. Please, go."

"What are talking about?" Violet asked as the two tried to stand.

"The blood. I took--" His eyes fluttered closed as the witch laughed.

"How does it feel on the receiving end?" she cackled. "Knowing that *your* life is being drained?"

The women got to their feet but were held back by the witch shouting, "Subsisto!" They were stuck, tears welling in their eyes as they watched, unable to aid their father as he lay dying.

Suddenly, from the hall leading to the kitchen, a severed head came flying into the living room, crashing into the back of the witch's head, and snapping her neck. She dropped, the light between her and Booth disappearing.

The witch dead and her spells broken, Rue rushed to her father's side. She listened for a moment, relief washing over her face. "He's alive. Just barely, but he'll be okay in a few hours."

Violet blew out a relieved breath, looking down the hall and seeing Kenton, covered in blood, his face burned, his torso stitching itself back together. He stood in the back doorway, leaning on the frame for support as he panted. Behind him, she saw a decapitated body on the ground, the closed umbrella she'd brought out to him sticking out of its chest.

Rue burned the witches' bodies in the outdoor incinerator while Violet got her father to bed. "I'm sorry," Booth muttered, eyes half-closed and voice little more than a whisper.

"Get some rest, Dad," she said, closing his blackout curtains.

"I didn't know they would track it."

"Track what?"

"The blood. I should have. I should have anticipated…"

"It's not your fault, Dad." She raised the blanket to his chin as his eyes closed. "Get some sleep."

She went downstairs where Kenton had sprawled on one of the sofas. She knelt next to him, brushing the hair out of his eyes. "You okay?"

"Never better," he wheezed, coughing and putting a hand to his chest.

"You can take my room. You should be comfortable while you heal."

"I'm perfectly fine here, love."

"But,"

"But, there could be more," he said, his voice lowering, his eyes stern. "The sun will be up soon and when the witches don't return, the others will surely take daylight as an opportunity to have their revenge. I won't leave you and your family unguarded."

Her features softened as she nodded. "All right, have it your way. But, sleep. You need rest to heal fast enough to be of any use to me." She winked.

CHAPTER 26

He laughed, coughing and clutching his chest. "I'll do my best to make a speedy recovery."

"Good," She pet his hair, staring into his Aegean eyes. "Because when this is over, I'm gonna fuck you so hard, you'll forget your own name."

He raised an eyebrow as she kissed him, her lips soft against his.

"Now, sleep." She stood, heading toward the kitchen as he closed his eyes, a sly smile on his face.

In the basement, Rue comforted an exhausted Iman. He shivered under the blankets on the cot, curled up and sweating. She reached through the bars with a wet cloth to cool his head, his fever still scorching. "It's all right, now," she told him. "You just try to sleep." His teeth chattered as he shook, an occasional tear sliding down his cheek. "Everything's okay."

"Not okay enough," Violet said, bounding down the steps, arms crossed. She cocked her head, a silent request for her sister to follow her upstairs. Rue nodded and the two went up the stairs and out the backdoor. The rain had stopped, the clear sky in its final moments of darkness before sunrise. Violet closed the door and spoke quietly, hoping the others wouldn't hear. "Are you sick of this shit?"

Rue clicked her tongue. "Girl, I'm three blocks *past* sick of this shit."

"There are more of them, right? How many did Ophelia say?"

"Fifteen total, I think."

"So, seven here, two at the loft. Six left."

"Six still coming for us."

"So, are we gonna wait for the next group of witch bitches to bust in here and get rowdy or are we gonna take this fight to them?"

Rue took her carabiner keychain from her belt loop and held it up for her to see. "Bitch, I'm already on my way."

Chapter 27

After cutting the fuel lines of all the cars in the driveway, Rue and Violet climbed into the trees next to the coven's house in New Jersey. Armed with a bag full of the strongest vodka from the bar and a handful of dish towels, they waited, preparing themselves for the coming fight.

"Are you sure about this?" Rue asked, looking to the sky as it filled with shades of orange. "You know how weak the sun's radiation makes us. Almost as weak as humans."

"Yeah, I know but *they* think sunlight *kills* us. Poofs us into dust like in the movies."

"They also think we don't breathe and our hearts don't beat. What's your point?"

"They don't know us. That's why they'll never see us coming. We won't burn, but they will."

"I hope you're right," Rue said, taking a bottle from the bag and handing it to her sister before getting one for herself. "Listen, if I don't make it--"

"I'll take care of Iman. One way or the other."

She nodded.

"And, if *I* don't make it--"

"Dad will lose his whole mind so don't even joke. I can't deal with the tantrum he'll throw if I let you die. Not to mention the whining your husband would do."

She laughed. "So, we just both have to get out of this unscathed."

"No problem." She took a swig from her bottle and stuffed a towel into the opening. Violet, too took a sip and prepared her bottle. They clinked their containers as if in cheers and took lighters from their pockets, igniting the flames and holding them to the cloths. Together, they threw the Molotov cocktails at the house, breaking windows and watching small explosions erupt inside. They hurried to make more, sending one after another into the smoldering home. Soon, the entire building was engulfed, the flames mimicking the colors of the sunrise.

The first witch to flee the house was enveloped in flame, her dress ablaze. She fell to the ground, trying to roll the fire out. After a few seconds with no success, she stopped moving, the flames overtaking her.

Two more fled the house, screaming when they came upon the smoldering corpse. Rue and Violet leaped from the trees, rushing toward the unsuspecting women. The witches joined hands but before they could utter a word, the sisters held their lighters in front of them, ignited the flames, and spit vodka like flamethrowers into the women's faces. Their screams lasted only seconds before they succumbed to their fiery fate.

Rue couldn't help but sing the chorus to Dragula while she went after another witch that ran from the building. She caught her, snapping her neck while Violet laughed at her sister's performance.

"What?" Rue said as the body dropped. "I can't have fun?"

She held her hands up and shrugged, still giggling. "You do you, fam."

"Is that it?"

"I don't know. I thought you said there were two more."

Rue leaned her head in the direction of the house. "I don't hear anyone inside."

"I'll check around." Violet walked to the front of the house, trying to listen for voices, breathing, or heartbeats. There was one sound aside from the roaring of the fire and smoke detectors. It was faint, but she was sure it was the sound of a heartbeat.

From the side of the house, she heard a woman's voice shout, "Volare!" Violet sped around the building to see Rue flying through the air, slamming against a tree so hard, the trunk cracked. She pounced on the witch, sinking her teeth into her neck. "Volare!" the woman said again, this time sending Violet flailing backward and slamming into the ground with a violent thud. The woman skulked toward her, arm outstretched in preparation for another spell, blood trailing from the puncture wounds on the side of her neck.

Rue raced to the witch while she was distracted, pulling her head back and tearing out her windpipe with her teeth then spitting out the bits. She flung the body away and ran to her sister. "You good?"

Violet grunted as she stood. "Good may be an overstatement but I'm all right." She brushed off her pants and straightened her posture. "Any more?"

They both listened for a few moments, the flames and fire alarm the only sounds they could hear. "I don't think so."

"Oh, thank fuck." She put her hands on her knees, bending over and taking a few deep breaths. "I'm exhausted."

"Same. That was an *ordeal*."

"Let's throw these bodies in the fire and get the hell out of here. I need a lie-down." She smelled her shirt. "And, a shower."

Rue laughed. "I wasn't going to mention it."

"Oh, like you're fresh as a fucking daisy."

They laughed, quickly tossed the bodies into the burning house, and hurried down the street to where they parked. They drove away, relaxing for the first time in what felt like forever.

"Just drop me at the loft," Violet said. "I didn't bring a change of clothes to Dad's. Plus, I really need to fix that front door."

She chuckled. "No problem. After, I'll call the insurance company about getting your living room fixed."

"Thanks." She looked down at her hands in her lap, her tone turning solemn. "Do you think they'll ever forgive me?"

"They like Lennon or they like all of them?"

"All of them, especially Ophelia."

"Bitch, I don't know. What you did was fucked *all* the way up. Spell or not."

"Yeah."

"I mean, she knows *why* you did it but--"

"No, I know. Believe me, if I were her, I'd never want to see me again."

CHAPTER 27

While Lennon slept, Ophelia remained sat up in bed, mindlessly scrolling through social media apps, her thoughts still racing. She put the phone down in her lap and rubbed her temples. She couldn't get the images out of her head; Marley tossing Rue around like a rag-doll without even touching her. Marley setting the room on fire with her mind. Marley levitating off the ground. She hated her and though she knew it was horrible to think, she was glad the witch was dead. However, she couldn't help but admire how strong she'd been. How in control. How powerful. She'd never once felt like that and the more she considered it, the more curious she was to find out how she could take some of that power for herself.

She picked up her phone and hit the icon for the search app. She paused, glancing over at Lennon to make sure they were still sleeping and not watching her. It felt wrong, what she was doing but she couldn't help it. It felt like something she *had* to do. She *needed* to take control of her life and this seemed like the perfect way to do it. No more relying on others. No more doing what someone else wanted her to. And, no more taking shit from *anyone*.

She typed in the search bar, *Introduction to witchcraft*. There were thousands of results. She clicked on the first one that wasn't an ad selling something. She took a deep breath, noticing the sun was coming up. *I'll sleep later*, she thought. *I have research to do.*

Chapter 28

Violet had gotten back to her apartment that day so tired, she didn't have the energy to shower before passing out in Ophelia's bedroom. She'd wandered in there, guilt gnawing at her insides like rabid honey badgers, hot tears slipping down her cheeks as she crawled into bed, smelling her pillow as she hugged it. Now that the threat to her life was gone, she was able to feel the full weight of what she'd done. She hated herself, so disgusted she couldn't even bring herself to apologize again. She had no right to be forgiven. As much as she wanted to go to the hotel and beg Ophelia not to hate her, she wouldn't. She'd leave her alone, let her speak to her when and *if* she wanted to. Then, she'd get on her knees and grovel.

After a nearly twelve-hour sleep, she woke up refreshed if not a little dazed from the events of the last twenty-four hours. She showered, threw on a sundress, got the door back up to the best of her ability, covered the broken window with trash bags and duct tape, and sat on the one dining chair that hadn't been broken the night before. She checked her phone. There was one text from her sister telling her that their father was feeling much better and that the insurance company would be there to inspect the following day between eight AM and noon. She sighed, looking over what used to be her living room. The walls and ceiling were charred. The TV, entertainment center, and video game systems were broken. The floor was stained with blood and the whole place smelled like charcoal. Her heart jumped as she remembered how close she'd come to being killed right there in her own apartment. The witch had had her. Had it not been for Kenton, she'd be dead.

"Kenton," she whispered to herself, her mind drifting to their time together in her father's backyard just before the fighting broke out. She'd spent years being angry with him for leaving her and more time than that trying to convince herself that she didn't even want him around. That having a soulmate was some kind of burden. That once she received her husband's bite, she'd lose part of who she was. She'd lose her freedom. But, sitting in the ruins of her loft feeling like a metaphor, she realized that not only was her life without Kenton over, she *wanted* it to be. The thought of sex with other people made her cringe now and even though it had only been a day since she'd seen him last, she missed him so badly, her stomach ached. After everything that happened the night before, she had a new perspective. Even with unlimited time, why would she waste another second not being with the love of her life? "What are you waiting for?" she asked herself. "Stop being stupid."

She jumped up, hurrying to the door, excited to make the trip back to Connecticut. "Oh, duh," she said, turning back to get her phone. She'd need to get a ride share since her sister had dropped her off and taken her car back to their father's. She'd just pulled up the app when a knock came on the door. Her breath hitched as she nearly dropped her phone. It was him. She knew it in her bones. He'd come for her.

She set the phone on the kitchen counter and tried to relax her breathing. Her heart was beating out of her chest, pounding louder in her ears with every step she took toward the door. Her pussy began to throb, already wet with anticipation as she reached for the doorknob. She turned it, blowing out a breath and pulling it toward her. As the door opened, he appeared, the intensity in his eyes burning hotter than the flames she'd seen the night before.

"Hello, love," he said, staring down at her from the threshold.

"You've healed?" she asked, swallowing hard.

"Yes." He stepped inside, closing the space between them. "Now, what's that you said about me forgetting my name?"

Sly smiles curled both of their lips as he removed his jacket and threw it to the floor. Her smile broadened as he unbuttoned his shirt, his eyes never leaving hers. "Don't you want to say something hot like, 'Your beauty drives me mad. I've thought of nothing since we last spoke but the feeling of my hands on your body'?"

He unbuttoned his cuffs and pulled off his shirt, the scent of his cologne, a mixture of grass, cardamom, and rose, enveloping her senses. He took her face in his hands, his expression turning serious. "The time for talking is through." He kissed her, both of them closing their eyes as she put her hands on his waist. His movements were slow but hungry, his tongue licking over hers as the kiss deepened. Her tongue massaged the underside of his, her hands wandering to his belt.

He kicked the door closed then stepped out of his shoes. She unbuckled his belt then yanked it out of the loops of his slacks, dropping it on the hardwood. Her dress had no buttons, so he tore it apart, down the center like a piece of paper. He pulled the shredded garment down her arms and tossed it away, her nipples hardening in the sudden cold as she stood naked in the air-conditioned room. His hands traveled down her body to her thighs. He spread them apart and lifted her, carrying her to the hallway as she wrapped her legs around his waist and her arms around his neck.

In her bedroom, he walked directly to the bed, not bothering to close the door. He lay her down, climbing on top of her, never breaking the kiss. She set her feet on the mattress, her legs spread wide. He unbuttoned and unzipped his pants, pulling them down with his boxers and kicking them off along with his socks. After a few more moments of kissing, he stopped to take off his sleeveless undershirt.

She watched him, the pale light of the moon and city street filtering through her window gleaming off his alabaster biceps, his muscular chest and narrow waist the sexiest things she'd ever seen. Her pussy flooded as he rested himself on top of her, staring down at her as he ran his hand up her left thigh. His brows furrowed and jaw tightened as he held himself back, his cock like stone as he slid it over her drenched pussy.

"I'm desperate for you," he told her, his voice deep and growly. "But, I have to be sure. Violet, darling, is this what you want?"

She moved herself against him, gliding up and down the shaft she'd never realized was so big. Her lips spread to its sides while her clit rubbed against the head sending shivers of pleasure up through her lower abdomen. "Yes," she said, her skin warming as she ran her hands down his back and to his ass. "Get in here."

Growling as he kissed her neck, he sank himself inside. She gasped, spreading her legs even wider for him as his balls pressed against her ass. He pulled out and pushed in, unhurried as he felt her clit swell against him. His forearms held his weight as he lifted his head, looking down at her body writhing beneath him.

She opened her eyes, looking at the space between them, watching his girthy cock move in and out of her, her pussy pulsing firmly around it. She bit her bottom lip, squeezing his ass, a low moan escaping her throat.

CHAPTER 28

He pulled up his knees, shifting his weight to them and grabbing her wrists. He raised her arms over her head, pinning them there with one hand and kissing her again. His free hand traveled down her body until it reached her arch, his thumb slipping between the folds and circling around her clit. He thrust harder, his balls slapping against her ass so hard, they could hear it.

Her body tensed with the first orgasm, her back arching and her toes curling. He stopped kissing her to watch her face, her features scrunching as she came. Her moans spurred him on, his movements now faster with even more force. He lowered himself to again kiss her neck, one arm next to her to shoulder his weight as he took the opposite hand away from her clit and used it to squeeze her ass cheek so hard, his nails broke skin.

She groaned in pleasure, matching his thrusts as waves of euphoria overtook her. She clenched around him, digging her fingernails into his shoulder blades as one orgasm ended and another began. He kissed up the side of her neck to her ear, his breath hot against her skin.

"It's forever now," he whispered. "From now on, we belong to each other." As he filled her, his fangs descended, his eyes going black. He grazed her neck with his teeth before piercing the skin, sinking his fangs into her veins, the warm fluid filling his awaiting mouth.

She gasped, her eyes flying open and then rolling back, the rapture of the moment overwhelming. She grabbed the back of his neck, holding him to her, crying out in ecstasy as she came for a third time. The world fell away, her skin tingling and her vision going dark. All there was was the two of them, no longer separate beings but one entity joined in eternal bliss.

He sucked hungrily, his arm now around her back, his hand holding her shoulder. He'd already come but he was hard once again, thrusting once more into his beloved. Soon, he heard her heart begin to slow and panicked. "Violet," he shouted, snapping her out of her lust-filled haze.

"What?" she breathed, her chest heaving.

"Are you all right, love? Did I take too much? I'm sorry, I couldn't help myself."

"I'm fine," she reassured him, touching his cheek.

He watched as the marks he'd left healed. A sigh of relief left his lips. He took her hand and kissed her palm. "I'm so sorry, darling. I would never--"

"I'm all right." She moved beneath him, encouraging him to keep thrusting. "Just still frisky." She lifted her hips, rolling him onto his back.

He laughed as she sat up. "Taking charge, are you, pet?"

"Well, I *did* promise to fuck you stupid."

"That you did."

She ground against him, her hands on his chest for balance. His hands ran up her thighs, to her hips, and then over her ass. He squeezed her, her cheeks separating, stretching her pussy as it swallowed his granite-hard cock. She rolled her hips, sliding clit-first down his shaft, her ass kissing his balls before rising up, hips forward. His eyes closed as he grunted, his muscles tensing as she continued, increasing her speed. She bounced on top of him, shifting to more of a twerk as she felt him throb inside her. He let out shaky breaths, his legs twitching as he opened them.

"What's your name?" she asked.

He panted, opening his eyes, sweat beading on his forehead.

"Tell me." A teasing grin spread across her lips as she grabbed his chin. "Can you say it? Say it for me. Tell me your name."

"I...ah, I--"

"Told ya." She swept her hand around to the back of his neck and pulled him up to a sitting position. She got off her knees, opening her legs around him using her feet to balance on the bed, holding him close and continuing to grind. He wrapped his arms around her, one hand on her back, the other on her ass. As they both came again, she grasped a handful of his hair, tilted his head to the side, and released her fangs, biting him as he'd bitten her, indulging in the glorious taste of his hot, rich blood.

He took a sharp breath, embracing her even tighter as he filled her again. He moaned, his body trembling as she drank.

"Just a little," she said, licking the side of his neck as the puncture marks healed. She scraped her teeth along the stubble of his cheek. "I just wanted to taste you."

"And, how was I?" he asked, catching his breath.

She smiled again, looking into his eyes, placing her hand on his cheek, and running her thumb over his lips. "Delicious."

Chapter 29

Rue didn't sleep. Instead, she paced the floor of her father's basement, occasionally reaching her arm through the cell bars to wipe Iman's forehead, neck, and chest with ice water. Throughout the day, he alternated between screaming in pain and falling unconscious; one minute throwing himself into the bars of his cage, sobbing, sweating, and shaking in agony and the next passed out on the floor or cot. Rue also cried, desperate to take his pain away and fearing the worst. As night fell, so did she, fainting from lack of sleep on the concrete in front of the cell, wash cloth still in hand.

Hours later, Iman awoke, his breathing steady and his hands no longer trembling. His head pounded and his throat was dry but he felt calm, the all-over nerve pain having finally left him. He sat up, his muscles aching with every movement. He rubbed his eyes and took a deep breath, the smell of iron so strong, it made his nose twitch. He realized it was the metal of the cage that held him and that if he could smell *that* this strongly, Violet's aversion to food made all the sense in the world.

He swung his legs over the side of the cot, the cold of the floor on his bare feet causing him to tense up. As his eyes adjusted, he saw Rue lying on the floor on the other side of the bars. He could hear her heartbeat and breathing, his body relaxing knowing that she was all right. He got down on his knees and crawled to her, taking the cloth from her hand and kissing her palm. He moved the hair away from her face and dragged his fingers down her cheek.

Her honey-brown eyes blinked open, her usually sharp-as-daggers eyeliner smudged and half worn off. "Iman?" She bolted up, getting to her knees and looking him over. She put her hand on his forehead, breathing a sigh of relief when she felt how cool his skin was. "Fever's gone. How do you feel?"

"Hungover," he told her, his voice raspy.

"That's normal. It'll go away in a few hours. How do you feel otherwise? Coherent? Any lingering unprovoked rage? Any more sharp pains?"

He shook his head. "I'm fine." He looked her in the eyes as his pupils dilated. "Just really, really hungry."

Twenty-four hours after her Initiation, Adia emerged from the cave a mile into the woods behind her house. The circle of candles in the clearing had burned out, signifying the ritual's completion. The night before, the coven had gathered, presented her with gifts of herbs to be used in future spells, the family grimoire, and fashioned her measure, tying her forever to her sister witches.

She wrapped the blanket around her shoulders, the only comfort item she'd been allowed during her stay in the sacred cave. She'd spent her time there meditating, becoming one with the nature that provided the magic she'd soon put to use. It was difficult at first, clearing her mind when her emotions had been so all over the place, her sister not bothering to show up to the ceremony disappointing to say the least. Marley had always treated her like an outsider, made fun of her because she "wasn't born of magic". She saw her as less than, not a *real* witch. Not even a real sister. She'd always thought it was because she was adopted but lately she'd begun to suspect there was more to it. It wasn't that she was adopted. It was that she was their mother's favorite. She called her her "modicum miraculum", her little miracle. Marley didn't *dislike* her. She was jealous.

Still, it wasn't Adia's fault she was the baby of the family and got more of their mother's attention. Jealousy is no excuse to miss something as important as your sister's Initiation. She didn't know if she could forgive her. After all, the Initiation is the biggest night in a witch's life. Marley might not have thought that she deserved to be made a full member of the coven, but that didn't matter now. She *was* a full member, born witch or not. She'd worked hard for her abilities and she was determined to become such a powerful witch that even Marley would be proud of her.

Adia gathered her gifts, the blanket, and the burnt-out candles in the box she'd brought with her and began the one-mile trek back to her house. It was only about fifteen minutes, but by the time she was near the tree line, her stomach had begun to rumble. She broke into a skip, thoughts of her mom's pancakes dancing in her mind. She couldn't wait to have breakfast with her mother and to rub her sister's face in the fact that she'd made it through her Initiation *without* her support. But, as the trees gave way to the clearing beyond, she was stopped in her tracks, dropping the box, her heart falling to her stomach.

Across the yard, remnants of the house stood charred and broken, the staircase leading to open air instead of the second floor. "Mom," she said, her voice broken. She screamed, running toward the site, "Mom!"

She got to what used to be the back door, now just a frame with a line of caution tape blocking the threshold. She tore it aside and stepped in, the sink and blackened appliances all that remained of the once grand kitchen. She shuffled through the rubble, stepping over hunks of wood that looked more like used-up firewood than building materials. Tears streamed down her face as she made her way to where the living room used to be. There, she could feel the absence of everyone that had been there the night before. They weren't only gone physically. Their spirits had also vacated not only the house but the mortal plane.

She dropped to her knees, her mouth agape in a silent scream. She clutched her stomach, bending at the waist and rocking back and forth as she inhaled sharply, choking on the fumes of sulfur and burnt flesh. She wailed, her grief echoing in the night. Outside, crows began to gather, flying in from all directions to land on every available surface. They, too cried out, their voices matching hers as she lamented. Their cries filled the air for miles, the call unmistakable to anyone that could recognize what it meant; the death of a coven.

Part 2
Rue

Chapter 30

"What the fuck, Violet?" Rue snapped through the phone.

"I'm sorry," Violet said, looking at the empty suitcase that sat open on the bed next to her. "I've been busy packing. I totally lost track of time." She edged closer to the end of the bed, her pants off and her legs spread wide. Kenton knelt before her, ignoring her conversation as his tongue continued its work.

"I get you're quitting to spend time with your man since he's back but you said you'd stay until I hired someone else."

"I know," She bit her lip to keep from moaning as Kenton's hands slid up underneath her shirt and settled on her breasts. "But, Paris calls. You know how overdue this honeymoon is."

He stood, pulling her ass off the edge of the bed causing her to fall back. She licked her lips and flashed a sly smile up at him as he whipped his belt off and quickly stepped out of his slacks.

"You're putting me in a really shitty position," Rue said, oblivious to what was going on on the other end of the call.

"I know and I'm really sorry but," She covered her mouth, silencing the gasp escaping her throat as he plunged himself into her. He grabbed her backside, thrusting hard as her hips rocked to meet his movements. "I really have to get this packing done. I'll see you before I leave."

"Fine, but don't expect to use me as a reference."

Violet ended the call and dropped the phone, stretching her arms over her head and grabbing the blanket. Kenton pushed her shirt up to her neck, exposing her breasts, her deep mauve nipples hard enough to cut glass. She covered them with her hands, squeezing the firm flesh around them.

CHAPTER 30

"Now, now," he said, pulling her hands away and pinning her wrists above her head. "Don't hide that perfect body from *me*." He bent down, kissing one breast, then the other, her back arching as he took a nipple into his mouth. He tore off his button-down and wrapped an arm around her waist, pumping harder as she trembled beneath him. She spread her legs as far apart as she could, knees bent, calves on his back. He lifted his head to meet her gaze. "You never have to hide *anything* from me."

He climbed onto the bed, dragging her up to rest her head on a pillow and stretching his legs as he lie on top of her. Her eyes rolled back as he kissed up her neck and she began to come. "That's it, darling," he breathed in her ear. "No holding back."

"Fuck," she said, her voice quiet and high-pitched. "*Fuck*." Fluid gushed from her as she climaxed, her body quivering as she held on to him. He grunted in her ear as he too finished, his teeth grazing her earlobe. Her muscles relaxed as he rolled to his side of the bed, both of them panting and covered in sweat.

"Your sister rang?" he asked as his breath steadied.

"Yeah. Nothing important."

"Good." He rolled back, settling himself between her legs. She bit her bottom lip and closed her eyes as he thrust into her again, removing her top and nuzzling her neck. "I'm not done with you, yet."

"The fuck is this now?" Rue griped, shoving her phone into her back pocket. As soon as she left the kitchen she was met with screams and the sound of bottles breaking. A crowd had formed in the center of the bar and at her height, she couldn't see over them to figure out what was going on. Blowing out an exasperated breath, she climbed onto the bar top and looked down at the mass of people that had gathered on the sometimes-dance floor. In the middle of the ruckus were two men, one leather-clad with a long beard, the other in a white tee shirt that looked half-drenched in what she assumed was beer. Through the noise, she couldn't make out what was being said but that hardly mattered because as she hopped down from her perch, the men's argument moved beyond words. The leather-vested man punched the other in the jaw. The smaller man quickly recovered and threw himself head-first into the other's chest. They locked each other in a bear hug, each one attempting to get the other on his knees.

Rue pushed her way through the crowd, her charcoal-black cat eye sharper than the broken glass at her feet. Without a word from her cherry lips, she grabbed the men by their hair and pried them apart. Laughter and a chorus of "Ohs" erupted from the onlookers as she dragged the two to the front door and pushed them out onto the sidewalk.

"You know the rules," she told them, voice calm but eyes fierce. "No fighting in my bar."

"He started it," the bearded man protested.

She scowled. "What am I, your mother? I don't care *who started it*. You're banned."

"We're sorry," the smaller man chimed in.

"Yeah," the other one said. "It won't happen again."

She folded her arms and sighed. "Fine. A one-week ban. But, if you haven't learned your lesson when you come back, I'll kick you out for good, you hear me?"

They both nodded.

"All right. Now, get the fuck out of here before I change my mind." She left them there, rolling her eyes as they pouted, and shooed everyone away from the mess on the floor. She got a broom and dustpan from behind the bar and swept up the shards of caramel-colored glass before using the rag in her waist apron to sop up the spilled beer. "Wild fucking animals," she muttered to herself, heading back to the kitchen to pick up the order she thought must be ready by now.

"Customers still rowdy?" Lou asked, setting a plate of wings on the line and taking down the accompanying ticket.

"Apparently."

"Not surprising."

"No?"

"Nah," He glanced at the next ticket and started work on the order. "It's too quiet. They need music to drown out the shit in their brains giving them anxiety."

She took the plate of wings. "That's what the booze is for."

He shook his head, his crow's feet exaggerated under the fluorescent lights. "Not enough these days."

"It's just one more night."

He put the second order on the line and took down its ticket. "Iman's better?"

"He thinks so."

"What'd you say he was sick with?"

"A cold."

"For two weeks?"

Maintain the lie, she thought. *No flinching*. "I'd chalk it up to man flu but you know how any little thing can mess up a singer's voice. He could feel fine but if his throat's even a smidge scratchy…"

"Yeah, I know. I see him drinking his tea and shit. I'll make sure to have some ready for him when he gets back."

"Thanks, Lou." She grabbed the second plate. "I better get these to where they're going before the next riot breaks out."

Two more fights, a round of vomiting party girls, and one flasher later, the bar was finally closed for the night. After locking up, Rue pored over the handful of applications she'd gotten since putting the help wanted sign in the window a week and a half before. Every applicant was qualified. Most were *overqualified* with degrees and years of work experience. Any one of them would be fine but for how long before they got a job in their preferred industry and quit, leaving her in the same predicament? "Just pick someone," she told herself, knowing that if she kept doing everything herself, she'd snap. She'd been angry with her sister for not coming in but the truth was, it wasn't her fault she was in this mess. She'd had two weeks to hire someone else and she couldn't do it. Not when she knew anyone she brought in would just leave at the first chance they got. She'd have to, though. She had no choice.

After twenty minutes of rummaging through her bedroom closet, Rue found the tiny blue box her mother had given her just days before she'd left. She took a deep breath and opened it. Inside, the thin gold chain covered the pendant. "Please don't be tangled," she groaned, plucking it from the box and holding it up in front of her. She let out a sigh of relief when the chain unfurled, revealing the winged scarab pendant dangling over her wrist. It was in perfect condition even after eighteen years. She placed it carefully back in the box and closed it, leaving her room and standing for a moment in the hall. She stepped into the guest room and gave it one last look, making sure the bed was made and the nightstand was dust-free. Her stomach fluttered with nerves. The next night, she'd pick Iman up from her dad's and he'd be staying in this room. He'd insisted and she'd agreed against her better judgment. She told herself, as he'd told her, it was because he needed more time away in a quiet place where he could get a handle on his heightened senses and thirst for blood. Deep down, though, she knew he was in control and that it was *her* that needed to get a handle on things. Having him so close would be a temptation she wasn't sure she could fight.

She'd gotten his things from across the hall, lined his guitars up on stands along the far wall in order of most played, and hung up what little clothes had been in his closet. She'd taken most of his clothes to her dad's two weeks before but he'd asked that his guitars stay with her for fear he might accidentally break them while adjusting to his newfound strength. Her heart raced as she pictured him playing, his well-developed forearms and long, slender fingers making her skin flush. She blinked the thoughts away, calling herself ridiculous as she headed across the hall.

CHAPTER 30

She knocked on Violet's door, not wanting to walk in and see something she couldn't unsee.

"Sister," Kenton greeted, opening the door and stepping aside to let her in. "We were just about to come say our goodbyes."

She slit her eyes. "Did you just call me 'sister'?"

"Of course. That's what you are, as I am your brother. What else *should* I call you?"

"Hey, Rue," Violet said, carrying a suitcase from her bedroom.

She gestured to her sister while holding her brother-in-law's gaze. "That."

He guffawed. "I didn't realize American families were so formal. Fine, I will call you by your given name at your request." He went to his wife and took the luggage. "I'll take that for you, darling." He kissed her cheek and headed to the door. "I'll meet you at the car?"

She nodded and stood in the doorway, watching as he walked away.

"Time to go, huh?" Rue said, the answer obvious.

"Yeah." She turned to face her, leaning on the door frame. "Flight to catch. You ready to get Iman tomorrow?"

"Not really."

She gave her a knowing look.

"Stop it."

She held her hands up in feigned innocence. "I didn't say anything."

"I know what you were thinking."

"Okay, then, I'll say it out loud. You're being ridiculous."

"Violet,"

"No, for real. You might be the one that always does the right thing and knows everything about everything because you're *so smart* but *I* know you. You're in love with that man."

"We're just friends."

"Bullshit."

"You know what would happen."

"Maybe, *eventually*. So what?"

"So what?"

"You're really gonna sit around wasting your hot years on a maybe?"

"Wasting my," she paused, folding her arms. "Bitch, I stop aging next year regardless. I'll be hot as all fuck *forever*."

"You're still wasting time. Time you could be spending letting Iman lay that pipe and *trust*, he is a skilled-ass laborer."

"I just threw up in my mouth a little."

She put her hands up again. "I'm just saying, there's no point in denying yourself. You want him, you should have him."

She shook her head. "You know I can't."

"Your call."

"Anyway, I stopped by to bring you a super late wedding present." She held out the box. "Mom wore it when she married Dad. She gave it to me right before--"

"I don't want it."

Her brows lifted in surprise. "But, it--"

"I don't care. I'm sorry, I appreciate you thinking of me and everything but I don't want anything from that woman."

"I know you're still mad and I get it but she's our mom and this was important to her."

"I don't give a fuck what was important to her. You know what wasn't important to her? Us. You, me, and Dad. *We* should have been important to her, not some useless piece of jewelry. You were what, eleven when she took off? Maybe you have a bunch of great memories of her that you want to hold on to but I don't. I was *five*." She stopped, holding back angry tears.

"I'm sorry," Rue said. "I didn't mean to upset you right before your trip."

"I know. You were trying to be nice. You're always looking out for me, even when I'm an ass. You've been doing it my whole life." She locked eyes with her, her expression serious. "You were my mom, not her. You took care of me, made sure I went to school, brushed my teeth, broke up with people that didn't treat me right. Remember Jimmy whats-his-name from tenth grade?"

She snorted. "Such a douche."

"Right?" Her features softened. "You were the one that was there for me. So, fuck Zahara and her damn jewelry. If I want to feel nostalgic, I'll go to Dad's. My old room is like a shrine to my youth. And, if I want something sparkly, I can buy it myself. My husband's *loaded* and he gave me access to all of his accounts." She winked.

Rue chuckled. "He's gonna regret that decision."

"Nah." She flashed a whimsical smile. "He loves me. Chump."

She laughed again. "Well, you should get back to him, then, before he comes to his senses."

"Yeah. You'll lock up?"

"I will."

She touched her arm before turning to go. "See ya next month."

"Have fun." When she was gone, Rue closed the door and headed to the kitchen, making sure her sister had remembered to stock the fridge for Lennon and Ophelia. They'd be back in two days and she wanted to make sure they had what they needed. She found almond milk, soda, various vegetables, butter, steak, and chicken in the refrigerator. In the freezer, there were pizzas, peas, carrots, two lasagnas, and a box of waffles. The pantry held bottled water, apples, oranges, bananas, maple brown sugar-flavored oatmeal packets, bread, peanut butter, pasta, and sauce. She wasn't super familiar with human eating habits, aside from what the patrons at the bar ordered from her limited menu, but it seemed like a good amount of food. Lots of options. She wondered if so many choices were overwhelming to humans or if they liked the variety.

She dropped onto a chair, placing the blue box on the dining table. She spun it between her hands, thinking about what her sister had said. Memories of her mother floated through her mind. Playing at the park, riding bikes, and snuggling under a blanket to watch old movies. She remembered the day she gave her the necklace and how strange her face looked. Anxious, like she knew it would be the last gift she ever gave her.

She opened the box, took the necklace from it, opened the clasp, and put it on. The pendant rested just below her clavicle, a golden beetle with a wingspan of an inch and a half. A comforting warmth washed over her as she touched the pendant. Violet didn't remember the good times with her mother but she did and yes, she liked holding on to them. Because, even though she left them, Rue knew she loved them. She knew it in her bones.

From the hall, she heard footsteps then her apartment door opening. She got up from the table, taking the box with her. She flung the door open and standing there was her father.

"Oh, hello, darling. I knocked but you must not have heard me. I, um," he took a step to the side so she could see past him into her living room where Iman was busy taking off his boots. "I thought I'd save you a trip."

She grabbed his arm and pulled him into Violet's loft, closing the door behind him. "What the hell, Dad?"

"I know I'm only meant to use my key in case of emergency but--"

"That's not what I'm talking about. Why is he here?"

"Well, he was getting antsy piddling around the house. To be honest, he was starting to get on my nerves." His eyes caught the glint of the necklace under the can lights. "What's this?" He gently lifted the pendant to get a better look. "Your mother's? I didn't know you kept it."

"I can take it off if it upsets you."

"Don't you dare." He smiled weakly as his blue eyes misted. "She'd want you to wear it."

"Dad,"

He took his hand away. "It's lovely. Besides, I wouldn't dream of influencing your fashion choices," He looked over her black tank top, torn jeans, and studded belt. "Such as they are."

She arched an eyebrow. "Are you making fun of my clothes?"

"Of course not, sweetheart. I understand how important it is for young people to express themselves."

"Uh, huh."

"Anyhow, your fledgling has grown stir crazy and as he's in full control of his faculties, I see no reason he shouldn't be home with you where he belongs. After all, *I* am not his sire, am I?"

She dipped her head and put her hands on her hips. "No."

"No." He sighed, tilting her chin to look her in the eye. "Oh, darling, there's no need for trepidation. He's fine. He won't be attacking anyone any time soon, I promise. Unless, of course, they deserve it." He winked and adjusted his lapels.

"That's not what I'm worried about."

"Oh?"

She chewed the inside of her cheek.

"Ah, you mean his crush on you."

Her eyes widened. "His what?"

"I caught him a few times flipping through pictures he'd taken of you on his phone. He didn't know I saw, of course. And, oh, the way his eyes lit up when you called. He was like a schoolboy."

"Jesus, Dad."

"What? I can't notice things? The boy's been haunting my house like a ghost for two weeks doing nothing but drinking bag after bag of blood and practicing Pahlavani in my yard. Do you know he had weighted clubs delivered? They weren't even in a box. The woman across the street asked if they were weapons. White people, I swear."

"Dad, you're white people."

"Yes, thank you, Rue, I'm aware of my lack of melanin. But, unlike my neighbors, I'm not actually terrified of every brown man holding exercise equipment."

"I know. You're very woke."

He rolled his eyes.

"What's Pahlavani?"

He closed his eyes and pinched the bridge of his nose. "Please tell me you're joking. Please, darling. I couldn't have failed you this much, could I?"

"I'm sure it's one of those things you mentioned in passing when I was a teenager and I just forgot."

He looked up to the ceiling. "For crying out loud. It's Persian Yoga, Rue. You took a class for six weeks."

"Oh, yeah! And then you pulled me out when I broke that kid's arm during wrestling practice."

"Yes. Perhaps twelve was too young to expose you to physical competition given your advantages. Still, your age was no excuse to harm an innocent child."

"He called me 'Too Few Rue'. He said I was tiny."

"You *were* tiny, dear. Still are."

She scowled. "Thanks, Dad."

"I'm sorry, sweetheart." He kissed her forehead. "I didn't mean to hurt your feelings. Your height is nothing to be ashamed of. You get it from your mother." Another small smile passed his lips. "You get so much from her."

"Yes, I know. The hair, the skin tone, the lips, the shortness. It's like you weren't even there."

He chortled. "Oh, you got plenty from me, believe me. You and your sister both. The shape of your hands, your delicate, button nose, and don't forget the snark. Your mother was very sweet. Not a drop of sass in her body. I, however, can't seem to help but be rude with my quips."

"Truer words."

He laughed and pulled her in for a hug, kissing the top of her head. "All right, dear. I must be off." He took a step back. "I have some business in the city and I need to wrap that up in time to open the museum." He opened the door and stepped out.

"What business in the city? You hate the city."

"Never you mind. Just tend to your sired." He turned to go but looked back over his shoulder. "By the way, not that you would take my opinion into consideration but your Iman is a good man. Choice of career aside, he's quite smart and very polite. I approve."

"Approve?"

As he walked away, he called back, "You could do worse."

"For fuck's sake," she whispered, leaving the loft and locking the door. She leaned against it, taking a deep breath, the butterflies in her stomach returning with wings of steel. She felt nauseous, her head spinning. "Get it together," she told herself. "It's just Iman. Nothing's changed." But, she was lying to herself and she knew it.

CHAPTER 30

In her apartment, Rue watched Iman unpack, leaning against his bedroom door frame, staying silent long enough to admire his ass when he bent to pick up a fallen tee shirt. She squeezed her eyes shut and cleared her throat.

He spun to face her, his expression brightening. "Hey."

"Hey." She chewed on her bottom lip for a second, their eyes locking. "The fridge is full. Dad's blood bag guy hooked me up. Said he'll make a delivery every Monday."

He chuckled. "You make it sound like a drug deal."

She shrugged. "It's not *not* like a drug deal."

"I guess." He hugged his arms, his gaze falling to the floor.

"You okay?"

"Honestly?" His eyes again met hers. "I have no idea. I mean, I was fine at your dad's but in a crowded bar? Not to mention Lennon and Ophelia right across the hall. They'll be..." He stopped, cringing at his own thoughts.

"They'll be what?"

The muscles in his jaw twitched and he held his arms even tighter. "Easy prey."

She marched toward him, reaching up and grabbing his chin, forcing him to look down at her. "You're not gonna hurt anyone, you hear me? What you are now doesn't change who you've always been."

"But, that night with those witches," His Adam's apple bobbed as he swallowed. "You saw what I did to them."

"The twenty-four hours after the change is brutal. Most people don't survive it. They either die in the transition or stay in it forever, like wild animals with fever and blood pressure so high, their hearts give out after a few days."

"But, not before they kill every person they come across. Your dad told me." He took her hand from his face and put it to his heart causing her stomach to flip. "I know I made it. I know I should be able to relax now but I can't. I still feel it in me, that blinding hunger. What if I lose control? What if I--"

"Nothing's gonna happen. As long as you drink enough from the bags, you won't be tempted to rip anyone's throat out. And, I'm here, right? You've seen what I do to people that *look* at O sideways. You think I'd let you kill her? She's like, my only friend besides you."

His eyes darkened as he swallowed again. He let go of her hand and sat on the edge of the bed. "Violet used to bite me during...you know."

She forced herself not to wince. "I know."

"And, other times. Random times. I don't know if she was just hungry or if some of that was..." He trailed off, his thick eyebrows scrunched and his gaze averted. "Do you have to be in the act to lose control like that?"

She shifted uncomfortably. "Yes."

"What if I hooked up with someone *once*," He looked back up to where she stood, her arms now crossed. "And, I'd *never* let it happen again. Like, it was a *huge* mistake but it still happened. If that person was around, would I be okay or would I be tempted to," He curved two fingers next to his face and made a hissing sound.

She took a step back, dropping her chin. "Oh. You and Ophelia."

"It didn't mean anything," he said, anxiety in his voice. "She was just trying to make Violet jealous and my mind was all over the place. I'd been drinking and--"

"You don't have to explain yourself to me."

"I know but," He stood to move toward her but she backed away.

"No."

He stopped. "No, what?"

"No, you're not any more likely to bite someone you've been with than you are any stranger on the street. It's a pheromone or hormone thing. You have to be actively banging one out for it to be a problem."

"Oh. Well, that's good."

"Yeah, so you should get some rest. Sun's coming up and I need you on all cylinders tomorrow. Turns out a music-less bar gets people twitchy."

"Rue,"

"I have some work to finish downstairs. Inventory. I'll see you tomorrow." She hurried out of the apartment and down the stairs, stomping through the empty kitchen, and closing herself in the bar's storage room. She sat on a case of napkins and covered her mouth, fearing that he'd be able to hear her too-fast breathing even there with his newly enhanced hearing. She rocked back and forth, the blue box crushed from being held so tight. "The fuck's wrong with you, bitch?" she whispered to herself. "Get it together. Stop being stupid." She knew what Iman and Ophelia's hookup was about. She knew they weren't together. Still, his confession was like a knife to the gut. "Stop it. You're just friends." Just friends. And, it would have to stay that way.

Chapter 31

Booth waited in his SUV, the tinted windows hiding him from passersby on the busy Brooklyn street. He was parked in front of an herbalist shop, the manager set to arrive to open at any moment. He slipped out of his jacket and set it on the passenger seat, glancing in the rear view mirror to reassure himself that the rope he'd brought along was still there.

From his jacket pocket, he heard his phone ring. With an impatient sigh, he answered it. "May I help you?"

"Hi," the voice on the other said. "I see that you're closed. Is that just for today?"

"No, ma'am. Sadly, we'll be closed for a few weeks. Perhaps a month. Family emergency. But, we'll have discount rates the week of reopening. If you sign up for our newsletter, you'll be notified."

"Okay, thank you."

"Have a lovely day." He ended the call and tossed the cell onto the seat, already regretting having the museum's calls routed to his personal line. He rolled up his sleeves revealing the British Red Ensign tattoo on his right forearm. "Any minute now."

Finally, the shop's manager appeared. She was an attractive woman of about forty, her light red hair hanging in soft curls down her back. She wore no makeup and a flowing flower print dress in earthy shades of green and cottage white. He watched her unlock the door and enter the building. She didn't lock it back but left the closed sign up, no doubt needing to ready the register for incoming customers. "Very good." He opened the glove compartment and pulled out a handkerchief, setting it in his lap before taking out another item, a bottle of homemade chloroform.

He doused the handkerchief and replaced the bottle, closing the compartment and exiting the vehicle. He beelined to the shop's door, clicking the remote on his key chain in his pocket as he went, opening the liftgate.

"Oh," the woman said, jumping at the sight of him and laughing at herself. "I'm sorry, I thought I'd locked the door. We aren't actually open, yet but if you give me one second, I'll be right with you."

"I'd say take your time," He sped toward and around her, grabbing her from behind and covering her nose and mouth with the poisoned cloth. "But I'm in a bit of a rush." After a few minutes of struggling, she went limp in his arms and he swung her up in a princess carry. His nose twitched at the overpowering scent of sage as he passed by a bushel of smudge sticks on his way to the door. He peered out through the glass, seeing no one close enough to cause any problems. Faster than humans can see, he took the woman from the building, threw her in the back of the SUV, hogtied her, duct taped the handkerchief to her face, and closed the door. Then, calmly, he got in the driver's seat and put his key in the ignition, letting out a relieved breath.

Next to him, his phone rang again. "Oh, bloody hell." He picked it up and declined the call. "Note to self, end this routing nonsense once this one's in the cage."

"Rue says the repairs are done so we can go home today," Ophelia told Lennon who sat at the small desk pouring coffee.

"Oh, thank fuck," they said. "No offense but being stuck in a hotel room with just you for two weeks has been a pain in the ass."

She looked up from her phone, brows furrowed. "Um, offense taken."

"You know what I mean."

"Mm." The phone chirped and she returned her gaze to the screen to read the next message. "She also says Violet left for her honeymoon and probably won't be back for a month."

"She left?" They stood, almost knocking over their cup by bumping their hip into the desk. "Without saying goodbye?"

"Rue says she wants to give me space."

"Pfft," They rolled their emerald green eyes, crossing their arms. "Coward."

"Accurate." She dropped the phone onto the bed she sat on and bent down to pull her bag from underneath it. She got up and began gathering clothes to pack. "It's good, though. I'm glad she's gone. I don't want to see her."

Lennon sipped their coffee. "You mean now or ever?"

Ophelia stopped, mulling over the question for a few seconds before answering. "I don't know."

It was after ten by the time Rue had gotten her emotions in check and decided to go upstairs to bed. Iman was asleep by now, she was sure and by the time they woke up, the awkwardness of their last conversation would be dissipated. She hoped.

She climbed the stairs and entered her apartment. It was quiet but for the sound of Iman breathing deeply in his room. Her shoulders relaxed and she placed the blue box on the bar, annoyed that she'd crushed it during her meltdown. From the hall, she heard Violet's door open and went toward the sound to investigate. There, she saw Lennon and Ophelia going inside, finally back from their exile at the hotel.

"I'm gonna have to buy a new console," she heard Lennon complain. "And headset. And controller charger. And..."

She went to a drawer in the kitchen and took out a check made out to them for five thousand dollars and walked across the hall. "The insurance covered it." She held out the check to Lennon who blushed but still looked irritated.

They snatched it from her hand. "Doesn't save me a trip to the store." They stomped off to their bedroom and shut the door hard.

"Is bitchy their default setting?"

"Kind of." Ophelia dropped her bag onto the kitchen table and leaned against a chair, the new dining set identical to the old, broken one. "Thanks for taking care of all this."

"What kind of landlord would I be if I let my tenants live in a burned-out hovel?"

"So, what's the deal, with Violet, I mean? When she comes back will her dude come, too? Or is he going back to England?"

"I don't know. I don't think *she* knows, yet. You know how she just does whatever the hell she feels like, no plan."

She looked down at her shoes. "Yeah."

"You don't have to move out if that's what you're asking. It's *my* building and I'm not about to throw you out on the street, especially after everything that witch bitch put you through. If V or her man has an issue with you being here, they can kick rocks."

"Thanks."

"Same rules as always. No rent but you have to pay your utilities. If I have to keep track of my bills and the bar's *and* yours my head will explode."

"Oh, of course."

Rue heard Ophelia's heart rate quicken at the mention of bills. *She quit dancing*, she remembered.

"Hey, I don't know what your plans are but Violet quit on me so I'm down a server. I know it's not your usual thing but the job's yours if you want it. Twenty dollars an hour plus tips, eight to close, Mondays and Tuesdays off. Those are the slowest nights."

Her head popped up. "I'll take it."

"Cool. I'm gonna go to bed now. All this sunshine is bad for my mood." She turned to go but stopped when her friend touched her arm.

"Wait. Is Iman doing okay? I know you said he made it through the change but--"

Her muscles stiffened. "He's fine."

"That's good," she said, the relief in her voice too clear for Rue to ignore. "I know you guys are a thing now and I just--"

She turned to face her. "We're not a thing."

She tilted her head in confusion.

"We're just friends."

"But, I thought when you turned him it was because you had feelings for him. And, I know he's had a thing for you since *forever,* so I just assumed."

Her toned sharpened. "*Friends*, Ophelia."

"*Okay*. Anyway, I don't want things to get weird so I feel like I should tell you something."

"I know you hooked up."

She froze. "Oh."

"It's not an issue."

"Um, okay. But, you should know it's not his fault."

"Fall in, did he?"

"I was upset and I kind of manipulated--"

"I don't need a play-by-play. I get it. He told me you were both in a weird head space about V's latest shenanigans and you wanted to make her jealous. He said you're not together and it won't happen again, blah freakin' blah. It's not my business. You don't have to explain."

"I wanted to punish her," she admitted. "Not just make her jealous but hurt her how she hurt me by dating that girl. I don't like Iman like that. You know that, right?"

"I know."

"Are you mad?"

She sighed. "No, I'm not mad."

"Are you sure?"

"I think we both know if I was mad at you, it'd be real clear."

"So," her bottom lip began to tremble. "We're still friends?"

Her features softened. "Yeah, girl. We're still friends."

She nodded, tears pooling in her eyes.

"Jesus, bitch. Are you *crying*?"

"No." She sniffed, blinking fast to keep her tears from falling. "It's just that you, Iman, and Lennon are the closest thing I have to," She sniffed again, brushing away

CHAPTER 31

the single tear that escaped her efforts at keeping it at bay. "I don't have people, you know?"

"Well," Rue turned her lip up in a playful grin. "I don't know if I technically count as *people* but I'm here." She did a silly jig and sang the chorus to Count On Me.

Ophelia giggled.

"Do you need a hug? Is this a hug moment?"

She nodded, more tears spilling down her cheeks.

She folded her into a hug, rubbing her back.

She squeezed her tightly and then relaxed.

"Seriously, though. You need to let me sleep. No one wants to deal with a cranky Rue."

She laughed, letting her go. "That's facts."

When Rue had gone, Ophelia unpacked and took a clean towel from the linen closet. "Do you need in the bathroom before I take a shower?" She asked, popping her head into Lennon's room, scrunching her hair. "That watered-down hotel shampoo was bullshit."

Lennon answered without looking up from their phone, the electronics store ad pulled up on the screen. "No, just don't take all the hot water this time."

She rolled her eyes and went to the bathroom where she was stopped in her tracks by what sat on the counter next to the sink: five bottles of her favorite body wash and two of the matching lotion. They weren't there when she'd left for the hotel which meant Violet had to have put them there. For her. "No," she told herself. "She doesn't get a pass just because she bought soap." She hung her towel on the hook on the door and turned the shower on. While she waited for the water to heat, she stripped down and took a long look at herself in the mirror. "You are not for sale and if you were, fancy soap wouldn't fucking cut it." She got in the shower, letting the water scald her skin, hot as hell just the way she liked it.

Chapter 32

Iman closed his eyes, blowing out a deep breath along with his nerves. He looked over the crowd, the bar so packed he was sure the fire marshal would shut them down any minute. "Good turnout," he said, adjusting the mic.

"Got the word out that we'd be back tonight on my socials," Brody said, plucking a few strings on his bass to test the volume of the amp. "I was in the other night for a drink and let me tell you, it was Woodstock ninety-nine in here. Your girl broke up *three* fights in *an hour*. I would've helped but I met a blonde and--"

"My girl?"

He gave him a knowing look then cocked his head in the direction of the bar. Iman followed his gaze to see Rue serving a beer to a long-haired guy in a trench coat.

"She's not my girl."

"Fine, your fantasy girl then. Point is, it was bedlam. These people are animals without tunes. You feeling up to it? Throat's okay?"

"Yeah, I'm good."

"Well, thank God. I was starting to consider getting a day job."

Iman chuckled. "Can't have that."

"No, sir." He tucked his long, black hair behind his ear and shuffled to his spot on stage.

Speaking into the mic, Iman addressed his bandmates and the crowd. "Everyone ready?"

Nods from the band and cheers from the audience put a smile on his stubble-covered face. "Let's do this, then." He belted the first line of Centuries, the band backing him up. The crowd went wild, shoving any residual anxiety out of his mind. The stage was where he belonged. This was home.

Thirteen songs later, he played a slowed-down, haunting version of There She Goes, his eyes falling on Rue behind the bar. He watched her without meaning to, the dim light bouncing off her hair and the curves of her body drawing his attention like a moth to a flame. Her black bra strap poked out from underneath her white tank top and as his gaze lowered he could see that she was cold. She disappeared into the kitchen and he tried to refocus. The song ended and he went into Late at Night, the last song of the set.

As the words flowed from his mouth, his mind wandered to thoughts of Rue, fantasies he'd had a million times now more intrusive than ever. He pictured her splayed on his bed wearing nothing but a come-hither stare. He imagined her underneath him, legs entwined with his, black-painted fingernails scratching down his back, pouty lips at his ear. As he sang the last few lines, imaginary-Rue came, grabbing his ass and biting his neck.

His eyes flew open, his erection jamming against the back of his guitar. No one could see it, luckily but he still felt embarrassed. More applause from the crowd as he unplugged from his amp and leaped from the stage, racing to the kitchen. As he booked it up the stairs, his want for his sire grew as did his hunger. He burst into the empty apartment, slamming the door, setting his guitar on the sofa, and speeding to the fridge. He took a blood bag and tore into it, not wasting time on heating the contents. He chugged it, then another, dropping to his knees as he opened a third. He sat on the floor, leaning against the still-open fridge and continuing to drink, his chest heaving and his pupils dilated.

Fantasy girl, he thought, taking one last sip. That's what she was. What she'd always been since the moment he'd stumbled into the bar to audition for the band three years before.

She'd worn a Weezer tee shirt and a spiked leather cuff bracelet. Her hair was pinned up in a faux hawk and her eyeliner was the same red as her lipstick.

"Name," she'd said without looking up from the paper on the bar top.

"Iman Ardavan," he'd told her.

She'd moved her pen down the page and stopped toward the end. "Says here you're the singer of Da Vinci's Cannon?"

"I was."

She'd finally looked at him, her honey-brown irises catching the beam of sunlight that spilled through the glass door. "What happened?"

He'd sat on a stool across from her and folded his hands. "Long story."

She'd dropped her pen. "I've got nowhere else to be."

"Do they?" he'd asked, gesturing to the band that talked amongst themselves on stage.

"They're busy complaining about the last guy. And the one before that. And the six before that. I don't think they even noticed you come in. Can't really blame them, though. Everyone that's auditioned so far has been mediocre at best." She'd placed a cool hand on his. "Please, for the love of fuck, don't be terrible. These guys won't play with anyone that isn't *perfect* and if I have to listen to them bitch one more time about how much they miss Dex, I'm gonna murder someone."

His heart had jumped at her touch. "Who's Dex?"

"The old singer. He was getting," She'd made grabbing motions in the air. "Handsy with some of the regulars so I...fired him."

"Oh."

"You're not a perv, are you?"

"No."

"Dope. So, what happened with your last band?"

"Short answer, our last tour almost killed us, literally."

She'd raised her dark eyebrows in interest.

"We were playing up and down the East Coast. Hole-in-the-wall places, house parties, stuff like that. We were getting paid *nothing*, sometimes just drinks but we were sure the exposure would be worth it. We were crashing in the van most nights, eating out of dumpsters. It was bleak but we kept telling ourselves that's life on the road. But, then December came. It was cold. I mean, *real* cold. We were stuck out in the Berkshires, nothing around for miles, in twenty-something inches of snow.

Roads not plowed or salted. We couldn't go anywhere. So, we did what we always did, parked and huddled under a blanket in the back of the van to wait it out."

"You froze?"

"Stage two hypothermia. Barely made it to a hospital in time. After that, I decided it just wasn't worth it. Touring, not music."

"Well, shit, if that story doesn't deserve a drink, I don't know what does." She'd set a glass in front of him and poured a finger of whiskey. "On the house, of course."

"Thank you but I'll save it for *after* the audition." He'd put his hand to his throat. "Wouldn't want to irritate the pipes."

"So professional, I love it." She'd banged three times on the counter to get the band's audition. "Yo, fellas, your next victim. Be gentle, he's recently thawed out."

The drummer had cast her a puzzled look. "You high again, Rue?"

"I haven't smoked in months and you know that." She'd turned her attention back to Iman, flipping her paper over and sliding it across to him. "Which one of these are you doing?"

He'd looked down the list of songs the ad had instructed auditioners to prepare and pointed to the one he'd been practicing.

"Got it." She'd again called to the band. "All right boys, we're doing Pop Evil's Work." She'd quieted her voice to speak to Iman directly. "They *just* learned this one so if they mess up, try to ignore it."

He'd nodded, getting up from his seat and heading to the stage. He'd brought the mic up to his level and did his best to ignore the butterflies he'd felt seeing Rue smile up at him from the bar. This was about the music and he'd needed to concentrate, no matter how hot the bartender was.

He'd signaled the band and they began to play, the thump of the bass vibrating the floor beneath him. He'd cleared his mind and given it all he had, mostly because he'd wanted the gig but partly because he'd hoped to impress Rue. He'd tried to keep his eyes off her while he sang but it was impossible. She was gorgeous. He'd had to close his eyes to focus on what he was doing.

When the music stopped, Brody had slapped him on the back. "The lungs on this kid!"

"And, the soul!" the drummer had said. "How old are you, man?"

CHAPTER 32

Iman had cleared his throat, hoping the older guys wouldn't dismiss him because of his age. "Twenty-five."

"Where'd you get that rasp? And, that *growl*?"

Brody had leaned his bass against the amp. "Fuck the growl. Did you hear that scream? Dude's a fuckin' banshee. Hey, Rue, cancel the rest of the auditions. This is our guy right here."

Iman had smiled from ear to ear, thanking the guys for their compliments. He'd looked to Rue who beamed up at him, phone already in hand. At some point, Violet had wandered in but he hadn't noticed her. Even sitting on the stool he'd once occupied, he'd paid no attention to her.

Now, sitting on the floor of Rue's kitchen, cold air at his back, flannel uselessly wrapped around his waist, he wished he'd never settled for Violet. She'd been his second choice, a consolation prize when Rue rebuffed his advances for the hundredth time. He'd been sure she liked him but her no-humans rule had been a roadblock he couldn't get past. *Until now*, he thought. But, who was he kidding? He saw how uncomfortable she'd gotten when he told her about the night with Ophelia. Fucking her friend after years of fucking her sister was probably the nail in his friend zone coffin. Still, he couldn't get her out of his head. She was all he thought about. If there was even a slim chance, he had to take it. He had to find a way.

Rue paced the alley, smoking her first joint in years. She'd given up the habit when her sister had started working for her full-time, not wanting to be a bad influence. Now that it was legal and Violet was out of town, she saw no reason to refrain considering how anxious she was. The craziness at the bar she could handle. Witches trying to kill her she could handle. But, Iman sleeping in the next room? That was another level of stress. She'd gotten past him banging her sister. She knew that wasn't serious and since she'd known the entire time he'd been living with Violet that that situationship was temporary, it had never really bothered her. The thing with Ophelia stung but after only twenty-four hours, she was already over it. She didn't want to be. She wanted to hold on to that jealousy, let it irritate her to the point that she'd stop having these feelings for Iman. But, no matter how many times she tried to force herself to imagine her friends together or tell herself it should feel like a betrayal, she didn't want him any less.

"He's not for you," she reminded herself, taking another hit. "You have to stop thinking about him like this." But, as the words came out of her mouth, memories of him from earlier that night filled her mind. His fingers wrapped around the microphone. His muscles rippling underneath his white tee shirt. The way his flannel hung over the back of his shredded jeans. The onyx curls that had fallen over one deep brown eye as he stared at her while breathily singing There She Goes. It wasn't a new phenomenon. He'd looked at her like that a million times, usually for just a second while singing a ballad. She was sure he didn't even realize he was doing it. "It doesn't mean anything."

She took one more hit and put the joint out with her fingers, pocketing it to save for another time. Her lips were numb and her arms felt like jello. "Strong stuff." She leaned against the bricks, a warm breeze like a kiss on her cheek. Her fingertips found her mother's pendant, the metal somehow comforting as the tension in her neck released. She'd stay there, alone, until she was sure the band's set was over. Hopefully, by the time she returned, Iman would be upstairs in bed. She didn't want to say something dumb while she was stoned out of her gourd.

Four hours later, the band had packed up and gone. Only a handful of patrons remained. The bar was quiet for the first time in weeks.

"So," Rue said sitting on a stool next to Ophelia. "How was your first night?"

"Good." She took a glimpse of the bundle of cash in her waist apron. "Not stripper money but I wasn't tempted to fuck a customer once."

"Um, good?"

She shrugged. "Huh." She leaned in and gave Rue's hair a sniff. "I didn't know you smoked."

"I don't, usually. I've just been a little wound up lately."

"PTSD from the witch attack?"

"No."

"You wanna talk about it?"

"Not really."

They sat in silence for a few moments, watching as the last few customers shuffled out the door.

"You ever like somebody but you knew it wasn't a thing? Like, it couldn't work out?" Rue blurted.

She frowned. "Like with Violet?"

"No, that was an ill-thought-out arrangement you never should've gotten involved in knowing how easy you are to catch feelings."

She crossed her arms. "I'm gonna ignore that since you're obviously high as fuck."

"I mean somebody that you care about and respect. Somebody that you'd do anything not to hurt. Like, a friend."

"Oh, you mean like your crush on Iman you're pretending doesn't exist?"

Her eyes widened.

"Don't get nervous, I won't tell him but I'm pretty sure he already knows."

"What do you mean?"

"Girl," She condescended. "How many times have I seen you wink at him or touch his arm for no reason? How many times have you had him help you with shit you could've easily handled yourself? Like that time you had him change your bathroom light bulbs?"

"They're high and he's like nine inches taller than me."

"You could've climbed on the counter or gotten a ladder or chair or something. It was an excuse to see him outside of work and you know it."

She bit the inside of her cheek.

"I'm just saying, if I can see how happy you get every time that fucker comes into a room, he can, too."

She chewed on her lip for a few seconds before again blurting out something she was sure she'd regret saying later. "How big is his setup?"

Ophelia cocked an eyebrow but answered honestly. "Eight inches, give or take. A little bigger around than a toilet paper tube."

"Nice."

"Pot makes you chatty."

She nodded.

"So, why can't it work out between you? You're into him, he's into you. You say you're not mad about our...mistake."

"I'm not."

"Then, what's the problem? V's back with her dude so she won't be trying to lay a claim to him. I have zero interest. That was a one-time thing that wasn't even about him. As far as I know, you don't have any other prospects so--"

"As far as you know."

She smacked her lips. "You got a fuck buddy I don't know about?"

She shook her head. "It's complicated."

"I bet it's not."

"It's really not. It's pretty straightforward. But..."

"But, what?"

Rue sighed, getting up from the bar stool. "It just wouldn't work. I have to put it out of my mind. Bury my feelings. Be Gen X about it."

"You're a Millennial."

"*But*, my dad is a million years old which basically makes him a Boomer which means he raised me the way he would have if I were Gen X."

"I don't think that logic tracks."

"I don't think *you* track."

Ophelia squinted at her. "You know that doesn't make sense, right?"

"What do expect? *I'm high.*"

She laughed. "Girl, go to bed. I'll lock up."

"Fine, *Mom*." She grabbed her face and kissed her cheek. "I'm gonna go upstairs, have a sensible dinner of O positive, brush my teeth like a good girl, and get some sleep." She spun on her heel and moseyed to the kitchen.

She laughed again, getting the keys from her apron and walking to the door. "Stoned Rue is a *trip*." She locked the door and brought the cage down. Once the place was locked up, she sat back at the bar and counted her tips. Her shoulders slumped. It was a tenth of what she was used to making per night as a dancer. Factoring in her hourly salary, she'd made two hundred and sixty dollars. At this rate, she'd be making less a week than she'd made every night at the club. It wasn't sustainable. But, she refused to go back to dancing. While it had been a great way to make money and she didn't have any negative feelings about stripping itself, she would never heal as long as she was in that kind of seductive environment. It was too tempting. She needed to work on herself, be celibate for a while and it would never happen if she was surrounded by so much readily available dick. She'd have to find another way to supplement her income. Maybe some work-at-home thing. An online side hustle. She needed to have enough money saved that she could get her own place *before* Violet got back.

Chapter 33

The next day, after an exhaustive job search and applying for seventeen online positions she knew she wasn't qualified for, Ophelia headed to the library where she pulled six spell books from the shelves. Too nervous about someone finding them at home, she looked through them there, setting herself up at a table in the back, far away from any windows. She'd scoured the internet for information but what she found was limited. Most articles were selling crystals, herbs, and vials of potions that for all she knew were just oregano oil. Of the few sites she found that weren't money grabs, five out of six said the best way to become a practitioner was to jump right in by doing spells yourself. It sounded simple enough but how could it be? She saw what Marley could do. There was no way that was as easy as saying a few words in Latin. There had to be more to it, right?

She opened the first book, excitement shooting through her like an arrow as she began to read. Rue would be pissed if she found out what she was doing but she didn't care. This was how she'd get her life back. This would give her control.

After skimming through book after book, one thing became clear: Spellwork wasn't just about the words. It wasn't just about the ingredients one used. It wasn't even mostly about genetics, although that played a part. Blood-born witches came into their magic much more easily, sometimes by accident. But, none of it was any more essential than the other. Those things mattered, of course, but they were secondary. What mattered most was intention. Well, intention and faith but faith she had. She knew witchcraft was real. She'd seen it. It was intention that she had to master. Setting her sights on a goal, what she wanted, no, *expected* a spell to do, and making it happen.

It was getting late. She had to be at the bar soon and since she couldn't risk taking the books with her, she instead took pictures of the spells she wanted to try. There were dozens and by the time she'd finished, put the books back, and left the building, the sun was down. She didn't have time to stop and eat without risking being late to her second night on the job, so she pulled a candy bar from her purse and ate on the way, her walk nearly a skip as she turned the corner. As night set in, she couldn't help but smile as she thought, *We're on our way.*

Lennon scrolled mindlessly on their phone for hours, too burnt out to put the new video game equipment together. It sat, still in store bags, on the dining room table while they lounged, legs crisscrossed on the sofa. Ophelia was already gone by the time they got back, not that they minded. After two weeks of hanging out with just her, they were exhausted. They refused to mask anymore and they were sick of being called rude. Iman had always been a good buffer but now he was across the hall and if they were being honest with themselves, he wasn't exactly a great friend, either. It had become clear to them that the only person they could stand for more than ten minutes at a time was Violet. Violet who hadn't spoken to them *once* since her husband came back. *And people call* me *rude,* they thought, rolling their eyes. "Fuck this." They went into their contacts and pulled up Violet's number. After a few rings, she answered, her voice chipper which annoyed them more.

"Lennon!"

"Hey."

"How are you? It's been a minute."

"More like twenty-three thousand but sure."

She laughed. "Are you feeling neglected?"

They looked down at their lap, their free hand fiddling with the frayed cuff of their jeans.

"I'm sorry. I promise we'll hang out as soon as I get back."

"You sure you'll have time? Won't be too busy with what's-his-name?"

"Kenton and no. I'm never too busy for you."

"Seems like you have been lately."

"You're right. I'm sorry. I should've called. I've just been...distracted." She let a giggle slip and Lennon ignored it.

"Where's your man now?"

"Asleep."

They looked at the time. "Isn't it only three there?"

"I think I wore him out. Again."

"Oh."

"So, how is everyone?"

"By 'everyone' do you mean Ophelia?"

She clicked her tongue. "Maybe."

"She's fine, as far as I can tell. Still mad at you, I think."

She sighed. "Understandable."

"It was pretty shitty of you, leaving without saying goodbye."

"I know. I just didn't know what to say. After what I did, how I acted. *You* still talking to me is a miracle but *her*? I wouldn't blame her if she never forgave me. But she's okay?"

"I think so. She took your old job at the bar."

"Oh, that's good. I could tell she's been tired of dancing for a while."

"Mm, hmm."

"You back to gaming?"

They glanced over at the bags sitting on the table. "Work in progress."

"And Iman? He back from my dad's?"

"Yeah."

"How's he adjusting?"

"I caught a little of his show last night. Seems okay to me but I haven't talked to him."

"What do you mean?"

"He's staying at Rue's."

"*Oh*," she said. "Isn't *that* interesting?"

"Um, no?"

"Come on! Has she fucked him, yet or is she being stubborn?"

They scrunched their face. "How would *I* know?"

CHAPTER 33

"What time is it there?"

They checked the clock on their phone and put it back to their ear. "Nine-seventeen."

"Okay, they should both be downstairs. You have that emergency key?"

"Yeah."

"Great. Go over there and tell me if you see anything."

"You want me to break in and snoop on your sister?"

"It's not breaking in if you have a key and it's not snooping. Just take a look around. You don't even have to touch anything."

They sighed and got up from the couch. "What am I supposed to be looking for? Vampires don't use condoms, do they?"

"Not usually. We don't carry disease and pregnancy for us is super rare."

They got the key from the kitchen drawer and walked across the hall to Rue's apartment. "How rare can it be if your parents had two kids?"

"Three out of four humans have kids. For us, it's more like one in a thousand."

They entered the apartment and closed the door softly behind them. "So, not really a concern, got it. What do you expect me to find, then?"

"Just check the bedrooms. Does it look like they've both been slept in?"

They peeked their head into each room, wrinkling their nose. "Neither bed looks made. Heathens."

She let out a frustrated sigh. "This bitch. Still being stubborn."

"Can I go now?" They looked around the living area, shuddering at its dark aesthetic.

"Yeah, I guess."

They locked up and hurried back across the hall, breathing a sigh of relief once in familiar surroundings.

"I can't believe she still hasn't fucked him."

"He's only been back a couple of days."

"A couple of days that close to somebody you're into is forever for us. She's gotta be losing her shit. I don't know how she's controlling herself."

"I know it's not my business but what's her deal? If she likes him,"

"She way more than likes him."

"Then why wouldn't she just," They paused. "I mean, we all know he has a thing for her. It's not like he'd turn her down."

"Like I said, stubborn. Like a fucking mule."

"Why, though?"

"Call it PTSD."

"An ex?"

"High school boyfriend," Violet told them. "Good dude. A real sweetheart."

"What happened?"

"Not my story to tell but let's just say, it was *bad*."

Chapter 34

Eleven years before, Rue had graduated valedictorian and was about to embark on her New York adventure, taking a year off school to figure out what she wanted to do with her life, out from under from her father's critical eye, and seven hundred and ten miles away from the only boy she'd ever loved. She had seven days to spend as much time with him as she could before their relationship turned into phone calls and too-few visits. So, she packed a bag, rented a cabin on Long Meadow Pond with the money she'd been saving from her summer job at the diner, and picked Ben up.

"Where are we going?" he asked.

"It's a surprise." She gave him a wink. "Buckle up. It's an hour drive."

"All right," He snapped his seat belt and ran his fingers through his messy blond hair, his eyes sparkling like sapphires in the midday sun. "But, remember, I have to be back by Sunday night to pack for Notre Dame. Plane leaves early on Monday."

"I know, I know," she teased. "Wouldn't want to mess up your free ride."

He chuckled. "Rue,"

"Mm?"

"I'll be back in time, right?"

She shrugged, stifling a giggle and starting the engine. "You trust me?"

He leaned in, taking her cheek in his massive hand, and pressed his lips to hers. When the kiss was broken, he rested his forehead on hers, both of their eyes still closed. "With my life."

She bit her lip, inhaling his scent, a combination of fabric softener and unisex cologne. "Are your parents home?"

"No." He moved his hand to her thigh, the skin exposed by the short cutoffs she wore.

She took a quick look around. Tall shrubs separated the long driveway from the neighbors and the sidewalk was far enough away that no one there would be able to see into the car. She turned the key, silencing the engine. "On second thought," She unbuckled his seat belt. "That can wait a few minutes."

"What are you--"

"Shh." She kissed him again. "You trust me, right?"

He nodded.

She unzipped his khakis and pulled them and his boxers down just enough, freeing his growing erection and wrapping her fingers around it. She gave it a few gentle strokes as his breath hitched in his throat.

He held onto the door handle, his eyes rolling back and closing. "I thought you said--"

"I know what I said but this doesn't count, right? Not if my shorts stay on."

Shaky breaths escaped his lips as he leaned back in his seat.

"Is this okay?"

He nodded.

"Can I...do more?"

"You can do anything you want."

She thought back to clips she'd watched on the internet, remembering the way the girls in the videos had tucked their teeth behind their lips. She'd practiced on a zucchini but this wasn't the same. It was much more delicate and seemed to have a mind of its own, pulsing in her hand and jerking itself toward his stomach. *You know what to do,* she thought. *It can't be that difficult.* She leaned over, bent down, and took his whole cock into her mouth.

He gasped, his left hand flying up in surprise. He looked down at the back of her head and softly touched her back, his approving groans quiet and uncontrollable.

She wasn't exactly sure how hard to suck but he seemed to like the amount of pressure she was using so she kept it up, bobbing her head up and down, stopping every once in a while to swallow excessive amounts of saliva. As she felt him get even stiffer, he frantically pat her back.

"Rue," he whispered. "I--I'm gonna come."

She stopped, massaging his balls and looking up at him. "Go for it." She went back to work, sucking a little bit harder.

"Oh, shit," he said, his voice husky. He grunted, his whole body jerking as if being electrocuted, hot semen jetting into the back of Rue's throat.

She sat up, swallowing the bitter fluid and wiping the slobber from her chin. She could hear his heart pounding as he rested, dick shiny and limp. "You okay?"

"I've never been better in my life."

She grinned. "All right, put it back in your pants. It's time to hit the road." She started the car and backed out of the drive while he got dressed.

He took her hand from the steering wheel and kissed the back of it. "You know how much I love you, right?"

She beamed, taking her hand away to turn onto the road. "If it's half as much as I love you, it's more than enough."

"It's way more than half."

"Is it?" she teased. "How do you know?"

"Because it fills me up from top to bottom and I'm twice as big as you. There's no way you could love me as much as I love you. It's physically impossible."

She laughed. "Oh, really?"

He smiled, dimples appearing on his cheeks. "What can I tell you? It's science."

She laughed again. "You'll have to show me where you read that."

He took his phone from his pocket and pretended to look something up. "I'll send you the link to the study right now. You think I won't?"

"You're ridiculous."

"You pronounced 'adorable' wrong."

She shook her head. "Silly."

"I mean it, though," he told her, his tone turning serious. "I really love you."

"I love you, too."

"I know you're worried about the long-distance thing but you don't have to be. We'll talk every day and see each other--"

"I know." She looked over at him and back to the road. "We'll figure it out."

He put a reassuring hand on her leg. "We will. You're it for me, Rue. You're the one."

She nodded, holding back tears she didn't want him to see. *We'll be okay*, she told herself. *We have to be.*

Once at the cabin, the two spent the rest of the day hiking the trails and relaxing in the solitude of the woods. They held hands and exchanged kisses as they walked, wandering the forest until the sun went down. "I can't believe you arranged all this," he said when they returned to the cabin.

"Why not? I'm hella smart."

He chuckled. "I know that. What I mean is, why didn't you tell me? I could've helped, or paid, or at least packed a change of clothes."

She held up her right hand, counting as she made her points. "I don't need help calling to make a reservation, I have my own money and I wanted to surprise you, and I packed for you." She picked up her suitcase from next to the door and put it on the coffee table at the center of the room. "See?" She opened it, gesturing to the folded polo shirts and slacks she'd swiped from her dad's closet. "I know they're not exactly your style but they should fit."

He flashed her an impressed smile. "You thought of everything, didn't you?"

"I don't do anything half-assed."

"No, you don't."

"Speaking of asses," She shimmied out of her shorts and pulled off her tee shirt, revealing the bikini underneath. "You wanna go swimming?"

"You didn't happen to pack trunks for me, did you?"

She dug around under the other clothes for a second and pulled out a pair of navy swim trunks. "You know I did."

"You're brilliant, you know that?"

She feigned humility. "I try."

He got out of his clothes and into the trunks while she grabbed two towels from the bathroom. They left the cabin, moving through the small yard to the dock. There, they held hands and jumped into the pond, the water only slightly cooler than the summer air above it. They swam for twenty minutes, splashing one another and admiring the moon's reflection on the waves they made. He dipped his head, slicking his hair away from his face and in the bright moonlight, his muscles shimmered in wet incandescence. The quarterback's body made Rue's skin warm, tingles in her pussy becoming throbs.

"You know," she said, reaching back to untie the strings of her top. "I saw yours."

His eyes widened as he wiped water from his face.

"It's only fair you see mine." She flung the top to the dock, her exposed nipples rock hard as she ran her fingers over her right breast.

He let out a shaky breath. "Jesus Christ, you're gorgeous."

"Oh, wait," her hands disappeared under the water. "It wasn't your chest I saw earlier."

"Rue,"

She pulled her bottoms from the pond and threw them.

"What are you doing, baby?"

She swam closer. "Nothing."

He put his hands on her shoulders. "Baby, I'm trying real hard to respect your boundaries here but--" He gasped as she slid her hand into his trunks and found his cock.

"I know. You're doing so well, too." She dunked down, yanking off his shorts, popping back up, and flinging them away.

"Is this a skinny-dipping thing or," He squeezed his eyes shut as his erection twitched at her touch. "You have to tell me what to do here, Rue. This is very confusing."

She wrapped an arm around his neck and teased his ear with her tongue. "What are you confused about?"

He growled under his breath as he resisted temptation. "You said you wanted to wait. You told me we *had* to wait."

"Do you want to wait?"

"I've waited since sophomore year. I'll wait as long as you want me to."

She looked him in the eye. "What if I'm tired of waiting?"

"You know how bad I want you but,"

"But?"

"I don't want you to feel like you have to do this because I'm leaving. I don't want you to feel pressured."

"I don't."

"Baby, are you sure?"

"This isn't about college or feeling like I have to do anything." She wrapped her legs around his waist and rubbed her pussy up and down his erection, the grunts leaving his throat making her even wetter. "This is about me wanting to be with you not in some vague future but right now. I don't know what's gonna happen later but I know that right now, right this second, I love you and you love me." She shivered against his cock, her pussy aching. "So, if you're sure, I'm sure."

"Rue," He wrapped an arm around her waist and grabbed her ass with his free hand. "I fucking love you." He kissed her hard, shoving himself into her, the two moaning in each other's mouths. She ground against him as he fought to keep them afloat. After a while, worried they'd drown, he swam them to the shore, lying her down and positioning himself on top of her. He thrust into her, over and over, his wet balls slapping against her ass. She came hard, her back arching as she met his movements. "God, I love you," he grunted in her ear, slamming into her as she cried out in ecstasy. "I love you so fucking much."

Back at the cabin, they snuggled naked together under a comforter on the floor in front of the fireplace, lying on their sides, shivering, her back to him. He kissed her cheek, worry tensing his face. "Baby?"

"Hmm?"

"I have a kind of awkward question."

"What's that?"

"How effective do you think pulling out is?"

She smiled to herself. "Don't worry about it."

"Okay but--'

"I went on the pill last month," she lied, knowing that since he was human, a pregnancy was impossible.

"Oh," His features relaxed. "So, you've been thinking about this for a while."

She squeezed his arm. "When have I *not* been thinking about it?"

"In that case," He brushed his lips along the side of her neck. "You ready for round two?"

"Ready and willing." She lifted her leg over his as he reached around, rubbing two fingers over her clit. She extended her neck, grabbing him by the hair and spreading her leg farther.

He groaned in her ear as he sank himself into her from behind, continuing to massage her clit. She sucked in a breath, rocking against him, the fire warming her chest as the blanket fell away. They went on like that for several minutes, Rue coming twice before Ben climaxed, this time coming inside of her. Again, he wrapped her in the comforter and his arms, both of them so spent, they fell asleep right there on the floor.

Hours went by, night becoming early morning. Rue woke up with a start, her chest heaving and stomach aching with a hunger she'd never felt before. She was starving.

She slipped out of Ben's embrace, picked up his tee shirt from the floor, slipped it on, and crept to the kitchen where she'd stashed a few blood bags in a pizza box. On it, she'd scribbled in permanent marker, '3/5/12', a date five months old. When Ben would inevitably open the fridge looking for food, he'd see the date and avoid the "pizza" like the plague.

"Where'd you go?" her boyfriend asked, sitting up and rubbing his eyes.

She froze. "Just looking for something to eat. There's nothing in here but expired pizza, though."

He looked over her shoulder to the window. "Nothing will be open this late. We'll get something in a couple of hours. Come back to bed."

"Okay, let me just get rid of the pizza. It's gonna start smelling up the place."

"Leave it." He got to his feet, picked up the blanket, and walked toward her.

She swallowed hard, her pussy flooding at the sight of his naked body.

"We should get some real sleep, in bed." He put the comforter around her shoulders and walked her to the bedroom. "I'll take the trash out after breakfast."

She reluctantly went with him, internally cringing at what she knew she'd have to do. There had been dozens of times over the two years they'd been together when she'd had to eat in front of him, choking down human food to avoid him thinking she had an eating disorder or worse, discovering the truth. She had trained herself through experience to hold it down for hours, waiting until she'd gotten home from their date or excusing herself to go to a bathroom to vomit up the contents of her stomach, an organ not equipped to digest it. She'd have to do it again, a few times a day for the next few days not to raise suspicion. It'd be worth it, though, to spend this time with Ben.

They snuggled under the covers, her head resting on his chest, the light musk of his skin filling her nose as she draped a leg over his. He kissed her head and rubbed her shoulder, his heart pounding under her ear like a drum.

"Rue," he whispered.

She ran her hand down his chest to his navel. "Hmm?"

"Are you tired?"

Her pussy pulsed as his fingers trailed up and down her arm. "Not really." She lifted her face to softly press her lips to his, reaching further down to find his dick already standing at attention. She rolled herself on top of him, sinking deeper into the kiss, and guiding him into her. He pushed her tee shirt up and squeezed her ass, unconsciously pumping up when she came down. Her uncovered breasts smashed against his chest, her arms above his shoulders, her face buried in his neck.

As she rode him, waves of rapture fogging her mind, the ache in her stomach grew more intense. Pain and pleasure permeated every part of her, flowing through her veins like adrenaline. She kissed his neck, letting her tongue slide over his salty skin. Her pussy throbbed around him, clenching and unclenching as she came.

She didn't feel her fangs elongate or pierce his artery. She didn't hear him gasp or feel his grip on her loosen. She only tasted the warm, sweet blood pouring into her mouth and down her throat. She trembled, the final punch of her climax stronger than any orgasm she'd felt before. She drank until her skin was hot and her belly was full. She only stopped when she felt his dick go limp and fall out of her.

"Oh, shit," she whispered, raising her head and looking at what she'd done. He'd gone pale, his eyes glazed over, his mouth agape. "Ben?" She lightly slapped his cheek. "Ben?!" He didn't respond. He couldn't. "BEN!" Tears streamed down her face as she put her ear to his chest. His heart was barely beating. He'd be dead within seconds. "No, no, no, no." She pulled her shirt down to cover herself and sat on her knees next to him, her hand shaking as she covered her mouth. Her heart and mind raced. This couldn't happen. She couldn't let it. "Okay," she said, trying to think straight while she hyperventilated. "It'll be okay. I know what to do."

CHAPTER 34

With her teeth, she slashed her wrist open and pushed the wound into Ben's slack mouth. "Come on," she told him. "Take it. Take it, goddamn it!" After a few seconds, lips closed over the vein. He began to suck, his dull eyes fluttering closed. "That's it. Take as much as you need."

Slowly, his skin regained its color. He weakly gripped her arm and continued to drink, his newly-black eyes flying open and looking up at her in confusion.

"I'm sorry," she whispered. "I'm so sorry."

When he'd had his fill, he passed out, the puncture marks on his neck healing themselves.

"Okay," she said again. "It's okay. Everything's okay." She jumped off the bed and tore through the closet. She found extra sheets which she used to tie his wrists and ankles to the head and footboards. She then ran to the kitchen, getting ice from the refrigerator door and putting it in a bowl with a splash of water from the sink. She snatched a hand towel from the counter and sped back to the room where Ben remained unconscious. "Shit," she said, putting the items on the nightstand and running back to the kitchen to check the time on the oven. "Three-ten." She set the timer for twenty-four hours just in case she forgot and took a breath. "It's okay," she repeated. "He's gonna be fine."

She dragged a chair from the kitchen table to the bedroom and positioned it next to the bed, sitting in it, and putting a hand to his forehead. He was already getting hot. She dipped the towel in the cold water and ran it over his face and neck. "Please be okay," she whimpered. "Please just be okay."

It was dawn before his first convulsion, the eruption of shaking and screams jerking Rue awake from an accidental nap. He thrashed against his restraints, wailing in agony while she sobbed, unable to help him. His muscles tightened and flexed, every vein bulging under his fair skin. He howled, his head and upper back rising from the mattress.

She covered her face, sobbing into her trembling hands. "What did I do?"

Finally, he fell back, losing consciousness again, the room going silent. She put the wet cloth on his head and checked his restraints. They were a little loose so she tightened them, making a mental note to do it every time he woke up and passed out. "I can handle this," she told herself, sitting back down. But, she wasn't sure she could.

Since she was small, her father had taught her the golden rules of turning people: Only if you love them and only if you have to. He'd always said, "Love is a risk worth taking." Even when her mom left, he never regretted marrying her. He kept all of their photo albums and she'd caught him flipping through them at least a dozen times over the years. Once, after catching her sister swiping some cash from his wallet, she'd found a picture of them together in Egypt where they'd met. "If someone you love is in great peril," he'd told her. "Or is stricken with an ailment that doctors can't remedy, it's within your right to try and save them. Be warned, though, that our venom and our blood are no guarantee. It ends more often than not in tragedy."

His words played over and over in her head as the day progressed, one violent outburst from her beloved after another making the hours drag. Night fell and the frenzied fits of rage continued. The sounds coming from Ben's throat grew more and more hoarse, guttural. His fangs burst through his gums and didn't retreat in his moments of forced sleep. After the timer went off, he was still burning up, no amount of fresh ice enough to take his temperature down even a bit. Growls like purring gurgled in his throat and at three-eleven, he woke up.

His eyes were wild, completely black, and unblinking. He let out a feral scream so loud, it shook the pictures on the walls.

"No," she whimpered, new tears filling her eyes. "Please, no."

He looked at her, chest heaving, his face twisted into something she didn't recognize. He yanked one arm toward himself, snapping the sheet. She leaped up, staggering back as he jerked his other wrist free, then his legs.

"Ben," she pleaded. "Ben, it's me."

He lurched out of bed, head crooked, staring blankly at her.

"Ben, do you know who I am?"

He moved toward her, one shaky step, then another.

"Ben," She backed into the closed closet door. "Ben, do you know me?"

He let out a ferocious roar, charging at her as she cried.

"Please, don't make me."

But, he couldn't hear her. Couldn't understand. Everything that made Ben human was gone. He wasn't Ben any longer. He was a wild animal.

He lunged at her and with her eyes tightly closed she threw her clawed hand in front of her to meet him, driving her nails into his chest, breaking through his sternum, and pulling his heart from his body. He fell at her feet and she dropped to hold him, weeping as she let the slippery organ fall to the ground. Shaking, she embraced him, her open-mouthed sobs silent at first, then deafening. Up to that point, he'd been the love of her life and she'd killed him.

She couldn't find a shovel, so she dug with her bare hands, a shallow grave deep in the woods where no one would find her lover's body. She wrapped him in the torn sheets, pushed him in, and covered him with dirt, her eyes bloodshot from hours of crying. She packed the car, got in, and drove home, wearing only Ben's tee shirt, covered in blood and earth.

The sun was just coming up when she got home. She hoped her family was asleep but didn't have the energy to check on her way to her room. She dropped her suitcase at her door and crawled into bed, the soft sheets providing no comfort.

"You're back already?" twelve-year-old Violet asked, wiping sleep from her eyes.

"Go back to bed," Rue said, her voice cracking.

"What's wrong?" She walked to the edge of the bed and pet her sister's hair.

Fresh tears tumbled down her filthy cheeks. "Don't ever love a human, V. It's *not* worth the risk."

She climbed in, getting under the blanket behind her and snuggling against her back. "It's okay, Rue. Don't be sad."

"Promise me," she demanded through sobs. "Promise you won't."

She pet her again, moving dirt-caked hair behind her ear. She kissed her cheek, hugged her arm, and rested her head on her shoulder. "I promise."

Chapter 35

It had been three weeks since Iman had turned and as Rue stared up at the ceiling, her black, satin pillowcase cool under her head, she blew out a puff of smoke, letting herself relax for the first time that night. She listened to his slow, steady breathing as he slept in the next room, her eyelids finally feeling heavy as she put out the joint now barely long enough to hold onto. *He's safe*, she reminded herself. *He made it.* But, her heart still jumped when she rolled on her side and saw the gap in her headboard where he'd broken a bar off escaping the restraint during his transformation. It was a reminder, not that she needed one, of how close she'd come to losing him.

She slipped her hand into the space, pressing her palm to the wall that separated the rooms. The Tyrian purple paint smelled faintly of latex but couldn't block the scent of Iman's agarwood aftershave. Not from the nose of a vampire with heightened senses. She breathed it in, closing her eyes as warmth spread through her abdomen. "No," she whispered, thoughts of him running through her mind. His eyes, his lips, his arms. She pictured the tattoo on his broad chest and the stubble on his face. "Just friends. *Don't go in there.*"

She rolled to her back, kicking her blanket off and fighting the urge to leave her bedroom and enter his. She tugged at the spaghetti strap of her cami as she lectured herself. *Bitch, don't you fucking dare.* But, the thoughts kept coming, one after another. His long legs, his tight ass, his perfect smile. She licked her lips as she pulled her top down, one breast peeking out. She squeezed it, able to keep herself from leaving but needing to quench her thirst for him somehow. *Good enough,* she thought, her fingers slipping inside her newly damp sleep shorts. It wasn't a solution to her *real* problem, her feelings for him, but it would stop her from acting on her current bout of lust. *Good fucking enough.*

CHAPTER 35

Iman woke to muffled moans from the other side of the wall, jealousy punching him in the gut as he assumed Rue must have taken a lover. He listened, expecting to hear two heartbeats but there was only one. He sniffed the air, the only scents hitting his nose Rue's English lavender soap and marijuana smoke. He closed his eyes, sighing in relief. *She must be dreaming*, he thought, but as the moans grew louder and the metal of her bed frame began to squeak, he realized what she must be doing. His eyes widened. *I shouldn't be listening to this*. But, how could he not? The building was silent otherwise so he had nothing else to focus his hearing on and if he made any noise himself, she'd know he was awake and might assume he'd heard her and feel embarrassed. The last thing he wanted was for things to be even more awkward between them. She'd been avoiding him since he'd moved in, no doubt because of the conversation she'd had with her father when he'd dropped him off. He hadn't meant to eavesdrop but just like now, he couldn't help but hear. Booth had told her about his feelings for her and while he was sure, deep down, she'd always known, things were different now. He was out of his arrangement with her sister and more importantly, he was no longer human. The harmless flirting that had gone on between them for years was suddenly, potentially not so harmless. There was nothing, as far as he knew, to keep them apart now. So, why was she still keeping him at arm's length? He was sure she had a thing for him. She'd never admitted it, of course, but there was something about the way her eyes twinkled when she looked at him. No matter what was happening, when she saw him come into a room, her whole mood lifted. That's more than friendship, more than general affection. That's love.

Wanting to respect her privacy, he wrapped his head in his pillow, covering his ears. Still able to hear every moan, every breathy sigh, every screech of metal as she moved, he held the pillow harder against his ears. So hard, his own heartbeat, now racing, pounded alongside hers. *Stop listening.* But, he couldn't and as his face flushed, he stopped wanting to.

He tossed the pillow to the floor, wondering how he'd be received if he knocked on her door. He imagined her inviting him in, wearing nothing but a sheet, taking his hand, and guiding him to the bed. *She wouldn't*, he thought. Still, his cock swelled, the image of her dropping the sheet playing in his head like a movie. He pictured her lying back on the bed, curling a finger as if to say "come here", and spreading her legs for him. He breathed in the lavender scent coming from her room and pretended he was there with her, face buried in her hair, cock buried in her welcoming pussy.

He pulled down his plaid sleep pants, the only thing he wore to sleep, freeing his throbbing erection. He gripped it gently, stroking to the beat of Rue's bed frame, imagining himself on top of her. Fantasy-Rue's pants of pleasure mimicked the real one's and as both versions of her came, Iman took a handful of tissues from the box on the nightstand, covering the head of his dick with them just in time.

He cleaned himself up, waited until it was quiet, crept out of his room to the bathroom, and flushed the evidence of his spying. He washed his hands and splashed cold water on his face before returning to his room. He listened again, this time purposefully, and was relieved to hear Rue's slow, deep breaths. She was asleep. She hadn't heard him leave the room. He rolled onto his side, pulling the covers up to his chest, and closed his eyes. As he drifted off, he again wondered why she was avoiding him. Why she wouldn't admit her feelings, and how much longer he could stand not being with her.

The stench of rotting flesh was becoming more than Booth could bear but the corpses of his victims served as a warning to the others. Every new witch he interrogated shared the cage with the bodies of the rest, the ones that refused to give him what he needed.

CHAPTER 35

He held the vial of crimson fluid up to the light and set it on a shelf with his collection. The woman, face tear-stained and wrist bleeding, sat with her knees to her chest in the corner of the cell, strands of golden hair stuck with sweat to her neck and cheeks.

"Why did you take that?" she asked, her voice scratchy.

"Blood of the covens." He turned back to look at her, his blue eyes like ice. "One witch from every coven on the eastern seaboard. Thirteen in all, once I've finished. Then, I can do the spell. That is, as soon as one of you gives me the final ingredient."

"A vampire doing a spell? That's not possible."

"Oh, it very much is. You lot like to think of yourselves as special, gifted. The truth is, like most things, all that's required is faith. Faith that what you're doing is just and believe me, there is no greater cause than mine." He crouched in front of her. "Will you be the one that gives it to me?"

She shrunk back, covering the cut on her wrist. "What?"

"The ingredient."

"What is it?"

"A word of power." He took a small notebook from his jacket pocket and opened it to a specific page. He held it out to show her. "For this spell."

She began to read. "This is a locator spell but," Her eyes widened. "Oh, my god."

"So, you see why it's so important to me."

She nodded, hugging her knees.

"Do you know the word?"

She shook her head.

He dropped his head and sighed.

More tears pooled in her pleading eyes. "It wasn't us."

"No, I don't suspect it was. But, it *was* your kind." He met her gaze, pupils now dilated, fury replacing calm in his usually relaxed face. "And, until I find the exact perpetrator, you will all suffer." He reached into the cell, grabbing her arm, and pulling her to the bars. Her head slammed into them, knocking her out instantly. He held her leaking wrist to his lips and drank. When her heart stopped, he stood, flipping the pages of the notebook until he found the name and address of the next witch on his list. His pupils returned to normal and he headed up the stairs and out of the basement, plugging the address into his phone's GPS. He thought about sitting down, taking a break. Maybe even getting some sleep. But, he couldn't. Not when he was this close. Just a few more witches and a single word. *So close*.

Chapter 36

Ophelia waited for Lennon to go to bed before attempting her first spell. Labeled "Bay Leaf Money Spell", she hoped it would bring her enough money for a deposit on a new apartment. She loved the loft but the longer Violet was gone, the more she dreaded her coming back. When she did, she'd have her husband in tow and the idea of seeing them together made her stomach churn. She was angry with Violet, hurt. Hell, traumatized but her feelings were still there, just under the pain, and no matter how much she wanted to hate her, the thought of her with him still made her jealous. She had to get out of there.

On her nightstand, she laid out what she needed for the spell: A bay leaf, tweezers, a lighter, a ceramic bowl, and a permanent marker. Using the marker, she wrote WEALTH on the leaf then drew tiny dollar signs all around the word, filling as much of the space as possible. Next, she picked up the leaf by the stem with the tweezers and picked up the lighter. She blew out a breath, her eyes closed as she set her intention, clearing her mind of all other thoughts. She imagined twenty, ten, and five dollar bills floating in a sea of black. She pictured herself counting the money, elated that she could afford to move out within a couple of weeks. *It's going to happen*, she thought. *It* will *happen*. She opened her eyes and looked at the phone's screen, not trusting that she'd memorized the spell well enough, and flicked the lighter. The end of the leaf began to burn and she recited:

"Power of bay leaf, I ask thee,
Through methods fair and just,
Bring abundant prosperity.
Through the fire,
Bring abundant prosperity."

The leaf burned to ash, its remnants gathering in the bowl. She set the tweezers on the nightstand and stood, taking the bowl with her to the window. She unlocked and opened it, birds chirping in the morning sun as she tilted the bowl and blew out the ashes, returning the leaf to the earth. She watched as they scattered, a strange peace washing over her. She'd never felt calm like this before and as she closed the window she realized what it was. *Hope.*

That night, the bar was slammed. Every table was full from open to close. She barely had time to clear when one group left before another sat down. It was so busy, she hadn't noticed how much people were leaving in tips. She'd just scooped up the cash and dropped it in her apron. It wasn't until she got back to the loft that she sat down and counted it. Her heart leaped in her chest as she looked over the piles of bills, separated into ones, fives, tens, and twenties. It was a little over eight-hundred dollars.

"It worked," she whispered.

"What worked?" Lennon asked, setting a bag of Mexican take-out on the table.

She gathered up the money and shoved it back into the apron that now sat on the chair next to her. "Nothing, just trying to be more talkative at work. Chipper, you know? Apparently, that's what people like in a waitress."

"Neurotypicals, maybe. I just want to give them my order and then be left alone." They pulled containers from the bag and placed one in front of Ophelia. "I made dinner."

She chuckled. "You *made* it?"

"I shlepped all the way to East Sixth because they were the closest Mexican place open this late and I fought the urge to eat it all myself on the way back plus I paid for it so yeah, I'd say I made it. Made it possible for you to eat it, anyway. You're welcome."

She laughed again. "Aw, thank you, Lennon. It's nice that you thought of me."

CHAPTER 36

"Mm."

She opened her container and lifted a quarter-piece of the quesadilla to her lips. She took a bite and did a happy dance in her seat as she chewed.

Lennon gave her a side-eye as they swallowed a mouthful of albondigas. "Good?"

"Yes, thank you. So, how's your game? Shooting a lot of zombies or whatever?"

They wrinkled their brows. "Are you trying to make small talk?"

"Kind of, I guess."

"You don't have to."

"I know I don't *have* to, geez. I'm just asking about your life. How are you? How are things? Did you have a good day?"

"I'm tired, my day was not terrible, and I don't know what you mean by 'things'."

She sighed. "Like, your game. Or people you've talked to lately. Or, maybe there's something in the news you want to talk about?"

"The news makes me hate life almost as much as I hate my parents so no, I don't want to talk about it. The only people I've spoken to today are you, the guy at the counter when I got dinner, and a girl walking her dog that bumped into me. She said, 'Sorry' and I said, 'No problem'. As for my game, I don't know which one you're referring to but it doesn't matter because I haven't been playing lately."

"Really? Why not?"

They took a sip of soda before answering. "I'm just not feeling it."

"Lennon," She put her hand on their knee. "Are you okay?"

They gave a confused glance at her hand then looked her in the eye. "I'm fine."

"Are you sure? Not doing stuff you usually love is a sign of depression. You know I'm here if you need to talk, right?"

"I don't need to talk."

"Really? Because that hating your parents comment--"

"You know what they did to me."

"I'm not saying you shouldn't hate them. I hate mine, too. I'm saying--"

"Are we trauma-dumping? Because I'm not in the mood."

"No, I'm *saying* if you need to vent or talk about anything, I'm here for you. It's what friends do. They listen, offer support. We're friends, right?"

They shrugged.

She took her hand away. "Nice."

They sighed. "It's just a lot of change lately. It's throwing me off."

She nodded, taking another bite. "Yeah, I get that."

"And, I can't even make a plan because I don't know what *Violet's* plans are. If she was here," They looked down at their napkin, tearing it into tiny shreds. "When I left Utah, I thought I had a year, two tops. I was sure I was gonna die or be dragged back, kicking and screaming. Do you know what Provo is like for someone like me? It's a dystopian hellscape wrapped in the Book of Mormon."

"I can imagine."

"You can't." They took another napkin from the bag and started to tear it. "Violet saved me. I know you hate her now but without her here, I don't feel safe. That probably sounds ridiculous to you after what she did but--"

"It's not ridiculous. I get it. And, I don't *hate* her. What happened just brought up a bunch of stuff for me, that's all."

They nodded.

"I don't know what she's gonna do. She might move her dude in here or they might go back to how it was before where he goes home to England and they just visit once in a while. Either way, I'm sure she won't cut you out. As much as I never wanted to admit it, we all know you're her favorite."

They half-smiled. "What about you? Are you moving out?"

She glanced at her apron and back at Lennon. "I think so."

"Like I said, lots of changes."

They went back to eating in uncomfortable silence, neither of them knowing exactly what would come next but both more than a little anxious about what the future held for them.

Chapter 37

The man peered through the bar's glass door, the fence obscuring most of his view. Inside, he saw Iman restringing his guitar, the black Les Paul Classic shining under the lights of the stage. To his left, a woman wiped down the bar, moving fast as if she was in a hurry. They were the only people in the room and even from the outside, he could feel the tension between them.

"You're still not talking to me?" he heard Iman ask, tilting his head so his right ear was closer to the glass.

"I'm not *not* talking to you," the woman answered.

"Could've fooled me."

She continued working.

He looked in her direction. "Am I making you uncomfortable?"

She stopped, her back to him. "Right now or in general?"

"Pick one."

She sat on a stool and spun to meet his gaze. "No, Iman, you don't make me uncomfortable."

"Then, why are you avoiding me?"

She put the towel on the counter and rolled her neck. "I don't know how to answer that."

"You could try honestly."

"Eh, doesn't seem wise."

"You can't be honest with me? Since when?"

"Since you moved in."

The man registered the flash of pain in his expression.

"Do you want me to move out?"

"No," she was quick to say. "No, you should stay."

"Because you think I'm not ready to be on my own?"

She dropped her head. "No. You're handling things as well as anyone could. I'm not worried about you, I just…"

He set the guitar on its stand and stood. "You what?"

She wouldn't look at him.

He stepped off the stage and walked toward her. "Rue,"

She shook her head and jumped up from her seat, backing away from him as he drew closer. "You didn't do anything wrong, okay? I'm not mad or upset or uncomfortable."

He cocked his head. "You're lying."

"Fine, I'm *a little* uncomfortable but it's not your fault and there's nothing you can do about it. It's just something I have to deal with. And, I don't want you to move out because I just don't. It's hard to be close to you right now but I'll get past it."

He closed the space between them, his voice softening. "Why is it hard?"

The man could see her eyes shine with forming tears as she backed into the swinging door next to the bar. "I have to go," he heard her say. "Turn off the lights when you leave."

The door swung closed with her on the other side, out of sight. Iman was alone, disappointment and defeat furrowing his brow. He took a bottle from behind the bar and poured a glass of what the man assumed was whiskey by the color of the liquid and drank it down. He poured another and replaced the bottle, releasing a disgruntled sigh.

The man's anger burned hot, his blue eyes glowing yellow, a growl rising in his throat. When Iman's head whipped around at the sound, he took off, speed walking to the corner and waiting impatiently for the "Don't walk" pedestrian signal to change. *Calm your shit*, he thought. *It's not a big deal.* He shoved his hands in his pockets and when the sign changed, he half-ran across the street, keeping that pace all the way back to his apartment.

CHAPTER 37

Once home, he locked the door and sat on the thrift store sofa, its blue and red stripes reminding him of a decade he was too young to actually remember. His feet tapped out of control as he clasped his hands together, his thumbs pressed to his scruffy chin. "Just relationship drama," he told himself. "No one's in any danger. You're overreacting." He ran his fingers through his wavy, light-brown hair, growling again, louder this time as his whole body trembled. "Calm the fuck down!" He stood, pacing the length of the studio apartment, his Doc Martin's squeaking on the hardwood. He fanned himself with his white tee shirt as he tried to slow his heart rate. "You're being crazy. Just relationship problems. Nothing to lose it over." He continued to pace but couldn't calm himself. Instead, he grew hungry.

He went to the white half-fridge and pulled out a package of raw hamburger, tearing away the cellophane, and digging his fingers into the cold meat. Handful after handful he devoured it, barely chewing, the meat sliding down his throat with no resistance. Soon, his muscles relaxed, his breathing steadied, and his heart slowed to its normal rhythm. He licked the myoglobin from his fingers and leaned on the kitchen counter, his eyes again shining in a xanthic hue.

Chapter 38

Ophelia crept down the hall, peeking her head into Lennon's room. Snuggled under a weighted blanket and surrounded by Squishmallows, they slept, orange light from the sunrise trickling in through half-closed blinds. Relieved, she went to her own room and retrieved the ingredients she'd hidden in her nightstand: chamomile flowers, marshmallow root, aloe, and powdered slippery elm bark. She took the herbs to the kitchen along with her phone and pulled up the picture of the healing spell she'd taken at the library. For weeks, the image of the witches healing Marley after the car accident played in her mind like a movie. She couldn't stop thinking about it. They'd literally cheated death and they didn't need to be made vampires to do it. For the last two years, she'd hoped Violet would turn her partly because she thought it would bring them closer together but mostly because she wanted to feel powerful. Strong. And, able to heal herself when she got hurt. If she could get this spell to work, it was one less thing the memory of Violet could hold over her head. One less reason to want her. One less thing holding her back.

She boiled a cup of water in the microwave then mixed a teaspoon of slippery elm into it. She put the mixture in the freezer to cool while she put chamomile and marshmallow root in the food processor to combine. She then added a splash of aloe juice and the cooled slippery elm. Her eyebrows scrunched. It looked thinner than the substance the witches had used on Marley. She looked at the spell again, making sure she'd gotten the proportions right. Everything looked correct. She tapped the counter with her copper-lacquered nails. *Something's gotta be off*, she thought. But, according to the spell, she'd done it exactly how she should have. She shrugged, deciding to try it regardless of thickness.

She checked the hallway, making sure again that Lennon was out of sight range. She didn't want them walking in on her with a knife to her arm. Not with their history of cutting. They hadn't done it since moving into the loft but she knew they were having a hard time with Violet gone and she, better than anyone, knew how easy it was to fall into old patterns when you're stressed. Hearing the light snoring coming from their room, she went back to the kitchen and took a steak knife from the block on the counter. She held her breath and using just the tip, she made a small cut on her forearm. She squeezed her eyes closed and gritted her teeth, managing to stay quiet through the pain. She set the knife down and opened her eyes.

She held a dishcloth under her arm to catch the drips of blood that slid down her skin. She'd have to wash the towel before Lennon saw it and asked what happened. She propped her bleeding arm on the counter and smeared the herbal concoction over the wound. It felt cool and slimy and had a strange sweet smell, like waffles mixed with flowers. Not terrible but definitely not good. *Hope this washes off.* She took a breath, clearing all thoughts but that of the cut closing itself from her mind. She held that image as she whispered the one-word spell, "Sana."

Immediately, her arm felt better, the stinging pain of the cut gone. "No way." She held her arm under the tap and turned the handle for cold water. As the substance rinsed away, her skin was revealed, completely healed. "Holy shit."

Too excited to sleep, Ophelia snuck out of the apartment and headed to 14th Street Park. It would be quiet this early and she thought it'd be a perfect place to try some nature spells, starting with The Absorption of Gaia's Gifts. Sitting on the grassy circle at the center of the park, she placed her hands on the warm ground, eyes closed, picturing white light coming up from the earth and wrapping around her hands and arms. She whispered the incantation:

"Give to me what nature allows,

with gratitude, I receive your gifts."

She repeated the words twice, warmth climbing up her arms, over her chest, and down her abdomen. Sweat beaded above her lip and at her temples as the warmth grew hot, raw power seeping in through her skin and into her muscles, organs, and blood. She could feel its strength, and knew it was too much but she didn't stop. She stayed, palms planted, absorbing all that she could handle. Sweat dripped down her back, soaking through her phases of the moon graphic tank top. "Gaia," she heard herself say, the words not part of the spell. "Thank you." Her eyes flew open and she fell back, hitting her head. "Oh, shit." She held her hand to her head and winced, sitting up and looking around to make sure no one had seen her. Only a few people sat at the pink tables on the other side of the circle and if they'd seen her odd behavior, they hadn't cared. She wiped her sweat-soaked face and caught her breath. *That was a rush*, she thought, taking her phone from her pocket and scrolling through the pictures until she found a weather spell. *Here goes nothing.* She cleared her throat, checked again to make sure no one was watching her, and whispered the words:

"Goddess of the West, hear my plea,

soothe the land with rain by thee.

Give us water fit to bring, here it be," She spat on the ground in front of her.

"Water of my body in offering."

She folded her hands in her lap and waited. Nothing happened. Seconds went by, then what must have been a full minute. Nothing. But, she would not be deterred. She knew it would work. She could feel it, an instinctual certainty that wouldn't allow her to move from her spot. Rain *would* come.

Suddenly, the overcast darkened, and a clap of thunder jolted her from her calm. Sprinkles hit her face and shoulders and as her smile broadened, rain fell in sheets, a sudden downpour that had the people at the tables running, covering their heads with their newspapers. Ophelia laughed, giddy as she put her phone back in her pocket and stood. She let the rain wash over her in a warm shower, face turned to the sky and arms outstretched. *I'm a fucking witch.*

Chapter 39

The sun was near setting when Iman woke, another erection fueled by dreams of Rue aching in his pajama pants. He got out of bed, intent on getting a blood-bag breakfast. Instead, he found himself in the hall, Rue's door ajar just enough that he could see into the room. He moved closer, his eyes fixed on her perfect form. She slept on her stomach, one leg straight and the other bent up, her tiny shorts barely covering her perky ass. The strap of her top had fallen off her shoulder, exposing all of her left breast except for the nipple which was smashed against the mattress. His boner twitched and he could feel the head of his dick dampen with pre-cum. *Stop looking at her, pervert,* he thought, forcing himself to look away.

He went to the kitchen and downed his breakfast, his condition not getting any better. He looked down at himself and shook his head. *This is out of control.* He tiptoed to the bathroom, pulled off his pajamas, and got in the shower, turning the cold water on. He shivered in the icy water, willing it to work its magic. After a few moments, his erection was gone. He breathed a sigh of relief and turned the faucet until the water became warm. He washed his face and hair and as he lathered his chest, his head jerked to the right, the sound of Rue's heartbeat getting his attention even through the noise of the shower. She was awake and she was listening at the door.

Rue stood in the hall, imagining what Iman must look like all wet and covered in suds, his tattoos glistening, his dark eyes cutting through the steam like a knife. She chewed on her lip, ear pressed to the bathroom door, Iman's heart beating faster than usual. Did he know she was there? Of course, he did. His hearing was as good as hers. *Stupid*, she thought.

She hurried back to her room, closing the door and hiding under her covers. "Get it together, bitch." Her heart pounded and her hands trembled, her throat going dry. She threw the blanket off and took a joint from her nightstand, putting it between her lips. She didn't like getting high before opening the bar but she had no choice. She couldn't let anyone see her like this, especially Iman. She picked up the steel skull and bones lighter, ignited the flame, and lit the joint. She took a long drag and held it, returning the lighter to its place. *Thank God for the dispensary*. She leaned against the headboard and blew out the smoke. A few puffs later and the tightness in her chest had evaporated. Her once tense muscles now relaxed, and her heart was beating at its normal pace. She'd almost forgotten to be embarrassed when she heard Iman's bedroom door close. Her stomach knotted as she listened, wondering if, when they saw each other later, he'd bring up the fact that she was a complete stalker.

She heard him walk from one end of his room to the other, then the squeak of his bed as he sat. After a few seconds, he began strumming his acoustic guitar. She recognized the song immediately as Until I Found You by Stephen Sanchez, her heart leaping to her throat as he started to sing. Why was he playing it? It wasn't on any of his set lists and until now, she didn't know he even knew it. Maybe he was practicing? Thinking of playing it at the bar sometime? Or, was he playing it for her, knowing she was listening? Was he sending her a message?

She put out the joint and covered her mouth as tears formed in her eyes. She hadn't cried in years but as she choked back a sob she knew she would again. The longer she kept Iman close but at arm's length, the harder it would be.

She managed to avoid him long enough to get to the bar where Lou had already started up the grill and fryers. Years of working in bars where food was served had given her a tolerance to the smell of human food but every night, that first whiff of fryer oil hit her like a truck and the pot was *not* helping her maintain her composure. She gagged, forcing down the bile that crept up her throat.

"You all right?" Lou asked from behind the line.

"Fine."

"Not pregnant, are you?"

"Not a chance in hell."

He snickered as she passed through the swinging door into the bar.

"Hey, Rue," Brody said from the stage, bass in hand.

"Hey." She nodded to the rest of the band and moved to the register, making sure everything was ready before she unlocked the door.

"My singer on his way down or is he," he exchanged glances with the others, all of them chuckling under their breath. "Running late?"

"He should be down any minute."

"Are you sure? Because we'd understand if he was, you know, *tired*."

She shot him a look on her way to the door. "The fuck are you talking about?"

"Nothing, nothing. Just that," He stroked his beard. "Nevermind."

"We have a little bet going," Bill, the drummer chimed in.

"A bet?" She lifted the gate and unlocked the door, flipping the sign to 'open'.

"Shh," Brody instructed, his shoulders shaking in silent laughter.

"Come on," Bill said. "I have last night."

Rue stood in front of the stage, arms crossed. "Okay, what's going on, guys?"

Brody contained himself and answered for the group. "Don't get pissed but we've been taking bets on how long it'll take you and Iman to, you know…" He made a circle with his thumb and index finger and used the opposite hand to put a finger through it.

She dropped her head and sighed at their immaturity. "Really, guys? You're middle-aged."

"Forty doesn't equal blind, boss lady. We have eyes."

"Yeah, Rue," Bill said. "It's not a mystery to anyone here. We all see the looks. Now he's living with you? It's just a matter of time. So, was it last night?"

"For fuck's sake, Bill."

"*Wild* Bill."

She rolled her eyes. "You really need to stop trying to make fetch happen."

He grunted while the others laughed.

"Seriously," Brody said, kindness softening his eyes. "You like him, right?"

"*I* think she does," Iman said, bursting through the swinging door to a chorus of "Oohs" and "Oh, shits."

Fuck, she thought. *Change the subject. Change the subject!* "Anyone seen--"

"I'm here!" Ophelia announced, coming in through the front door. "I had some errands. Just gonna run up to get my apron and I'll be right down."

"I'll get it for you," Rue said, entering the kitchen before Ophelia could protest. "She all right?"

"Fine," Iman told her. "Just afraid to talk to me."

"Why, what'd you do?"

He moved closer, looking back to see the guys ignoring them as they got situated. "Nothing, she's just avoiding me like the damn plague. Do you know what her deal is lately?"

"Not really."

He squinted, hearing her heart beat faster. "You're lying."

She smacked his arm, lowering her voice. "Don't use your vamp hearing on me."

"I can't help it."

"Fine," She glanced over his shoulder to make sure she wasn't coming back. "There may or may not be another dude in the picture."

CHAPTER 39

His Adam's apple bobbed as he swallowed, a muscle twitching in his jaw. "Another dude?"

"I don't know. She said it was complicated, then said it wasn't, then said she had to push down her feelings for you but wouldn't say why. She wasn't making a lot of sense."

He hugged his arms.

"I promised I wouldn't tell you she's into you so you didn't hear any of this from me."

He nodded.

"I mean it. I do *not* want to get on her bad side."

"I won't say anything."

She sighed. "I see you're upset but don't be."

"Because we're just friends?" he scoffed.

She clicked her tongue. "Friends my ass. No. Listen, I don't know what's going on with her or if there's some guy waiting in the wings but I *do* know that that girl is into you and I mean *deep in.* She's just...guarded."

His jaw twitched again. "Like Fort Knox."

She touched his arm. "Give her time."

Again, he nodded again.

"Got it!" Rue said, placing the apron on the bar. Ophelia went to grab it and tied it around her waist just in time for the first customer to walk through the door.

Iman took his place on the stage and adjusted the mic, his eyes falling to Rue who greeted the customer who'd sat down at the bar with a, "What can I get you?"

As more people poured in and the band began to play, Rue noticed her hands were once again trembling. *Seriously, bitch?* She took a beat, retreating to the kitchen. How long could she keep this up?

Chapter 40

Rue and Iman's drama aside, Ophelia was feeling great. Powerful. In control, for once. *She'd made it rain.* She was on top of the world and nothing could bring her down.

As the night went on, she was thrilled to see the big tips were still coming. Twenty dollars here, forty there. One group of businessmen left a hundred and fifty dollar tip. It still wasn't stripper money, but it would be enough. Things were falling into place and soon she'd be out of Violet's apartment once and for all.

Her shift went by fast, the late-night crowd all but gone as it got closer and closer to close. Just twenty minutes left and she could get back to what she really wanted to be doing; trying more spells.

"Can I get you ladies another round?" she asked the group sitting in the corner booth. There were five women, all in their early twenties, with elaborate eyeliner, bright clothes, and hair to match. *Gamer girls*, she thought, remembering the video chat she'd walked in on between Lennon and some of their "work friends". They'd been talking strategy. Or maps. She couldn't remember. But, these girls looked just like them, down to the fake, henna freckles. They were smashed which hopefully meant a big tip for her.

A girl in a cat-ear headband elbowed the girl next to her, a pale girl with a shy smile, orange space buns on her head, and a black and white striped cut-off shirt barely covering her nipples, the underside of her breasts poking out the bottom. She giggled, nudging the cat-eared girl back. "We're fine for now."

"Okay. Let me know if I can get you anything else."

"We will," a few of them said in unison. She left the table, glancing back to see the orange-haired girl staring at her, her hand covering her mouth as she laughed.

CHAPTER 40

The fuck was that? she thought, not sure if she was flirting or just out-of-her-mind wasted. She blew it off, focusing on the next table who settled their tab and left, leaving a fifty dollar bill on the table for her. She shoved it in her apron, flattened her skirt, and turned to go to the kitchen. She was sure there weren't any orders waiting but she wanted to check, just in case. There was nothing on the line and Lou was already starting to wash dishes in the back.

"Hey," a whisper came from behind.

She jumped, spinning around to see the girl with the space buns. "Oh, hey. Listen, you're not supposed to be back here. Do you need something else?"

"Kind of." She licked her lips, looking her up and down. She dragged a finger down Ophelia's arm. "Are you, by chance, into girls?"

Her throat went dry, all the fluid in her body seeming to move south. "Sometimes."

She came closer, her tequila breath hot against her cheek. "Is now maybe one of those times?" She licked her earlobe and slid her hand down to hers.

Her heart raced, her pussy tingling. "Maybe."

The girl took her by the hand to the stairwell just behind her. They went up ten steps, just enough to be out of Lou's sight if he came back to the line. The girl kissed Ophelia's neck, up her jaw, and then brushed her strawberry-flavored lips softly against hers. Ophelia stifled a moan as the girl reached under her skirt and slid her fingers between her panties and her skin. She slipped two fingers between her folds, gently pinching her clit between them as she massaged her. Ophelia returned the favor, unbuttoning the girl's shorts and slipping one hand inside, the other on her right breast. The girl dove her fingers inside, working her G-spot before sliding out to circle over her clit. Ophelia matched her movements, the girl squirting in her hand and all over her jean shorts.

"Holy shit," the girl whispered, sounding surprised at how hard she'd come. "That deserves more than hand stuff." She dropped to her knees, pulling Ophelia's black panties down. She stepped out of them and rested one foot on a step two higher than the other one, opening herself up to be devoured. The girl wasted no time, pushing her skirt and apron up around her waist and putting her tongue to work. She grabbed her ass as Ophelia leaned against the wall, placing her dry hand on the back of the girl's head.

This is dangerous, she told herself. Lou could see them. If he walked too close to the stairs, he'd *definitely* see them. Or, worse, *Rue* could see them. Lou would be embarrassing but Rue would fire her on the spot or worse. She knew what happened when that girl lost her temper and neglecting her server duties to hook up with a stranger at work would absolutely piss her off. *Girl, what are you thinking?* She held onto the railing, biting her lip to keep from making noise as she started to come. The girl licked faster, then sucked hard on her clit, throwing Ophelia's raised leg over her shoulder and pressing two fingers into her, rubbing her G-spot. She grunted, shaking, hardly able to keep her balance as the explosion of her climax surged through her. She, too squirted directly into the girl's eager mouth.

She stood, wiping her face and buttoning her shorts while Ophelia got back into her panties and pulled her skirt and apron back down into place. She took a few steps down and turned to look up at Ophelia who was still catching her breath.

"Nice meeting you." And, with that, she was gone, down the steps and out of the kitchen.

"Uh, you, too?"

When she had regained her composure, she went back out into the bar where she saw the girl and her friends giggling as they left. As they neared the door, she heard the orange-haired girl tell the others, "I told you I could bag the hot waitress."

She stood there for a second, shame slapping her in the face like it always did when something like this happened. She shook it off, putting it away to be dealt with later. She went to their table, collected the bill and thirty-six dollar tip, and made her rounds.

Back at home, tips counted and Lennon in bed, she finally let herself feel the weight of what she'd done. Sitting on the floor next to her bed, she cried. She'd been doing so well. She hadn't had any sexual contact in weeks and for the first time maybe ever, she'd been proud of herself. Now, with one random hookup, that feeling was gone, replaced with guilt, self-loathing, and disgust. She was so angry with herself she could scream. All that work, staying out of the clubs, taking a lower-paying job, avoiding temptation at every turn, up in smoke. "Weak fucking bitch," she said, shaking her head. "Fucking weak."

Her eyes flicked to the half-dead flowers sitting in the vase on her nightstand. She glared at it, that sense of calm she'd felt at the park coming back. She quieted her mind and said the word she'd seen in one of the library books. "Vivo." The flowers immediately came back to life, the colors brightening and the leaves unwilting. She wiped the tears from her face, her resolve returning. She *was* powerful, not weak at all. She could do anything she wanted to. She just had to get her libido in check.

Chapter 41

Ophelia fiddled with the zipper on her bag, holding it close, the leather acting as a security blanket. She glanced around the room, a community center turned meeting spot for people like her. She sat in the metal folding chair, using all of her willpower to keep her leg from shaking. A dozen others sat in similar chairs, the furniture making a circle so no one person felt more or less important than the others and they could all feel seen. It was her turn to speak and with all eyes on her, her heart thumping in her chest, she tried to get the words out. Tried but all she could do was clear her throat.

"You need some water, sweetie?" the kindly older woman sitting next to her asked.

She nodded. "Yes, thank you."

She got a bottle from her beach bag and handed it to her.

She opened it and took a sip.

"Throat dry?" a man sitting across from her asked.

"Dryer than a nun on Sunday," she said, taking another long sip.

The others laughed quietly.

The man crossed one leg over the other, resting his ankle on the opposite knee. "Happens to all of us the first time."

The woman pat her shoulder. "It does. But, this is a safe space. You can say whatever you want to. No judgment."

The others nodded in agreement. She recapped the water bottle and sat it on the floor next to her. She never thought she'd be here, spilling her guts to a bunch of strangers but it was what she needed. She knew it was. Still, opening up about her past, tearing open old wounds wasn't something she looked forward to doing. She

CHAPTER 41

clutched her purse again, taking a slow breath. After a few seconds of silence, she began.

"Hi, I'm Ophelia and I'm a sex addict."

"Hi, Ophelia," the others greeted.

"My story's probably a lot like some of yours. Started having sex when I was nine, by choice when I was thirteen. At fifteen, I ran away from my abuser, spent some time tricking, living on the streets. Started dancing at sixteen, moved in with a guy I met at the club. That went as well as you'd expect. Shitty relationship after shitty relationship, always moving too fast, moving in with them after a couple of weeks. Taking off when they showed their true colors."

Understanding nods from the others eased the tension in her shoulders.

"I recently ended things with this chick. I mean, *I* didn't end things, they just…ended. Badly. And, I loved her, like, *really* loved her but the whole time we were together, I cheated on her *constantly*. At least once a week with some random person I met at the club." She held back tears of shame and went back to fidgeting with her zipper.

A woman with a clipboard a few chairs away who she assumed was the director gave her a concerned glare. "And, did you use protection?"

She looked down, unable to contain the tears, letting them drop onto her bag instead of running down her face and ruining her makeup. In a hushed voice, she answered, "Almost never."

"Why do you think that is?"

"I looked it up," she admitted, turning her face back to the others but not looking any of them in the eye. "I know it's either because I have no impulse control when it comes to sex or because I don't care about myself but…"

"But, what?" the man asked.

She looked directly at him, his kind eyes and relaxed manner comforting somehow. More tears spilled down her cheeks as she told him, "I'm pretty sure it's both."

The woman next to her put her hand on top of hers and gave it a quick squeeze. "You wouldn't be here if you didn't care at least a little."

Chapter 42

The man whose eyes flashed yellow slipped into the bar as the last customer walked out. The only people left in the building were Iman, distracted with getting his guitar in its case, and Rue who was busy wiping down the bar. "We're closed," she said, but as she lifted her eyes to meet his gaze, her stomach dropped. There was something about him she recognized. His vibe. His *smell*. She stepped out from behind the bar, dropping the towel and taking a few apprehensive steps toward him. As she drew close, fear rising in her throat like bile, their eyes locked, she lowered her voice to almost a growl. "I said, *we're closed*."

He tilted his head as if confused by her hostility. "I know, I just…" His gaze shifted, rising to where Iman had turned to face them. The singer hopped down and walked toward him, a broad smile turning up his lips.

"Dylan?" he said, pulling the man in for a hug and patting his back. "What are you doing here?" He pulled away and pat his shoulder. "I thought you and the guys were upstate."

"We were. Things got…weird."

"You'll have to fill me in. Rue, this is Dylan, the bass player in my old band. Man, it's been too long. How have you been? How--" He stopped, his features scrunching in confusion. His hand covered his heart as he took a shaky breath. "What is this?" He looked to Rue for clarification.

She shrugged.

"What is this I'm feeling?"

"I feel it too, man," Dylan told him. "I've been feeling it since I found out where you were playing these days. I came looking for you to see if you had an idea of what it was."

Rue cocked an eyebrow, arms crossing over her chest. "What does it feel like?"

Iman answered but didn't take his eyes off his friend. "I don't know, it's like...it's like how I felt about my mom before she died."

"Exactly," Dylan agreed. "Like a...bond? Like best friends but more."

Rue took a step back. "And, you felt this from upstate?"

"Yeah. And, I mean, no offense, we're on good terms but we haven't talked in years. I wouldn't even call us friends anymore, not *really*. But, now..."

Iman nodded. "Yeah, I agree. It's like all of a sudden, I realize I've been missing you. *A lot.*"

"Soulmates," Rue told them, dropping her arms to her sides.

They looked at her like she'd just told them the sky was purple.

She sighed, annoyed she had to explain. "Soulmates are usually linked romantically. People in a past life were so into each other, they couldn't let go, even in death. So, they find each other, or try to, in every life after. But, sometimes it's a family-type thing. Like a mom whose baby died so they feel cheated and meet up in the next life. Or something. No one actually knows for sure but that looks like what's going on here."

"How do you know that?" Dylan asked.

"My dad told me."

"And, how does he know?"

She shot him an insulted glare. "He's old as fuck and crazy smart."

"I think she's right," Iman said. "You don't feel like an old friend to me. You feel like," He slapped his shoulder. "A brother."

"Yeah." Dylan smiled at Iman. "Soulmates, huh? As good an explanation as any, I guess."

"Come on," Iman clapped him on the back and led him to the bar. "Drinks on me."

Rue watched the men sit and locked the door, flipping the sign to closed. *Soulmate*, she thought, keeping her sight trained on the newcomer. *But, that's not all he is.*

Chapter 43

Ophelia stashed that night's tips in the shoebox under her bed with the rest of her savings. It was at a little over six thousand. It was probably just enough but she wanted to get to ten before looking for a place. She pushed the box back to its hiding spot and sat on the bed, breathing out the stress of the day. Work had gone fine, it was the SAA meeting that had her stomach in knots. Talking about old traumas had brought up a lot of feelings she'd wished would've stayed buried, even if it meant she'd never heal. *No*, she thought. *I need to keep going, at least once a week.* As much as thinking about her past pained her, it was good for her to work through it. Plus, in that room, more than anywhere else, she didn't feel alone.

Still in her work clothes, she curled into a ball on her side, letting salty tears smear her mascara and stain her pillow. *It's okay to feel it*, she reminded herself. *You're safe now. It's okay to remember.* But, she didn't want to. Didn't want to pick at old wounds. Didn't want to study the scars and relive the trauma. She didn't want the burden. She didn't want the pain.

She woke up six hours later, the morning sun shining a beam of unwanted light through a crack in her blinds. She hadn't meant to fall asleep, in her shoes and on top of her covers. She'd just been too exhausted to move.

This is bullshit, she thought, throwing her legs over the side of the bed and stomping to the mirror hanging on the back of her door. She used her fingers to fix her hair and smoothed her clothes, deciding to shower and change later. She needed a distraction. She needed to feel in control. She needed more power.

She remembered an article she'd read online about a specific book of spells. It was hard to come by and not a lot was known about exactly what kind of spells it included, but according to the article, it was highly sought after. She took her phone from the charging pad and did a search. After a lot of dead ends, she finally found a store that carried it, a small occult shop on East 14th. She grabbed her bag, took a quick bathroom break, and headed out.

Ophelia's nose wrinkled as she walked into the shop, the smell of burnt sage and lavender hanging in the air like fog. Every bit of wall space was filled with shelves holding candles, Buddahs, and jewelry displays. Tables of crystals took up the center of the room, everything from amethyst to zircon. At the back, a white-haired woman in a red and gold sari sat at a round, wooden table, tarot cards splayed in front of her.

"Can I help you?" a pretty African-American woman said from behind the counter that held the cash register. Her braids were up in a bun and her short stiletto nails were painted white with black tips. She wore a black tank top, several silver necklaces, and a stainless septum ring. *Hot*, Ophelia thought, immediately getting mad at herself. *Bitch, focus*.

"Yeah, I'm looking for this book." She pulled up the picture on her phone and showed the screen to the girl who looked to be in her mid-twenties.

Her eyes turned to saucers. "Uh, yeah," she stammered. "We have it. It's on that back wall next to the pentagram stuff." She pointed to a shelf with a dozen or so leather-bound books. "They don't print it anymore so it's a used copy but it's in good condition. No missing pages or anything."

"Thanks." She beelined to the back of the store, ignoring the older woman at the table who watched her every move. She scanned the titles and found what she was looking for tucked behind three other spell books as if it had been hidden. She took the hefty tome from its spot and ran her fingertips over the unassuming cover. She smiled, whispering the words on the spine to herself, "Cartea Diavolului."

At the counter, the cashier clasped something between her hands, holding it close to her mouth as she muttered something under her breath. As Ophelia put the book down in front of her to pay, the woman unclenched her hands, revealing a clear quartz crystal hanging by a sterling chain.

"Take this," she said, holding it out for Ophelia.

"I just need the book."

She shook her head. "If you're set on using that, you need this. Trust me." She slipped the chain over Ophelia's head, the crystal dangling over the center of her chest. "No charge." She flicked her gaze to the older woman who nodded.

Ophelia looked at her then back to the woman at the counter. "You sure?"

"Girl, yes. And, whatever you do, don't even *open* that book unless you're wearing it."

The women at the shop had freaked her out. Why were they so insistent that she wear the necklace when working with the book? And, why did they look terrified when she left with it? She shook it from her mind. Weird looks from two chicks at an out-of-the-way occult shop weren't going to deter her from doing the spells in the book. She wanted to do more than make it rain and re-alive wilting flowers. She wanted to do everything Marley could do.

After a few hours of studying the book in her room, memorizing the spell she'd been dying to try for weeks, she hid it in her closet and stepped out onto the fire escape. She closed her eyes, breathing in the evening air and taking in the energy of the world around her. *You can do this*, she thought, blowing out and opening her eyes. She scanned the alley below, making sure no one was there to see. It was empty.

CHAPTER 43

She cracked her neck and recited the words, "Lejer ca pene, plutesc." *I hope I pronounced that right.* In seconds, she was off her feet, floating up from the iron egress. "Holy shit." She levitated higher, passing the roof of the building, her elation turning to panic. *"Holy shit."*

She swam through the air until the roof was underneath her but she still rose higher. *How do I get down? Fuck, how do I get down?"* Her mind raced, the building getting farther and farther away. "Stop!" she shouted. "Just stop!" Her intention changed, she froze, her body hovering, her heart beating a mile a minute. *Intention. It's all about intention.* She took a breath, picturing herself slowly floating down to the roof. She imagined the sound of her shoes hitting the gray surface and the feeling of stability. Soon, her thoughts became reality and she was safe on top of the building.

She got down on her knees, panting and sweating. "Oh, thank fuck." She caught her breath, her fear turning to joy. She laughed, her hand on her heart, the chain warm against her palm. "I did it. I really did it."

She got to her feet and went to the door that led to the stairwell. She pulled but it was stuck. "Locked." She dropped her head and took her phone from her pocket, pulling up her contacts, and hitting call. "Shit."

"Yeah?" Lennon answered.

"Hey, are you home?"

"Yeah, why?"

"I got locked out. Can you come let me in? I'm on the roof?"

There was a moment of silence.

"Uh, please?"

"On my way." The line went dead. A minute later, Lennon appeared, holding the door open.

"Thanks," Ophelia said, walking toward them.

"What are you doing up here?"

She stopped. "Nothing weird."

They quirked an eyebrow.

"I just needed to be alone for a while. Somewhere quiet."

"Try again."

She pursed her lips. They knew her too well. She'd only been up here a handful of times and only when Violet had wanted to have sex outside. She'd never gone to the roof alone. Why would she? It was nothing but concrete covered in bird shit. Unable to come up with a lie on the spot, she decided the best thing to do was tell the truth. Or, a bit of it, anyway. "I went to an SAA meeting. It was…a lot. I needed to clear my head."

"Oh," They looked away and made a funny expression that to Ophelia looked like embarrassment, though she'd never seen them embarrassed in her life. "Well, good for you. I, um," They awkwardly pat her shoulder. "I'm proud of you."

Her brows lifted in surprise. "You're…proud of me?"

"It's a big step for you, so, yeah." They tapped her shoulder again. "Good job."

"I…what?"

"What? I can be nice."

"Since when?"

"Let's not make a big deal out of it."

They went inside and began the walk down the stairs. Her lips turned up in a small smile. "Whatever you say."

Chapter 44

Rue fumbled with the glass she was trying to clean, nearly dropping it three times before giving up and putting it in a bus tub under the counter. She leaned on the bar, every nerve in her body standing at attention as she tried and failed to ignore Iman's stare. He sang Don't Wait directly to her, his gaze glued to her so intensely, even the handful of customers that lingered at the end of the night noticed. They looked between them from their booths and tables as if in expectation, the anticipation in their eyes mimicking the hope she knew Iman felt. It was clear as could be, his feelings for her on display with every performance. It was just a matter of time before things came to a head and she'd have to tell him, to explain why they could never be together. Why, no matter what she felt for him, no matter how much she wished things could be different, they just weren't meant to be. She'd been avoiding it, knowing the conversation would be hard. Knowing it would break his heart.

"You okay?" Ophelia asked, standing next to her behind the bar. "You look like you're gonna hurl."

She shook her head. "Nope, not okay in the slightest."

She looked over at Iman and stage and back at her boss. "Yeah, I'm surprised he hasn't jumped you, yet."

She held her fingers to her temple and squeezed her eyes shut. "Please don't give me mental images. I'm barely holding it together."

She leaned in and whispered, "Girl, just fuck him."

"Bitch," she said a little louder than she meant to. She glanced around to make sure no one was paying attention and lowered her voice. "You have no idea how bad I wish I could."

"So, what's stopping you? The mystery dude you won't tell me about that no one has ever seen that I'm pretty sure you're making up?"

"I didn't make anyone up. And, I don't know if there's a dude. It's," she sighed heavily, rolling her eyes.

"Complicated, I know."

She sighed again, needing to change the subject. "*Anyway*, just a heads up, Iman's old bandmate is in town. If he comes in here, steer clear."

She cocked her head. "Windowless van vibes?"

"Something like that." She allowed her eyes to wander back to Iman who still stared, his voice sending shivers down her spine. "I need a break. You need a break? Let's take a break." She took Ophelia's hand and led her through the kitchen to the service door, calling to the cook as they passed, "Lou, can you watch the bar for a minute? Thanks!"

He popped his head up from behind the line. "Can I *what?*"

"You're the coolest!" The women hurried outside, the door slamming closed behind them. Rue took a half-smoked joint from her pocket and lit it, taking a long drag and offering it to Ophelia who shook her head. She blew out the smoke and leaned against the building, her hands still shaking.

"You know this isn't healthy, right?"

"It's just pot. Relax."

"I don't mean that. I mean Iman. Look at you, quivering and shit."

"I don't want to talk about it, okay, please?"

"You can't tell me you don't love that man."

"Bitch, I said please."

"Fine." She put her hands up in surrender. "So, what's the deal with Iman's friend? Bad news?"

She took another puff and held it as she answered. "Just trust me."

"All right." She stood next to her, leaning on the wall and waving the smoke out of her face. "Can I ask you a question?"

"Not if it has to do with Iman."

"It doesn't."

"Then shoot."

"What's with you and guys like that?"

"Guys like what?"

"You know, rapey."

"Oh," Rue blew out a final puff and put the joint out with her fingers, putting it back in her pocket. "I don't think Dylan's rapey, just...dangerous, maybe."

"Okay, other guys, then. Creepers, perverts, abusers. I appreciate you looking out for me, I do, and no shade. They're trash but since I've known you, they've been like," She took a quick glance around. "Your favorite snack."

She shrugged. "That's true."

"So, why? Not saying they don't deserve it and a girl's gotta eat but it seems like it's more than that. It feels..."

"Personal?"

She closed her mouth, swallowing the lump that jumped to her throat. "Oh, I didn't mean to...I'm so sorry. I didn't know. If you ever need to talk--"

"Oh, no!" Rue said, touching her arm. "No, no, I wasn't..." She paused, trying to find the right words, knowing her friend's history and not wanting to upset her. "No one hurt me."

"Oh." She unclenched her jaw, relief apparent in her tone. "I just thought...you know, because you said--"

"No, I get it. Sorry, it just," She tucked her hair behind her ears. "It's a little hard to talk about, even after all this time. I can tell you but, trigger warning."

She nodded. "Go ahead. I'm curious."

"All right but, seriously, it's fucked up."

"When I was nineteen, I finally made it to the city. I'd meant to come the year before but I was not in a good head space. Anyway, I just got a job at a bar on West 44th, a real fancy place. Black walls, green padded high-back chairs, white button-down uniform, the whole thing. Pretentious as fuck. So, it was me and two other girls, both in their early twenties. Angela and Miranda. And, the manager, Jasper. Jasper was a real hardass, OCD, and real particular. Made us keep our hair in high ponies, said we had to keep our makeup natural, and we couldn't wear shoes that made noise. They had to have rubber soles so our walking didn't 'ruin the ambiance'. Said no matter how rude a customer was, we always had to keep a smile on our faces. We were *so* pretty when we smiled. He was a real douche, gelled back hair, pinky ring, you know the type.

So, since I wasn't twenty-one yet, I couldn't serve drinks alone so Miranda let me shadow her. She showed me the ropes, taught me how to make the prohibition-era drinks the customers there liked, even split her tips with me until I started making my own. We started talking after hours while we cleaned up. She told me about the college classes she was taking and how she wanted to be a vet. I told her about my dream of opening my own bar someday, how it wouldn't be like where we worked. Not stuffy and boring. It'd have live music, a relaxed atmosphere, and food people actually *wanted* to eat, not the microscopic, plant-based bullshit we had there. She was the first person I told I wanted my own bar and she was really supportive. She was a good friend to me." She paused, biting the inside of her cheek. "She was a really good person." She swallowed her emotions and continued.

"I barely knew Angela. She was super quiet, kept to herself but she was nice. Always asked how I was, stuff like that. But, we didn't really talk. One night, I saw her come out of Jasper's office and she looked *pissed*. I asked what was wrong but she just told me nothing which was an obvious lie but I didn't want to push. If she was in trouble with the boss, that wasn't my business. When she didn't show up the next day, me and Miranda assumed she got fired. But, when we asked Jasper what happened, he said she called and quit. We asked why and he just said, 'beats me'. For days, we speculated. Did he yell at her about her uniform? Her shirt *was* a little wrinkled when she came out of his office and he was a stickler for looking 'professional'. Did he catch her stealing? Had he given her a warning and she was too embarrassed to come back? We had all kinds of theories.

"Then, a few nights later, after closing, he ordered Miranda into his office. Said it was urgent. I was wrapping silverware for the next day, listening to my MP3 player because, you know, twenty-thirteen. I thought I heard a bang so I took my earbuds out and that's when I heard Miranda scream. I dropped everything and ran to the office. It was locked and I could hear her yelling at him to stop and when I tell you my stomach dropped to the fucking floor, I kid you not, I almost fell over. I was like, fuck this job, fuck this door, I'm breaking it down. So, I kicked it in but they weren't there anymore. They'd gone out the service entrance door that was at the back of the room. I ran out there and I saw Jasper running down the alley and Miranda on the ground, blood all over her face, one of her eyes swollen shut, her shirt ripped open." She took the joint from her pocket, her hands again starting to shake. She lit it and took a puff, offering it to Ophelia who took it this time, taking a drag, her own hands beginning to tremble. Rue blew out the smoke and continued.

"Her heart was weak but still beating so I called nine-one-one and waited with her 'til the ambulance came. She was so messed up, eyes rolled back, not moving. I thought about turning her but I didn't want to risk it. Not after..."

"After what?"

She wiped away a tear she hadn't realized had fallen. "Nevermind." She took another drag and passed it back to Ophelia. "At the hospital, I told myself the doctors knew what they were doing. That she'd be okay. For a little while, she was. She woke up, told me what happened. She said Jasper told her to give him head. Said it was *'in her job description'*. Said if she didn't do it, she'd get fired just like Angela. Piece of shit. So, she said she quit but he wouldn't let her leave. Blocked the door. Forced himself..." She stopped, choking back more tears. She took a breath, calming herself.

"While he was," She gritted her teeth, unable to say the words. "He had his hand over her mouth. She grabbed his wrist and bit him so hard, she drew blood. That's how she got away. She went outside to run but he followed her, slammed her head into the side of the building. She didn't remember anything after that until she woke up at the hospital."

"Oh, my God."

"She said we had to stop him from doing it to anyone else. She said we had to make him pay. I agreed. Then, some woman came in, I think it was her mom. She kissed her head and asked where the doctor was. Asked what happened. Before we could tell her, Miranda's eyes just...went out. Like someone flipped a switch. They called it an intracranial hematoma. I remember I was crying, like a fucking faucet, watching her mom melt down, smelling my friend's blood on my clothes from when I tried to wake her up in the alley. I remember thinking what happened to her was my fault because if I hadn't been listening to that stupid MP3 player, I would've heard her sooner. I thought it was my fault she was dead because I was too chicken shit to turn her. But, that was bullshit. I wasn't the one who hurt her. I wasn't the one to blame. *He was.* It was like a switch flipped in me, too. I wasn't sad anymore. I mean, I *was* but in that moment, I was pure rage. And, I remembered what she said. He had to pay.

"So, I went back to the bar and because he was a smug son of a bitch, he was there, in his office, doing paperwork like nothing happened. He put on a whole performance, said he was *so* glad I was okay and could I believe what happened to *poor* Miranda? He said a mugger attacked her while he was out making a bank deposit and he was *worried* they got me, too. I was like, 'A mugger?' And he was like, 'That's what the cops think'. He said it also could've been a jilted lover or a stalker and I interrupted his bullshit with, 'Or a pervert boss that doesn't know how to take no for an answer.' He scoffed at me and was all, 'You think I'd hurt one of my own employees?' And I was like, 'No, I think you fucking killed her.' He looked freaked out. I guess he hadn't heard the news because he was like, 'She's dead?' And I said, 'Yeah. I know the rules are a little fuzzy to someone like you, but even you have to admit, murder goes a smidge beyond boys will be boys.' That's when he dropped his mask.

"He got real creepy, like a serial killer, you know? He said, 'You shouldn't have come back. There's no one here to help you.' And I was like, 'You think I need help? Why, because I'm five-two, a hundred and ten pounds soaking wet, all tits and ass and not much else? No real muscle mass or weapons? Just a dumb, helpless girl trapped in a room with a six-foot, slightly overweight Neanderthal in a cheap tie?' He got up from his desk like he was gonna do something, walked toward me all skulky. He looked genuinely surprised when I closed the door and locked it. I said, 'I'll tell you a secret, you fugly piece of shit. I'm not the one of us who's trapped.' He walked over and was like, 'I'm gonna enjoy making you scream' And I laughed in his face like, 'Bitch, I won't be screaming but I'm kind of sick of your voice so I'm gonna do myself a favor and make sure you don't, either.' And, then I flew at him, like, feet off the floor *flew*. Like I was hundreds of years old or something. I let myself *loose.* Wailed on him. Got him on the ground and beat the ever-loving fuck out of him. Just yelling like, 'You like that, asshole? You like being on the other end of a beating? Why aren't you smiling? You should really smile more.' I'm telling you, I went *off*. I didn't even bite him. I was so disgusted by this dude, even his blood smelled like garbage. So, I got up and took all the money out of his wallet. I was like, 'You know what? Fuck you *extra*. I'm taking all your shit. Call it severance. Now, I'm no thief but I was that night. I took it all. The register money, everything in the safe. I didn't give a fuck. I took that make-him-pay shit *literally*.

"I was gonna leave him there. I really was. I was gonna hurt him, take his money, and take off. What was he gonna do? Go to the cops? Unlikely. He knew I knew what he did. No way he would've risked going away for murder over a few thousand dollars and a beat down, especially when he'd have to admit he got his ass handed to him by a tiny teenage girl. His ego wouldn't allow it. But, then," She thinned her lips.

Ophelia took one last hit and handed the joint back. "Then, what?"

"I was on my way out. I opened the door, on my way to the bar to get the stuff I'd left earlier. I was *this* close to being out of there when I heard this motherfucker laugh. It was mostly a cough, kind of gurgly from the blood in his throat, but it was a laugh. I went back and was like, 'Bitch, what's funny?' He couldn't open his eyes but he was looking at me, you know what I mean? And taunting me. He was like, 'There'll be more girls.' And I was like, 'The fuck did you say?' And he said, 'There will always be more girls.' Bitch, no. I was *not* having that on my conscience. There would absolutely fucking *not* be more girls."

She gulped, almost afraid to ask. "What'd you do?"

" I went back to the bar, got a bunch of bottles, dumped that shit all over him, and lit a match."

"Jesus."

"He had it coming."

"No, he definitely deserved it. I understand, just…I mean, *Jesus*."

"Listen, I know I'm violent or whatever. But I'm not--"

"Scary. Scary is what you are."

She frowned. "You're scared of me?"

"Not usually but let's just say, I would *not* want to piss you off."

Chapter 45

Rue's story had given Ophelia nightmares but also a new understanding and respect for her. She *was* violent. Brutal even, but she had her reasons. Plus, she'd always looked out for her. She was like an avenging angel…with fangs.

While Lennon slept in the next room, Ophelia studied her new book. She remembered the freaked-out looks on the shop girl's face when she bought it and wondered what the big deal was. She could feel how powerful it was, the spells inside giving off an energy all their own. But, it didn't feel *bad*. Just strong. And, she needed all the strength she could get. Rue wouldn't always be around to protect her. She needed to be able to look out for herself.

The levitation spell hadn't gone one hundred percent as planned but she just needed to learn to control it. In the meantime, she had her eye on another spell, one that could come in handy in a lot of situations, including when some creeper got grabby. She sat cross-legged on the floor reading the word over and over, checking a translation app to make sure she got it right. She held out her hand, took a deep breath, and said, "Ardeat."

With a whoosh, her blanket erupted in a blaze, her bed in front of her engulfed in copper flames. She scooted back, mouth agape and mind racing. She was so stunned, she didn't hear the fire alarm go off or Lennon screaming as they burst into the room. She only noticed them when white foam sprayed over the fire, suffocating it and filling the room with a cloud of irritating smoke. She coughed and waved it away, the smell making her feel sick.

"The fuck are you doing in here?" Lennon shouted over the alarm.

She coughed again. "You got here fast."

"Duh. After that Marley girl's bullshit, I put one of these things in every room. Under the sinks, in the hall closet, in my room."

CHAPTER 45

"But, not *my* room?"

The alarm quieted and they put the fire extinguisher down. "I didn't want you to think I was paranoid. Seriously, what were you--" Their eyes fell to the floor next to her and she knew by the look on their face what they'd spotted. "Are you fucking kidding me?"

She hurried to stand. "It's not what you think."

"It's *exactly* what I think. You're messing with," They lowered their voice to a near whisper. "*Magic?* After what happened? Are you *trying* to get your ass kicked? Rue is right across the hall. If she finds out--"

"But, she won't find out, right?"

"Your blanket--"

"I can get another blanket. She never comes in here, anyway."

"She'll smell the fire. She probably heard the alarm. She could be on her way *right now*."

She bent to retrieve the book and hid it in the back of her closet under some clothes. "I'll tell her I left a candle burning. She'll buy it, trust me. She's so preoccupied with *not* banging Iman, she won't care less."

"Bitch,"

"Please, Lennon? I need this."

"What for?"

She pleaded with her eyes, begging without words for them to understand. "I'm just really tired of feeling powerless. Helpless. I need this for *me*."

They folded their arms, pity in their eyes and an exasperated sigh on their lips. "Fine. I won't say anything but if she finds out, I didn't know shit, you hear me? I had no idea what you were up to."

She nodded emphatically.

"And, I want to go on record as saying this is the absolute dumbest thing you've ever done, and I've seen you do some epically stupid shit."

"Noted."

They pointed at the bed. "And, I'm not helping you clean that up."

Luckily, Rue and Iman slept through the entire ordeal: the fire, Lennon's lecture, and Ophelia's clean-up procedure which included buying a new blanket and throwing out the charred one. It was late afternoon by the time Ophelia left for her SAA meeting. While there, she had a hard time paying attention to other people's stories, her thoughts consumed by the fire. It was the second spell in a row she'd messed up, not because they didn't work but because she couldn't control them. She needed to learn how to rein her power in and fast before she or someone else got hurt.

After the meeting, she stood to leave, following the others to the door to go. As they filed out, one of the women, a cute brunette with a perky smile stopped her.

"I like your quartz," she said.

"Sorry?" Ophelia said, not hearing her, her mind on more important things than small talk.

"Your crystal," She pointed at her necklace. "Clear quartz. Great for protection. You practice?"

Her ears perked up. "Yes. You?"

She touched her chest. "Wiccan, going on three years. You should meet my group. Even more than these meetings, those ladies saved my life. It's so important in our healing journey to feel empowered, you know?"

Her heart skipped. "I *do*."

"I'm heading over now. You want to come? I know the girls will love to have you."

"Sure, thanks!" She followed her a couple of blocks to the same park where she'd tapped into the earth's magic and made it rain. There, sitting around one of the pink tables, were four women, all in their mid to late twenties, all wearing the same type of flowy dress as the girl from her meeting. Courtney. She was pretty sure that was her name though she hadn't really been paying attention when she'd introduced herself at that first meeting.

CHAPTER 45

"Blessed be, everyone," Courtney said as she pulled two chairs over to join them.

"Blessed be," the others greeted as the two sat.

"This is Ophelia, another practitioner."

"Hi, Ophelia," the women said in unison.

One of the women flashed a beaming smile and took a cookie from a plastic container on the table, holding it out to her. "Oatmeal butterscotch?"

Ophelia took it politely. "Thank you." She took a bite as the woman introduced herself and the others. "I'm Sam, this is Evie, Scarlet, Izzie, and you know Courtney. I'm kind of the designated mom friend of the group so if you need anything, just let me know."

"Um, thanks." She swallowed and took another bite.

"Go easy with that, now. Half is all you need."

"All I need?"

"Didn't Courtney tell you?"

"Oops," Courtney said, looking embarrassed and taking a cookie for herself.

Evie chimed in, "Sam's cookies are...special."

"Oh," Ophelia said, sitting the remainder of her cookie on the napkin Sam had put in front of her.

"Sorry about that," Courtney said, her mouth full. She swallowed, taking two bottles of water from the cooler on the ground next to her and handing one to her. "I can't believe I forgot to warn you."

"It's fine," she said, taking a sip of water, wondering how long it would be before the cookie kicked in and if she had time to get back to the loft before it did.

"I was just excited to introduce you to everyone." She turned her attention to the others. "She's a survivor, like us."

Sympathetic nods from the group.

"And, she practices."

"I see," Sam said, gesturing to her necklace. "I love your quartz. And, on a silver chain. Smart."

Ophelia crinkled her brow. "Smart?"

"Silver is best for transferring energy," Evie told her.

"Yes," Sam said. "Makes the crystal's power even stronger. Easier for you to access."

"Oh, right." She took another sip of water, hoping they didn't notice how much of a newb she was.

"So, what's your school?"

"My school?"

"Of magic. You know, Elemental, Rune, *Blood Magic*."

The others winced.

"Don't even joke," Courtney giggled.

Sam laughed. "I'm sorry. *Obviously*, not Blood Magic."

She squirmed in her seat. "Obviously."

"What, then?" Izzie asked, her hazel eyes twinkling in the late-day sun.

"Elemental, I think."

"You think?" Sam asked.

"Well, I haven't been um, practicing for long. I hadn't put a label on it."

"Oh, well that's okay. What do you do? Make herbal remedies? Work with crystals? Read Tarot?"

"Well," She cleared her throat, her mouth starting to go dry. "I did one herbal thing, a healing spell. This is my only crystal and I just wear it. I haven't done a spell using it or anything."

"A healing spell?" Evie asked. "Like oregano oil?"

"No," She took another sip of water, her mind already going fuzzy around the edges. "A wound-healing spell."

"Wound healing? Did it work?"

"Yeah. I cut my arm and it healed it right up."

"Oh," Izzie said, looking to the others in confusion. "Anything else?"

"Mostly stuff that doesn't go right. I tried a fire-in-hand spell but my whole bed blew up. I levitated but went *way* too high. I did do a good job of making it rain, though. Of course, that was right after Gaia gave me a bunch of nature magic. Nature power? Whatever. *That* worked properly, at least."

They stared at her, slack-jawed, puzzled expressions covering all of their faces.

"What?"

"Oh!" Courtney nearly shouted. "She's messing with us."

"Oh," Sam said, laughing and taking a cookie from the container. "You almost had me."

CHAPTER 45

The others laughed, too, Courtney patting Ophelia's back.

"Gaia," Evie said, shaking her head.

"*Levitating*," Scarlet said, almost choking with laughter, her mouth full of pot-cookie.

"You're hysterical," Izzie chuckled.

Goddamn it, Ophelia thought. *They're not witches. They're stoners with a cottage core aesthetic*. She guzzled down the rest of her water and stood, hoping she'd make it home safely. "If you ladies will excuse me, I have about three hours before I have to be at work and I need to sober up."

"Ooh, take a nap. That always works for me," Courtney said, handing her another bottle. "And, drink more water. Flushes it out."

"Thanks." She opened it and took a gulp. "Nice meeting you all."

"See you later!" Sam called as she walked away.

She rolled her eyes. *The fuck you will*.

She made it home, crashing on the couch, her legs like jelly. She took her phone from her pocket and hastily wrote a plea for assistance, posting it in a handful of New York-based social media groups claiming to be for witches. She asked for help in controlling her magic, hoping that someone somewhere would know something useful. When she was done, she set an alarm for two hours, got relatively comfortable, and passed out.

Chapter 46

Just blow right by, Rue thought, seeing Iman sitting on the sofa from her spot in the hall. *He's reading something on his phone. He might not even notice I'm here.* She took a few steps into the living room, the door in her sights. Just a few more steps. Maybe ten and she'd be out of the apartment.

"You leaving?" he asked, not looking up from his screen.

So close. "Just heading downstairs. I need to get there early for the delivery guy." She walked faster, reaching out for the doorknob. She was almost there, her fingertips just touching the brass fixture.

There was a brief silence cut by Iman's somber question. "You know I'm in love with you, right?"

She stopped dead in her tracks, eyes glued to the door, her body going cold.

He put his phone on the coffee table and stood, talking as he made his way to where she was.

"You know, right? How I feel about you?"

Her throat had gone so dry, she could barely speak. "Iman,"

"It's not an innocent crush. It's not *just* that I think you're gorgeous. And, it's *definitely not* a friendship thing." He stood next to her, placing his hand on the door. "I love you."

"You shouldn't." Her voice was quiet and though she turned to face him, she couldn't bring herself to look up at him. She didn't want to have this conversation. Didn't want to hurt him. But, the time had come. She could tell by his tone, he was done waiting for answers.

"Give me one good reason why not."

"Iman, please."

"Is there another guy?"

"What?" She finally lifted her head to look at him. "No. I mean, it's not--"

"Then what? You don't love me?"

Her lip quivered. "We're friends."

"For how long?"

"How long, what?"

"Have we been friends? Three years, give or take? You think I don't know when you're full of shit? We are *not* just friends and we both know that."

"Iman,"

His features softened as he tucked her hair behind her ear. "I know you love me. You wouldn't have turned me if you didn't. You wouldn't look at me the way you do if you didn't. And, your heart wouldn't be racing so fast right now it could win a marathon if you didn't."

Tears pooled as she fought to keep them from spilling.

"So, give me a reason, one good reason why you keep me at arm's length."

She averted her glance.

"*One.*"

"Because we're not soulmates," she blurted, her voice shaky but certain.

He blinked. "I said one *good* reason."

"Um, that's a *really* good reason, bro."

"How is that a good reason?"

She shook her head. "You don't get it. Somewhere, there's a guy. *The* guy. He could show up any minute and when he does--"

"*If* he does. He might never. For all you know, he died years ago or it could be a family thing like me and Dylan."

"Could be but I don't know that."

"No, you don't. So why are you putting us through this?" He pet her hair and tilted her head up, forcing her to look him in the eye. "Why are you letting a future maybe keep us apart when you know we belong together?"

Her tears rolled down her cheeks as she used every bit of willpower she had to hold herself back from kissing him. "Because I've seen what happens when a romantic soulmate shows up. I know what it does to people. Violet married Kenton *the day they met*. She *had* a girlfriend. Dropped her like NASA dropped Pluto."

"Okay, but Violet's hardly--"

"That's what happens. You get obsessed. You stop caring about whoever you're seeing. You forget how you felt about them. You hurt them."

"Rue,"

"I won't do it. Hate me if you need to. Be mad at me. Call me ridiculous or dumb or whatever combination of colorful adjectives you want. But, I will *not* hurt you like that." She shoved him out of the way and opened the door to leave, keeping her eyes locked on his. "I would rather die."

Iman drained his third blood bag in a row, his emotions fueling his hunger. After his confession and subsequent rejection, he didn't know how to feel. *Of course*, Rue was trying to protect him. That's what she did. No matter what it did to her, she always looked out for the people she cared about. She told him what she did as a warning, hoping it would cool his feelings for her. But, knowing why she was keeping her distance, that she was trying to spare him more pain in the future, made him love her even more.

"You fuck Rue, yet?" Lennon asked, entering the apartment unannounced.

He dropped the empty bag into the trash. "Hello to you, too."

"I'm just curious."

"Are you, or are you spying for Violet?"

They put their phone in their baggy jeans' pocket. "It can be both."

"Uh, huh."

"She called and asked *again*, but I really *am* curious."

He sighed and took a seat on the sofa. "No, I haven't."

"Really? The hell are you waiting for?"

"Uh, consent?"

"Sure but, come on." They sat next to him. "I'm Ace and the tension's giving *me* stress."

"Sorry to be a nuisance."

CHAPTER 46

"Just do the thing."

"The thing?"

"The thing girl's like. Take charge or whatever. Throw her up against something. Infantilize her. Choke her a little."

"I'm *not* going to *infantilize* her. And, *choke her?* What are you talking about?"

"I read a study that said fifty to fifty-eight percent of women in their twenties like being choked during sex. Is that not a thing?"

"Uh…"

"Another study said sixty percent of women fantasize about being dominated and the most common pet name for a significant other is baby with derivatives like baby girl and baby doll ranking high on the list of--"

"You researched women? What for?"

They stared blankly. "The 'tism."

"Ah."

"Plus, I've lived with women my entire life and I cosplayed as one for almost two decades. I'm not saying I'm an expert but I *am* saying, based on statistics and what I've observed, women like dominate men and I've walked by enough open doors to know that's you when you want it to be."

His cheeks went hot with embarrassment as he ran his fingers through his hair and cleared his throat. "Can we maybe not talk about what you've seen me…doing?"

They shrugged. "I just don't get it. I thought love was supposed to make people happy."

"It is, ideally."

"Then why aren't you happy?"

He rested his head on the back of the couch. "Because she's pushing me away."

"But, you love her."

"Yeah, I do and it's fucking killing me."

"It doesn't make sense."

"Love isn't always what you want it to be. Sometimes, it's heartbreak, and suffering, and pain worse than death. Literally. I've been starved, nearly frozen to death, electrocuted. I basically died and went through hell to come back and it was *nothing* compared to this. To love someone who you *know* loves you back but can't even look you in the eye…it's torture."

They were quiet for a second then awkwardly pat his knee. "Sorry."

"She's just hung up on the whole soulmate thing. Thinks it'd be worse to dump me later than never be with me at all. I think that's," He leaned forward and rested his forehead in his palm, his elbow on his thigh. "Who am I kidding? It's noble as fuck, is what it is."

"That's her problem?" Lennon nearly shrieked. "Violet told me it was something important but *this*? This is stupid. What if her meant-to-be guy never turns up?"

He shrugged.

"Huh. Well, anyway, Violet said--"

"No offense but I'm not really interested in anything Violet has to say right now. After everything, I'm pretty much Violet-ed out."

Their voice went stern. "She told me to tell you that Rue is stubborn and paranoid and that even if she drives you crazy, you shouldn't give up on her."

He dropped his hands into his lap and sighed. "I couldn't if I wanted to."

***

"The hell happened to you?" Rue asked, opening the bar's door to Brody.

"You remember that blonde I met a few weeks back?" he said, trying to scratch underneath the cast he now wore on his right arm.

"No." She locked the door and walked with him to the bar where she poured him a whiskey.

"Thanks." He held the glass up as if in cheers and gulped it down. "You remember. Long legs, belly shirt, butterfly tramp stamp?"

"Not ringing any bells, dude."

"I swear, if they aren't covered in tattoos and living in your apartment, you don't pay any attention."

"Get to the point, Brody."

"Okay, so we've been hooking up, right? And, she's, I mean," He made an expression somewhere between excited and confused. "Let's just say, Gen Z is a different breed."

"Dude, gross."

"Relax, she's twenty-five, not sixteen."

"Still, you're old enough to be her dad."

"I would've had to have her when I was *fifteen*."

"Like that doesn't happen *every day*."

"All right," he said waving his good hand around like he was trying to forget about the age gap. "*Anyway*, things got a little out of control last night."

"I *guess*."

"She got in this latex getup, started spanking me and shit. Put a ball gag in my mouth and then--"

"I *really* don't need the details, bro."

"Oh, right. Sorry. Point is, I can't exactly play one-handed. I'll be down for probably eight weeks."

"Well, fuck."

"I'm sorry, boss but," He gestured to his cast. "What are you gonna do?"

"No, it's fine. Obviously, your health comes first. We'll figure it out."

"I hate leaving you in the lurch like this, after how shitty things got when your boy was out sick and everything."

"Please stop calling Iman my boy."

"All right, touchy, touchy."

"We'll find someone to fill in, don't worry. Just take care of yourself."

"Problem!" Rue announced, bursting back into her apartment. Iman stood in the living room, guitar case in hand, on his way to go to work.

"What's wrong?"

"Brody let some dominatrix break his damn arm so he won't be able to play for two months. We're gonna have to hold auditions for a temporary replacement and that's gonna be a pain in the ass but you get a night off...or sixty, depending on how things go so, happy vacation."

"A domin-- Do I want to hear this story?"

"I doubt it."

"Okay. Listen, it's gonna be fine. Dylan plays. He can sub in for a while. I can text him right now."

"I don't think that's a good idea."

"What? Why?"

"I just...how is he? Behaving himself?"

"Behaving himself?"

"Yeah, like, does he seem okay to you? Is he calm or have you noticed anything weird? Violent outbursts, maybe?"

"No, he's fine. What are you talking about?"

"Nothing, just," She chewed on her lip. "I know he's your soulmate bestie but I still think you should be careful."

"Why?"

"Nothing," she huffed, not wanting to upset him twice in the same night. "It's fine. Text him. Just keep an eye on him."

"Uh, okay. Do you not like him or something?"

"No, I'm sure he's dope."

He crossed his arms and arched an eyebrow.

"It's nothing. I just think we should be, you know, careful around him, that's all."

"Why?"

She nervously tapped her foot, her pointed boots clicking on the hardwood. "Call it instinct."

Chapter 47

Dylan thought he'd have a hard time getting back into the swing of things, not having played in months. But, by the third song, it felt like old times, him on bass, Iman at the mic. They played some of the songs they had back in the day: Ain't No Rest For The Wicked, Everybody Talks, and The Plain White T's version of Will You Still Love Me Tomorrow. As his nerves faded, he was able to focus on the crowd, gauging their response. Thankfully, they seemed to like him or, at least, not notice that he wasn't the usual bass player. They danced and drank, some happily singing along, others bobbing their heads from the booths. Yes, just like old times.

Just as he got comfortable being back on stage, he was jolted from his calm by the sight of a woman; the most beautiful woman he'd ever seen. She had long, tight curls and brown eyes so big he could get lost in them. She wore a white tee shirt and black skirt under a waist apron and a crystal necklace that sparkled under the dim lights. As she passed by the stage, empty drink tray in hand, the scent of vanilla wafted to his nose. He couldn't take his eyes off her. She was too gorgeous.

He tried to concentrate, tried to stay focused on the music, but his eyes kept wandering to where she was. For the rest of the night, he'd find himself staring and force his eyes away only to look again. He thought he saw her steal a look at him a few times, too but he couldn't be sure. When the bar cleared of customers and the last song had been played, he fought to hold himself back. But, with nothing left to distract him, her scent proved too strong to ignore. It wasn't just the smell of her vanilla soap or lotion, it was *her*. Her pheromones. They called him, beckoned him like a siren to a cliff. She had him in a vice grip and she didn't even know it. She stood in front of the bar, wiping down the counter, back to the stage. His mouth nearly watered as he gawked at her smooth, strong legs, his body aching to be between them.

No longer able to control himself, he leaped from the stage, bounding toward her, his instincts taking over. From behind, he grabbed her by the shoulders, smelling her hair.

"What the--" She whipped around, her breath hitching as she looked at him. Standing only about an inch taller than her at five-seven, their eyes locked, her pupils dilating. He gently cupped the back of her head and buried his face in her neck, taking a long whiff. He felt her relax against him as he wrapped his free arm around her waist. He heard her breath quicken, felt her skin warm, and her fingers trace up his back. She was aroused.

Rue burst through the swinging door, racing to snatch him by the back of the shirt and fling him to the stage where he crashed into the drum set. He ran back but she had planted herself between them, blocking him from the waitress. His eyes flashed yellow, a low growl in his throat. Rue's eyes went black, her fangs descending as she hissed.

"What the fuck?" Ophelia asked, shaking her head as if coming out of a dream.

"That was gonna be my question," Iman said, coming out from backstage where he'd been putting the amps away for the night.

Rue drew back her teeth and returned her pupils to normal. "Get your boy out of my bar before I get a newspaper and boop this fucker's nose for bad behavior."

Dylan seethed, his chest heaving as he struggled to calm down.

Iman separated them, standing between them with a hand on Dylan's chest. "A, what?"

She rolled her eyes. "He's a werewolf. That was a dog joke. Keep up."

"It's not what you think," Dylan defended.

"Really?" she mocked. "Because you were just sniffing my friend like a goddamn fire hydrant."

Iman blinked, looking to his friend. "You're a *what?*"

Dylan took a step back, crossing his arms as he regained his senses. "Oh, big deal. You're a *vampire.*"

"How do you know that?"

Rue smacked her lips. "He's got super strong canine senses. He can probably smell your blood breath a mile away."

"Ooh," Ophelia said. "*That's* why you told me to be careful around him."

CHAPTER 47

"Yeah, and of course, you didn't listen."

"Hey, I was just standing here."

"Standing like a goddess in a world not good enough for her," Dylan said, his lips turning up in a sexy half-smile.

Her cheeks warmed.

"All right, Casanova," Rue huffed. "Take it outside, along with your boner. Jesus fuck. No one needs to see that."

Ophelia gave the crotch of his jeans an approving glance.

Iman pushed him toward the door.

"Wait," he said, planting his feet. "I'm not what you think I am."

"You're *not* a werewolf?" he asked, keeping a hand firmly on the back of his neck.

"Well, I *am* but I'm not part of a pack. I don't kill people or eat their hearts or anything. I wasn't born like this." He looked to Rue for approval as she was obviously the alpha of the group. "Let me explain."

Iman, too looked at her, his eyes searching her features. Dylan could tell he wouldn't let him stay or release his grip on him unless she felt safe. *He must really love her*, he thought. *To choose her over his soulmate.*

"Fine," she said through gritted teeth. "But, if you attack my friend again, I'll put you down like you have rabies."

"I wasn't attacking her," he said, eyes falling on the waitress again. "I could never." He cleared his throat. "So, it was back in February…"

"Me and the guys were camped out in the van after a shitty gig upstate. The campground was empty except for us but there was a fire pit with a grill over it so we had a fire going and were eating our canned ravioli when we heard a weird noise coming from the woods. Like a growl. Malcolm got in the van because he thought it was a bear but Kenny's dumbass wanted to investigate. He disappeared in the trees and started screaming so me and Anton went to help him but by the time we got there, he was gone. All we saw were these glowing, yellow eyes. They shined like a cat's in the dark. We thought Malcolm had to be right about it being a bear, up on its hind legs because it was tall. At least six feet. But when it got closer, we could see that thing was no bear.

"It was a guy just real hairy with claws and a mouth full of pointy teeth. I thought I was tripping, like our stash was spiked with angel dust or something. But, we both saw it. That thing was *feral*. So, we hauled ass to the van and started screaming for Kenny. It was *maybe* thirty seconds and something crashed into the roof. We looked out the window and didn't see anything so Anton went out there. He came back in *shook*, locked the door, and said we had to go *now*. Kenny was dead.

"He didn't have to tell me twice. I climbed up to the front seat but by the time I got the keys out of my pocket, the sliding door was *ripped off* and Anton's head was torn right off his body. Malcolm was screaming at me like, 'Go! Get us the fuck out of here!' So I put the key in the ignition but," He paused, hugging his arms. "It got quiet."

Iman rubbed his friend's shoulder, his eyes glossing.

"I looked back and Malcolm's chest was in *ribbons* and the monster was in the van with me. I saw it stick its hand *in* him and take out his heart. It bit into it like a fucking apple. I knew I wasn't getting out of there alive unless I did something so I got an emergency flare from the glove compartment. I must've made a noise because it looked up at me and *pounced*.

"It yanked me to the back, dragged me through my friends' blood, and bit down on my shoulder so hard, I swear I heard bone crack. It took out chunks of flesh like I was a goddamn chicken leg."

"Jesus Christ," Ophelia whispered.

"While it was distracted *eating me*, I got the flare lit and shoved it in the fucker's gut."

"You killed it?" Rue asked.

"No. It ran and I got the hell out of there. Ditched the van because how could I explain that? By the time I hitched a ride to the clinic, I was healed. Now, I'm not the brightest bulb but it doesn't take a genius to figure out what had just happened to me. So, I did some research, figured out how to handle this," His eyes scanned Ophelia. "For the most part."

Rue didn't look convinced. "And, the full moon?"

"I go back to the woods."

"To eat campers?"

He looked her in the eye, jaw clenched. "To find the piece of shit that did this to me and rip him the fuck apart."

"Hot," Ophelia said. Iman and Rue glared at her. "Did I say that out loud?"

Dylan winked at her and turned his attention back to Iman. "So, you're a vampire now. How'd that happen?"

He cocked his head in Rue's direction.

"You did this to him?"

Rue crossed her arms. "Well, I wasn't about to let him *die*, was I?"

He raised an eyebrow.

Iman explained. "A witch electrocuted me with a TV."

"Damn. Sounds painful."

"Like fire through the veins."

"Ouch."

"Yeah."

"So, are we cool, or…"

Rue squinted, pursing her lips. "I guess I won't kill you *for now* seeing as Iman would be super upset and I *suppose* you can keep playing with the band until Brody comes back *but* if I catch you doing anything remotely murdery, we're gonna have an Old Yeller situation, do you understand?"

He nodded, trying not to laugh at the reference.

"Fine. Now, get out of here before I change my mind."

"Come on," Iman said, clapping him on the back. "Let's get you some dinner."

"All right. And, you can tell me all about the witch thing."

"It's a long story. You sure you want to hear it?"

"So bad."

They chuckled and left, Rue locking up behind them.

"You hear that?"

"Yeah," Ophelia said, sitting on a stool.

"*Werewolf*. So, keep your distance."

"He didn't seem that bad to me."

"Sure, right *now*. But, I'm telling you, when the moon is full, they are wild fucking animals. They can rip their own mother's throat out and not remember doing it."

"Shit."

"Trust me, I know you think he's cute but it is *not* worth the risk."

"Okay, I hear you."

"Do you?"

"Girl, yes. I just got out of a thing with a monster. No offense."

"None taken."

"Believe me, I'm not trying to get into another 'will they kill me in my sleep or won't they' relationship."

Chapter 48

Stop, Ophelia thought, trying to get the memory of Dylan pouncing on her out of her head. She stared up at the ceiling, her new blanket softer and more cozy than the old one. Her room still smelled like smoke but she didn't mind. It was a welcome reminder of how powerful she was, even if she wasn't yet in full control.

Don't she told herself, but the memory lingered. His hands on her, his breath on her neck, his skin hot against hers. He *was* like a wild animal, all sex and violence. Seeing something he wanted and not hesitating for a second to take it. *No*. She couldn't let herself go there. She couldn't get caught up with some dude she just met, especially when he could be a bloodthirsty killer. On the other hand, pretty much everyone she knew was a monster. She herself was becoming a powerful witch, something even vampires were afraid of. Still, she was supposed to be avoiding temptation. *But,* fuck *he's tempting*.

She decided she wouldn't sleep with him, no matter how hot he was. *But, there's no harm in thinking about him while I handle my own business, right?* She slipped her right hand underneath the covers, closing her eyes and letting her mind drift back to the memory. *No harm at all.*

She woke up a little after noon, the air conditioning fanning her face and sending a chill up her exposed arm. She rubbed her eyes and picked up her phone, checking for messages. She had a comment on her post in a witch group. She'd almost forgotten about it but was excited to see a response.

It was from someone calling themselves SarahGood2005 and it read:

Witch here. I can help you with control IF you're the real deal. DM proof?

"Hmm." She got the spell book from its hiding place and looked through the pages, touching the necklace that hung around her neck to make sure it hadn't fallen off in her sleep. "What could I," She stopped, the perfect spell catching her eye. She memorized it, repeating it in her head until she was sure she had it down.

She set the phone up against her lamp and sat on the floor in front of it, putting a bunch of small objects in her lap: A tube of lipgloss, a pen, and a pocket knife she carried for protection. She reached over to hit record and took a calming breath.

"As my mind commands,

give me the power of movement.

Telekinesis stronger than my physical body,

so mote it be."

One by one, she floated the objects, her hands remaining on the floor. She concentrated, imagining each one drifting in different directions. However, instead of slowly drifting, they shot off, hurdling away. The lipgloss smashed against the wall. The pocket knife flew into the closet and the pen embedded itself into the door behind her. She dropped her head in defeat then looked up at the camera. "You see my problem?"

She stopped recording and uploaded the video, hoping against hope that this Sarah could help her and wasn't just another wannabe. She sat on her bed, hugging her pillow. "Fingers crossed."

The phone chimed with a message. It was the witch.

Finally! I was beginning to think I was the only legit witch left. I can absolutely help you out. Meet up?

Yes, thank you! She wrote back. *I have some time today. Just name a time and place.*

Her heart sank as she read the next text, recognizing the address right away. "Oh, fuck me."

Chapter 49

"I don't enjoy hurting you," Booth said, wiping his blade on a handkerchief. The latest witch in his cage sat against the bars, her black hair matted with blood and her white crop top stained crimson. "I want you to know that. I'm actually a very gentle man, usually. Well reformed of my warrior ways. I hadn't bloodied my hands in over two hundred years. I *buy* my food, you see. But, you witches," He tsked. "You've pushed me. I've been moved passed run of the mill desperation and squarely into the tranquility of blind revenge. Your sisters," He gestured to the pile of bodies opposite it her, the stench of which had begun to attract flies. "They either could not or would not give me what I needed. I should feel something for what I did to them. Guilt. Shame. Remorse. But, I feel nothing. It seems I am once again the man I was before. Before I knew what it was to be loved. All I feel now is a cold rage. A determination rooted in anger. I don't *enjoy* hurting you, but I can't say in honesty that I mind."

"Please," she whimpered. "I would tell you if I knew. I swear."

He sighed, putting the knife in his jacket pocket and looking down at her, feigned pity in his expression. "I believe you."

Relief and a spark of hope glinted in her eyes as he unlocked the cell. He extended a hand and she took it, using his arm to pull herself up to standing. "I hope you find what you're looking for."

He clutched the back of her head, leaning it to the left, his irises going dark. "Believe me when I tell you, you do not."

She screamed as he bit down, emptying her veins of what remained after twelve hours of torture. When he finished, he flung her body onto the pile and wiped his mouth on the handkerchief. As he lumbered up the steps, he lamented to himself, "This is getting exhausting."

Chapter 50

Ophelia stood in the shadow of the tree line, her stomach doing somersaults. The two-story house, or what was left of it, had been demolished. Now, in its place was a construction site. Lumber in organized piles sat around a tarp covering the basement. A dumpster and three porta potties lined the right side of the driveway and at the back of the yard, almost to the woods sat an old RV. That's where the witch, whose real name was Adia, had wanted to meet. Was it a trap? Did she know she had been there? That it was her that told the vampires where and what Marley was? And, who was she to Marley? Had she been there that night? Rue had been sure she and the others had killed all the witches there but they obviously hadn't. Who was Adia and why did she want to meet here?

Maybe I should just go, Ophelia thought, her nerves and common sense urging her to take off. *I shouldn't be here.* But, as risky as talking to this girl was, what choice did she have? She was a real witch with real skills and Ophelia *needed* to learn to control her magic. This girl was her only lead. She blew out a deep breath and walked carefully into the yard and toward the RV. *Guess I'm rolling the dice.*

Before she could knock on the red and blue striped door, it flew open, a girl in cutoffs and a baby pink lace-up tank corset top smiling like she was greeting her best friend.

"Ophelia?" she asked, hopping a little.

"Yeah." Her stomach hit the floor. It was her, the young girl from that night. She *had* been there. *Shit.* "Adia?"

"Yes! Hi! Come in!"

She joined her inside, her heart pounding so loud in her ears, she thought the girl might hear it. *Be cool.* "Nice RV."

"Thanks! Nineteen eighty-nine Winnebago Itasca Spirit." She waved her hands around like a game show host. "Bed up there, bathroom over there, little kitchen here, and," She sat at a tiny booth against a window and pointed across the table for her to join her. "Seating for two."

She sat. "Cool."

"I can't tell you how happy I am to find another witch. I've been looking for *weeks*. I'll be texting with someone, sure I've found my people, and then BAM! Ghosted."

"Yeah, I thought I found a group but turns out they were more into the aesthetic than doing real magic."

"Oh, yeah," she said, rolling her eyes. "Those chicks are everywhere lately."

"Yeah." *I'm okay*, she told herself. *She doesn't know. She would've killed me by now if she did.* But, she had to be sure. "So, building a house?" She pointed out the window to the lumber in the yard.

The girl's face darkened. "Rebuilding. The old one burned down. Everything but the basement was trashed."

"Oh, I'm sorry. If you don't mind me asking, what happened?"

"Booze, according to the investigators. They were partying pretty hard before I left. They must've spilled something and knocked over a candle. I was in the woods doing my binding ritual and when I got back," Her eyes misted. "Everyone was gone. It must have been before the ritual was complete because the crows came."

"The crows?"

She nodded, brushing away a tear. "As far as the universe is concerned, the coven is dead which means I'm the only one left. They all died. My cousins, aunts, my mom." She sniffed back more tears. "My sister."

Ophelia forced down a lump in her throat. "Your sister?"

"Marley."

She almost threw up.

"I hated her a lot of the time but she was still my family, you know?"

"I'm so sorry. Are you okay?"

She wiped her cheeks and offered a small smile. "I'm okay. My mom had this RV in storage so I'm living in it while construction's going on. Insurance covered everything plus I'm the sole living benefactor of a *lot* of life insurance policies which means I can grieve without any other real stress. I miss them but they take care of me, even now."

She felt her muscles relax a bit. *She thinks it was an accident. Thank God.*

"Enough depressing stuff. What spells do you need help with?"

"Oh," She cleared her throat. "Um, almost all of them?"

She giggled.

"First, I did the sana spell and it worked but the potion or whatever was thinner than I thought it would be. Like, basically liquid."

"What kind of aloe did you use?"

"Just aloe juice from the drug store."

"Mm. That'll work in a pinch but the thicker the 'potion or whatever' is," She flashed a teasing grin. "The stronger it'll be. It stays in place better so it has time to really work on deep wounds. Next time, try aloe gel straight from the plant."

"Oh, duh," she said, laughing at herself. "I should've known."

"What else?"

"The control thing. That's my biggest problem. I did the A-R-D-E-A-T spell and it blew up my whole bed."

"Ah, so you just want like, a little fire?"

She nodded.

"Yeah, that spell literally burns everything. What you want," She held up her palm. "Is ignise." A ball of flame erupted in her hand.

"Holy shit."

"Stinguo." The fire went out.

"*Holy shit!*"

"Try it."

"Okay." She held out her hand, cleared her mind, pictured the fireball forming, and said the word. "Ignise." A fireball burst in her palm. "Oh, my God! It worked! And, it doesn't even hurt. Just feels a little warm."

"That's because it came from you. It's part of you."

"What's that word you said to put it out? Stinguo?" It extinguished. "Ha! That was awesome!"

"Great job! You're a natural. I mean, right? You were born to magic?"

"Oh, no. I just started practicing."

CHAPTER 50

"What do you mean, *just*?"

"Like, a month ago?"

Adia blinked. "I'm sorry, did you say *a month ago*?"

"Um, yeah?"

"There's no way."

"Uh, I promise."

"No, I'm telling you. I wasn't born to it, either and it took me my whole life to get this good. And, I was raised in the most powerful coven in the tri-state area. For you to just *pick it up*," She shook her head. "No. You are a natural-born witch if I've ever seen one and I've seen plenty."

"Really?" She was shocked. No one in her family did magic, as far as she knew. Although, her grandmother had died before she was born and her mom had spent most of her time half-dead in one heroin stupor after another. If magic ran in the family, there'd be no way for her to know.

"Girl, *yes*. That's probably why your spells are too strong. It's because *you're* strong. That much raw power takes extra effort to rein in. It's always been there, dormant. Now, you've let it loose. Like a water balloon being broken. That magic just goes everywhere. What you want to do is try letting out a little at a time. My sister had this same problem during her rebellious-teen phase. Too many hormones, not enough discipline."

They both chuckled.

"The guys are back from lunch," Adia said, looking out the window.

Ophelia followed her gaze and saw a line of trucks pulling into the long drive.

"Can't do magic in front of the normals. They'll get spooked. Meet back here same time tomorrow? I'll help you with the, what was it? Levitating?"

"Yeah. I just kept going up. Scary."

She laughed again. "Too powerful for your own good."

She smiled.

"See you tomorrow?"

"Yes. I'll be here."

Powerful, she thought as she headed home, the backseat of the ride share smelling like old fast food. And, she always had been. All she'd had to do was tap into it, the power that she was born with.

For the next week, Ophelia spent her afternoons taking lessons from Adia, practicing spells alone in her room, and studying the book she'd gotten at the occult shop. She was exhausted at work from the lack of sleep but at least the brain fog was keeping her from lusting after Dylan. For the most part, anyway.

Saturday night, the bar was packed. The crowd loved the new bass player, one woman flashing him as the band played Heart Shaped Box. Ophelia felt a pang of jealousy when she saw Dylan blush at the sight. In trying to avoid looking at him, she saw Iman staring so hard at Rue, she thought he might burst a blood vessel.

Rue poured drinks, pretending not to notice but Ophelia knew she did by how tight her lips were pressed together. *The drama on this bitch*, she thought. She weaved through the crowd to the bar where she set her tray down.

"Two shots of whiskey and two beers for table three," she told Rue. "And a shot of vitamin D for you."

She got glasses and a bottle and started pouring the whiskey. "I can't actually give you a face right now because I'm busy but *side eye*."

"I know you see him looking at you."

She put two bottles of beer on the tray and popped them open. "He's always fucking looking at me. I told him we can't be together but he just keeps staring. I don't think he even knows he's doing it half the time."

"Is it hard to clean?"

"Is what hard to clean?"

"The cobwebs off your kitty."

"Bitch," Rue leaned on the counter, her chin to her chest. "I swear to fucking Christ."

"Fuck the boy," she said, her voice just above a whisper. She picked up the tray and stifled a laugh. "Before you get dust bunnies."

As she walked away, Rue called after her, "I'll have you know, my kitty's pristine." A man at the bar choked on his drink. She glared at him. "Mind your business."

Chapter 51

As the sun rose, Rue wrapped her naked body in the flannel she found draped over the arm of the couch. She put its collar to her nose, breathing in Iman's woodsy scent. She held it closed, pretending the cloth against her skin was his touch, wandering to his bedroom door.

He'd left it open. Like an invitation, perhaps. She watched him sleep, his arms above his head on the pillow. His chest rose and fell, the wings of his Faravahar tattoo resting over his umber nipples. His blanket had been kicked off and as her eyes drifted to the bulge in his boxer briefs, she felt herself get wet.

Bitch, what are you doing? She thought, shaking her head. *Get your dumb ass to bed.* She turned but before she could take a step, Iman had sprung out of bed and sped to block her path.

"Don't go."

Her cheeks flushed. "I'm sorry. I was just--"

"I know what you were doing. Watching me sleep, trying to keep from coming in. I've heard you, more than once."

"I...I'm..." She didn't have words. What could she say? There was no denying what she'd done.

"I've done it, too."

She blinked up at him. "What?"

"I've stood outside your door, listened to you breathe. Listened to your heartbeat. Touched the wall between our rooms and pretend you could feel me." He moved closer. "Touched myself while I listened to you come."

Warmth spread through her abdomen, her pussy now so drenched she thought she might soon be standing in a puddle.

CHAPTER 51

He ran a finger over the collar of the flannel, sending chills up her spine. "This mine?"

She felt her grip on the shirt loosening, unable to stop the words from coming out of her mouth. "You want it back?"

They locked eyes, her resolve fading faster than cheap hair dye. He leaned down, so close their noses were almost touching. "Tell me to stop and I'll stop."

Slowly, he brushed his full lips against hers, threading his fingers through the hair just above the nape of her neck. Her body relented, her hands letting go of the flannel entirely and rising to rest on his shoulders. The shirt fell open, and as he deepened the kiss, he lifted her with his free hand, her legs wrapping around his waist.

He carried her to the bed, lying on top of her, the thin fabric of his boxer briefs the only thing separating them. She felt him stiffen and rubbed herself against him, soaking through the cotton. Her pussy throbbed, desperate to let him in. As they made out, he slipped two fingers over her clit, between her lips, and inside. She moaned into his mouth, touching his cheek, every part of her tingling.

He kissed her neck and up to her ear, his breath hot on her skin, and whispered, "Should I keep going?"

She clenched around his fingers, her hips rocking involuntarily. His hair on her cheek sent shivers through her body, her legs spreading more for him. Her clit swelled as he massaged it, an orgasm already imminent.

"Are you ready for me?"

Her eyes flew open, all of her anxiety flooding back. "Stop."

He froze. "Stop?"

"Yeah, stop."

He pushed himself up onto his knees and slid off the bed to stand. She got up, covering herself with the flannel.

"I'm sorry," she said, walking to the door. "I shouldn't have let that happen."

He followed her, again blocking her path. "Tell me you don't love me."

"Iman,"

"Tell me. Tell me right now that you don't love me and that we're just friends and that's all you want us to be. Tell me and I'll drop it. I'll move out. Maybe crash at Dylan's. I'll give you some space and we can both move on."

His words stung. "Iman, please, just let me go to bed."

"*Tell me.*"

She bit her lip, her body trembling, her voice quiet. "I can't."

He stepped closer, his voice softening, too. "Why not?"

Tears pooled but she refused to let them fall. "Because I don't want to lie to you." She gently pushed passed him and went to her room, closing and locking the door.

He followed, balling a fist and pressing it and his forehead to the door but not knocking. He listened to her on the other side, getting into bed, adjusting her covers, and flicking her lighter. He sat on the floor, back against the door, and after a few seconds, he smelled the smoke from Rue's joint. Soon, he heard her muffled sobs and he, too, began to cry.

Chapter 52

"Hey!" Adia said, hopping out of the RV.

"Hey," Ophelia replied, bouncing from one foot to the other. "The construction guys gone for the day?"

"Yeah, apparently they've adopted a DWPF policy."

"A what?"

She chuckled. "Don't work past five."

"Oh," She laughed. "Well, good. Can't risk anyone seeing."

"Okay, enough with the secrecy. What was so important you wanted to show me right this second?"

She grabbed her hand and pulled her a few feet away from the RV, a goofy smile plastered on her face. "I've been practicing, like you said." She closed her eyes, her arm stretched in front of her.

"What are you--" She stopped, frozen, the sound of metal screeching getting her attention.

The RV jostled, then lifted, floating a few feet off the ground.

She whispered, "*Oh, my God.*"

It lowered slowly to its spot in the yard, squeaking as it settled.

"Are you kidding me?!"

"Right?!" Ophelia grinned, dropping her arm.

"Girl, get in here!" She led her inside, all but shoving her into the booth. "That was unbelievable!"

"I know! I don't need the words anymore. I can just *make shit move*."

"You're already as good as me! Better, even."

"I wouldn't go that far."

"I would. Here," She reached into a small cabinet next to the mini fridge and took out a huge, leather-bound book, setting it on the table and sitting across from her. "You should study this."

"What is it?" She ran her fingertips over the raised symbol on the cover, its three swirls strangely familiar.

"The symbol or the book?"

"Both."

"The symbol is the triskele. It represents the three realms: Earth, Sea, and Sky. Also, the triple goddess: The Maiden, Mother, and Crone. The spirals portray the generative power of the womb. The *book* is my family's grimoire." She opened it, pointing to the first page. "These are the names of my ancestors going back to Sarah Good who was the first to write in it. Then, her daughter, Dorcas, and so on and so on until we get to me." She pointed at her own name near the bottom of the page.

"You," She swallowed. "You want me to read this? Are you sure? Isn't it like, sacred?"

"Sacred to the coven." She tucked her dark, wavy hair behind her ears. "I'm hoping *we* can be a coven."

Her eyes lit up. "Really?"

"Well, yeah. I mean, I know we're only two and that's not a *coven* coven but," Her eyes glossed. "I've been kind of lost, if I'm being honest. But, hanging out with you, doing magic, I feel...not as alone."

She pat her hand and nodded. "I totally get it. Of course, we can be a coven. I'll start reading this as soon as I get home."

The two smiled, bonded in magic and a shared yearning to belong. For the moment, they were content, their friendship cemented.

CHAPTER 52

Ophelia got back to the loft with only a few minutes to spare before she had to clock in for work. She stashed the grimoire in her closet and grabbed her waist apron, checking to make sure it was empty of last night's tips.

"Hey," she heard from behind. She spun around, her heart leaping to her throat, Violet's slender frame standing in the doorway.

"H--Hey. You're back."

"Just for a few minutes. Needed to pack the rest of my stuff. Kenton bought an apartment on West seventy-second so…"

"You're moving out? For good?"

"Feels like the right thing to do."

She realized she was clutching her apron to her chest and as much as she didn't want to appear frightened, she couldn't relax her arms.

"Rue's gonna let you stay as long as you want. The bar makes enough money, she doesn't need to charge rent." She laughed under her breath. "She said, 'Tell Ophelia the place is hers as long as she stops hassling me about you know who.' Keep an eye on her for me, will you? She's not exactly acting in her own best interest with this whole depriving-herself-of-dick thing."

She nodded.

Violet rubbed her arm, something Ophelia had seen her do in the past when she was nervous. "You know how sorry I am, right? About everything."

"I know. I'm not *mad*. It was the spell."

"I don't mean just that stuff. That's bad enough but I mean all of it. Keeping you and Iman here like a fucking harem, taking so much blood you'd be sick, making you feel weird about eating. None of that was okay. You deserve better than that. I had issues and I took my shit out on you. Used you. That was fucked up and I'm really sorry."

She dipped her head. "I don't know if I can forgive you."

"I expect you won't. *I* wouldn't. What I did, especially under Marley's spell was next-level shitty. I'm kind of a trash bag."

She snorted. "Can't disagree."

"For real, though. I want you to hear one thing before I go and I mean *really* hear it." She closed the space between them, resting her hands gently on her shoulders. "Just because I couldn't love you the way you needed me to *doesn't* mean you don't deserve to be loved. You're smart, and kind, and beautiful as fuck. Anyone would be lucky to have a second of your attention. Don't settle for someone that treats you like shit. Look at me."

She lifted her gaze, tears forming in her eyes.

"You deserve to be fucking worshiped."

"I'm ready," Lennon said, poking their head in.

"You're leaving?" Ophelia asked.

Violet stepped out. "I'll give you two a minute."

"Yeah," Lennon said, hovering in the doorway. "She has an extra room and you know how she gets when she doesn't eat."

"So, you're gonna keep being her meal delivery service? After everything she did?"

They pursed their lips, hugging their arms. "She's my best friend."

She watched as they walked down the hall, picking up a box near the front door. The two left, locking the door from the outside.

She sat on the end of her bed, tears trickling down her cheeks. *No*, she thought. *No blubbering. I still have Rue and Iman.* She wrapped her fingers around the crystal hanging from her neck. *And, now Adia. I have people.* But, as she got up and made her way to the living room, standing at the door on her way to work, she'd never felt more alone.

Chapter 53

Ophelia pulled herself together, waiting at the bar for Rue to unlock the door for customers. The band was setting up and her boss was somewhere in the back dealing with a distributor and as the minutes ticked down to opening, she hoped she could keep from losing it until after her shift.

Dylan hopped down from the stage and stood in front of her, his head slightly tilted as he studied her face. "What's wrong?"

"Hmm? Nothing, I'm fine."

He crinkled his nose. "You're upset."

"My roommate moved out. Both of them, actually. It's fine. If Violet didn't leave, I was going to. It's no big deal."

"You sure? You sound…lonely."

"Maybe. A little."

He got close, sniffing the air around her. "I know what you need." He dashed off, disappearing behind the swinging door.

A few seconds later, she heard Lou yelling, "Get out of my kitchen! Don't touch that! I said GET OUT!"

"Sorry, geez," Dylan said, reappearing holding a bowl. He placed it on the bar in front of her, handing her a spoon.

"What's this?" she asked.

"A hastily made ice-cream sundae. Vanilla ice cream, hot fudge, nuts, and an ungodly amount of whipped cream."

Her chest warmed. "You made me this?"

"You need a dopamine boost. Booze would do the trick but that's a slippery slope. Sugar's safer." He winked. "And, it tastes better."

"Thank you."

"You're welcome. I better get back up there before Iman blows a fuse. He's extra on edge today. Vamps and their tempers, I guess."

"Right. Well, have a good show."

"I always do." He went back to the stage, picking up his bass.

Was he just nice to me for no reason? She wondered, taking a bite of the messy sundae. *Could he be an actual nice guy?*

Rue burst through the door, pointing to the bowl. "I know that was like, a gift or whatever, so I won't make you pay for it but you have about thirty seconds to get it eaten before I unlock that door.

She nodded, shoveling ice cream and toppings into her mouth as fast as she could.

"And, you," She turned her attention to Dylan. "I'm watching you."

As she stomped toward the door, Dylan nudged Iman's arm. "You two are touchy today. Something in the water?"

"We're fine," he all but growled.

He threw his hands up, backing away. "Okay."

"Let's do this."

"There aren't even people in here, yet."

"She's letting them in right now."

"Dude, are you okay?"

"ONE, TWO, THREE, FOUR!" The drummer jumped at the command and kicked things off, pounding out the intro to Down With The Sickness.

As Dylan sang backup, he and Ophelia exchanged confused looks. She shrugged and he subtly shook his head.

"Clean that shit up," Rue hissed, walking around to behind the bar as a crowd formed in front of the stage.

Ophelia picked up the bowl. "Girl, what's with you two?"

"What do you mean?"

"I know vampire emotions are heightened but you're acting crazy."

"*You're* acting crazy."

"Are you high?"

"I wish."

"Did you have a fight or something?"

"Drop it."

"Rue,"

"I said fucking drop it."

Thirteen empty vials littered Booth's kitchen island, their contents mixed in a bowl next to a map of the United States. He dumped the blood on the outer edge of the map and recited the spell: "Akhir mawqie lizawjati." He looked down at the notebook where he'd scribbled down what the witches had been hiding from him; what he'd needed for nearly two decades and had finally found: the word of power. "Meithrus."

The combined witches' blood smeared itself down the map, moving at a snail's pace. "Come on," he griped, his patience worn thin. Finally, it stopped, settling on a small town in New Jersey.

It was a construction site, a half-built frame with piles of building materials scattered around the yard. At the back was an old RV, something Booth might've driven to tour the country with his wife before the girls were born. He broke in, rummaging through the living quarters and finding nothing but clothes and food. Someone was living there and if it was the last thing he did, he would find them.

In the woods, Adia hid, a ball of energy readied in her palm in case the stranger discovered her location. After ten minutes of ransacking her tiny home, he got back in his car. She made a note of his license plate and watched him speed away, letting the energy dissipate. Who was he and what did he want? And, why did she hide instead of fight? She had been trained in self-defense, magical and otherwise by her mother. She wasn't afraid. She should have attacked. After all, he was invading her home. So, what about the man had kept her from defending her space? What made him different than any other criminal? There was something odd about him and she was determined to find out what it was.

Chapter 54

Rue did her best to keep busy, avoiding looking at the stage as much as possible. But, as the band played a cover of Bush's Mouth, she could feel Iman's eyes on her, burning through her like hot pokers. When she got a break in customers she accidentally let her eyes wander, meeting the singer's intense, cat-like stare. She was flooded with emotion, love and lust pumping through her veins like blood.

"Did you two have a fight or what?" Ophelia asked, snapping her out of her trance.

"Oh, thank fuck," she whispered, blowing out a relieved breath. She concentrated on her friend, answering her question. "Or what."

"You're acting crazy. You should just--"

"I am begging you not to finish that sentence. I can't afford the imagery."

"Yo, baby!" a man at the end of the bar called, waving his empty beer bottle in the air. "Can I get another?"

Ophelia's features scrunched.

Rue sighed, grabbing a bottle from behind the bar and popping off its top. She walked over and sat it in front of him.

"Thanks, sweetheart." He licked his lips as she walked back.

"Perv," Ophelia muttered, flicking two fingers toward him. His beer toppled over, spilling into his lap.

Rue's eyes saucered as did Ophelia's when she saw that she'd been caught.

"It's not what you think," she stammered.

Rue's attention snapped to Iman again as he played Only Love Can Hurt Like This, staring daggers at her as his husky voice delivered the first line. She listened, transfixed, her eyes wandering to the steel ball choker around his neck, down to his black Henley, and over the muscles in his arms. When the band was a little over two minutes in, she stepped out from behind the bar. She felt her legs carrying her but she couldn't stop. She was compelled, intent on heading to the stage, to rip his clothes off right there. To confess her love for him, consequences be damned. She took a step toward the stage but was shaken to her senses by Ophelia's pleading voice.

"It's not a big deal. It's not--"

She snatched her by the arm and dragged her through the kitchen, up the stairs, and into the loft, slamming the door behind them. "What in the ever-loving fuck?"

"Please, just listen. I can explain."

"I just have one question. Did you suddenly develop tele-fucking-kinesis or are you a goddamn *witch* now?"

She gulped. "Which answer gets me less dead?"

She pinched the bridge of her nose.

"Both, kind of. But, really the second one. I just did some research and then started doing spells, practicing, learning control. I'm not a monster, I promise. I just--"

"You're rambling."

"I'll stop if this is a stop-or-die situation but I really don't want to. You have no idea how bad I need this, Rue. Please."

She crossed her arms.

"Are...are you gonna kill me?"

"Jesus, no, I'm not gonna *kill you*, stupid. I'm just thinking," She tapped her foot.

She shrunk back. "About ways to torture me?"

"What? Bitch, for real. Get a grip."

"What? You can be *real* scary."

"Calm your tits, I'm not gonna hurt you."

"Oh." She glanced around awkwardly. "So...what are you thinking about?"

"I heard of a spell once, not sure if it's real or a myth. Super old. Supposedly, there's a way to find your soulmate."

"Uh, yeah, I read about it. Hold on." She took her phone from her pocket and swiped through her photos until she found it. "Yeah, it's right here."

"Awesome. Do it."

"You want me to do a spell?"

"Is it something you can do? Say it is because I'm about ten seconds away from hopping Iman like a fence in front of the whole bar."

"What does that have to do with--"

"Why do you think we're not together?"

"I thought you had some guy in the wings."

She shook her head.

Her brows lifted. "Ooh."

"If there's a dude out there taking his sweet ass time to show up and be the love of my life, I need to know that *now*."

"Uh, okay." She read over the spell. "I need a world map."

Rue disappeared in a blur, returning in seconds with a folded map.

"All right, then." She took it and spread it out on the dining table and glared at the screen, biting her lip.

"What's the problem?"

"It needs one more ingredient but..."

"But, what?"

"It's...frowned upon."

"Bitch, I am horned up with nowhere to go not to mention the absolute hell I'm putting Iman through. I don't care if it's frowned, spit, or shit upon, I will get that ingredient if I have to kill someone to do it."

"It's not hard to get, just--"

"Great. What is it?"

She swallowed. "Your blood."

"How much?" She elongated her fangs. "We talking a finger prick or you need me to open a vein?"

"You're not even thinking about it?"

"Did you not hear the desperation in my fucking voice? No, I don't need to think about it. How much?"

"Just a couple drops at the top center of the map."

"Not a problem." She slashed open the end of her finger and dribbled a few drops onto the paper. She sucked on the wound until it healed while Ophelia read from the screen.

"Haec mulier's destinatus amentis, innexa per totum tempus, revelare praesens locus."

The blood vibrated on the map like a cup of water left on a loudspeaker. In a hushed voice, Rue asked, "What's it doing?"

Ophelia shrugged.

After a moment, instead of slithering to a location on the map, it rose into the air, hovering over the table in front of them. "What the fu--" But, before Rue could finish her sentence, the floating liquid flew at her, smacking into her forehead. She wiped it off and glared at Ophelia. "No, seriously. What the fuck?"

"I don't know." She squinted at the picture on her phone. "It should've," She stopped. "Oh."

"Oh, what?"

"I'm sorry."

"About what?"

"I'm just the messenger."

She clenched her fist. "If you don't start explaining, *I'm* gonna have a message for *you*."

"It says, 'if the blood returns to the body from whence it came, the soul therein was born...complete'."

"Complete?"

"It's saying you have no other half. You're whole, all by yourself."

Her eyes widened. "No soulmate?"

She shook her head.

"Are you serious? Are you *sure*?"

"Yeah. Are you okay? Feeling sad or...homicidal?"

She burst out laughing.

"It's funny?"

"Funny, no. Dope as shit, yes."

"Um, huh?"

"Watch the bar." She raced out.

"Watch the," She ran after her. "Did you say, '*watch the bar*'?"

Downstairs, Iman's guitar rested on its stand while he gripped the mic, belting the chorus of Heart's Alone. Dylan nearly dropped his base when Rue burst in, yanking Iman from the stage, and dragging him away. Ophelia emerged from the kitchen a few seconds later, giving him a thumbs up to let him know everything was all right. He took the mic, casting the waitress a questioning stare.

She raised her eyebrows, dropping her chin a little.

He mouthed, *Oh* and snickered, the band playing the outro a little sooner than expected.

Upstairs, Rue threw Iman into the sofa so hard it scooted back on the floor a few inches. She locked the front door, kicking off her boots.

He thinned his lips, his brows furrowed. "Are we fighting or flirting?"

"Neither. Different verb." She began peeling her clothes off, starting with her leather bodice top. "Also starts with 'f'."

He sat up straight. "Have you been drinking?"

"No." She whipped off her studded belt and unbuttoned her jeans. She watched his Adam's apple bob as he swallowed, his knuckles going white as he gripped the arm of the couch. He was holding himself back and as she slid out of her pants, she heard the quietest of growls emitting from his throat.

He stood. "What about your soulmate?"

"Doesn't exist. Apparently, I have no ethereal connection to anyone."

He took a step toward her, arching an eyebrow. "Really?"

"Yeah. And this thing between us, anything could happen. No guarantee it'll work out. It's a roll of the dice but I'm stark raving cocoa puffs in love with you. Always have been, even when I wouldn't admit it to myself. So, I'm throwing my kitty at you. You gonna catch it or..."

He scooped her up, sitting her on the kitchen island's concrete countertop. He held her face as his hungry lips crashed into hers, their tongues entangling as she pulled his shirt up. He flung it off and kissed her again, pulling off his boots, dropping his pants and boxer briefs, and stepping out of them. He pulled her to him, getting her ass half off the counter, his cock pressed against her slick pussy.

He stopped, looking her in the eyes. "Are you sure?"

She dragged her chrome-painted nails through the stubble on his face, her free arm slung over his shoulders. "You love me, right?"

"More than I've ever loved anything."

"So, get me to that couch, and let me give it to you like a goddamn present."

The right corner of his lips turned up in a sexy half grin. "Yes, ma'am." He carried her to the sofa, sitting down and positioning her on top of him. His fingers combed up the back of her hair, holding her close as they sank into a deep kiss.

She wrapped her fingers around his cock, stroking it as she kissed his neck, causing his eyes to roll back. She slid herself up his shaft then tucked his tip into her, lowering herself down, both of them gasping, years of unrequited emotions finally being expressed as she took all of him into her.

She grabbed the back of the couch for leverage, grinding against him, her hips' back-and-forth movements being dictated by his pelvic thrusts. She rode him like a horse, his fingertips sinking into her thighs, their chests pressed together so firmly that they could feel each other's heartbeats.

Her walls clenched around him, pulsing as she came, her body trembling in pleasure. As the waves of ecstasy subsided, she lifted her hips, kissing down his body until her knees hit the floor.

He gasped again as she went down on him, his hands in her hair, his face toward the ceiling. He grunted as he came, filling her mouth with his bitter fluid.

She stood, swallowing and wiping the corners of her mouth.

"Where are you going?" he asked, sitting forward and running his hands up her legs.

"I was gonna get you a blood bag. This is the first time you've had sex since turning. Aren't you hungry?"

He looked up at her, a mischievous twinkle in his eye. "Not for food." He grabbed her ass, pulling her closer.

"Oh," she said, raising a brow.

He pulled her down onto the sofa, laying her back and spreading her legs in front of him. His mouth went to work. She was a ripe plum and he was a man starved.

CHAPTER 54

She moaned as her pussy pulsated, her arms over her head, draped over the arm of the couch, her body stretched and her back arched. His hands skimmed up her body, over her breasts, and back down, resting on her hips.

With vampire speed, he stood, hoisted her up, and carried her back to the island. He wrapped his arms around her, plunging himself into her throbbing, wet pussy. She held onto him, quiet moans escaping her lips with every powerful thrust.

She shivered with another orgasm, her skin prickling.

"Already?" he asked, his voice husky in her ear.

She smiled. "Maybe if you keep going, it'll happen again."

He kissed her tenderly, his cock pulsing inside her. "Challenge accepted."

He sped her to her bedroom, sitting her up against her headboard. Up on his hands, he slowed his movements, pulling almost all the way out of her before diving back in, holding himself there for a moment, then repeating the motion. He nuzzled her neck, his breath on her skin making her heart flutter. Soon, he quickened his pace, panting in her ear, contented groans and heavy sighs from both of them as he grew even harder.

He lifted his head to look at her, his irises going black and his fangs protruding. She held his gaze, tilting her head. She'd never been bitten but in that moment, she wanted nothing more. He leaned in, opened his mouth wide on her neck, and bit down.

His tongue glided over her skin as he began to suck, his mouth filling with his lover's blood. Her body quaked, her final climax stronger than anything she'd ever felt. She was nearly convulsing, pure rapture sparking through every inch of her as she gushed, his venom like molly mixed with cocaine. He too came, his semen surging into her with the force of a burst pipe. She went limp, her heart slowing and her eyelids fluttering closed.

"Oh, my God," Iman breathed, pulling away, blood trickling down his chin. "Rue? Rue!"

"Hmm?" She couldn't open her eyes. She was floating on a cloud of ecstasy and exhaustion.

"Hey, are you okay?" He lightly tapped her cheek. "Baby, can you hear me?"

She tried to answer him but words wouldn't come. She was drifting, unable to move. She couldn't feel anything but the complete contentment of being with the man she loved. Finally.

"*Shit.*" He sprung up, super-speeding to the kitchen and grabbing two bags of blood from the fridge. He raced back, tearing one of the bags open on his way. He held it to her lips, urging her to drink. She did. Sighing with relief, the tears that had gathered in his eyes fell. She finished the bag and by the time he'd gotten the second one to her her lips, her eyes had opened. "I'm so sorry," he said, wiping the blood from his mouth and chin. "I didn't mean to."

"It's okay," she told him between sips. "I wanted you to."

"You did?"

She offered a weak smile, taking the bag out of his hands and sitting up straight. "I think," She thought of Ben and the night they'd spent together, hoping that the last thing he'd remembered was the bliss that came from her bite. "I needed to know how it felt."

He held her face, his palms on her cheeks, his long fingers in her hair. "I'll never hurt you again."

She touched his arm. "I believe you."

He kissed her softly, on the lips then on the cheek. "I love you."

"I love you, too."

"I called you 'baby'," he said as if just realizing it.

"You did."

"Is that okay or is it...infantilizing?"

She chuckled. "It's fine."

"You sure?"

"Yeah." She brushed a few stray curls out of his eyes. "I kind of like it."

Chapter 55

Booth returned home, his suspicions all but confirmed by the state of the property he'd just visited. He sat in the car, seething, his hatred sinking to depths he didn't think possible. He screamed, slamming his hands into the steering wheel until it bent. He thought that he should cry. That it was the normal response to what he'd discovered. But, he couldn't. He wouldn't. Not until he had his revenge.

He went inside, marching like a soldier on a mission to the basement where more than a dozen witches' corpses lay rotting. Two by two he lugged them to the outdoor incinerator, burning them to ash, the smell of their charred flesh his only comfort. When all were disposed of, he got to work destroying all evidence of their time there, using a vinegar solution to clean the floor and bars of the cell and spraying insect killer to rid the basement of flies. He put the map away and washed the bowl he'd used for the spell, the witches' blood going down the drain the last thing reminding him of their presence. He showered, put on fresh clothes, and made a cup of tea, his usual calm demeanor restored.

He picked up his phone and called his oldest daughter who, despite their tendency to butt heads, always soothed him, her kind nature so much like her mother's, even if it was at times overshadowed by the excessively strong sense of justice she inherited from him. As she answered, her voice weak, he noticed that the sun had come up.

"I'm sorry, darling. Did I wake you?"

"No," she said. "But, it's early. Why are you up?"

"There's something that requires discussion. Call your sister. Come to the house."

"Are you okay?"

The tension in his jaw lessened, the concern in her tone touching. "I'm fine. Just gather your sister and come home. We need to have a family meeting."

Rue and Violet sat across each other at the kitchen island while Booth stood at the end, the basement door behind him.

Violet waved her hand in front of her nose. "Why does it smell like poison in here?"

"Just a little pest problem in the basement," her father told her. "I took care of it." He turned his attention to Rue. "Are you sure you're all right? You look unwell."

"I'm just tired," she lied. "I should've been in bed two hours ago."

"Tired," Violet said, a knowing twinkle in her eye. "Is that what we're calling it these days?"

"Fine, I let Iman bite me while we were banging and he got carried away. Happy?"

"Yes!" She raised her fists in the air as if in victory. "Finally!"

Booth cringed. "Must we speak of this?"

Rue crossed her arms. "Not if I can avoid it but you know how she is."

"Come on!" Violet rested her fists on the counter. "You're together now, right? Please tell me you're together."

"Yes, we're together."

"Woo hoo!"

"All right, girls. As much as I love hearing about my daughter's sex lives and, believe me, it's my favorite topic of conversation, there are much more pressing concerns."

Violet laughed. "Never too early to bust out the sarcasm, huh, Dad?"

"It's late for me, actually. I've been up all night. Before I begin, I must ask for your forgiveness. I've been keeping things from you. For years now, in fact."

They sat up straight, their full attention now on their father.

"This will be hard to hear, so prepare yourselves. It has to do with your mother."

CHAPTER 55

"I don't want to hear it," Violet snapped.

"But, you must."

"She fucking left us. Her kids and her husband. Her *soulmate*."

He rubbed his forehead. "Violet, your language."

"Fuck my language, Dad. And, fuck her. I don't want to hear *anything* about that bitch."

His eyes darkened, the look on his face making her freeze. "I realize you're upset and you have every right but if you speak of my wife like that again, I will slap you so hard, your unborn children will feel it."

The women stared at him, neither ever having heard him so coldly angry. He'd never threatened either of them. Never raised a hand to them. Never even raised his voice. But, in that moment they believed he meant what he said.

Rue broke the silence, her voice quiet, quivering under the weight of her question. "Is she back?"

Violet swallowed, folding her hands in her lap.

Rue looked her father in the eye. "Did she come back?"

"No, darling, I'm sorry." He touched her cheek, his stern look going soft. "I don't think she'll ever come back."

She sniffed back tears, her fingertips grazing the necklace she still wore. "Why not?"

He placed his hands on the island's top, leaning on it for support, exhaustion and despair threatening to overtake him. "I don't believe she can."

Chapter 56

Ophelia woke with a start, having crashed on the couch after getting the bar closed, a job she hoped she'd never have to do again. She'd been exhausted, stressed to her limit by drunks trying to tussle, people ordering complicated cocktails she didn't know how to make, and kicking people out at closing that did *not* want to go. She didn't know how Rue did it night after night.

The loft had never been this quiet, her thoughts the only thing she could hear. She looked at the time, grimacing at how early in the morning it was. She'd need more sleep if she was going to make it through another night of work in twelve hours' time. She went to her room, intending on going to bed. But, the book in the closet called to her, Adia's family grimoire full of new and interesting spells for her to try. "Just for a few minutes," she said, retrieving the book, knowing full well she was lying to herself. She sat on her bed and flipped through the pages, lighting up as she skimmed. Even the names of the spells were intriguing: Summoning of Shadows, Tremblement De Terre, Ferventi Sanguis. There were instructions for making love potions, herbal remedies, and sleeping aids. There was even a spell to stop time.

Near the back of the book, several pages were stuck together. She tried to gently pry them apart but they weren't glued. They were sealed with magic. "A binding?" She went to her other book, sure she'd seen an unbinding spell when she'd been studying it a few days before. "Yes," she whispered, finding what she'd been searching for. She held her palm over the stuck pages and recited the words, "Per mea verbum, nulles amplius ligatus." She peeled the pages apart, now able to read what had been hidden. "Gotcha."

CHAPTER 56

"Your mother didn't leave because she was feeling overwhelmed by her life as the note she left would have us believe," Booth said, his daughters at the island watching him pace. She left to protect us."

"Bullshit," Violet muttered.

Rue shot her a look. "Would you shut the fuck up, please?"

He continued, "I searched for her for years, long after I told you I'd given up. When I ran out of leads, I went to Egypt. As you know, Zahara came from a long line of born vampires, their generations supposedly going back to Sekhmet, though I'm sure that's not entirely true. I'd hoped that she might keep contact with them, at least but they were of no help in finding her. They said if she'd gone, she had good reason. But, they did inform me of a war that's been quietly raging for centuries between some of the older vampires and a handful of covens. Your mother was part of a collective. A spy, so to speak. Her people in Edfu weren't sure what she was working on specifically but if she'd been doing her duty, she would have kept a record. So, I came home, rifled through her belongings. Eventually, I came across a bank statement for a safety deposit box, the account in her maiden name. When I'd gained access to it, I found this journal." He placed the book on the counter between them. "Inside are details of her exploits. She describes the witches she'd tracked. Covens that kidnapped, tortured, and killed vampires. Covens that she then slaughtered."

"Holy shit," the women said in unison.

"In the final few pages, she goes on to say she thinks she's being followed. I believe she left in the hopes that whoever was following her wouldn't find where she lived. To keep them from discovering *us*."

Rue mindlessly fidgeted with her necklace. "So, she was hunting down witches for *decades*? How did we not know about this?"

"Apparently, there's a hierarchy to these things."

"Okay, but that was years ago. Why has she stayed away this whole time?"

Booth held each of his daughters' hands in his, his chin dropping to his chest. "The witches that were following her," he said, his voice cracking. "I believe they killed her."

"What is it?" Kenton barked, wrapping himself in a Baroque pattern robe, its Italian silk cool on his skin. He opened the blinds for light as he marched through the West 72nd Street apartment, his annoyance at being woken in the day exacerbated by the harsh rays of the morning sun. "Bloody hell." He went to the door, the visitor on the other side beating on it like a drum. He called to them as he unlocked it, "This better be bloody well important!" He swung the door open, surprised to see Alexander standing in front of him.

"It is, old friend." He pat him on the shoulder and pushed his way in, not waiting for an invitation.

"Alexander!" His tone went from irritated to delighted. "What are you doing stateside? I thought you hated the colonies."

"This isn't a social call, I'm afraid. Have you got anything to drink? Scotch, preferably, though an Irish whiskey would do."

"Of course, have a seat." He gestured to the long, white sofa across the room and closed the door. Alexander sat as Kenton went to the liquor cart and poured two glasses of his favorite single malt. He handed his friend a glass and sat next to him, taking a sip of his drink.

Alexander gulped his drink down, his eyes bloodshot and cheeks flushed.

Kenton placed a comforting hand on his back, turning his body to face him. "Are you all right?"

"Not entirely, no."

His jaw clenched. "More hunters?"

He shook his head, holding his glass in his lap.

CHAPTER 56

"What, then?"

"It's Florin."

His eyes widened, his stomach dropping.

"He's returned."

Chapter 57

Ophelia read the once-forbidden pages three times, unable to process what she'd learned. Her heart was beating out of her chest, her mind racing. "*What the fuck?*" She put the book down, standing and pacing around her room, her stomach churning. "It can't be," she said, not really convincing herself. "It can't be, right?" She sat back down on her bed, picked up the grimoire, and read through the pages one more time.

Skye, of the Coven of Good, September 2004

Strigoi #29 was more difficult to capture than the others. It killed two of my sisters and left me with a gash so deep, it healed in a scar even with treatment. This one is strong. If any of them can survive the cure, it's #29.

First attempt:

#29 could detect the blackthorn, juniper, and nightshade in the pig's blood by smell even with onions added. It refuses to drink.

Second attempt:

#29 continues to refuse the cure.

October 2004

Third attempt:

#29 continues to starve itself. It no longer tries to escape. It appears sick. It will be dead within the month if it doesn't drink.

Fourth attempt:

#29 has lost consciousness. We strapped it to my bed and fed it the cure through a feeding tube. It had two seizures, thirty minutes apart but unlike the others, it didn't die. We'll run tests to see what makes this one different.

November 2004:

Blood work on #29 showed high levels of HGH which could potentially explain its strength. More analysis is needed. Also detected were increased levels of hCG. Further testing will be done asap.

Upon internal inspection of #29, it appears it is, in fact, pregnant. This shouldn't be possible. Vampires are made by bite; a transfer of the magic that made the first. A vampire pregnancy is unheard of. We'll monitor this new development closely.

December 2004:

#29 remains in what looks like a coma. We feed it the cure twice a day through the feeding tube. Research indicates that without human blood, vampires will die. The pig's blood shouldn't be keeping #29 alive but it still has a heartbeat, though barely. Before #29, we didn't know vampires had heartbeats. We'd never been able to monitor them closely. We aren't sure if this is common or a side effect of the pregnancy.

January 2004:

#29's pregnancy has become more active. We've monitored kicks by touch and sight. #29's seizures continue with every feeding.

February 2004:

No change.

March 2004:

No change.

April 2004:

#29 seems to be gaining strength. Color has returned to its face. We hoped it was a sign that the cure had worked but when electric stimuli were introduced, its fangs showed themselves.

May 14th, 2004:

#29 regained consciousness. It removed its feeding tube and broke free of its restraints. It slammed itself against the barrier spell, demanding to be freed. I told it we were trying to cure it, to make it human again. It laughed at me, claiming to have been born as it was. It said there was no cure and our attempts were killing its kind. I couldn't argue but pleaded with it to calm itself for the sake of its offspring. It yelled at me to keep away from its child. While I was distracted, my young daughter ran into the bedroom, through the barrier. I screamed for Marley to come back but the beast had her. It said it wouldn't hurt her if I let her go but vampires can't be trusted. I said, "#29, please," and it snapped at me, saying its name isn't #29, it's Zahara. As much of an interesting specimen as #29 is, my daughter's safety comes first. I said, "Confractus", breaking its neck. Before it could recover, I got an ax and chopped its head off.

I used the blade to open up its abdominal cavity and pulled the infant out. I spilled Holy Water on its leg to no reaction. It had no teeth, let alone fangs. I've run every test I can think of. The child appears human. The cure didn't work on the mother, but miraculously, it saved the child.

This is a major breakthrough. Sharing this information with the Howe and Wildes Covens is the right the to do. But, I won't. This record will be hidden. The child nor anyone outside of the Good Coven will know the true identity of the vampire's baby. From now on, she will only be known as my daughter, Adia.

Part 3
Ophelia

Chapter 58

Ophelia spent the day in a mild panic, alternating between disbelief and terror. She paced the living room, still in her work clothes from the night before, hours of thinking over what she'd read getting her no closer to knowing what to do with what she'd learned. Adia wasn't just the sister of the witch who had tried to kill her and her friends, she was also Rue and Violet's sister. Not only that, but her adoptive mother killed their mother, the woman Violet had spent her entire life hating for abandoning them. What would the vampires do if they found out? And, what would Adia do if she knew the truth about who she was?

"I have to tell them," she said to herself, leaning on the dining table. "Just...not yet."

A knock came on the door, the noise like a shock wave through the quiet of the apartment. She jumped, her heart skipping a beat. "Who is it?" she called as she shuffled to the door, her legs tired from hours of walking around the loft.

"It's Dylan," a voice from the other side of the door called back.

She froze, her heart pounding like a hammer. "One second!" She ran to the bathroom, checking herself out in the mirror and rinsing her mouth out with antiseptic mouthwash. She touched up her curls and swiped her lips with black cherry gloss. "What are doing, ho?" she whispered, giving her reflection a disapproving glare. "You're supposed to be staying away from him, not trying to look cute so he'll like you." She sighed, hurrying back to the front door, replaying Rue's warning in her mind, *I know you think he's cute but it is not worth the risk.*

She opened the door, her stomach fluttering as his piercing blue eyes stared into hers. For a moment, they just looked at one another, not saying a word, the air between them electric.

CHAPTER 58

"Sorry," He cleared his throat, holding out a dessert box. "I thought you might need another sugar boost so I picked up some baklava from a place on 9th."

She took the gift, warmed by the thoughtful gesture. "That's so nice, thank you. I love baklava."

"I know. I asked Iman. I hope that's not weird."

"You asked about me?"

"I did. He said you also like chocolate-covered almonds and shortbread but this seemed the fanciest."

"You trying to impress me?" she flirted.

He smiled, his laugh embarrassed but his body language confident. "Always."

"I'm supposed to be staying away from you."

"Because Iman's girl says so?"

She nodded. "She's protective."

His eyes twinkled as he teased, "What is she, your mother?"

"Closest thing I ever had to one."

"Really?" He leaned on the door frame, his brows knitting together. "The vampire with the anger issues?"

She laughed. "Sounds ridiculous but she looks out for me. Cares about me. Believe me, I know how messed up it sounds but," She shrugged. "She's family."

"Huh. Well, I wouldn't want to come between family. I should go."

Her stomach dropped. "Giving up already?"

"Never." He leaned in, pressing his lips against her cheek and taking a step back. "Just switching strategies."

"Sup, Fido?" Rue said, taking two bottles of tequila from a crate and placing them on a shelf behind the bar.

Dylan clenched his jaw as he sat on a stool. "I'm gonna ignore that insult."

"Probably wise."

He folded his hands on the counter, hoping to get through the conversation before she had to open the bar, giving her an excuse not to have it. "Since you're kind of the HBIC around here, I was hoping we could talk."

She continued working, never looking in his direction. "About what?"

He cleared his throat. "Ophelia."

"No," she said, still busy with unpacking bottles.

"No, what? To talking?"

"To dating her. Not that I would try to stop her if she wanted to get with you but I *could* hurt you a little. Take out a kneecap, hide your favorite chew toy."

"What is your problem?"

"Is that really a question?"

He held back a growl, not wanting to give her any more ammunition. "I know you think I'm--"

"I don't *think* anything. You're a werewolf, by choice or not. You came here wanting to plead your case, tell me your intentions are honorable, that you really like her."

"Yes."

"That you wouldn't hurt her."

"*Yes.*"

"Bullshit."

He fumed, gripping his hands so tight, he hurt himself. "I wouldn't--"

"I don't know if you're lying to me or yourself but we both know you have no control. Before you even met her, you pounced on her like a rabid squirrel. You were damn near humping her leg. What's gonna happen when you're alone with her? You get all horned up and she says 'no'. Can you honestly say you wouldn't--"

"*I wouldn't.*"

She sighed, leaning on the bar and looking him in the eye. "Listen, I don't think you're a bad guy. You actually seem very sweet and Iman has vouched for you a bunch of times. But, Ophelia has been through an ungodly amount of horrific shit and the last thing she needs is another monster getting in her pants and ruining her life."

His lips thinned and his cheeks went hot.

"No shade. I'm a monster, too, and not just because of the fangs."

CHAPTER 58

"What do you mean?"

"Do you need a drink? I need a drink." She got two shot glasses and filled them with whiskey. "Probably not the smartest thing since I'm running on four hours of sleep and had most of my blood drained last night but cheers, anyway." She clinked his glass and threw her shot back.

"You, what?"

"You gonna drink that?"

He glanced at the drink and then back at her. "You okay?"

"No but what else is new? I have work so no time for whining. For real, drink it or it's mine."

He pushed it toward her.

She gulped it down. "This morning, I found out my mom didn't just take off when I was kid, she was fucking murdered by witches with a hate-on for vamps and instead of dealing with it, I'm here because God forbid I take five minutes to process an emotion."

"Oh, I--," He cleared his throat again. "I'm sorry."

She shrugged, putting the glasses in the bus bin under the counter. "Yeah, I'm a dumpster fire on wheels and I'll probably take it out on some creep later. Kill them in an alley, justify it to myself so I can ignore the twinges of guilt. I'm not any better than you. I'm probably a lot worse." Again, she leaned on the counter, her eyes so focused on his, it was as if she were looking into his soul. He shifted in his seat, the intensity of her stare making him uncomfortable. "The difference between what I am and what you are is I know what I'm doing when I'm doing it. I have a choice. You don't. You're a slave to your wolf. It's not your fault and it sucks but I don't want my friend in the crosshairs when you can't rein yourself in. Monsters like us shouldn't get involved with humans. We will hurt them. Every time." She took a step back and crossed her arms. "That being said, she's a grown woman, and as much as I think everyone would be better off if they just did what I told them to, it's her decision. She can do whatever, or whoever she wants. But, if you're looking for my blessing, you won't get it."

That night, Dylan backed Iman while he sang a synth-free cover of Enjoy The Silence, Rue's words repeating in his mind. *A slave to your wolf.* Was she right? He *had* lost control the night they met and it was taking all his willpower not to let it happen again, her scent driving him crazy as she passed the stage, tray of beer bottles in hand. The only thing keeping him from losing it at her apartment earlier was the overpowering smell of mint and antiseptic. Now, though, the vanilla and pheromone combination had him so distracted, he almost forgot the lyrics he was meant to sing. He imagined dropping his bass, running to her, bending her over the bar, and taking her, hard and rough, pulling her hair with one hand, and sliding his other up her shirt.

Stop it, he thought. *Focus on the song.* He pulled his eyes away from her, looking over at Iman who stared at the bartender as he sang the chorus. He noticed her looking back at him, a sly smile on her lips. The gazes between the new lovers ignited resentment in him, flickering like the start of a fire that, left unchecked, would burn out of control. He wanted what they had and he wanted it with Ophelia.

I can do this, he thought. *Even if it's hard. She's worth it.*

Chapter 59

"Vocare umbra ad vitum," Ophelia chanted, eyes closed and palms up at her sides. She took a breath, trying to focus on the spell but her mind was preoccupied with what she'd read in the forbidden pages of Adia's grimoire. Standing in the witch's backyard, knowing what she knew had her on edge, to say the least. She had to tell her, right? And Rue and Violet, not to mention their dad. They deserved to know. Needed to know and *soon*. The longer she kept the truth to herself, the angrier they'd all be at her for hiding it. She just had to find the right time, the right way to fill them in. It would be a shock and if she wasn't delicate, she could end up on the wrong side of an angry vampire or worse, losing the only witch friend she had.

"Holy crap!" Adia said.

"What?"

"Open your eyes!"

Ophelia gasped, her heart leaping to her throat. From the trees surrounding the property, shadows rose concealing the once-bright morning sky in a black haze, giant, faceless creatures the shape of men blanketing everything they touched in a sea of darkness. "It worked," she whispered, astounded that even only half-concentrating she was able to pull it off. "Summoning of Shadows." The shapes began to move, walking in silence toward the treeline. "What are they doing?"

"Whatever you want them to."

In unison, the four creatures took hold of four trees. The earth shook as they yanked the trunks out of the ground, roots and all.

Adia's jaw dropped. "No freakin' way."

They set the displaced oaks gently on the forest floor and then stood upright as if awaiting orders. Ophelia beamed up at her creations, her anxiety about Adia's true parentage replaced by pride. She let her hands fall and gave the command, "Evanescet." The shadows dissipated, vanishing in the light of day.

"Seriously!" Adia nearly shouted, her eyes wild with excitement. "Who are you?"

"Huh?"

"It's driving me crazy. There's *no way* you're just some newbie witch that *happens* to be powerful as balls. That's not how it works."

She shrugged. "It is, though, apparently."

"No. It takes years, *decades* even to get that spell to work, and even then, the shadows can't touch things, let alone rip freakin' trees out of the ground. My mom couldn't even do that and she was a direct descendant of the most powerful Salem witch. You're *someone* and we have to figure out who."

"Why?"

"*Why?*"

She stared blankly.

Adia sighed. "Because different family lines are naturally better at certain things. Spellwork, nature magic, telekinesis, etc. If you knew which coven you're from, you could work more specifically and really live up to your potential which, from what I can tell, is unlimited."

"*Okay*, but I don't have anyone to ask."

"No family?"

"None I'm willing to speak to."

"Hmm. There's a spell but it's…a lot."

"What do you mean?"

"It requires a coven to perform it."

"I thought *we* were a coven?"

"Technically no. Just a 'working couple'. For the Hidden History spell, we need at least three but four's better. Plus, you'd *really* have to trust us. It's super personal."

"Personal, how?"

"It's basically a time walk. You'd go back through your family members' experiences with magic starting with yours and ending with the first witch in your line. Every spell you and your ancestors have ever done. Well, not every spell. Just the important ones. Spells that like, defined their relationships with magic. And, we'd be there with you, seeing it all."

CHAPTER 59

She chewed on her lip, thinking about who she knew that might be willing to help out. "Do they have to be real witches or can they be like, witch enthusiasts?"

Adia giggled. "*Witch enthusiasts*. That's hilarious." She quieted her laughter to answer the question. "They just have to have a basic knowledge of how mystical energy is shared. Sit still, calm the mind, and let you take what you need."

"All right. I'll do it."

Her face lit up. "Really? Awesome! But, it's gonna take a while to find people to help. I looked *forever* before I found you."

"I think I might know someone."

Burnt sage and cinnamon perfumed the air inside the occult shop, welcoming her like a hug from an old friend. It was empty of customers but for her, the room so quiet that the bell on the door caused the cashier to jump.

"Sorry," Ophelia said, approaching the counter. "I didn't mean to startle you."

"That's okay," She shook her head, laughing at herself. "It's been so dead in here today, I've kind of been off in my own little world. So, you're back. I see you're still wearing that crystal."

"Yeah. It's...comforting. I never take it off."

"Probably smart, especially if you're messing with spells from that book."

She glanced around. "Where's the older lady? The one with the cards."

"Veda? She only comes in once in a while, does readings. She'll be in tomorrow if you want your cards read."

"That's okay. I was just wondering, do either of you," She leaned in, lowering her voice. "Practice?"

She snickered. "You don't have to say it like it's a secret. Not in here. And, yeah, I do. Veda doesn't. She's not like us."

"Like us?"

"Witches."

She smiled. "Oh."

"She's psychic, or so she claims. I'm Irie, by the way."

"Ophelia."

"So, Ophelia, what can I help you with today? Herbs? Crystals? Another forbidden book?"

"I was actually hoping you could help me out with a spell. I'm trying to figure out where my magic comes from. The girl that's been showing me the ropes says she knows how to do it but we need more people to perform it."

"The Hidden History spell?"

"Yes! You know it?"

"I know *of* it. It can be dangerous if you don't know what you're doing. Takes a lot of juice."

She checked the door to make sure no one was coming in before holding her hand out and using her mind to float Vera's table.

Irie gasped.

She set the table down and put her hands on the counter. "Juice I've got. It's a coven I'm lacking. You in?"

Irie laughed. "Well, shit, how could I say no to *that*?"

She flashed another smile and took the piece of paper she'd written Adia's address on out of her jeans pocket. "Meet me here at six."

There was a new face at Ophelia's SAA meeting that afternoon and as he described the reasons for him being there, his porn addiction and how it had driven his wife away, the ungodly amount of money he'd spent on websites and sex workers, she couldn't help but be distracted. All she could think about was the spell she'd be doing later that day. She hadn't wanted to admit it to herself, but she *needed* to know where her magic came from. Adia was so sure she'd inherited it and while her parents were garbage, maybe there was someone in her family tree that wasn't.

CHAPTER 59

Someone who wasn't abusive or neglectful. Someone she could be proud to call family. Someone powerful.

When the meeting ended and she made her way to the door, she was stopped in her tracks by a beaming Courtney.

"Hey!" She said, grinning from ear to ear, blocking Ophelia's path.

"Hi," She observed the half-crazed look in her eyes and wasn't sure if she was just happy or having a psychotic break.

"Can I talk to you for a second?"

"Sure. Everything okay?"

"Better than okay." She led her to a corner, glancing around to make sure no one was listening. "So, you remember that day you came to hang out with me and the girls? Sam's group?"

"Yeah."

"And, you rattled off a list of spells you said you did and we all laughed?"

She tried to hide the annoyance that threatened to creep into her voice. "Uh, huh."

Courtney paused, seeming to notice Ophelia's aggravation. "You weren't kidding, were you?"

"No."

"I knew it! You're a real," She looked around again and lowered her voice. "A real witch."

"I am."

"Sorry, it's just, none of us have any real power. The others think magic isn't real. It's all fun and placebo effect but when you said all that stuff about spells and Gaia, you were so straight-faced. I thought you had to be telling the truth so I did a little digging into that wound-healing spell you were talking about." She reached into her bag and pulled out a vial of what Ophelia recognized as healing serum. "I can't freakin' believe it but it works. How?"

She shrugged. "Magic."

"Can you show me? How to practice for real, I mean?"

"I don't know if I'm good enough to teach someone else." She should have left it at that. Everything in her was telling her to leave, blow her off, and get to Adaia's. But, the heartbroken look on Courtney's face gave her pause. She was just like her.

Abused, lonely, and desperate to feel in control. She sighed. "I guess I could try. Here," She took a pen and an old pharmacy receipt from her purse and scribbled down her address. "Come by tomorrow and we can try some spells."

She took the paper, bouncing in place with glee. "Thank you! And, don't worry. I won't tell the girls. They'd just call me crazy, anyway."

"They seem pretty closed-minded for people claiming to be witches."

"To be honest, I don't think they'd know a real witch if one was sitting on their face."

She laughed.

"Do you think I'll ever be a real witch, like you?"

"I mean, you got the healing spell to work so you're not *not* a witch." *Four is better*, she remembered. "Hey, you down to try a spell right now?"

Chapter 60

Ophelia and Courtney arrived to find Adia and Irie already getting to know each other, sitting cross-legged on a blanket in the yard and chatting. Between them sat a vintage, silver chalice engraved with the triple moon, and a bottle of tequila.

"She's kind of young to be drinking, isn't she?" Courtney whispered.

Ophelia shrugged.

"I've been doing spells using booze since middle school," Adia said as the two approached.

Courtney blushed. "Sorry. I didn't think you could hear. I wasn't being judgmental, just--"

"It's okay." She giggled, patting the blanket to offer them a seat. "If I was thirty and saw a teenager with a bottle of liquor, I'd be concerned, too. But, I promise, it's not to get wasted," As they sat, she filled the cup, a mischievous grin on her rosy-brown glossed lips. "This time."

"Is this everyone?" Irie asked.

Ophelia and Adia nodded.

"You sure it's enough? This spell is pretty hardcore."

"It's plenty." Adia took out a pin that had been stuck through the sleeve of her shirt, dipped it in the alcohol, and held out her free hand. Ophelia rested her hand in Adia's awaiting palm, letting the girl stab the tip of her index finger.

"What the hell?" Courtney gasped.

Adia squeezed a few drops of Ophelia's blood into the chalice while Courtney looked on in horror. "What are you doing?!"

"Sorry to just get right to it," Ophelia said. "But, I have work in a few hours and it's an hour and a half drive back to the city."

"Shit, sorry," Adia said, swirling the contents of the cup. "I'm Adia, this is Irie. Don't worry, we'll do the whole 'nice-to-meet-you' thing next time. Assuming you both want to join us permanently. You might not after this. This spell is pretty intense. Who knows what kind of deep, dark family secrets Ophelia's got buried in her ancestors' closets."

"Shut up," Ophelia said, the two of them laughing.

Courtney furrowed her brow. "Her what?"

"Okay, everyone take a sip, Ophelia last." Adia took a swig of the concoction and passed the chalice to Irie who hesitated but drank before handing it to Courtney.

"Are you serious?"

"Relax," Adia told her. "The alcohol kills any germs...probably."

Courtney held the cup, her eyes wild as she looked between the women. "You're doing *blood magic?*"

"Okay," Ophelia huffed. "Someone has to tell me what the deal is with blood magic. Why does it freak people out so much?"

"Are you kidding? Blood is *life*."

Adia rolled her eyes. "Here we go."

Courtney ignored her. "When your blood is used in a spell, it can open you up to all kinds of evil forces. Trickster demons, malevolent spirits, *the dead*. If something malicious gets a whiff of it, they can use it as a tether. You can get possessed or haunted or--"

"Old wives' tales," Adia interrupted.

"It's true."

"It's not. My family has been using blood in spells since they came over on the freakin' Mayflower. Nothing's gone wonky in, what, four hundred years? Not since Sarah, anyway."

"Who's Sarah?"

"Sarah Good, as in, Salem."

Courtney and Irie raised their eyebrows.

"So, you see I'm not some weak-sauce newb that doesn't know what she's doing or what she's talking about. Unless you're actually summoning something *on purpose*, blood magic is perfectly safe."

CHAPTER 60

The two looked skeptical and with the spell at risk and time running out, Ophelia offered some anecdotal evidence to support Adia's claim. "I did a locator spell using my friend's blood. A soulmate finder thing. Nothing terrible happened."

"See?" Adia chirped. "It's fine. Listen, this spell will tell us where Ophelia's magic comes from. Who she is. She deserves to know who her ancestors are, doesn't she?"

Ophelia pleaded with her eyes, hoping that Courtney would put aside her apprehension. If she didn't, she might never know where she came from or how she so easily came to possess her magic.

Courtney stared into the cup, her brows knitted together and her lips pursed. She glared at the women and sighed. "Fine, but if I get cursed or something, I'm coming for you bitches." She took a small sip and passed the chalice to Ophelia who flashed a grateful smile.

"Wouldn't *I* be the one cursed in this scenario?"

"Jesus, no one's getting *cursed*," Adia mocked.

Ophelia chuckled and finished the cup, wincing as she put the empty vessel back on the blanket.

"All right, let's get this show on the road." Adia held her palms up at her sides. "Join hands, close your eyes, and clear your minds."

The others did as instructed.

"Last chance to back out."

"No backing out," Ophelia assured her. "I'm ready."

She blew out a breath, cracked her neck, and recited the spell: "Monstra nobis praeterita, vetera revela, initium videamus."

The sky darkened as wind whipped around them, leaves blowing into their hair and the chalice falling on its side. Courtney yelped as thunder clapped, the would-be witch trembling. Ophelia gripped her hand tighter, knowing that if she broke the circle in her panic, the spell wouldn't work. After a few seconds that felt like hours, the void their minds had been looking into began to fill with images; memories that weren't their own. Everything was scrambled, at first. Then, as the real world fell away, the visions aligned themselves in proper order. They saw Ophelia in her kitchen, healing herself with the serum she hadn't made quite right, then in the park making it rain and again, floating above her building. As Ophelia's experiences with magic faded, another's came into view. Ophelia thought she was ready to see it but as she saw the face of her mother as a child, emotion gripped her. *Can I handle this?* she thought, but as the vision continued, she realized she had no choice. She had to see it. She had to know. *No going back now.*

Ophelia's ten-year-old mother sat at a small kitchen table, Michael Jackson playing quietly on the radio, a bowl of sugary cereal in front of her. Her braided hair was secured with rainbow bubble hair ties and as she scratched under the short, puffy sleeve of her yellow dress, a crash from another room made her jump. There was yelling, her stepfather's booming voice carrying through the apartment so loudly, she almost didn't hear her mother's cries.

She stood from the table, tip-toe-ing in her white, patent leather shoes to the hallway. There, through the half-open bedroom door, she saw her mother, eye swollen and lip bleeding.

"George, please!" the woman begged. "There's no one else, I swear!"

"Don't lie to me, woman!" he shouted, towering over her as she cowered on the bed, belt in hand. "Darrel told me you were makin' eyes at him *at church*. You got no shame! I should kill you for embarrassing me like that."

"I didn't look at--"

"Shut up!" He raised the belt, bringing it down hard across her cheek. She fell back into the pillows, covering her face. "I shoulda known. My father told me not to marry you. Said you were damaged goods. Said you looked like the kinda bitch that would end up makin' a fool out of me. Said one man would never be enough. That it? This dick ain't enough for you?" He ripped open his dress shirt revealing the sleeveless undershirt underneath. "Maybe you just need a reminder of how good it is."

"George, stop this now," Ophelia's grandmother pleaded. "Our baby's in the kitchen. She might hear--"

"*Your* baby! Not mine. Let the little bitch hear. Maybe if she sees what happens to cheating sluts she won't turn into one." He unbuttoned his slacks.

"No, George. Don't. Please."

"That's not what you were sayin' last night."

"Please!"

As the girl watched him climb onto the bed, holding her mother down and pulling at his pants, sweat beaded at her temples. Her breathing quickened and her eyes slit. The room shook, pictures falling from the walls, windows rattling.

"What the fuck?" the man said.

The girl trembled, her body stiff, her fists clenched. She let out a scream and as the windows and mirror shattered, the man flew off the bed, across the room, and into the wall, his head hitting it so hard, it left a hole in the drywall. Blood splattered and as he fell, the light in his eyes dimmed.

The woman screamed, jumping up and rushing to check on her abusive husband. She held her fingers to his throat.

"Oh, my God," she whispered, looking up at her daughter as the room quieted. "He's dead."

The child's eyes became saucers. She backed away, tears spilling down her cheeks. "I'm sorry. I didn't mean to. He was hurting you and--"

"It's okay, baby," she told her, crawling to her and pulling her into a hug. "I understand. It was an accident." She took her by the shoulders and looked her in the eye. "We'll wait til dark, put him in the trunk of the car, dump him in the Hudson. We'll say he left, thought I was cheating. It'll be all right."

She nodded, wiping fresh tears from her face.

"It's not your fault, baby. It's these gifts. We can't use 'em, okay? They're too strong. People get hurt, you understand?"

As she nodded again, the vision faded, giving way to another.

Ophelia's great-grandmother sat on a tufted, high-backed sofa, its French-blue fabric decorated in tiny silver flowers. Next to her was a young white woman, her cheeks red and eyes puffy, her bright red lipstick cracked over chapped lips.

"I don't know what else to do," the woman sobbed. "I know it's a sin but--"

"It's all right, child," her great-grandmother said, patting her hand. "I don't judge. Here," She took a vial from the end table's drawer. "Take this before bed. You'll feel sick and have some cramps but it'll be over in a few days."

She took it, staring at the tiny bottle with hope in her eyes. "What is it?"

"Just some herbs. Never you mind. It'll bring on your monthly, that's what's important."

"You sure it'll work?"

"You're not the first young girl to come to me and I haven't had any complaints. I trust you'll be discreet?"

"Yes, of course. Thank you, Miss Shirley." She reached into her purse and pulled out a wad of cash. "And, you won't tell anyone I was here?"

She took the money and slipped it into the drawer. "There's not a person alive who could get it out of me. Now, go on home. I'm sure your mama's worried."

She shook her head. "She thinks I'm seeing His Girl Friday with Barbara and Kay. I should be getting back, though. It's getting dark." She rolled the vial between her fingers, new tears pooling in her green eyes. "Do you think I'm doing the right thing?"

"Not for me to say. Not my business."

"I know but--"

"Listen here. People have their opinions on these matters and I don't dare speak mine in public but I will tell you this: I've seen more girls' lives ruined by boys with nice smiles and false promises than I care to count. You need not be one of them when you hold an alternative in your hand."

The girl nodded, put the vial in her purse, and squeezed the other woman's hand. "Thank you, Miss Shirley. I think you just saved my life."

The image disappeared and a new one took its place.

"Your life line is long," Miss Shirley's grandmother said, tracing the palm of the man sitting across her in the dimly lit room, the candles nearly burned out from a long night's use. "You'll be an old man when your time comes."

"And, my wife?" he asked. "Does she truly love me?"

"I can not see how she feels but see here," She pointed to the small line under his pinky. "Only one marriage line. She is to be your only wife. And, above it, here." She pointed to four faint lines. "These represent your future children. I see four."

CHAPTER 60

"Four?" A broad smile replaced the worry on his face. "Are you certain?"

"You see the lines as clearly as I do."

"Yes, but I do not know their meaning."

"Your wife will give you four healthy children, Mr. Perkins. Now, whether she loves you truly or she just loves your money is beyond my perception. Either way, you will have a long, full life."

The palm-reader's grandmother, a blonde, blue-eyed woman with a French accent, argued in the night with her father on the shores of St. Domingo. A tall, African man stood beside her, his head down, his hands wringing. The crashing waves weren't loud enough to drown out her demands as she shouted, the young woman insisting on her lover's freedom.

"He is a man like any other, though you and your heathens treat him otherwise. I will have him as my husband or I will not marry at all."

"Then, do not marry!" her father scoffed. "I can as easily send you to a nunnery as I can down the aisle."

"Then, perhaps to live is a burden I can not bear. I will as soon walk into the sea than be one more second without being Obazee's wife."

"Do it and he will be hanged for murder."

"Then we should both be free from under your thumb."

"Damn it, Colette! This is not what we left home for!" He took her by the shoulders, shaking her and screaming in her face. "We came here to escape the Corsican Fiend and have a chance at a better life."

"Don't you see, Father? That's what you've given me. Here, I've found love. Happiness. If you take that from me, you're no better than the Ogre himself."

"Sir!" a man holding a lantern called as he and two others approached. "Everything all right?"

"Wonderful," Colette said, rolling her eyes. "Your henchmen have come to aid you in tormenting me."

"Everything is not all right, Laurent. This slave is attempting to kidnap my daughter. Put him in The Hole."

"That's a lie!" she shouted, but the men didn't take their orders from *her*. They moved closer, violence in their eyes. Obazee didn't run, instead holding out his hands as if accepting defeat. "Stop!" She flung her hands in front of her, pushing her father away. She stepped in front of her lover, planting herself between him and her father's minions.

"Step aside, Miss," one of them told her, his voice low and commanding.

She stood firm, chin high. "I will not. If you must take him, you will take me, as well."

He looked to his boss who waved his hand.

"Take her, too, then. Lock her in her bedroom and stand guard at the door."

"Yes, sir."

"No!" Colette snapped. "Stay back!"

As the man gripped her arm with one hand, the other was suddenly covered in flame, the glass of the lantern shattering and the fire spreading up his arm. Soon, his entire body was engulfed as were the two others. Their screams pierced the night air as they feebly tried to put themselves out, running into the ocean only to die there, blistered and steaming.

"Oh mon Dieu," the girl's father whispered, making the sign of the cross. "You have your mother's curse."

As she watched the men's bodies lying limp in the water, Obazee lifted his head, taking Colette by the hand, and gently turning her head to look her in the eye. "Listen to me now," he said, his deep voice soft and clear. "You are not cursed. You are an Aje. Where I come from, you would be respected and admired, not feared."

"Go!" her father all but begged. "Leave this place and never return. There's a cargo ship leaving at first light for New Orleans. Be on it."

"Father, I didn't mean to--"

"Just go! If I see you again, I'll have to lock you away like I did your mother." He turned his back to them and ran.

CHAPTER 60

Colette's mother rocked her newborn to sleep, her own eyelids growing heavy. As the infant went quiet, the woman sat, positioning the child on her shoulder and taking a sip of tea. She had misjudged how exhausted she had been and as she drifted off, her cup tilted, then fell, spilling scalding liquid onto the thinly-clothed baby.

Colette screamed, wailing in pain as her mother jolted awake. She, too, cried out, waking her husband in the next room. She jumped up, letting the teacup fall and break on the floor, and rushed the baby to the sink where she undressed her. The burns were severe, the infant's back, sides, and legs an unimaginable shade of red.

"What's going on out here?!" her husband barked. She ignored him, holding her daughter close. He hurried to them, gasping at the sight of the infant's burned skin.

Her mother closed her eyes, her voice nearly a whisper as she said, "Cictriser." Slowly, Colette's crimson skin returned to its usual alabaster and as her crying stopped, her mother opened her eyes, her husband in front of her as pale as a ghost. "It's not what you think," she pleaded as he backed away.

"Witch," he muttered.

"Henri, please,"

"You harm our child to do your magics."

"I did not!"

"You deny what I can see with my own eyes?"

"It was an accident. I only did the spell to heal--"

"You admit it! A spell. How could I not see it? I've married a witch in league with the devil."

"You misunderstand! It's nothing like that!"

He snatched the baby from her arms. "You're a blight on this house." He stormed away, uttering under his breath, "And I'll have you removed."

What came next was a sea of women, one after another, all practicing various forms of herbalism and midwifery. They stayed hidden, working their spells in secret, only sharing their knowledge and power with family. The line of mothers and daughters seemed never-ending, going back sixty-two generations in total. Finally, Ophelia and her coven came to the final witch, the first in her line.

She was pale with bright blue eyes and raven hair that fell loose down her back. She wore a black dress gilded at the hem and a gold necklace that's rectangular pendant was adorned with a ruby-eyed dragon. With her teacher, a thin, bald man with sallow skin and rotting teeth looking on, she performed her spell. "Dod." The two stood in a meadow, the sound of wind through the tall grass mingling with her breath. The teacher snarled, impatient as they waited.

"Again," he demanded, but she just smiled, eyes closed as the first butterfly fluttered toward them, resting itself on her shoulder. Another came and another, more and more floating up from the grass and out of the trees, encircling them in yellow and blue wings.

"Very good," the old man grumbled. "But--"

"Shh."

He grit his teeth, ready to reprimand her but before he could speak, a fox scurried past. A family of rabbits hopped between them, then a weasel and three badgers. Soon, they were surrounded by stoats, red squirrels, and deer. The animals stood as if awaiting orders, the man's astonished eyes wide at the sight. As the woman's eyes opened, he cleared his throat, shifting his weight from his leg to his staff. "Excellent work," he said. "But, you must be quicker. Your brother's enemies are many and we must be stronger. If not--"

"I understand," she said, the confidence on her face turning to determination. "I'll do anything you ask. Anything to save my brother and all he's built."

"Good, because what is needed is not for the faint of heart."

"I know."

"Listen to me, girl," He waved his hand, sending the animals back to the forest. "You must be sure. I have every confidence that you can perform the spell required but unless you are willing--"

"I'm willing." She stared, her eyes locked on his. "I understand the risks and I tell you now, there is nothing I wouldn't do to help my brother win this war including providing him an army."

The man nodded, reaching into a pouch that hung from the belt of his cloak, and pulling out a small, glass vial. "This is your brother's blood. Mingle it with your own and they'll be bound to you both, faithfully doing your bidding. When the war is won, they won't want to go back. It will take all of your strength and mine to drive them back."

She took the vial and removed its cork top, taking a deep breath and holding out her hand for the sorcerer to cut, his dagger sharp and quick. She cringed at the searing pain, spilling the vial's contents onto her wound and kneeling. He moved to stand beside her as she squeezed the combined blood into a pool on the ground.

"Make haste, child," he said, looking anxiously to the north. "Rheged approaches."

She closed her eyes again, blowing out a deep breath and beginning the incantation in Welsh. "Gythreuliaid dod allan." The ground beneath them shook as the sky darkened, wind whipping her hair as the old man held fast to his staff. "Cymhorth mi ymladd," she continued, louder to be heard over the thunder that clapped and the rumbling of the earth. "Ennill canys yr mi teulu." Her eyes flew open as she said the final words, her face scrunched and her body trembling. "Gwnewch fel y gorchymynaf."

A chasm appeared before them, the ground opening up with a roaring moan. She stood, the two stepping back, making way for what was to come. Soon, creatures of malformation and torment clawed their way up the walls of the fissure, screeching and reeking of sulfur. Dozens came then hundreds. By the time the last stood on solid ground, there were several thousand.

"An army of demons," the teacher said.

She looked them over as she replied, "As you wished."

The monsters hissed and snapped, their twisted bodies dripping in primordial ooze.

"Silence!" she ordered. The crowd of demons went quiet. She turned to the sorcerer, a smirk on her pink lips. "The war is ours to win."

"Holy shit!" Courtney yelped as the four women came out of the vision.

"Whoa," Irie muttered under her breath.

"I knew it!" Adia exclaimed, her face beaming as she looked at Ophelia who was too stunned to speak. "It was the only thing that made sense. I knew you had to be--"

"I have to get out of here," Courtney said, scrambling to her feet and setting her eyes on Ophelia. "Can you get a ride from someone else because honestly…it's too much." She darted to the driveway.

Adia frowned, whispering as she stared at Courtney fleeing, "Vestigium."

"What's *her* problem?" Irie asked.

"Scaredy-cat," Adia said, shaking her head.

Courtney got in her car and sped away, leaving the others to reflect on what they'd just seen.

"You all saw that, right?" Ophelia asked, unable to believe what she'd just discovered.

Irie nodded. "Oh, we saw it."

Adia bounced with excitement. "Plain as day."

Ophelia looked down at her shaking hands, her voice trembling. "I'm…I'm…"

Adia's smile grew wider. "A direct descendant of the most powerful witch of all freakin' time!"

Chapter 61

Ophelia came home to find Dylan waiting in the hall. He held a bag of fast food and her gaze as she stepped closer to unlock the door.

"You look happy," he said, flashing a smile.

"You know what? I think I *am* happy." She opened the door, gesturing for him to follow her inside. She closed the door as he placed the bag on the kitchen table and took out its contents.

"That's really good. I'm glad to see you with a smile on your face after that whole evil-witch-trying-to-kill-you thing."

"Yeah, Marley was a bitch but not *all* witches are evil, you know."

"Oh, I know. I had a witch friend in high school. She's a doctor now." He pulled out a chair for her. "I know you have to work tonight and I thought you might need a quick dinner."

She sat, looking over the feast of cheeseburgers, chicken tenders, and fries. She hadn't noticed how hungry she was until that moment, the discovery of her ancestry so exciting, that all she'd felt since in her stomach was butterflies. She looked at the clock on the oven, realizing she only had a few minutes before she had to get downstairs. "Thank you."

He sat to her left, picking up a burger, unwrapping it, and taking a bite. "Oh," he said, getting up from his seat. He pointed to the fridge. "You mind?"

She shook her head and he opened the appliance, taking out two cans of soda and setting them on the table. She picked one up, opened it, and took a sip. "Thanks."

"So," He took a sip of his drink and put the can back on the table. "Does this count as our first official date or should I plan something nicer?"

She met his flirtatious stare, her mouth turned up in a half-smile. "I don't know. What did you mean earlier by 'switching strategies'?"

"Well, I know how important Rue's opinion is to you so I--"

She burst out in laughter, almost choking on a fry. "You talked to *Rue*? About *this*? Oh, that couldn't have gone well."

"It did not," he said, laughing a little himself. "Not terrible, though. I don't think she hates me, she's just looking out for you. It's nice. She cares about you. I just have to win her over, that's all. Show her I'm not the monster she thinks I am."

She hesitated, needing an answer but afraid to ask the question. She swallowed, her brows scrunching as she got up the nerve. "Do you think that's true?"

"What?"

She gulped again, her nerves getting the better of her. She liked him, no denying that. He was sweet, thoughtful, and hot as all hell. But, what if Rue was right? What if he really was dangerous? "Do you think you're...safe?"

His face tensed as he folded his hands on the table. "Honestly? I don't know. I like to think I have this werewolf thing handled, that I can keep myself from going over the edge. But, sometimes I get so angry. It's hard, you know? Keeping myself in check. But, I've done okay. I haven't hurt anyone."

She nodded, her expression still anxious.

"Hey," He scooted his chair closer to hers. "I would never hurt you. I swear."

"I want to believe you."

He put his hand on her leg just above her knee, his touch sending shivers up her spine. "I promise you, I will never let anything happen to you. Whether we're together or not, nothing will hurt you as long as I'm around, not even and especially me."

She watched as his eyes fell over her, looking down her body to where his hand still sat and up again as he lifted his head to smell the air around her. His fingers pressed harder into her flesh, her heart beating faster as her skin warmed. Their eyes locked, the heat between them undeniable. With trembling fingers, she touched his cheek, leaning closer, her lips begging to meet his.

"I should go," he said standing up and backing away.

"What? Why?"

"Because I really want to kiss you right now and I shouldn't."

She stood, taking a step toward him. "It's okay. I want you to."

He shook his head. "Full moon's tomorrow. I'm extra...feral."

CHAPTER 61

"Sounds hot."

"I said I wouldn't hurt you and I meant it. If I kiss you now, I can't guarantee I'll be able to stop so I won't risk it." He took her hands in his and kissed them. "I like you. I want this to work. We'll have another date, a *real* one someplace fancy with dim lighting and overpriced drinks in a few days. Deal?"

She nodded.

"Okay." He kissed her forehead, lingering there for a few seconds before turning to go. He opened the door, waved goodbye, and closed it behind him.

She dropped back into her seat and popped a handful of fries in her mouth. *A legitimately good guy,* she thought. *Fuck, I'm gonna fall for this man like space junk into the ocean.* With only ten minutes to finish eating and get to work, she scarfed down the rest of her burger, a handful of tenders, and the remainder of her soda before brushing her teeth and changing into her work clothes, getting out of her newly damp panties. She looked for a clean pair but her underwear drawer was empty. She looked at her reflection in the mirror, making sure her skirt covered everything. *Going commando, I guess.*

She grabbed her waist apron and tied it on, stepping into her slides and running out the door.

Throughout the night, Ophelia and Dylan exchanged flirty glances. From the stage, he watched her work, his lust for her growing by the minute. As the crowd dwindled and his set came to an end, his longing for her intensified. He could smell her from the stage, her pheromones calling to him. She wanted him, he was sure. At dinner, she had been turned on and had he given himself over to his desires, he could have had her then. *No,* he thought, squeezing his eyes shut. They hadn't even been on a real date, yet. Hadn't even kissed. But, with the bar now empty and the scent of vanilla and arousal filling his nose, he couldn't stop himself. He hopped down from the stage and went through the swinging door where Ophelia was saying goodnight to the cook. The man left through the service door and Ophelia locked it back, her back to Dylan who could no longer rein himself in. He rushed to her, pinning her to the door, her body flush with his. She jumped, craning her neck to see who had trapped her. He kissed her neck, growling in her ear as he ran his hands up her legs and under her skirt.

"Dylan," she breathed, her muscles relaxing. He moved his hands up, feeling for panties so he could swiftly remove them but found none. He growled again, dragging his teeth over her soft skin and sliding his fingers between her folds. She gasped, her face pressed to the cool, metal door. He kicked her legs apart, throwing her off balance, forcing her back to arch and her hips back, her ass now firmly against his aching manhood. He dipped one finger into her well, then two, massaging her G-spot.

"What are you doing?" she whispered, palms against the door and pussy dripping.

He tore open his jeans, pulled them and his boxer briefs down just enough, and gripped his now-twitching erection. "Oh, fuck," she said as his fingers circled her clit and his cock teased her opening. He slid himself up to his fingers then back, his shaft spreading her lips, the movement of her hips urging him to continue.

"I shouldn't be doing this," she said. "I shouldn't let you."

He ignored her words, responding only to her body, the wetness of her, the swelling of her clit, and the way she moved against him. He continued to rub himself between her lips, moving his hands up her shirt and squeezing her breasts.

"*Shit*," she whispered, slipping a hand under his cock and pressing it harder against her clit, swiveling her hips. "Don't put it in," she told him, sliding herself along his shaft.

"I have to," he grunted, biting her earlobe.

"*Don't.*"

His fingers dug into her hips as she continued to grind, precum seeping from him and coating her skin. He shook, fighting against every nerve in his body that begged him to fuck her. It was all he wanted and he wanted it more than he'd ever wanted anything. Her opening was *right there*. One quick motion and he'd be inside, feeling her all around him, encased in her warm grip. He could do it now, as she was about to come. They could come together. All he had to do was shove himself inside.

He roared, backing away and fixing his pants. She spun around to see his eyes glowing for just a moment.

"I'm sorry," he said, the guilt of having those thoughts causing his voice to quiver.

"For what?"

"That was too close. I almost..." He shook his head, fighting back tears and swallowing the bile that crept up his throat. "Rue was right. I'm a monster."

She grabbed his face, forcing him to look her in the eye. "I told you not to put it in and you didn't. You respected my boundary. You didn't do anything I didn't want you to."

He pulled her hands away and stepped back, his face reddening and his voice raised. "I pushed you against a door and touched you without consent. I rubbed myself against you. And, you have no idea the twisted shit I was thinking. My head is *fucked*. This wolf shit--"

"Hey," She cupped his face in her hands again, the tears he'd been holding back now falling to her thumbs. "You didn't hurt me."

Again, he took her hands away. "But, I could." He wiped his tears and sniffed, averting his gaze. "I'm gonna take off for a couple of days. Full moon and everything. I'll see you after."

"Dylan,"

"It's okay." He backed into the swinging door, opening it. "I know what to do."

"I say fuck him," an older woman at Ophelia's SAA meeting said after hearing Ophelia's story about the night before.

"Carol," the director warned.

"What? That was porn-level hot."

"Oh, my God, it *was*," Ophelia said, crossing her legs. "But, the point is, as hard as it was,"

"No pun intended," Carol said, giggling under her breath.

Ophelia ignored her. "I set a boundary. I never set boundaries. I'm proud of myself. Now, my question is, did I need to set that boundary? I know I'm supposed to be abstinent for a while but I really like this guy. He's nice and honest and he cares about me. Like, *actually* cares. I don't want to give him up. What should I do?"

"Do you feel ready for a new relationship?" the director asked.

"I don't know. How do I know?"

"Everyone's recovery is different. Most people need a couple of months of complete abstinence in the beginning but it's not for everyone. There's no one-size-fits-all answer."

"For crying out loud," Carol said. "Just let the girl fuck him."

"*Carol*,"

"She's not using his dick to self-medicate. She likes him. And, he sounds like a decent guy which," She glanced around at the men in the circle. "No offense, but is like finding a needle in a haystack full of dog shit." She looked Ophelia in the eye, her expression serious. "Take my advice. Relationships are always a roll of the dice so if this guy seems worth the gamble, I say, ante up."

Chapter 62

Dylan drove to the campsite, the sun nearly set by the time he got there. Like every month, he stuffed himself full of raw meat, hoping it would be enough to satiate the wolf's hunger and in turn ensure he wouldn't hurt anyone. Anyone, that is, aside from the creature that turned him. The monster that made him this way.

As the sky darkened, he walked deep into the woods, sniffing the air for traces of his enemy's scent. Finally, after all this time, he caught it, the smell of his maker. He darted in its direction, all thoughts of self-preservation gone as his mind was consumed by the memory of what he'd done to Ophelia. She could say it was consensual all she liked but he knew what he'd done. He'd forced himself on her. Crept up from behind when she was alone and put his hands on her body. More than his hands. He'd lost control, been taken over by his wolf's instincts. He couldn't let that happen again. Couldn't put her in danger. He had to end it, once and for all, by killing the wolf that made him a monster.

Part of him hoped that killing the beast would end his curse. Make him human again. But, that's not how it worked and he knew it. Still, even if all it did was give him some closure, it was enough. That thing had killed his friends and made him someone he didn't recognize sometimes. It being gone would give him a sense of peace and maybe then he'd be better able to stifle his urges.

In the distance, he heard a branch snap. He barreled toward it, his muscles already aching with the beginnings of his transformation. As he ran, his joints popped from their sockets, his shoulders first, then his knees and hips. He fell, spine curved, black claws breaking through his elongating fingertips. He growled, trying desperately to hold it off. He needed to find the wolf in the woods first. He couldn't risk getting this close only to wolf out and run off, aimlessly wandering the forest like he'd done so many times before. He wanted to see the thing with human eyes before giving himself over to his other half.

A low growl perked up his ears. He crawled toward it, coming upon a small clearing with a tent and ashes from a fire that were still smoking. It had only recently been put out. Was this where the wolf had been living or just where it had gotten its last meal? His forehead hit the ground as his spine stretched and cracked, the vertebra tearing open the back of his tee shirt. Blood poured from his nose as it broke, expanding to form a small snout. He cried out, rolling to his back as he felt his chance at killing the wolf slipping farther away with every cracked rib. It would only be a few more seconds before his mind would go dark, his wolf taking over. Once he blacked out, he'd have no control. He'd wake up in the morning with no memory of the night's happenings and with the knowledge that he, once again, had missed his opportunity.

Suddenly, a pair of glowing eyes appeared from inside the tent. He sat himself up as best he could, squinting to see as he yanked off the shreds of his mangled shirt. He heard himself let out a deafening growl as the beast approached. It was him. It was the wolf that turned him. He was fading but as his teeth grew and sharpened, he forced himself to his feet. With the moon overhead and one last moment of lucidity, Dylan sprang forward, his body colliding with the wolf. As his eyes shined in an unnatural blue glow, his vision went black. He was all but gone, his wolf now in the driver's seat. The last thing he was aware of before letting go completely was the distinct snap of a bone breaking.

***

He awoke to the sound of birds chirping, sunlight burning his eyes. He looked down at himself, relieved and then horrified. His body was human again, just like every day after a change, but his skin was covered in blood. It was everywhere; on his chest and arms, soaked through his torn jeans, and caked under his fingernails. He looked around, realizing he'd strayed far from the campsite. He tried to smell

CHAPTER 62

the ashes from the put-out fire but it was impossible through the overwhelming stench of the blood that coated him from head to toe. He stood and took in his surroundings, including the position of the sun and the markings on the trees. He breathed a sigh of relief, recognizing where he was. He headed south, making his way through the greenery back to the ravaged campsite. The place was trashed, the tent torn to bits. As the wind picked up, he caught a whiff of his enemy's scent. He followed it a few yards to the east into the woods. There, in a pool of blood and bile, lay a fifty-something-year-old balding man. He was nude, his face and chest clawed open, his internal organs ripped out and scattered haphazardly around him. Dylan's face scrunched in confusion as he got closer, kneeling next to the body and sniffing the man's head. It was him, all right. He was the wolf he'd been hunting all this time.

He scrambled back, the gravity of what he'd done hitting him like a ton of bricks. He'd managed to kill the beast that turned him. He'd freed himself, finally, of the shadow that had hung over his head. But, now, staring into the empty eyes of the man who was the wolf's other half, he felt sick. He hadn't just killed a monster. He'd killed a person. Someone just like him. He could have been anyone; a teacher, an accountant. A father.

"What did I do?" he whimpered, covering his mouth and crying, the coppery taste of the man's blood still lingering on his tongue.

Chapter 63

Ophelia sat at the kitchen table, drinking coffee and wrestling with the decisions she needed to make. As far as starting something with Dylan went, she had pretty much made up her mind. Ready for a relationship or not, she was into him and no amount of red flags or lectures from Rue could get him out of her head. It could all blow up in her face but it was a risk she was willing to take.

As for coming clean with Rue and Adia about their shared DNA, she still didn't know how she'd go about it. Which should she tell first? Should she say anything at all or just show them the pages in Adia's grimoire? Would they want to know each other or would revealing the truth lead to more bloodshed? Would Adia come after the vampires for killing her family or would the vampires kill Adia for being part of the coven that tortured and killed Zahara?

"Rue," she whispered to herself. Rue, even at her most menacing, put her family first. She wouldn't hurt Adia, Ophelia was sure. She'd know whether telling the others would be a good idea or not. She'd know how they'd react. "She'll know what to do."

As she swallowed her last sip of coffee, a knock came on the door. When she opened it, she was surprised to see Courtney in the hall, panic on her face.

"Hey," Ophelia said, waving for her to come in. "You come to practice spells?"

"Kind of," she said as Ophelia closed the door behind her.

"You look freaked. What's wrong?"

"Your ancestor. You know who that was, right?"

"I do! How crazy is that? Everything makes sense now. Adia said--"

"That's another thing. That girl. Do you know who she is? Because I did some digging and turns out her coven is notoriously bad news."

She swallowed hard, the look in Courtney's eyes telling her to run. "What do you know about her family?"

"From what I've heard, they're sadistic. Evil on a level you only read about in horror novels. I'm sorry, Ophelia. I like you but that coven can't get hold of your kind of power."

She stepped back. "What are you talking about?"

She clapped her hands together and shouted, "Suffocare potentia!"

She coughed. "Wha--" She couldn't talk. She couldn't breathe. It was as if a pair of invisible hands were wrapping around her neck, constricting her airway. Crushing her windpipe. Her hands flew to her throat but there was nothing she could do. Nothing tangible to grab onto. She fell to her knees, her vision going blurry.

"What's going on?" Courtney asked. "I'm just binding your powers. It shouldn't hurt. What are you doing?"

"Ch..." Ophelia grunted as her eyes began to bulge. "Choking."

"What?! No! I'm just...I don't understand! Did I do it wrong? I'm sorry! How do I stop it?"

Finis, she thought but, "Fff," was all Ophelia could say. She was out of air entirely and if Courtney didn't end the spell, she'd die. She looked around, hoping to see a pen lying around. If she could just write it down, get the newbie witch to say it, she'd be saved. But, she saw no pen. No paper. Nothing useful except, maybe her empty coffee cup.

With her telekinesis, she flung the mug at the front door, its loud crash giving her hope. She fell to her side, the room starting to go dark. With no time to waste waiting, she threw the coffee pot then the blender, broken glass clattering to the floor in razor-sharp shards. *Please*, she thought. *Please hear me.*

"What the fuck is this now?" Rue barked, flinging the door open.

Help, Ophelia mouthed, her hands on her throat.

"I don't know how to stop it," Courtney said through tears. "I was just trying to bind her powers. The nutjobs in the Good Coven can't have them. Do you know what kind of sick shit those people do out on their death compound? The stories I heard about people being kidnapped, experimented on. They go in that place but never come out. Of course, Adia isn't afraid of blood magic. She's a freak from a family of freaks. They *kill* people. I had to do something. I couldn't let you get mixed up with those people. I couldn't let them get your magic. I couldn't..." She stopped, covering her mouth.

"Ophelia," Rue said kneeling next to her. "How do I stop this?"

A tear trickled down her cheek as she shook her head. There was only one way now and they both knew it.

Rue stood, stepping toward Courtney. "Nothing personal." Without another word, she snapped the woman's neck, turning back to Ophelia before the body hit the floor.

She gasped, her lungs filling with air and her vision returning.

"I was asleep," Rue complained, pointing at the window. "You see that bright ball of bullshit in the sky? That's the sun. We aren't exactly besties. But, now I'm up, dragged into your witch drama. You want to tell me what that bitch was going on about?"

She stood on wobbly legs, grabbing a water from the fridge and taking a drink. "It's," she rubbed her throat, her vocal cords still scratchy. "Complicated."

"I bet it's not. What's the Good Coven and why was this girl scared of them getting your magic?"

She took a deep breath, sitting at the table, and preparing herself. *This is it*, she thought. *Time to come clean.* "I was having trouble with spells. They'd work but like, too well. I couldn't control it. Little fires turned into big ones. I almost floated off into space. It was--"

"I'm sorry, what?"

"Never mind. Anyway, I needed someone who knew what they were doing to help me so I looked and finally, I found Adia. She's been awesome, helping me with control, giving me new spells to try. We did a walkabout sort of thing where I found out about my ancestors who, turns out, are like, mythically powerful. Adia is my friend."

She leaned against the wall, crossing her arms, annoyance clear in her tone. "That's super. Friends are great. Is there a point coming?"

"Adia was part of the Good Coven. Good being the last name of the first witch in her line going back to Salem. I mean, not her *actual* line. Her coven's line. Those people were fucked up but she's not like them. She's nice."

"Right. So nice that your friend here almost killed you for having anything to do with her."

"I swear, she's not like the others."

"But, they're her coven. Her family? So, how different can she be?"

She cleared her throat and took another sip of water. "You have no idea."

"And, they're cool with you practicing magic with her? I thought covens were all cloak-and-dagger."

"They don't really have a say."

"Why not?"

She looked her in the eye, her heart pounding and her palms sweating. She braced herself, hoping she could get through this conversation without getting her ass kicked, or worse. "Because you killed them."

The tracking spell Adia had put on Courtney led her to a bar in the city. It was closed but the lock on the service entrance door had been broken. "That's not sus at all," she muttered, entering the building. For two days, she'd followed Courtney, worried what she'd do after finding out who Ophelia was. She'd looked so terrified, there was no way she'd just go home and forget about it. And, she didn't. She'd gone snooping, asking about her and her family in witch circles. Now, she was here, in a closed bar in the middle of the day, miles away from any other place she'd tracked her to. She was up to something. She didn't know what, but her gut told her she had bad intentions.

She peeked through the swinging door. When it was clear to her that the bar was empty, she set her sights on the stairway. *What's up there?* she thought, taking the first step. As she ascended, she could hear voices. She recognized Ophelia's but not the other. Courtney must have come to confront her but if she did, why couldn't she hear her? She got to the landing and sleuthed to just outside the door to an apartment. From inside, she heard the mystery woman shout something that grabbed her full attention.

"Marley?! After what that bitch did to us?"

"Adia's not like that, I told you!" Ophelia said. She sounded scared. Desperate. Adia pressed her ear to the door. How did they know Marley and what did she do to them?

The mystery woman answered her question by giving Ophelia a guilt trip. "She almost killed us! I had to turn Iman or he would have *died!* You have no idea what that put me through. I get that you're all into this witch shit now but *them*? They hate us. They kill us. They *hunt* us. Why the fuck would you make friends with one of them?"

"Can I help you?" a deep voice came from behind. She jumped, turning to see a tall man standing in the doorway of the apartment across the hall.

"Are you," Her throat was so dry, she could barely speak. "Iman?"

He tilted his head as if listening to something she couldn't hear. "Yeah. Do you need something?"

"No, I was just, um, looking for Ophelia. We were supposed to hang out but it sounds like she's busy. I'll just text her later."

"You sure?"

"Uh, huh. See ya." She hurried to the stairwell, acid in her throat. She raced down to the kitchen and bolted out the service entrance, her heart like a jackhammer in her chest. "Holy shit," she whispered, running out of the alley. "Holy fucking shit."

"I don't want to hear anymore," Rue snapped, opening the door.

"But," Ophelia pleaded.

"Not buts. Maybe later once I've calmed down but right now, I can't handle any more buts. Not one but. Not even a cheek."

"Rue, please."

CHAPTER 63

"I have to go make sure Lou isn't here early so I can burn this body. Then, I'm going back to bed because it's one in the afternoon and I'm fucking tired." She blew through the hallway and down the stairs, ignoring Iman who rubbed his temple.

"Do I want to know?" he asked.

"Probably not," Ophelia said, guilt gnawing at her as she looked over Courtney's corpse. "Basically, I've been doing magic and a witch came to bind my power which led to an uncomfortable conversation about who I've been doing magic with and Rue got pissed and left before I could tell her the most important part."

"Witches?" Iman's eyes flashed black causing Ophelia to jump.

"Okay, put your scary face away. It's not what it sounds like...mostly."

"Sorry," he said. "I didn't mean to...I'm calm. Just, after everything that happened..."

"I get it. And, I promise, I'll explain everything but right now, Rue has to listen to me. I have to tell her about Adia."

"Adia? Like the song?"

She shrugged.

"So, Adia's a witch? She was here to do spells or something?"

"No, this," she gestured to the body on the floor. "Was Courtney. A super new, half-assed witch who almost killed me trying to bind my magic because she's afraid of Adia getting it."

"That's...wow. But, no, I meant the girl I caught eavesdropping while you were on the receiving end of Rue's mood."

"What?"

He shrugged, holding a hand out to his side. "About yea high, dark hair, looks fourteen."

"She's eighteen and *fuck*." She grabbed her purse and left the apartment, not bothering to close the door. "Please don't tell Rue."

"You want me to hide something from *Rue*? Are you high?"

"Fine, just don't tell her Adia was here until she's done incinerating my friend slash almost murderer. Should give me enough time to leave without her seeing where I'm going."

"Where are you going?"

"Rue isn't the only person that deserves an explanation."

Chapter 64

"Adia," Ophelia called, opening the door to the RV.

"Vampires?!" the girl said, waving her hand causing Ophelia to fly back and onto the ground outside.

She grunted, sitting herself up. "I probably deserved that."

"You're friends with *vampires*?" She stepped out and stood over her, letting her stand before holding her hand in front of her, scooting her back a few feet.

"Yes, but--"

"They killed my sister, didn't they?"

"Yes, but in their defense, she tried to kill them first."

"Duh! They're *vampires*. My coven has been hunting them *forever*. They're *monsters*."

"Monster being a relative term."

"What's that supposed to mean?"

"Did you kill vampires with your coven? Do you now?"

"No. I wasn't allowed. Too young plus they always thought I was--"

"Tainted?"

"What?"

Ophelia moved closer, bracing for another hit and hoping one wouldn't come. "Do you know who your real parents were? Your mom hid the pages but I found them. The grimoire's in my bag. Just read it and you'll underst--"

"I'm not reading shit but I *am* going back to your place *after* I've gathered some weapons and prepared a few attack spells. Then, I'll finish what Marley started."

"You can't hurt them," Ophelia told her, desperation in her voice.

She looked at her, eyes like steel, and with a flick of her wrist, tossed her into the side of the RV, holding her there with her mind. "I'm pretty sure I can."

CHAPTER 64

"You don't understand."

"The fire wasn't an accident, was it?"

"Adia,"

"*Was it?*"

"No."

"And, you told them about me so I'm next on their hit list, right?"

"No," she said, struggling to free herself from Adia's telekinetic grip. "They won't hurt you. Not once they know who you are."

"What are you talking about?"

"That girl I was talking to. Her name's Rue."

"The vampire that turned the guy in the hallway. I don't care what her name is." She closed the space between them, her nose just inches from Ophelia's. "In a few hours, she'll be fucking dead."

"What do we have here?" a voice called from the driveway. Two women approached, both in their mid-twenties, both blond, and both slinking toward them in a way that gave Ophelia chills. There was something in their eyes. She'd seen it a million times before: the look of a predator.

"Do I know you?" Adia asked as they closed in.

"Adia, right?" the first woman asked.

She nodded.

"We were friends with your sister, Marley. She told us all about you."

Ophelia's eyes widened, her stomach dropping. "Adia, let me go."

She ignored her. "What about me?"

The second woman stepped closer. "What you are." She tilted her head. "Do you not know?"

Sweat beaded at Ophelia's temples as she fought the spell but it was no use. She wasn't going anywhere until Adia wanted her to. "Adia, please. I can't help you like this."

The first woman scoffed. "There's no helping this," She looked Adia up and down. "*Thing.*"

"Excuse me?" Adia said, crossing her arms.

The woman flashed a sinister grin, twirling a bit of hair between her bright red nails. "Marley said you were off limits until your mom died but since she's gone…"

"We were just going to kill you," the second woman said. "That was always the plan. Marley's plan."

"My sister," Adia said. "Wanted to kill me?"

"Of course. You're a freak. No, what did she used to say?"

The first woman answered her companion's question with a laugh. "An *abomination*."

"Oh, that's right. Abomination. Anyway, we were all supposed to get rid of you once your mom died but then Marley got herself killed, too so we were going to do it ourselves but then--"

"But, then, our priestess said you might be the key to ending vampires once and for all. She thinks your blood is the cure. Or it could be used to develop a cure? I'm not a hundred percent. Point is, we should have been here right after your coven burned but our priestess needed to figure out exactly how much of your blood she'd need. Turns out, she needs all of it."

"But, there's nothing that says you have to be alive before she takes it, so..." The golden-haired witch flicked two fingers, snapping Adia's neck. The girl's body fell, her hold on Ophelia releasing upon her death.

"Movere!" Ophelia shouted, sending the two flying backward. She bounded toward them as they hurried to stand but she held out her palm, holding them down with her mind.

"Volare!" the first woman said, flinging Ophelia backward, her back crashing into a palette of lumber.

"She's strong," the second woman said as the two got up and stepped closer.

The first woman nodded in agreement as she addressed Ophelia. "And, who might you be?"

She stared them down, the sky going dark, thunder clapping overhead. She raised a hand toward the clouds and made a fist, rage in her voice as she told them, "I'm a le Fay."

She brought her fist down like a hammer, a bolt of lightning following, streaking through the sky and down to just behind the witches that threatened her. They jumped, scrambling to run but she wouldn't let them go. Not after what they did. Not after they killed her friend.

She brought down another bolt, this one striking so close between them that the hems of their dresses singed. They bolted for the woods, Ophelia hot on their tracks. She chased them, unsure of what she'd do if she caught them. She wasn't a murderer, was she? She pictured Courtney's lifeless corpse on her living room floor, guilt twisting in her stomach like a knife. She wasn't the one who actually killed her, but she was dead because of her. Because Rue saved her, *again*. More guilt crept up her throat like bile as she wondered how in the world she was going to tell her that not only did she have a human sister but that she, just like Zahara, had been killed by vampire-hating witches. Rue would be crushed and it would be Ophelia's fault because she couldn't protect her. If she had told them sooner, if she had explained who Adia was even just a day sooner, she might be alive. Now, instead of hosting a long overdue, albeit awkward family reunion, she was chasing down her friend's killers with no idea what she'd do with them when and if she caught up to them. But, the plan or lack thereof didn't matter. She had to keep running. Had to get to them. Had to stop them before they circled back to gather Adia's body and use her blood for whatever creepy experiment they had planned.

She could see them, just a few yards ahead. As she ran faster to catch up, a strange breeze blew by her left side. Seconds later, she saw a wild-eyed Adia tearing into one of the women's throats, stripping away flesh, blood splattering in her face. Ophelia stopped cold, her stomach flipping in terror as Adia grabbed the second screaming woman by the hair and sank her newly formed fangs into her neck. She drank, dropping the body when she was finished.

"Holy fucking shit," Ophelia whispered, the new vampire's black eyes setting on her.

She snarled, edging toward her, fangs out and face devoid of humanity. She pounced, leaping toward the witch who backed away.

"Somnus!" Ophelia said. Adia fell in a sleeping heap to the forest floor. Ophelia tentatively stepped closer, making sure the sleeping spell was holding. "What the fuck?" She listened to the girl's breathing slow and watched as her fangs retreated back into her gums. "Well, ain't this some shit."

Ophelia dragged a half-asleep Adia through the bar's service entrance, dropping her to a seated position on the stairs leading to the apartments. *No more procrastinating,* she told herself, texting Rue to meet her in the kitchen. She expected her to come from upstairs but instead, she came in through the swinging door that led to the bar and she wasn't alone. Following closely behind were Violet and Booth.

"Shit," she whispered, still not sure how to explain everything to Rue, let alone the entire Witcomb clan. She cleared her throat, hoping the fear in her stomach wouldn't make itself known in her voice. "Hey, everyone. What are you all doing here?"

"Family meeting," Rue said, her arms folded over her chest. She glared at the groggy girl on the steps then back to Ophelia. "You brought her *here*?"

"I had to. Just let me explain."

"That won't be necessary," Booth said, stepping forward and taking notice of the girl on the stairs. "Is this the witch?"

"Yes, but--"

He zoomed past her, grabbing Adia by the throat and lifting her. He slammed her into the wall next to the staircase, the rage in his eyes sending terrified shivers up Ophelia's spine.

"Mr. Witcomg, no!" she begged, but he ignored her, addressing the glossy-eyed girl in his grasp.

"I thought there was no more revenge to be had but here you are, dropped in my lap like a gift. One last member of the coven that went after my girls. That killed my wife."

"It wasn't her. She isn't a hunter. Please stop!"

Adia slowly came to, her eyes focusing on the man in front of her; the man she'd seen breaking into her RV. "You."

He tilted his head, studying her face. "What are you?"

CHAPTER 64

"Dad?" Rue said, stepping closer to see whatever it was he was seeing that gave him pause.

He leaned in, the scent of something familiar on the girl's skin. He stared into her eyes, their amber seeming to startle him as he took his hand off her throat. "Who are you?"

"She's your daughter," Ophelia blurted.

"What?!" the others said in unison.

Adia's eyes went wide, then rolled back as she again lost consciousness.

Booth caught her and set her back on the steps, leaning her head against the wall. "That's not possible."

"The fuck are you talking about?" Violet said, her tone causing Ophelia to jump.

"Zahara was pregnant when the witches took her," she told them. "They force-fed her some potion they thought would make her human but it only worked on the baby. They hid what they'd done. Hid her. I found their records in their grimoire."

"What's wrong with her?" Rue asked.

"No one was ever supposed to know about her. Huge scandal. But, Marley blabbed and tonight, some other witches showed up and snapped her neck. They think her blood can cure vampirism or something."

"Then, how is she alive?" Violet wondered.

"I guess her vamp genes weren't *gone*, just...dormant. She woke up and tore those bitches apart. I did a sleeping spell to get her here without getting eaten but it's wearing off."

Booth crouched in front of the sleeping girl, his hand over his mouth and tears forming in his eyes. His voice softened as he looked up at Ophelia. "Are you certain?"

"Yeah," she said, reaching into her bag and pulling out the spell book. She flipped to the previously fused pages and handed it to him. "It's pretty disturbing."

He stood, reading through the heartbreaking entries, a single tear sliding down his sullen cheek.

"Is it true?" Rue asked.

He closed the book and wiped his face. "Yes, darling. It seems to be."

"Holy shit."

"We should get her home." He gave the book to Rue and swept Adia up in a princess hold.

"To be clear," Ophelia said, blocking his path to the service door. "You're not gonna hurt her, right?"

"No," he said. "But, she will kill every human she comes across, starting with you, if I don't get her somewhere safe so do kindly step aside."

She swallowed hard, moving out of his way. He took Adia outside, Rue and the grimoire following. Violet, however, stayed behind, her arms crossed and her lips thinned.

"You're not going with them?" Ophelia asked, her stomach flipping, being alone with her ex giving her as much anxiety as anything else that happened that day.

She shook her head.

"Why not?"

"She might technically be one of us but she's also one of them. Raised by them to hate us. To hunt us. There's a war going on between witches and vampires. What are the odds she lands on our side?"

"You're her family."

"So were they," she said, her cold stare making Ophelia nauseous. "And, we killed them."

Chapter 65

Ophelia climbed the stairs, still shaky, not because of the events of the day but from speaking with Violet alone. When she'd gone, she'd let out a sigh of relief, surprising herself. She hadn't realized just how much her ex still got to her. Still gave her anxiety. Still frightened her.

At the top of the steps, she found Dylan sitting in front of Rue's door. He looked disheveled, his clothes wrinkled, and his hair a mess of dirty blond curls. When he spotted her, he jumped up, clearing his throat. "Hey."

"Hey," she said, unlocking her door. "You okay? You look..."

"Like shit, I know."

"I was gonna say tired but sure, we can go with that. What are doing sitting on the floor?"

"I was waiting for Iman. Guess he's out."

She opened the door and stepped inside. "You're welcome to wait here. Looks like Rue won't be opening the bar tonight so..."

"I don't think that's a good idea. After what I did--"

"I told you, I'm fine and you clearly need to talk to someone. I might not be your soulmate bro-friend but I do know how to listen."

He dropped his head and followed her inside, closing and locking the door as she put her bag on the table.

"Sit down. I'll get you a water."

"Thanks."

She got a water from the fridge and handed it to him before sitting next to him. "What's going on? This about the wolf? Are you hurt?"

"I'm fine, all things considered. Not hurt, just fucked up." He took a sip of water and put the bottle on the coffee table.

"Did you, um--"

"Kill him?"

She nodded.

"Yeah. I did." He looked down at his hands, his usually bright eyes shadowed in mournful regret. "I don't remember most of it but I did it. I killed the thing that made me like this."

She put her hand on his thigh, seeing the guilt on his face.

"I thought I'd feel better, you know? Like, unburdened somehow. But, when I woke up and found his body," Tears welled as he spoke but didn't fall, his voice steady and his expression sullen. "He had reverted to his human form. He was just a man. He was just like me."

"Not just like you," she said grabbing his hand.

He glared at her hand on his but didn't move it. "Exactly like me. The only difference between us is I never killed anyone until him. And, I'm worse because I planned that shit out. I went looking for him for months. *I wanted him dead*. For all I know, what happened to me and my friends was a complete accident. He might not have even remembered doing it. That could've been the first time he'd hurt anyone, just taken over by his wolf. That's what happens. The moon comes out and we disappear. Nothing left but the monster. And, that's what I am. I'm a monster and a murderer. I'd turn myself in except next month, I'd end up tearing my cellmate to shreds."

"Stop," she said, touching his face. He lifted his eyes to meet hers, a single tear finally making its way down his cheek. "You're not a monster. You're probably the sweetest person I've ever met. You're kind and thoughtful. You're honest. You barely know me and you care about me more than anyone ever has."

He moved her hand away, his cheeks reddening as more tears threatened to come. "How I feel about you doesn't make me a good person."

"And, wanting to avenge your friends' deaths doesn't make you a bad one."

"I killed that man and that has me all kinds of fucked up but you know what's worse? I'm selfish." He took her hands in his, kissing them as more tears fell. "I should be protecting you from me. I should leave and not come back and I don't mean the apartment. I mean the city. The state. Shit, the country. I want to shelter you from the parts of me that could hurt you or worse. I tried to leave, even packed a bag but when I thought about never seeing you again, I got this pain in my chest. It was so strong, I thought I'd die. I know I should go, but--"

She put her lips to his, a jolt of electricity running up her spine. He took her face in his hands, deepening the kiss, her tongue massaging his as her hands rested on his hips. For a moment, she forgot about Adia, the witches in the woods, and even Violet. She floated on a cloud, Dylan's lips on hers, the world around them suddenly meaningless.

He pulled away, shivering with desire. "I should go."

She grabbed his face, her eyes determined and her voice soft. "Don't you dare leave me." She kissed him again, sinking into him like a warm bed. The circumstances were crazy and she hadn't known him for long at all. Still, as she basked in his kiss like the sun on a summer's day, she couldn't help but think, *He's the one.*

"Darling," Kenton said as Violet entered their apartment. "You look troubled. What's happened?"

She locked the door and crossed to the sofa, dropping down next to him on the plush upholstery. "A bunch of stuff. Distract me."

"I'd love nothing more but I must go to Romania."

"Romania? *Now?* What for?"

"My sire has called for me and I can not refuse."

She sighed. "Bad timing but okay."

"I'm sorry, darling but Florin will not be ignored."

She rolled her eyes. "I get it. There's just a lot going on right now."

He touched her cheek. "Tell me."

She took a breath before explaining. "Apparently, I have another sister who's half vampire, half witch, and her blood is the magic ingredient in a spell to cure vampirism and Ophelia's doing magic now which I have to just let go because every time she looks at me with her big puppy eyes, I feel guilty all over again so lecturing her is *not* a thing, not that she'd listen to anything *I* say and who can blame her? So, Dad and Rue took Adia, that's my new sister's name, home to Connecticut because she's in full transition and you know how *that* goes and I know I should be there but it's so much so fast and all I want to do is curl up with a bottle and listen to you tell me I'm pretty."

He chuckled, tucking her hair behind her ear. "Sorry to disappoint, love, but I would never call you 'pretty'. You're beautiful. Stunning beyond measure. Pretty doesn't begin to do you justice."

A weak smile crossed her lips. "That's it. That's the good stuff."

He laughed again and kissed her tenderly, squeezing her hand. A quiet growl sounded in his throat as he pulled away. "If I did not have to go, I would ravage you right here in the parlor."

She bit her lip, tracing a finger up his arm and to his chest. "You don't have time for a *quick* ravaging?"

"Afraid not, love. I've procrastinated too long, already. Come with me."

"To Romania? Pass. Eastern Europe gives me the heebies."

He shook his head, holding back another laugh. "It's a beautiful country, I assure you. Lush forests, the Carpathian Mountains--"

"You're trying to tempt me with nature? Did we just meet?"

He snickered. "Medieval castles, one of which we'd be visiting. More history than you could take in in one trip. The museums we could visit. Please, darling. You'd love it and the thought of being away from you is breaking my heart." He stuck out his bottom lip in a feigned pout.

She giggled. "You could ravage me on the plane?"

His eyes twinkled as he kissed her hand. "Repeatedly."

"Now, *that's* tempting but I should really go to my dad's, figure out this whole Adia thing. I don't know if she's pro-vampire or against at this point and if she gets rowdy and turns on my dad or Rue, I should be there too, you know," She ran her finger across her throat. "Besides, hasn't your sire been MIA for like, centuries? Whatever he wants, it's probably important. I wouldn't want to distract you with my wiles."

He laughed. "Your 'wiles'?"

"Yeah, you know," She stuck out her chest and winked.

He laughed harder, his hand on his stomach. "Yes, you're probably right. Your wiles are quite distracting. Fine, I'll go alone…begrudgingly." He leaned in, his hand running up her thigh. "But, when I return, I will have you in ways you've only dreamed of."

Her lips turned up in a teasing smirk. "You promise?"

Chapter 66

"You put her in the cage?" Violet asked, storming into her father's house through the back door, her eyes locking onto her sister sitting at the kitchen island.

"Duh," Rue said, not looking up from her phone. "If she's one of us, she'll be twice as strong as a turned vamp and if she kills herself losing her shit, Dad might have a mid-century crisis."

"Not to mention her magic shit." She sat across from her, dropping her purse on the counter.

Rue looked up, setting her phone down and letting out an exhausted sigh. "Nice of you to finally join."

"I wasn't a hundred percent on coming but I figured better to show up than to get a lecture."

"You might get one, anyway. After we got her locked down, Dad went on a family-above-all rant. Said no matter what those witches did to her, she's our sister, blah, blah."

She clicked her tongue. "Girl, she was *raised* by those people. She's so brainwashed I bet if we stood close enough to her, we'd smell bleach. Dad in bed?"

"Yeah, you know him and his human schedule."

She nodded. "So?"

"So, what?"

"What do you think? You think she'll be cool with all this vampire stuff or will she turn on us? Set us on fire, liquefy our organs or some shit?"

She shrugged. "No telling. So far, her talking has just been incoherent scream-rambling and sleep-babble. Not for sure but I think some of it was in Latin."

"Well, that's not disturbing or anything."

"Not as disturbing as how fast the bitch is going through blood bags. Three times as many as Iman when he turned and it's only been half a day."

"Shit."

"Yeah." She yawned, stretching her arms in front of her. "Mind taking over Adia-watch? I know it's only four but I'm beat worse than Clarence at the end of 8 Mile."

She scrunched her eyebrows. "Huh?"

"You know, the final battle?"

"What battle?"

"The rap battle. Bitch, are you serious?"

She shrugged.

Rue shook her head. "For fuck's sake. Watch a movie once in a while."

"*Anyway*, yes, I'll make sure little sis doesn't break out of her cell and go on a killing rampage."

"Thank fuck." She stood from her place at the island and walked toward the living room. "I already pulled the emergency blood from the deep freezer. It's thawing in the fridge but if she needs it, just nuke it for a minute or so."

"Okay. Night."

"Night."

With Rue upstairs, the house was eerily quiet. The sudden loneliness Violet felt caught her off guard and while she knew there were three other people there, the house had never felt so empty. A chill went through her as she looked around the kitchen she'd spent countless nights in, watching her father drink cup after cup of tea, never understanding how he could stomach it. Like booze, it was liquid and therefore digestible but just the smell of it was enough to make her gag. She suspected her father only still drank it after all these years as a 'fuck you' to the Colonists that threatened to burn his house down for being a Loyalist and the Rebel soldier that turned him. She knew from the stories he'd told her that that was his motivation for staying in the States after the war. No one would push him from his home. "Spiteful, petty, and stubborn," she said to herself with a laugh. "That's my dad."

She looked around again, nostalgia and melancholy blowing through her like wind. Just as her unjustified ennui threatened to bring her to tears, a sharp clang sounded from the basement. She crept down the steps to see Adia in the cage, bashing her fist against the iron bars, her hair as wild as her eyes.

"Libero," the hissed. "Liberum me!"

"Hey, little sis," Violet cooed in the calmest voice she could muster. "You doing okay?"

"Libero me hinc!"

"I don't know what you're saying but you need to calm down. You're gonna wake Rue up and trust me, that's never a good idea."

"Futue te ipsum!"

She cautiously stepped closer, the baby vampire's features becoming clearer in the dim light of the basement. She had amber-brown eyes, a small, upturned nose, and full lips. Her cheekbones were high and her expression dripped with self-righteous rage. "Yep," she muttered, seeing Rue and herself in the girl's face. "Definitely one of us." Even her hair was the same chestnut brown, though instead of wavy, it was straight and so dishevelled, she could see the tangles from yards away. Her clothes were drenched in buckets of sweat and her voice was so hoarse from shouting it was hard to make out what she was saying, not that she'd be able to decipher the words, anyway. To her father's dismay, she never bothered learning Latin.

"Fututus et mori in igni!" Adia knelt down and gathered several empty blood bags that littered the cell floor. "Ede faecum!" She stood and began throwing the bags in Violet's direction. One after another they hit her as she backed away.

"Okay, okay! I get it!" She sprinted up the stairs, grabbing two fresh blood bags from the fridge, and bringing them back down, tossing them through the bars, not daring to get close enough to be grabbed.

The girl growled at her, looking disappointed but tearing into the first bag, anyway. She drank it down at lightning speed and opened the next, sitting on the floor, still staring daggers at a perplexed Violet.

She couldn't help but feel sorry for her. Never having to go through the pain of transition, she could only imagine how scared and miserable she must feel, especially after growing up hating the very thing she was becoming. She had so many questions but clearly, this was not the time to ask them. The girl was rabid, just as Iman had been. She assumed since she was born of two vampire parents, that there wasn't a chance of her not making it through but Rue's experience with Ben still haunted

CHAPTER 66

her. It was the reason she'd never turned anyone. Looking at Adia now triggered memories she'd rather forget. Rue covered in dirt, her tear-stained cheeks, and the crack in her voice when she begged her never to fall in love with a human. She didn't know her new-found sister at all but in that moment, seeing her drop the blood bag and rest her forehead on the bars in exhaustion, she prayed that she'd be okay.

"It's about half over," Violet said, kneeling to her level. "You'll feel better soon."

"Is it true?" Adia asked, the first coherent thing she'd said all night. "What Ophelia said?"

"Which thing?"

"About my mom. What she did to yours."

A lump formed in her throat. She swallowed it and sat cross-legged on the cement. "Yeah, I think so."

"And, your mom is my real mom?"

"Yeah."

"That's why my sister hated me so much. Wanted to kill me. Had people on fucking standby waiting to off me as soon as my mom died."

"Jokes on them," Violet said with a chuckle.

A small laugh escaped her scratchy throat. Her face fell as she looked up to meet Violet's gaze. "I never killed anyone before."

"Trust me, those bitches had it coming."

"Still. This is what I am now? A murderer that kills people to survive?"

She tilted her head. "Is that what you think? That we have to kill people to live?"

"Don't you?"

"Girl, no. You see the trash all over the floor? That's from living donors. I don't kill people to eat. Neither does my," She paused, correcting herself. "*Our* dad. We drink from those bags or we have people that *willingly* feed us. It takes some control not to take too much from them but it's not that hard. My friend, Lennon feeds me. They live with me so I never have to worry about where my next meal is coming from."

"Like a pet?"

"No."

"Sounds like a chicken you get eggs from."

"*Lennon is not a pet*. Or a *farm animal*. They're more like," She thought for a moment. "A private chef that also happens to be the best friend I've ever had."

"Oh."

"What?" she asked, noticing the confused look on her face.

"Nothing, just...you're defending them."

"So?"

"They're human, right?"

"Again, *so?*"

"I thought vampires hated humans. Think of them as food and nothing else. Want to string them all up in blood farms. Breed them like cattle."

"The fuck?" she yelped. "Girl, your brain's been scrubbed with steel wool, hasn't it? Jesus fucking Christ. Who got high and thought that crazy shit up?" She shook her head. "No, bitch. None of that is accurate."

"You say that, but you locked me in a cage."

"That's to keep you from going ape shit and butchering more people like the witches that attacked you. And, to keep you from hurting yourself. The transition is bonkers. Trust me, it's for your own good."

"I don't know *who* I can trust anymore." She scraped at the rust on one of the cell bars with her fingernail.

"Ophelia," she said plainly. "I know she kept all this from you for a little while but she was just afraid. After what Marley did to us, she had good reason. If you're not ready for the whole vamp-family thing, stick with her. She cares about you, I can tell. Plus, she has lots of experience with vampire shit." She slit her eyes to let her know she was serious. "Just don't hurt her or I'll have to hurt you back."

Adia's eyes widened, fear tingeing her face. "She's a friend of yours?"

Violet relaxed her features and sighed. "Honestly, I don't even know anymore."

Chapter 67

Ophelia snuck past the sofa where she'd left Dylan sleeping the night before, not putting her shoes on until she was in the hall. She didn't want to wake him after what he'd been through but she needed to check in with Irie to make sure Courtney hadn't contacted her after the Hidden History spell. She was probably being paranoid since they didn't know each other, hadn't met until right before the spell, and as far as she could tell hadn't exchanged contact information but after what happened, she wanted to cover all of her bases.

As she walked the twelve blocks to the magic shop, her mind drifted to Dylan. He was a walking contradiction, sweet and gentle but also unbridled and sexy as all hell. She thought about him pressing her to the door, his hands wandering her body, his growl in her ear making her shiver just by thinking about it. She was starting to regret not letting things go past kissing the night before.

The bell on the door rang as she stepped into the shop, the sage and lavender scent knocking her thoughts back to the present. The store was empty of customers and when she didn't see Irie at the counter, her heart leaped to her throat. Had Courtney tracked her down here and told her she planned to confront her? If she knew what Courtney had been planning, knew when and where she was going, and then didn't hear from her again, she'd be suspicious, wouldn't she? She'd assume she'd done something to her. *She'd know.*

Just when she thought she might have a full panic attack right there in the store, the older woman in the sari emerged from the stockroom. Maybe that's where Irie was, just doing some backroom work while there were no customers. She breathed out slowly, telling herself to stop overreacting and making ridiculous assumptions.

"Excuse me," she said to the now-seated woman. "Is Irie working today?"

Without looking up from the tarot cards in her hands, she simply said, "Lunch," and pointed to the chair across from her at the little table.

"Oh, thank you but I don't need a reading. Do you know when Irie will be back?"

The older woman looked up, her eyes blazing as if she'd been insulted. Again, she pointed at the chair, the look on her face so severely serious, Ophelia was terrified to refuse again. She walked to the table and sat, the woman on the other side already shuffling her cards.

Without a word, she drew three cards and placed them in front of the witch, her eyes widening with the last.

"What does it mean?" Ophelia asked, examining the beautifully decorated cards. The first portrayed a man and a woman, one floating above the other. Above the man were fluffy clouds and a bright sun and below the woman was a sea of red fire. The second card was labeled, 'The Chariot' and featured a woman on a throne flanked by two sphinxes. The last card showed a knight on a horse carrying a black flag.

The woman placed a finger on the first card and began to explain, her accent so thick, Ophelia could barely make out the words. "The World. It represents the ending of a cycle. A pattern has finally been broken. You're letting go of who you once were and are embracing a new version of yourself." Her eyes flicked up at her for just a moment. "Spirit says you should be proud of how far you've come."

Next, she pointed out the second card. "The Chariot. It indicates an upcoming battle, usually with yourself, a decision that needs to be made. In this case, however, Spirit says it's literal. A physical battle. It's big. Ugly. And this," She tapped the final card. "Death. Someone close to you will die. Soon."

She almost choked on her spit as she swallowed the lump in her throat. "*Die?*"

The woman nodded, scooping up the cards and placing them back in the deck. As she shuffled again, a card fell from the center of the deck as if it had a mind of its own. She squinted down at it before relaxing her jaw. She picked it up and turned it to face her. "The Lovers. Spirit insists that you know you have a strong connection to someone you've met recently. There is real love there, love that can be trusted."

She stared, dumbfounded, wondering how many grains of salt she needed to take with this reading. Before she could ask a follow-up question, Irie ambled in, taking a long sip of soda from a fast-food cup. "Thanks." Ophelia hurriedly got up from her seat and moved to meet her at the crystal display in the center of the room.

"Hey," she said, doing her best to sound nonchalant.

"Hey," Irie said, finishing her drink and setting the plastic cup on the counter. "Need help finding something or you want me to schlep back out to Jersey for another spell?"

"Neither. I was just wondering if you'd heard from Courtney. She's not responding to texts. I think she ghosted me."

"You mean the scared-of-witches witch from the other day?"

She snickered. "Yeah."

"No, I haven't and I don't expect to. Can I be blunt?"

She nodded.

"Girls like that shouldn't be practicing, period. If you're afraid of what you're doing or worse, looking down your nose at it, you're just asking for trouble."

She swallowed. "Trouble?"

"Spells going wrong or not working at all. Spirits getting pissed off. Don't tell her I said it because I'm sure she'd get offended but that girl needs to stick to herbal tea and rock collecting. Leave real magic to people that can handle it. Speaking of, if you ever *do* need me for another spell, I'm down. Unlike coward-ass witch wannabes, I'd love to work with a descendant of Morgan le Fay."

Her eyes brightened. "Really?"

"Of course! You're witch royalty. Any practitioner worth their salt would be crazy not to jump at the chance to work a spell with someone of your caliber."

"Thanks," she said, her cheeks growing warm. "I'll keep that in mind."

The bell on the door chimed as a woman with a pink ponytail entered the store.

"Back to work," Irie said, picking up her cup. "I'll see you later." She walked around the counter with the register, tossed her cup into a waste bin, and cleared her throat before addressing the new customer. "Can I help you find anything?"

Ophelia's goodbye wave was met with a nod of acknowledgment from her friend and as she left the building, she breathed out a long sigh of relief. Irie didn't know anything about Courtney's plan and she didn't suspect a thing about what had gone on when she'd tried to enact it. Now, all she had to worry about, besides helping Dylan through the trauma of killing the wolf that turned him, was Adia's transition.

She checked the time on her phone. Dylan would be awake soon if he wasn't already. She decided to head home, assuming the Witcombs could handle Adia. After all, they were there for Iman when he turned and he was fine. Adia had a whole family to help her get through the next few hours but she was all Dylan had. *I'll check up on her later*, she told herself, already halfway back to the loft. *I'm sure she'll be fine.*

Ophelia hurried home, her desire for Dylan growing with every step. By the time she got to her door, the ache in her nether region was unbearable, her inner walls throbbing to her heartbeat and her panties as wet as if she'd just pulled them out of the wash. *Fuck the SAA rules*, she thought. *I deserve something healthy, a relationship where I'm the other person's priority instead of an afterthought or a punching bag. I'm allowed to be happy.*

She walked in, finding Dylan in the kitchen tossing fruit together in a large mixing bowl, his strong hands covered in juices. "Hey," he said, turning to see her locking the door and stepping toward him. "I hope you don't mind. I thought you might be hungry when you got back so I made fruit salad." He looked at the mixture. "Well, kind of fruit salad. Just strawberries and mango. I can't eat mango on its own since I got turned. It tastes like flowers. Sit down, I'll get you a bowl."

She did as he told her, watching his shoulders jitter as he washed his hands in the sink. "You didn't have to do that," she said, noticing the involuntary rasp in her voice. He heard it, too, spinning to see the wanton look in her eyes. "It's really nice of you to make me food."

He cleared his throat, reaching into a cabinet to find two bowls. He set them on the counter and opened a drawer, looking for forks. "It's no problem."

"You've done that a lot, bringing me food."

He turned to face her again, placing the forks in the empty bowls. "Maybe I just like feeding you."

CHAPTER 67

She cast him a knowing glance and stood, walking around the dining table and hopping up to sit on it. Now, directly in front of him, she could see where his jeans were starting to get tight. "You really like me, huh?"

His brows knitted together, his voice lowering an octave as he said in a tone so serious, she felt her heart jump, "I more than *like* you."

She flashed a mischievous grin, her fingers moving to unbutton the first few buttons of her shirt. "How much more?"

She could see his Adam's apple bob as he swallowed, his eyes lowering to her slowly opening top and back up to her lips as she wet them. "I don't think there are words to describe how much I'm into you." He pushed away from the counter and stepped closer, running his hands over her knees and up her thighs, pushing her legs apart and standing between them. "From the second I got a whiff of you I was hooked. Something about your pheromones or something." He leaned in, inhaling deeply as he ran his nose up the side of her neck. "*It's primal.*"

"Like an instinct?" she asked, getting her arms out of her shirt and tossing it away. "So, you have no choice?"

He slid his hands up her hips to her waist, his lips just under her ear as he answered, "There's always a choice. I just see no reason to fight what every cell in my body is telling me is true."

Her breath hitched as his lips brushed her neck, his right hand moving up to cradle the back of her head. "And, what's that?"

He kissed up her neck to her cheek, his lips hovering over hers as he answered, "That *you* are *everything*."

She stared into his eyes, the tension in his shoulders as she ran her fingers over them letting her know how hard he was working to restrain himself. "You don't have to," she whispered. "Not anymore."

"I don't have to what?"

She bit her bottom lip, gliding her hand up the nape of his neck and lacing her black-lacquered nails in the soft waves of his hair. "Hold back." She slammed her lips to his, throwing an arm around his neck and pulling him even closer. Their tongues danced as they embraced, their arms wrapped so tightly around one another, they could hardly breathe. Soon, his hands glided up her back, his nimble fingers making quick work of the hooks of her bra. Once it was unhooked, she slid out of it, dropping it to the floor and pulling his shirt up over his head. He got out of it as she unzipped his jeans and pulled them down, his eyes flashing yellow as he went in for another kiss.

He kicked his pants and socks away, standing in nothing but red boxer briefs as he unbuttoned her leather pants. She put her hands on the table, lifting herself enough that he could get her pants down past her ass. He got them down to her knees, taking her shoes and socks off before pulling them the rest of the way off, kissing her harder, the thin fabric of their underwear the only thing separating them now.

As they continued to make out, a knot of realization tightened in her gut. He didn't know she was a witch. As much as she didn't want to ruin the mood, she thought she should tell him before things went further, just in case. She really liked him and she didn't want to start their romantic relationship off with a secret.

He kissed down her neck to her chest, the heat of his skin on hers testing her resolve. "Dylan," she breathed. "Dylan, wait."

He pulled back. "I'm sorry," he said, shaking his head. "I went too far, didn't I?"

"No," She grabbed his face, giving him a reassuring peck on the lips. "Something you should know about me, when it comes to us, there's no such thing as too far."

His eyes changed again as he dragged his hands up her naked thighs. "What's wrong, then?"

"Nothing's wrong, I just think I should tell you something…*before*."

"You want me to wear a condom? I don't have one on me but I can make a store run if--"

"Oh, um," she said, another realization hitting her. It hadn't even occurred to her to bother with a condom. She'd been tested after her encounter with the gamer girl and she was clean. She'd also gotten a birth control shot while at the clinic and it had been more than a week so she was sure she was protected. Still, she didn't know anything about his past or what he could potentially be carrying. "That's not what I was thinking about. I just got tested and I'm on birth control but if you have something…"

"I don't. I can't."

"Oh, right. Wolf healing stuff."

"Mm, hmm. So, what is it?"

She touched the light hair on his chest, letting herself get distracted for just a second before answering. "I don't know how to say it except to just say it. Um, I'm a witch." She held her breath in anticipation of his response, hoping she didn't just ruin everything.

His face relaxed. "Is that it?"

"Yeah."

"Okay." He kissed her, his hands in her hair and his body pressed to hers.

She pulled back. "Wait, that's it? You're not freaked out?"

"Baby, I'm a werewolf. My best friend's a vampire. Promise not to turn me into a frog or something and I'm good."

"Are you sure?"

"Yeah. So, you do magic. It's not a big deal."

"It kind of is."

"Ooh," he said, his lip turning up in a flirtatious grin. "Should I be nervous?"

She held her hand up then made a fist, thunder crashing on her whim.

His smile broadened. "Okay, that was hot as fuck."

She beamed as he kissed her again, wrapping her legs around his waist.

He slid a hand under her backside and lifted her off the table. "Where?"

She pointed down the hall to her bedroom and carried her there, lightly sucking on her neck as he went. Before she knew it, she was on her back and out of her panties, Dylan hovering over her while he threw his boxer briefs to the floor. He again focused on her neck, breathing in her scent and kissing her as she reached down to guide him into her, gasping as he sank deep inside. Quiet growls escaped his throat as he began thrusting, his face in her hair and her hands on his ass. With their bodies flush, Dylan only pulled out halfway before diving back in, his movements and girth taking Ophelia to the point of climax in only a few minutes. She wasn't usually the just-lay-there type but she was enjoying taking his massive dick without putting in any effort. She wondered if that made her selfish but as he trembled on top of her, his heavy breath shaky in her ear and his growls getting lower and louder by the second, she decided he was having a good enough time that her worries were unfounded.

He raised himself up enough to look her over, horror spreading across his face when he caught his reflection in her eyes. In the dim light of her room, the blinds blocking out most of the afternoon sunlight, his eyes glowed yellow, their pupils enlarged. He squeezed them shut. "I'm sorry," he said. "I don't want to scare you."

She touched his cheek and swiveled her hips, encouraging him to continue. "I'm not afraid. I know you wouldn't hurt me."

He opened his eyes, thrusting harder as she drew her legs up. He looked down at her, his face serious. "I never will." He flattened himself against her, pumping into her and sniffing her neck.

She met his movements, unable to be still as she started to come. "Swear?"

He kissed her neck and whispered in her ear, "On my life."

Chapter 68

Kenton stood outside the ten-foot iron gate that led to his sire's impressive if not a little over-the-top castle. The forty-thousand square foot stone structure, situated in the middle of a dense forest stood as proudly as it had the last time he'd been there more than two hundred years prior. The gate was open, he assumed because Florin had been expecting him and as he made his way up the long, wooden bridge towards the fortress' main entrance, his nerves began to get the better of him.

As his sire, Florin had been a kind of father figure to Kenton whose actual father had died when he was a child. He taught him how to fight, to hunt, and to hide what he was. As a human, he'd been a soldier in his Queen's army but once he'd been made a vampire he had to learn to use his heightened senses and enhanced strength to his advantage instead of being overwhelmed by them and Florin had made sure he did. He'd offered him a home, a family of sorts, not to mention the gift of immortality. He was grateful, of course, and his devotion to him was matched only by his devotion to Violet but, standing before the heavy, oak doors of his maker's ancient home, anxiety gripped his heart like a fist. Florin was a hard man, ruthless and unforgiving. Not necessarily quick to anger but absolutely unrelenting when crossed. He'd burned an entire village to the ground over an insult, massacred a nobleman who dared to levy taxes on him, and waged wars on royal houses that he deemed unworthy of their titles. He'd never raised a hand to Kenton, himself but the threat was always there, ever lurking, one wrong word away.

When he'd disappeared, Kenton had been angry. He'd felt abandoned. Betrayed. But, if he was honest with himself, there was also relief, the need to walk on eggshells removed giving him a sense of freedom. After a few decades, the resentment faded to indifference and he lived his long life without fear. Without judgment. Without apprehension. Now, those old feelings returned, slapping him in the face like an icy hand. He fought to maintain his composure, remembering how insufferable his sire found signs of weakness in his progeny. He wouldn't let him see him sweat. He'd show confidence and exude power, no matter how he felt inside.

After a few calming breaths, he gripped the knocker and slammed it into the struck plate three times, admiring the iron wolf's head that held the ancient hoop.

"Come!" Florin ordered, his deep voice booming even through the thick, wood door. Kenton went inside, allowing the eight-foot-high door to close itself behind him. He couldn't have prepared for what he saw in the grand entry or in the great hall just beyond it. He covered his nose at the stench, bodies of men in bulletproof vests littering the floor, their blood and bile staining the antique rugs. Kenton took in the garish scene, looking past the ornate meeting table to the fireplace where his sire stood, a hand on his hip and a boot in a puddle of what used to be a human head.

"I'm late to the party, I see," he said, stepping around the rest of the corpse to stand in front of him.

"Only by a few moments. Nothing I couldn't handle alone."

"I see. Hunters?"

"Yes. The third group in so many days." He was only an inch taller than him and yet, he towered over him, his presence so overwhelming that Kenton felt small by comparison. He was regal in brown leather pants, a ruffled linen shirt, and a knee-length, silk-lined coat with bear-fur trim. Black curls hung to his broad shoulders and thick eyebrows sat above his slate-gray eyes, the flames from the fireplace reflecting in them as his gaze settled on his progeny's face. "You look well."

"As do you."

"Looks can be deceiving." He gestured to the table. "Sit."

He did as instructed, pulling out a chair next to the head of the table where Florin took his seat. He sat and scooted to the table, its medieval mahogany shining in the glow of the fire. Only a minute inside the castle and Kenton had begun to sweat. Between the fire and heat of summer, he was burning up. He wouldn't complain, of course. He knew better.

"How have you been, Kenton?"

"For the past two hundred years or just recently?" He regretted it as soon as he said it, clenching his hands in his lap as he waited to be reprimanded for his snarky attitude.

Florin chuckled, raising an eyebrow but showing no signs of anger. "I only wish to hear of your *current* state of well-being."

He relaxed his hands and swallowed before answering. "I'm well. And, you?"

"Rotting from the inside, actually."

"What?"

"Refresh my memory," Florin said, pulling his coat closed over his chest. "What have I told you about my past? How I was made?"

"Nothing, sire."

"Nothing? Are you sure?"

He thought back, four hundred years of memories taking a while to get through. "Fairly certain."

"Interesting. Well, I'm sure I had my reasons, trivial as they seem in hindsight. I'm sure I thought I was protecting you, or myself but it's time you know."

He leaned in, listening intently as Florin began his tale.

"When I was twenty, I was killed by a pack of wolves in these very woods. I forget how many thousands of years ago it was. Time loses meaning when you're as old as I am, you see. My wife was of the old religion, a powerful enchantress but not a necromancer as such things don't actually exist. She was beside herself with grief, her sisters of no comfort though they tried to ease her pain with spells of some sort. She refused to bury or burn my body, to her sister's dismay. After three days of letting me bloat and fester, she resorted to desperate means to bring me back. She summoned something, something dark. In exchange for freeing the being from its prison, it granted her request. I was reborn, immortal, and invulnerable to illness or injury, gifted with the powers of the demon that resurrected me. Furious and afraid, my wife's sisters drove us from our home. We fled to Dacia where we had six sons and a daughter before my wife succumbed to illness of the lungs. She had aged seventeen years but I remained as youthful as the day I died. My children were as I am, their lust for blood as unrelenting as my own. Without my wife to ground us, we grew wild, feasting on village after village, killing for food and for sport. Inevitably, the human hordes came for us, killing one of my sons. We'd been fool enough to think we were invincible. Proven wrong, we scattered across Europe, hoping that a single one of us would be less likely to be discovered. We lost track of one another, then but I know they lived at least long enough to discover how to make more of our kind as I did. Eventually, I found myself in Kemet where I made the acquaintance of a woman named Sekhmet. She didn't fear me as others did. She found me intriguing. She was a queen, strong and fierce, and quite possibly the most beautiful creature I'd ever laid eyes on. I wished nothing but to please her but gifts of jewels and silk meant nothing to her. What she craved most was power...so I gave it to her. I made her as I am, my only condition being that she refrain from making more like us. Anonymity, to this day, is our greatest defense. We were happy, for a time. But, as her children began to age, she realized the burden of immortality. She couldn't stand it, the thought of watching her children wither and die. So, she betrayed me and turned them. Her eldest son went mad, butchering hundreds before I put him down. Though I had no choice, my love could not forgive me and I was again alone."

Kenton could feel how wide his eyes had become but he couldn't for the life of him hide his shock. "You're telling me you're the first? The first vampire?"

"I'm telling you much more than that." He adjusted his coat again and Kenton noticed how blue his fingernails looked against the paisley fabric. "As Sekhmet's descendants became many, they too were hunted. They formed armies of spies to stalk and butcher those that would do them harm. Over the millennia, threats have come and gone but Sekhmet's line has remained vigilant, snuffing out hunters, covens, and the torches and pitchforks crowds. I, too raised an army of sorts, siring the strongest of men to defend our kind if need be. We infiltrated governments and spread propaganda condemning witches, turning humans against each other and forcing covens to stay hidden and isolated. The war between our kinds seemed to have been won. Then, at the end of the last century, the witches became emboldened. They developed communities, shared secrets. They joined forces and came for us once more. They not only kill us but run vile experiments, torturing us in the futile attempt at finding a cure."

"Is that why you've summoned me here after all this time? To find the cure before they do? Because, I assure you, it's not a concern."

Florin blinked. "Not a concern?"

"No, sire. They need the blood of a girl who was cured while in the womb but she has recently turned. She is now, as she was always meant to be, a vampire. Her blood is useless to them."

He cocked his head, his shoulders relaxing a little though his hands still held his coat tightly closed. "You have personal knowledge of this?"

"Yes, sire."

"Interesting."

"Sire, may I ask a...delicate question?"

"No need. I know what you want to ask." He sighed and leaned forward, the directness of his eye contact making Kenton shift in his seat. "You're wondering why I'm so unwell. I'll tell you." He paused as if preparing himself. Kenton had never seen him shaken. He was a pillar of strength and stoicism. Now, behind the cold grayness of his eyes, Kenton saw something he never thought he would in his sire. He saw grief.

"You don't have to. If you're uncomfortable--"

"I'm dying."

"You're...what? How?"

"A witch put a hex on me. With every human I kill, a part of me dies. A lobe of my liver, a bit of my spleen. A chamber of my heart. For two centuries, I'd kept myself locked away, sleeping as the years quietly passed. But, in the late nineteen nineties, I was awoken by a group of hunters that had come to murder me in my bed. After disposing of them, I tried to go back to my slumber but more came. Every few years, more hunters come and with every one of them I kill, another part of me is destroyed. *That* is why I've called you here. You are my most trusted and most capable progeny. I need you to do what I can not."

"What do you need?"

"Protection and a way to lift this curse. It's of the utmost importance. *I can not die.*"

"Of course, sire. The girl, the one the witches are after, was a witch before she turned. I'll take you to her. She might know a way."

"All right. Thank you." His face hardened, the seriousness in his stare causing Kenton's hair to stand on end. "There is one more thing I need to tell you."

Ophelia's phone chirped with a notification, waking her from the best sleep she'd gotten in months. Next to her, Dylan slept on his stomach, his left arm draped over her chest. Even in his sleep, he needed to be near her, or so she hoped. She took her phone from the nightstand and checked her messages. Rue texted: *Adia made it. She's doing fine. Don't think she's feeling us, tho.*

She blew out a sigh of relief, her guilt for not being there fading as she put down the phone and lightly stroked the hair on her lover's arm. For the first time maybe ever, she felt at ease. There was no tension in her muscles, no need to walk on eggshells, and no desperate need to prove herself worthy. She didn't have to fight for anyone's attention or even try to attract it. With Dylan, she could just *be*.

After a few blissful moments of contentment, her hunger made itself known, her stomach growling so loudly she thought it might wake her companion. She slid out of bed and into a tee shirt, tip-toeing to the kitchen where the sort-of fruit salad still sat on the counter. She scooped some into her bowl, grabbed a fork, and began to eat, the fruit so sweet it was almost like candy. She stood leaning against the counter, looking out into the living room. The apartment felt smaller, not as empty as it had since Lennon moved out. It wasn't just because she didn't feel lonely anymore, it was because she didn't feel alone. With Violet, even on their best days, she knew she wasn't really *with* her. It was temporary. She was little more than a side piece. Every relationship she'd had felt basically the same, every partner having one foot out the door from the start. Dylan was different. She could tell by the way he looked at her that he was all in.

"I wouldn't eat that," he said, emerging from the bedroom and sliding into his jeans, his light chest hair and triangle tattoo on full display. "It's been sitting out for hours. It's probably turned."

She shrugged, taking another forkful. "Tastes fine to me."

CHAPTER 68

He walked over to her, kissing her cheek and popping a strawberry into his mouth. "I wish I could make you something more substantial. Carb heavy."

Her eyes lit up. "Like, fries?"

"Oh, I'd love some fries right now." He looked at the clock on the oven, his face falling in disappointment. "I don't know of any places open at four A.M., though."

A mischievous grin brightened her face as she took his hand and led him to the front door. "You know what's definitely *not* open right now? The bar."

He followed her down the stairs to the bar's kitchen. "You think Rue would mind?"

"I doubt she'll even notice. She's busy with some heavy family drama. We'll just clean up when we're done."

"All right, then. While I'm getting the fryer turned on, can you grab me potatoes, garlic, parsley, salt, pepper, butter, and olive oil? Oh, and some parm?"

"That's a lot of stuff for fries," she said, her eyebrows lifted in excitement. "You making something fancy?"

He grabbed her hand and drew her to him, wrapping his arm around her waist and kissing her. "Only the best for you." He smacked her ass as she walked away.

"Okay, Daddy," she giggled, going into the walk-in while he got the fryer going.

Soon, he had steak fries frying and a skillet simmering with the other ingredients. He pushed the garlic around the pan with a silicone spatula, Ophelia trying not to drool at how amazing it smelled.

"Where'd you learn to cook?"

"Here and there," he said, setting the pan aside and turning off the burner before pulling the fries, dumping them in a mixing bowl, and sprinkling a good amount of salt on them. "I started working in restaurants in high school, washing dishes, bussing tables, stuff like that. I ended up at this great out-of-the-way burger spot in Brooklyn. The summer after graduation, I got a chance to work on the line and I fell in love. The pressure was invigorating. Stressful as anything but I felt alive, you know? But, then, the band booked a tour, then another, then more and more gigs came and I couldn't let the guys down. I had to stick with it but I missed working on that line. Still miss it, to be honest, but what are you gonna do?"

"What do you mean?"

"It's kind of difficult keeping a steady job when you have to call off a few days every month. I can get away with it for two or three months saying I get migraines but eventually, bosses get sick of not being able to depend on me and I get canned. So, I make deliveries for money. Work when I can." He dumped the contents of the skillet over the fries and tossed them, making sure they all got coated. He then used a microplane to grate fine shavings of Parmesan over the steaming fries and tossed them again.

Ophelia got two forks and handed him one while simultaneously stabbing a fry and shoving it into her mouth. She waved at her open mouth in a futile attempt to cool it down.

"You okay?" he chuckled.

"Hot," she said, finally able to swallow. "That's incredible."

"You like it?"

"*Love it.*" She blew on her next bite before taking it, her eyes rolling back. "So good."

He smiled, taking a bite of his own. "Glad I impressed you."

"You really did."

"Hey, I have a question, since you've been around vamps longer than me. Is it true what they say about garlic?"

"Like, does it keep them away?"

He nodded.

"Not really. They don't like the smell of it, or of any food, but especially strong things like garlic and onions. Eating a lot of it might be enough to keep vampires on the street from biting you if given other options but if you're the only snack available, they won't hesitate."

He laughed. "I don't know how I feel about being considered a snack by my best friend."

She licked the oil from her lips. "What about by me?"

He raised a playful brow. "You think I'm a snack?"

"The snackiest."

He set the bowl down, pulled her close, and kissed her gently. "*That* I'm okay with."

Chapter 69

"Dad still taking her on a trip down memory lane?" Violet asked, sitting across from Rue in the kitchen and straining her neck to get a peek into the living room down the hall where she could see her father and new sister sitting next to each other.

"Yeah," she said, covering her mouth as she yawned. "He's been going through the old photo albums, telling her stories, mostly about Mom. She legit didn't think we could be photographed."

She rolled her eyes. "After decades of experimenting, you'd think witches would know us at least a *little bit*."

"I swear to God, they get half their information from old books and monster movies. Like, how did it not occur to them to question some of that stuff? If it defies the laws of physics, it's probably made up. Dumbasses."

"To be fair, some of what we do doesn't make sense. Kenton can fly, for fuck's sake."

"Touche', I guess. Where is he, anyway? I thought he couldn't *stand* being away from you for five minutes."

She laughed at her sister's teasing tone. "He can't but Florin 'summoned' him and you know how old-as-shit vampires are about their sires."

"Florin?" she asked, almost choking on her own spit. "Like, *Florin*, Florin?"

She shrugged.

"Like, from the stories?"

"What stories?"

"Bitch," Rue said, dropping her head in exasperation. "You have to remember this. The vampire-creation story Dad told us growing up. Florin, the first vampire, made by a demon and a witch thousands and thousands of years ago. How do you not know this?"

"Ooh," She tapped her lips with a finger while she put the pieces together. "He *did* say he was meeting up with him in Romania."

"It *is* him! Holy crap, I thought he was a myth."

"Who's a myth?" Booth asked, entering the kitchen with an empty tea cup and saucer.

"Florin."

"Oh, yes, well, no one knows for sure. You know how stories change over the years. I'm sure the Florin story has its roots in a bit of truth."

"I don't know about the story's details but Florin himself is real, apparently."

He raised a curious brow as he set his dishes in the sink. "Is he?"

Rue turned to Violet. "Do you want to tell him?"

She shook her head. "No, go ahead. You look way more excited about it than me."

She swiveled in her seat to face her father. "He's alive and your son-in-law's sire."

"Really? Hmm."

She was taken aback by his calm reaction. "Don't get too excited. Wouldn't want you to strain something."

"No, no, it's very interesting. I just have other things on my mind at the moment." He gestured toward the living room where Adia sat alone on the sofa.

"She still doesn't trust us?" Violet asked.

"You can't blame her," Rue said, giving herself a quick neck massage. "She was raised to think we're monsters, to hate us. That doesn't get undone in a couple of nights, family or not."

"Would you talk to her?" Booth asked. "Please, darling. I'm afraid that nothing I say is reaching her."

She groaned as she stood. "Fine, but I'm telling you right now if she spells my lips shut or something, I'm going home." She walked down the hall, grumbling to herself, "My whole sleep schedule's off. I don't even know what day it is anymore. Got me out here playing therapist to a baby vamp with more issues than Sports Illustrated when I should be working. The bar's losing money every minute I keep it closed. Regulars are probably pissed." She straightened her shoulders as she entered the living room where she found Adia staring at one of her parent's wedding pictures. "Hey."

"Hey," the girl said, not looking up. "They look really happy here."

"They *were* really happy, 'til the witches kidnapped and murdered her."

Her face scrunched as if the words physically hurt her.

"Sorry," Rue sat next to her, leaving half a cushion of space between them. "That was out of pocket. I just haven't been getting much sleep. How are you feeling?"

"Overstimulated."

"Valid."

She glanced back toward the kitchen and sighed, closing the album. "He wants me to be okay with everything, be a daughter to him, a sister to you. I'm just not there."

"I get it. After how you were raised, I'm surprised you haven't tried to kill us all, already."

"You're not how I thought you were. Vampires, I mean. You have marriages and families and happiness. Jobs. Whole lives. Aside from the drinking blood to live thing, you're pretty much like everyone else."

"No lies detected."

"So, what's the fighting about? Why do witches hate you," She paused. "*Us* so much?"

"I imagine it's because we kill people so often."

Her eyes widened. "Violet said you don't actually do that anymore."

"She doesn't. Dad doesn't. I though, have a hard time controlling my anger when dudes get handsy. I'm trying to be better, just drink from bags but the city's full of predators. Sucks for them that I'm apex." She thought for a moment. "I might have a vigilante complex. Anyway, vampires are just like anyone else. Most drink from blood bags but some have donors they drink from regularly."

"Like Violet with her friend, Lennon."

"Yeah. Others kill, either because of anger issues," She pointed to herself. "Or because they like it, like serial killers but that's *maybe* one percent of us."

"Do you...like it?"

"Not even a little. To be honest, I kind of hate it *and* hate myself for doing it. The guilt is real, even if I think they deserve it."

"Do you feel guilty about Marley?"

Her eyes showed pity but her voice was full of scorn. "I know she was your sister but what she did to us was pure fucking evil. She tricked Violet into falling for her, turned her into an abusive bitch, then tried to murder her, me, and our friends. She got what she deserved. For the record, though, I didn't kill her or your mom. Kenton did but if he hadn't, I would have."

Tears pooled in Adia's eyes as she held tighter to the photo album.

"Listen," Rue said, feeling sorry for the girl. "If we had known about you, things would've been different. Dad never would've left you with those people."

"But, I was human. In a house full of vampires, I would've been dinner."

She stared daggers at her, holding herself back, fighting the urge to slap her in the face. "You would have been fine. Dad would have protected you the way he's always protected me and Violet. We would have loved you."

Tears tumbled down her cheeks as she looked into her big sister's eyes, *her* eyes. Their mother's eyes. "I don't know where I belong anymore."

She rubbed her shoulder, tilting her head in sympathy. "This is gonna sound harsh, but I'm gonna go out on a limb and say maybe you don't belong with the people who are actively trying to murder you when you have a full family right in front of your face."

She snickered under her breath as she wiped her face. "You're probably ri--"

"Shh."

"What?"

She stood, straining to hear the footsteps coming up the drive. "Not this shit again."

The door burst open, a man in tactical gear having kicked it in. He and six more rushed inside, guns pointed. Adia jumped from her seat, Rue standing between her and the hunters. She recognized one of the armed men as her cook, betrayal stinging like a bee.

"*Lou?*"

"Sorry, boss," he said, his tone sarcastic. "I try to stay out of politics but when your old man here," He pointed to Booth who, along with Violet, joined Rue in blocking the hunters from getting to Adia. "Started rounding up witches, I had no choice."

"The fuck are you talking about?"

"I'll handle this, dear," her father said, stepping in front of her. "Take your sisters outside."

Lou cocked his rifle. "No one's going anywhere until you tell me what you did with those girls."

"Well," he took off his glasses, giving them a quick cleaning with a handkerchief and putting them back on. "I killed them, of course."

"The fuck?" Violet muttered.

"I needed their blood for a locator spell," he explained. "Specifically, a *final* location spell." He stepped forward, his voice calm, his demeanor defiant. "You see, your kind kidnapped, tortured, experimented on, and murdered my wife along with countless others. I wanted to know where my Zahara had taken her last breath. Now that the coven that killed her is dead, I have no quarrel with you. However, if you feel inclined to do me harm, take your best shot but leave my girls out of it. They're innocent in this."

Lou scoffed. "*Innocent?* You know how many scumbag rapists I've seen Rue *eat*? She doesn't hide it as well as she thinks she does. I'm not saying they didn't deserve it but innocent, she ain't. Now, the higher-ups say I have to bring that one in alive," He pointed his gun at Adia, then back to Booth. "I'm gonna kill the rest of you for revenge, of course, but her blood is the cure for you freaks and since witches made you vamps, they see it as their duty to clean up their mess."

"Jokes on you, dick," Violet scoffed.

"Shh," Rue warned.

Lou scowled. "How's that?"

Rue stepped closer but still behind her father. "*Nothing*."

"Ooh," Adia whispered. "I'm useless to them now, aren't I?"

Violet clicked her tongue. "Pretty much."

Rue sighed. "What part of 'shh' do you two not understand?"

"Well, I'll be damned," Lou said, studying Adia's face more closely. "You made her one of you."

Adia crossed her arms in anger. "No, actually, your people did when they *snapped my neck*. Killing a fellow witch for her blood? That's messed up."

"You were never a witch. Not really. You were always one of them. Now, you'll die alongside them."

Before he could get a shot off, Booth snatched the gun from Lou's hands, bashing him in the nose with its butt. As he dropped, shots rang out, the six hunters edging toward them. Bullets flew into Booth's chest as he ordered his daughters to run.

The women raced to the kitchen, bullets whizzing by, Rue pushing the other two from behind. "Get her out of here," she told Violet who nodded, grabbed Adia's hand, and led her out the back door. The two bolted through the yard to the woods behind it. Once in the safety of the trees, Violet stopped.

"What are you doing?" Adia asked. "They're right behind us."

"Keep going. Find a place to hide. We'll come get you when it's over." Violet turned to head back but Adia grabbed her arm in protest.

"Are you crazy? You could get killed!"

"Rue and Dad are back there! I have to help them." She twisted her arm free, rushing off in a blur.

"Violet!" she shouted, but she was already gone

Chapter 70

There was blood splattered on every surface. Walls, furniture, and flooring all doused in crimson and gore. Kenton and his sire stepped through the open doorway to find the living room littered with bodies, torn-off limbs, and discarded organs. In the center of the room, the bullet-riddled corpse of Booth Witcomb lay face-up on a pile of wood that used to be a coffee table, its empty eyes fixed on the hallway.

"Violet," Kenton whispered, following the dead man's gaze. He leaped over the decapitated body of a gun-holding hunter, running through pools of blood and slipping on a link of intestine. He fell to his knees, going ghost-white as he came upon her body, his beautiful wife, snuffed out by a wooden bullet to the heart. He patted her cheek in desperation. "Violet, darling," Tears sprang to his eyes as he took her hand in his, examining the flesh caked under her nails. "That's my good girl, fighting back." He kissed the cold back of her hand before pressing it to his forehead, his head bowed as he began to sob.

Florin pat his shoulder as he passed on his way to the kitchen where another hunter's body lay on the floor, its throat ripped out. Next to it was the body of a woman with the same features and long, dark hair as the one Kenton was mourning. This one had a stake plunged into her chest, her body crumpled in front of the back door as if she was trying to block someone from exiting; the hunter, Florin presumed.

He kicked the hunter's corpse out of the way and knelt next to the woman, touching the wings of the gold beetle pendant that hung around her neck. "Interesting." He quickly glanced back to where Kenton still wept. "I can't just leave this here," he muttered to himself, wrapping his slender fingers around the stake, gripping it tight, and yanking it from the body.

He watched in awe as the muscle and skin repaired itself. "Fascinating." After a few seconds, her eyes flew open, her hands flying up to her chest as she gasped for air.

As she sat herself up, coughing with her first few breaths, Kenton rushed in. "Sister," he said, taking Florin's spot as he stepped away. "Are you hurt?"

Rue looked down at herself, her hands, arms, and clothes soaked with blood, rubbing her chest in disbelief. "I don't know. I thought--" She stopped, her eyes saucering with realization. "Adia. I told her to run. If they catch her..."

"How many were there?" Florin asked.

"Seven."

He and Kenton exchanged worried glances. "By the looks of things, I'd say six met their ends here."

"One's still out there," Kenton seethed.

"I have to find Adia," Rue said, her voice straining as she tried to stand.

"You should rest," Florin told her, gently pushing her back to a seated position. "I'll find the girl." And with that, he darted out the back door, not bothering to close it behind him.

"Who the fuck's that?" she asked.

"His name is Florin, my sire."

"The first? Huh. I thought he'd be wizened and shit. He looks like a teenager."

"He was only twenty when he was raised but I assure you, he's no child."

Her eyes fell to the hallway where her sister's body lay. "They killed them." Tears streamed down Rue's cheeks, cutting through the hunter's blood speckling her face like freckles. She looked down at her shaking hands, bits of hunter still stuck under her mossy green painted nails. "They had wooden bullets and..." She noticed the blood-stained stake on the floor a few inches away. "Seriously, what the fuck?"

He took her face in his hands, his lip quivering but his eyes blazing with rage. "Someone once said, 'Justice and revenge are not the same thing.' I say vengeance is where the twain shall meet. Today, we grieve. *Tonight, we* will be the hunters. Every one of them will pay for what happened here in blood. Are you with me, sister?"

She nodded, her nostrils flaring and her cheeks going red. "Tonight."

CHAPTER 70

Florin stalked the woods behind the Witcomb house, the light of the early morning sun filtering through the trees a welcome sight, even if it did leave him feeling a little weaker than usual. Though he spent most of his long life in the shadows, he indulged in the occasional daytime walkabout. This time of day was his favorite, just after sunrise, when the world was still quiet but lit up, beaming with color and life. He only hoped he'd have the chance to see more mornings like this.

"Interiacio!" He heard from above before being lifted off his feet by an unseen force and thrown backward into an oak tree.

"Retained your magic, I see," he quipped, adjusting his coat.

"Who are you?" Adia demanded from the safety of a tree several feet away, hidden high up in its crown of leaves.

"I won't hurt you," he promised, looking up into the canopy. "I came with Kenton, your brother-in-law. I just want to make sure you're all right."

"I'm fine."

"You can come down. I won't bite."

"Sounds like something a vampire would say right before they--"

"My name is Florin. I assure you, I mean you no harm."

"Florin?" She shimmied down to a low branch and hopped to the forest floor. "Like, the first vamp?"

His lips turned up in an impressed smile as he buttoned his coat. "You've heard of me?"

"Sure. No offense but I kind of thought you were a myth."

"No offense taken. You're a bit of a myth, yourself. The girl whose blood can end vampirism once and for all."

"Yeah, not anymore." She flashed her fangs.

"I see. Your blood is no longer cured, therefor it no longer *is* the cure." He stepped closer, reaching out to brush a few wayward wisps of chestnut hair away from her eyes, warmth spreading from his chest to his abdomen. She was stunning, her cognac-brown eyes glowing in sunlight. He was mesmerized by her beauty, so much so that when she batted his hand away, he didn't flinch. He simply cleared his throat and held his hands in front of himself, hoping she'd forgive his forward nature. "When word of your transformation spreads to the covens, you'll have an even bigger target on your back. The witches will be coming for you, whether you were once one of them or not. Will you fight with us, then? To protect yourself and others like us?"

She crossed her arms. "Depends. Did my dad make it? My sisters?"

"One of them did," he told her, trying to appear sympathetic. "The one wearing the scarab."

"The bug necklace?"

He nodded.

She dipped her head. "That's Rue. She sent us out, me and Violet. She tried to save us."

"And, she succeeded, at least, in part."

She shook her head. "Violet went back. I begged her not to but she wouldn't listen. Now, she's gone. And, her-- *our* dad."

"Yet, here you stand, a survivor, a vampire with the gift of magic. Harness your power and no one, witch, vampire, or otherwise will be able to stop you. You, dear girl, are a creature unlike any other. You can put an end to this war, not the way the witches thought, of course, but *your* way. Show them what you're made of. Make them wish they'd never heard the name Adia."

She squeezed her arms tighter, her lips pursed and her glare skeptical. "You said Rue's okay?"

"She took a stake to the chest, but she's recovering nicely. I'll take you to her. I found her blocking the kitchen door, protecting you, I imagine. Will you do her the same courtesy?"

She released her arms. "They'll never stop coming for me, will they? The witches."

He shook his head and held out his hand. "They haven't stopped coming for *me* and it's been...well, I can't quite remember how many millennia it's been."

She blew out a resigned breath and took his hand.

CHAPTER 70

He began leading her back to the house, that warm feeling flooding through him once again. "Your sister will be glad to see you alive."

She made air quotes with her free hand. "Alive."

He chuckled. "From what I hear, this is how you were meant to be born. Believe me, you are very much alive."

"Yeah," She rolled her eyes. "As a freakin' vampire."

"More than that. *You* are a force of nature."

Chapter 71

Ophelia was jolted from bed by the sound of a door slamming. Dylan, too, sprang up, rubbing his eyes. She moved to get out of bed but he held her back, sniffing the air.

"Stay here," he said, sliding off the mattress and into his jeans. "I smell blood. A lot of it." But, before he could get his pants zipped, the bedroom door flew open, Rue storming in, covered in dried blood.

She stopped and looked the two over, an exasperated sigh in her throat. "Remind me to lecture you about *that* later," she said to Ophelia, pointing at Dylan.

"What happened?" Ophelia yelped. "Are you okay?"

She covered the hole in her shirt. "*No.* You stink. What is that smell?"

"Garlic, probably. We had a late-night snack before going back to bed. What--"

"Gross."

"What the hell happened?"

"Later. I'm gonna go shower. I have people-gristle all over me. I just came by to tell you you have a new roommate. I set Adia up in Violet's old room."

"What? Why?"

"I need her close but not in the same apartment, just in case. If they come looking for me, she'll have time to get away and if they come looking for *her*, I'll be able to get the jump on them."

"But--"

"You're friends, right? Besides, you're a witch now. If she gets fangy, just spell her to sleep or something."

"But, what if--"

"No arguments. It's just until me and Kenton take care of this witch thing once and for all." She spun on her heel and left the apartment in a flash.

"The fuck happened last night?" she muttered.

"I don't know but that was a lot of blood."

"I saw."

"No, I mean, a lot of *different* blood. Hers plus at least five others."

"Jesus."

"What's she mixed up in?"

"Oh, you know," She sighed and lay back down. "Vampires v witches. Tale as old as time."

He got in next to her, wrapping her in his arms and kissing her head. "Never a dull moment around here, huh?"

"Not lately, no."

"Well, vampire, witch, goblin, or whatever, nothing's gonna hurt you. Not while I'm around."

"Really?" she teased. "And, how long do you plan on being around?"

He tilted her chin up to look her in the eye. "For as long as you'll have me."

Meanwhile, in her new bedroom, Adia paced, hands on her hips, confusion in her heart. Vampires killed her old family and witches killed her new one. Neither side seemed to have any sort of moral compass, just loyalty to their own and hate for the other. In a world where no one is good or bad and right and wrong depend on one's perception, where did she belong? Not with the witches that were trying to kill her, obviously but were the vampires much better? "They protected me," she reminded herself but was that enough? Her whole life she was taught to fear and despise vampires. Now that she was one, she wasn't sure where her loyalties lay; with the sister that saved her or the magic she was raised in. "Both," she decided. "Like Florin said." She flopped onto the bed, kicking her shoes off and staring at the ceiling.

She closed her eyes to sleep but she couldn't stop thinking about the tall vampire with the gray eyes, his crafty smile, and his fingers grazing her cheek. She never thought she'd be attracted to a vampire, let alone the oldest and most dangerous, but here she was, fantasizing about kissing him, touching him, and letting him touch her. Booth had told her that her emotions and senses would be heightened now but she hadn't expected to feel like *this*, especially right after two more of her family members were killed. But, there Florin was, in her head like a goddamn incubus. She wondered if she'd see him again and if she did, what she would do. Would she be able to control herself or would she give in to her dark desires? She grunted, covering her face with a pillow. "Why does he have to be *so hot*?"

Across the hall, Iman slept while Rue showered, still unaware of the events of the night. She'd shelter him from it, for now, the thought of talking about it making her cry all over again. It took her almost an hour to scrub away all the blood. She used a washcloth and even a toothbrush to get every speck of hunter out from under her nails. Once clean, she wrapped herself in a towel and wandered to the living room where she stared blankly out the window, cars full of people in rush hour traffic like ants so many stories below. She felt numb, cold. Dead inside. It was normal, she knew, but she also knew that if she let herself slip into this depression, let it overtake her, she wouldn't have the strength to do what needed to be done. Kenton was right. The witches had to pay. But, she would be in no condition to fight, to protect Adia, if she was disassociated on the couch for who knows how long. She needed to feel something, *anything*. It was literally life and death.

"Hey," Iman said through a yawn. "How's everything with your new sister? Your text was pretty vague."

She remembered the last text she'd sent him. *Adia made it through the change. See you soon.* How long ago was that? Five hours? More? She couldn't keep track. "She's sleeping at Ophelia's."

CHAPTER 71

"So, good, then?" He kissed her cheek and rubbed her back.

She looked up at him, his chocolate eyes like pools she could get lost in, deep and warm. "Do you love me?" she blurted.

"You know I do."

She dropped her towel, her skin glistening in the sunlight through the window. "Show me."

His voice lowered as he leaned in, taking on the rasp she was used to hearing when he sang. "Yes, ma'am." He kissed her, long and deep, his tongue like an explorer in her mouth. As he removed his clothes, she let herself feel it, her lust for him. Every sensation, every touch, every penetrating kiss. In no time at all, she was wet, her body reacting to him with the heat of a burning building.

She didn't know how they'd made it to her bed but she was grateful to be on her back as her legs felt like jelly. He kissed her neck as she guided him inside, her troubles melting away with every achingly slow thrust. Her hips instinctively swiveled to meet his movements, his growl in her ear giving her goosebumps.

Soon enough, night would fall and she would join with Kenton in tracking down her ex-cook and the witches that sent him. There would be more battles, more death, more pain. Until then, though, she would indulge in her lover's body and in sleep, gaining strength for the fight to come.

Chapter 72

The summer sun beat down on Kenton's pale neck, his head hung low, his black button-down doing nothing to protect him from the UV rays. He stood over his wife's fresh grave, her father's just next to it in the garden of their Connecticut home. He'd buried them hastily, the tall shrubbery along the sides of the yard hiding what he was doing from the neighbors. He wasn't sure if it was the right thing to do in the long run, legally speaking but it was the most respectful thing he could think to do, given the circumstances. With the threat of another attack hanging over his head and the desperate need for revenge burning in his chest, there simply wasn't time to come up with a story the police would believe. They'd want to investigate, do autopsies. They'd suspect him of the murders or worse, discover what they truly were. He couldn't risk it. Violet and Booth deserved a proper burial, consequences be damned.

"The hunters' bodies have all been burned," Florin said, taking his place next to Kenton. "I'll call for a cleaner to deal with the mess inside. They're very discreet, one of us."

"Thank you."

"I'm very sorry for your loss, meu fiul. Truly."

Again, without raising his head, he simply said, "Thank you."

"I know the pain of losing the woman you love, your soulmate. There was nothing I could do when my Silviana passed. You can't fight a disease, at least not once it's won. But, *you* can fight the evil that took *your* wife. You can take your revenge and save the rest of us while you're at it *if* you're up to it. So, are you, my boy? Are you in a condition to once again be my right hand?"

He slowly raised his head to look at his sire, his bloodshot eyes brimming with fury and despair. "Point me like a weapon in any direction and I will not fail you."

"Good," He patted his back and rubbed his shoulder. "Because I know just where to start."

Lou stood outside the New Rochelle mansion, its stuccoed exterior and Spanish-tiled roof more fitting southern California than the New York suburbs, though he would never mention it. It was home to the High Priestess of the Howe Coven, arguably the most powerful witch in all of North America, if not the world. Everything the hunters did was on her command and punishment for failure was at her discretion. Letting Adia get away, he knew, was an unforgivable offense and as he trembled, taking one last shaky breath before knocking on the oak and iron Tudor-style door, he said a silent prayer, wishing for forgiveness and mercy.

"Hunter," a woman greeted after opening the door, barely looking at him before wandering off. He recognized her as a Howe witch and as part of the coven, she was not to be insulted in any way so he stifled the urge to roll his eyes and entered. The foyer led to a winding staircase of honey oak and wrought iron while the walls shone in a white so bright, that he regretted not bringing sunglasses. To his left was an archway leading to a sitting room and there, as if waiting for him, was the Priestess.

She sat on a white chaise, wearing a white dress, and drinking a glass of white wine. She looked like a model in a home catalog, the aesthetic all important, it would seem. Her dark curls hung loosely over her bare shoulders, the ringlets perfectly imperfect. She licked her full, red lips and set her glass down, her jade-green eyes flicking to him. She was so stunningly beautiful, he would have been aroused by the mere sight of her if he wasn't so terrified.

"Hunter Lou," she said, her velvety voice cutting the silence like a knife. She looked him up and down, her relaxed expression turning to disgust. "Don't sit on my furniture in those clothes."

"Oh, of course, Priestess," he said, looking down at his blood-stained tactical vest. "I-I'm sorry, I should have gone home and changed but I wanted to come straight here to--"

"Tell me of your failure?"

He swallowed, then cringed at the audible *gulp*. "Yes, Priestess." He clenched his hands behind his back, hoping she wouldn't notice how badly he was shaking.

She sighed, taking another sip of wine and putting the glass back on the end table. "Tell me what happened."

He moved to stand in front of her, head down in embarrassment and fear. "We arrived at the location at approximately 0500, and announced our intention to take the girl, Adia with us. She was then removed from the house by the vampire, Violet while our team neutralized the male vampire. There was a skirmish with Rue, the ringleader of the nest. During the fight, Violet returned alone. Upon interrogation, she refused to disclose the girl's location. In the end, we put down all three vampires that were protecting the girl."

"But, she got away and your men are all dead," she said, sounding bored.

He cleared his throat. "Y-Yes, ma'am, but there's more."

She raised an eyebrow in interest.

"The girl," He swallowed again, preparing himself for the worst. "She's been made vampire."

A deafening silence filled the room, the air heavy with the Priestess' disappointment. She didn't move, didn't speak. She didn't seem to react at all. But, he could feel it, the weight of her disapproval, like being at the bottom of the ocean with no way to swim to the surface. Sweat beaded at both of his temples as the room's temperature suddenly increased by at least twenty degrees. It got so muggy he could hardly breathe. His heart raced as he wondered if this was his punishment. Would it get hotter and hotter until he cooked like meat in an oven? Was she intending to do this or was she out of control? He couldn't die like this. He had to do something but what? She was his Priestess and he was at her whim.

"Priestess," he croaked, his throat suddenly bone dry.

She sighed again, the temperature of the room returning to a comfortable seventy degrees. "Do you have any idea where the girl ran off to?"

"There's only one place left she could be hiding. I would have checked but there's another vampire that lives in the building. I'd need a team."

"Of course." She shook her head and finished her wine.

"Priestess, if you don't mind me asking," She shot him a look that told him she absolutely did mind but he was too curious not to ask, anyway. "If this girl's blood is...tainted, what do we do now?"

She stood, getting close enough that their noses nearly touched. He squeezed his hands tighter, begging in his mind for the encounter to be over, praying that she wouldn't kill him or worse, make an example of him. Every nerve stood on edge as she opened her mouth to speak. His limbs went cold and he was sure he'd pass out any second. "We'll do as we've always done. If we can't cure them, we'll kill them."

"E-Even the girl?"

"*Especially the girl,*" she hissed. "We can't have a rogue vampire with the magic of the Good Coven running around looking for revenge. We just slaughtered the last of her family. She'll be coming for us...if we don't get to her first."

Chapter 73

Dylan stared up at the ceiling, unable to get back to sleep after Rue's impromptu wake-up call. Hours had passed since she'd left and Ophelia had drifted off, her head on his chest. Adia, the new vampire Rue had dumped in the next room, also slept, her deep breathing audible to his heightened sense of hearing through the thin walls. Based on how long he'd been lying there and how full his bladder felt, he guessed it was about noon. There was no sense in trying to go back to sleep at that point. No matter how tired he was, he needed to get up.

He gently rolled Ophelia away and slipped out of bed, admiring how beautiful she looked as he pulled his jeans on. He crept out of the room, tip-toe-ing to the bathroom. When he finished, he washed his hands and headed to the kitchen to see if there was something to make for breakfast. He was trying to decide if he should bring Ophelia breakfast in bed or let her sleep when he got a whiff of something he wasn't used to smelling in this building this early in the day: humans.

He left the apartment, sniffing the air in the hall. It wasn't coming from Rue and Iman's place but it was definitely stronger. He followed the scent downstairs, out of the kitchen, and into the bar. There, he saw five men, all in black tactical gear, some carrying what looked like water guns. He recognized the one in the lead as the cook who'd yelled at him when he'd made Ophelia a sundae. He sized them up, their outfits not exactly screaming 'casual'. He grabbed a bottle from the counter as a weapon, just in case. They were obviously looking for trouble.

"Lou?" he asked, unsure if he was remembering his name correctly.

"Bass player," Lou said.

"Can I help you with something, fellas?"

Lou tilted his head, his eyes slits as he pointed his weapon, pulling the trigger, a stream of water hitting Dylan in the cheek.

CHAPTER 73

He wiped it away. "Seriously?"

"Stand down," Lou told the others. "He's not one of them."

"What is that, Holy water?"

He blinked. "You know about them?"

"Yeah. So, what, you came to demand a raise or, uh, is this like a murder thing?"

"I already handled Rue."

"You sure?" He lifted his ear. "Cause I can hear her heart beating from here."

"The fu--" He stepped closer, studying Dylan's face. "Ooh. You're not one of *them*. You're something else. Something *wild*, am I right?"

"Yeah, I'm definitely something. What do want, Lou? Shift doesn't start for like, seven hours."

"It's not your concern, mutt."

"Well, that's not very nice. Pretty insulting, actually. Downright rude."

"*Step aside.*"

He glanced back at the swinging door. "You boys hungry? Breaking into a bar seems a little dramatic when diners exist. Restaurants, bodegas, food trucks. Lots of options that don't require catching a charge...or these hands."

"Get out of the way!" a man behind Lou demanded.

"Yeah, I won't be doing that but nice work trying to be intimidating. Really, good job. I especially like the way you're mouthing off while hiding behind cook Lou, here. Very brave."

"Quiet," Lou said to the man before turning his attention back to Dylan. "We're not here for you. If Rue somehow managed to get back here after I staked her, I'll take her out, too but all we're really after is the witch. Get out of the way and this will all be over in a few minutes."

"The witch?" Dylan said, nostrils flaring.

"Yes. We'll be on our way as soon as she's dead. You can go back to sniffing asses or whatever you people do when it's done. All we want is the witch."

He dipped his head, shaking it as if saying 'no'. "Now, that's too bad. See, I'm pretty fond of her. We're kind of a thing. Still new but intense, you know? So, I'm gonna have to ask you boys to," He made a swirling motion in the air with his left index finger and whistled. "Turn yourselves around and get the hell out of here."

Lou fumed. "Get out of our way, dog. We didn't come here for you but make no mistake, we will put you down before putting a bullet in your bitch's head if you don't move."

He smacked his lips, again shaking his head. "That was really the wrong thing to say." In one fluid motion, he slammed the bottle down against the side of Lou's head then swung it up across his chin.

"Kill this fucker!" the second man shouted. The four holstered their water guns and drew their real ones, training them on Dylan.

He used the unconscious cook as a shield, throwing him into the others.

"Fuck!" the second man said as stray wooden bullets pelted their leader. His body dropped, blood pouring from a wound in his lower abdomen, the only part of his torso not covered by Kevlar.

Dylan used the distraction to his advantage, dropping down and sweeping the second man's leg, knocking him on his back. His eyes glowed yellow as he stood, stomping on the man's head and punching another in the face. He yanked the rifle out of the final commando's hands and bashed him in the nose with its butt. He snarled, ripping off the man's arm. Another sat up, taking a knife from his vest. Dylan used the limb like a baseball bat to hit him across the face, knocking him out cold.

They were all down but he didn't stop. He couldn't. They were after Ophelia and he would *not* let them get to her. He broke the bottle against the bar top and used its sharp edges to slit one of their throats. He smashed two of their heads against the floor until he was sure they were dead and used the fallen knife to stab the unconscious man in the neck. By the time he got to Lou, he was so blind with rage, he didn't hear his friends run into the room or Ophelia's scream as he dropped to his knees, grabbed Lou's head, and tore it clean from his body.

"Jesus fuck," Rue said, her arm stretched out to keep the others from getting closer to Dylan and his mess.

"Dude," Iman said. "Hey, you okay?"

He growled, chest heaving, his golden eyes shining in the dim light of the closed bar. He hunched over the mutilated corpses, like an animal guarding its dinner.

"See," Rue snapped. "This right here is what I was worried about. Ophelia, go upstairs."

CHAPTER 73

"Girl," she said, stepping out from behind Rue's arm. "That is *not* happening."

"Bitch, are you stupid? *He's feral.*" She gently kicked Lou's decapitated head over to see its face. "Did us a favor, looks like, but still."

"Hunters?" Iman asked.

"Yep."

"You'll need a new cook," Ophelia said, inching her way toward Dylan. "Dylan can cook."

Rue grabbed her arm and pulled her back. "Do you have brain damage from the fight with Marley or are you just dick-whipped? Christ, I thought it was just white chicks that had no fear of wild animals."

"He's not an animal," she defended, yanking her arm away. "He was protecting us." She moved closer, taking small steps toward him. "He won't hurt me."

"Is it drugs?" Rue asked, turning her gaze to Iman. "Is she on drugs?"

He shrugged, eyes fixed on his friend.

Ophelia knelt in front of Dylan, slowly holding her hand out. He sniffed in her direction, his jaw relaxing. He edged toward her, his growls turning to whimpers. He smelled her palm, up her arm, and to her neck. The others watched intently as his eyes reverted to their usual sky blue and a pained breath escaped his lips.

"I told them to leave," he muttered, his voice again human. "I didn't want to...I'm sorry."

Rue sighed with relief. "The fuck, man? I was *this close* to ripping your heart out."

He touched Ophelia's cheek. "They said they were here to kill you."

"Me?" Ophelia took his hand in hers. "Why?"

"Did they mention her by name?" Adia said, entering through the kitchen's swinging door.

He looked up at the group as if noticing them for the first time. "Lou said 'the witch'."

Adia blew out a nervous breath. "They meant me. These are Howe hunters."

"Howe hunters?"

"Men born into some covens aren't allowed to practice magic, logic being that the power goes to their heads. They get all world domination with it. Instead, they're trained to be vampire hunters. You can tell they're Howe by the H tattoo on their right hands. See?" She pointed to one of the bodies. The others nodded in acknowledgment. "They wouldn't be here unless the Priestess sent them which means she knows what and where I am. When they don't come back, she'll send more."

Dylan leaned in to quietly ask Ophelia, "I thought she was a vampire?"

"She's both."

"That's possible?"

"Apparently."

"Are you shaking?" Rue asked. "Shit." She poured a shot and walked it over to Dylan.

"Thank you," he said, gulping it down.

"I see the guilt on your face," she said, crossing her arms. But, *this*," she gestured to his blood-soaked clothes and the corpses littering the floor. "Is not okay."

Ophelia stood to face her. "Didn't you *just* come home covered in people-parts? How are *you* the morality police, exactly?"

"Wait, what?" Iman asked.

"Nothing," Rue snapped. "That was different."

Ophelia scoffed. "How?"

She sucked on her front teeth then grunted. "Fine, it's not *that* different. Just, go get your man cleaned up while mine burns these bitches."

Ophelia and Dylan retreated upstairs while Rue found a pen and notebook, slamming them on the counter.

"Adia, get your pubescent ass over here."

"Eighteen is hardly pubescent," she said, sitting at the bar.

"Fine, your barely-legal ass, then." She slid the writing supplies across to her. "Write down every coven you know that even *might* be involved in this shit. I want names, addresses, favorite restaurants, everything. Any location they could be hiding out in."

"Okay," She shakily took the pen and began to write. "What are you gonna do?"

She picked up the receiver to the bar's landline and looked her dead in the eye. "Protect my sister."

As she dialed, Iman snatched the receiver from her hand.

"The fuck, bro?"

"Are you gonna tell me what the fuck is going on or am I supposed to just--"

"Later." She took the phone back. Her features softened as she touched his arm. "I promise."

He glared at her for a few seconds before turning, walking over to the pile of corpses, and hoisting one over his shoulder. When he left the room, she dialed Kenton's number.

"Sister," he answered after five rings. "Excuse the delay, I was a bit preoccupied."

"Hey, you and Grandpa Vamp still stateside?"

"For the moment."

"You interested in a little payback?"

"I believe you know the answer to that."

"Good." She watched as Adia scribbled at hyper-speed. She'd already filled one page and had turned to another. "I have some info for you. I'll text you tonight with a list. You start at the top, I'll work my way up from the bottom."

※

Kenton picked a bit of gristle from his teeth, kicking a dead body out of his way as he moved through the house, listening for the sounds of hiding witches. The only heartbeats left were his and his sire's, the latter's slower than it should be as he drank from a freshly-killed witch. There were twelve bodies in all, the entire coven, he assumed. He dropped to a blood-stained sofa, lying back on the cushions, exhausted from hours of slaughter and feeding. He listened to Rue explain what happened at the bar and was relieved to hear that she was all right. She was the only family he had left, aside from Florin. Come hell or high water, he would make sure she was safe.

"I look forward to tonight's to-do list. Thanks, love." He ended the call and shoved his cell in his back pocket, closing his eyes for the first time in more than twenty-four hours.

"I believe that's all of them," Florin said, wiping his mouth on a handkerchief. "Who were you speaking to just now?"

"My sister-in-law. Hunters paid her a visit. She was saved by a werewolf, of all things. How she managed to domesticate one is beyond me."

"In my experience with the beasts, there's only one thing that can tame them."

"What's that?"

"The same thing that tames us all."

"What, love?" He scoffed, putting his hands underneath his head for better support.

"Don't underestimate its power. It brought me back to life, remember."

"I seem to recall you telling me it was a demon that raised you from the dead."

"Yes, technically." He slumped in a chair, wrapping himself in his coat as if it were a blanket. "But, had it not been for the love of a devoted woman, that demon would never have known I existed. I'd be rotting in the ground as we speak."

"Rotting? You'd be completely disintegrated by now."

"Mind your tone, boy."

His eyes flew open. "Apologies, sire. I forgot myself."

"An understandable lapse in judgment, given the day you've had. Rest now."

"Yes, sire." He closed his eyes again, rolling to his side and hugging himself, hoping the vision of his wife's bullet-ridden body would fade as he drifted to sleep.

Ophelia leaned against the bathroom door frame as Dylan showered, his bloody clothes soaking in peroxide in the washer. She watched him get himself clean, the red-tinted water swirling down the drain getting clearer and clearer. *Is it fucked up that this is turning me on?* she thought, his rippling muscles glistening through the steam-covered shower door. He leaned his forearms against the tiled wall under the shower head, head down, letting the near scorching water roll down his back.

"I really didn't mean to kill them," he said, his voice so low, she could barely hear it over the running water. "I was just gonna rough them up a little, maybe knock them out and call the police. But, the wolf," He stopped, rubbing his eyes as tears mingled with the water on his face. "It took over. I kept picturing them with their guns pointed at you and I--" He turned his face to her, wiping the steam from the glass so he could see her. "I couldn't let them get to you." He leaned on his arm again, his shoulders trembling as he silently sobbed.

She stripped down and opened the shower door, joining him. She massaged his shoulders as he cried and when he got himself together, he turned to face her.

"I should go," he said, water at his back. "Rue was right. I could hurt you."

"You wouldn't."

"You saw what I did, *what I am*. I'm a monster."

"Aren't we all?"

"No," He took her face in his hands. "You're not. You're human and good."

"And strong." She held a hand up, telepathically sliding him back against the wall, the faucet digging into his spine.

He looked stunned as he regained control of his body and moved close to her.

"Witch, remember?"

"Yeah, but--"

"I don't think you'd ever hurt me. I trust you completely. But, if you ever tried, I can protect myself." She ran her hands over his chest and down his body, his eyes closing, a growl in his throat.

"What are you doing?"

She pulled him with her as she backed into the wall, opening her legs just enough to let his sudden erection slip between. She rubbed its head against her clit, one hand on his cock, the other on his shoulder. "Comforting you?"

He buried his nose in her neck, breathing her in, his hands on the wall to steady himself. "Are we crazy?"

"Probably." She wrapped one leg around his waist, opening herself up to him. He sank into her, kissing her neck and squeezing her thigh. He panted in her ear as their slippery bodies collided, water tickling her ass with every thrust. She matched his movements, throwing both arms around his neck for stability. Her legs shook with her first orgasm and as she felt like she might slip, he grabbed her waist and held her close, grunting into her hair.

"Are you ok?"

"Yeah," she breathed. "Keep going."

He growled again, his cock throbbing inside her, growing even harder. "I'm close."

"Come in me," she said, her hand gripping the back of his neck. "I want you to."

Another low growl left his lips, his eyes flashing yellow as his teeth lightly scraped along her jawline. She came again, a rush of fluid trickling down their legs. "*Fuck*," he whispered, quickening his pace. "I'm gonna marry you, I swear to God."

She smiled as he came, his words warming her heart as much as the heat from the running water warmed the rest of her. *Yes*, she thought. *He's definitely the one.*

Chapter 74

"Watch her," Rue said, shoving Adia over the threshold into Kenton's apartment.

"Um, what?" Lennon asked, turning off the TV and putting the remote down on the sofa next to them.

"I need her somewhere safe until I handle some things so just keep her here and text me if there's an emergency."

"Like what?"

"I don't know, murder? Threats of murder."

"The fuck?"

"Not from me," Adia assured.

"No," Rue said. "I gave her a blood bag before we left. She's good for a while."

"Again," Lennon said, standing to meet them. "*The fuck?*"

"I can't explain right now. I have witches to butcher. You should both be safe here until I get back." She turned to go but was stopped dead in her tracks by what Lennon asked next.

"Where's Violet?"

Her jaw clenched as she fought back tears, saying the only thing she could that wasn't a total lie. "My dad's."

Adia shot her a look to which Rue responded by subtly shaking her head.

"I'll be back as soon as I can," she called from the hall as she sped away, leaving Adia to close the door.

"*Okay,*" Lennon said, moving closer. "And, *who* are you?"

"Adia. Rue's sister, turns out."

"And Violet's."

"Mm, hmm." She nodded, lips tight, her stomach dropping at the intensity of their eyes. "I-I like your hair. The purple suits you."

"It's fading."

"Oh, well, still. It's nice."

"Where is Violet, *really*?"

"Uh, Connecticut."

"Bullshit. I'm not *great* with facial expressions but you don't have to be neurotypical to recognize the head motion for 'no'. Rue doesn't want you to tell me where Violet is. Why?"

She gulped. "I don't know."

"Yes, you do!"

Adia took a step back. "I don't *know* but I'm *guessing* she doesn't want to upset you. She probably wants to explain things when there's more time. Help you."

Their eyes were slits as they prodded. "Help me to what?"

She swallowed again, a twinge of sadness in her voice. "Grieve."

Their eyes widened as they stumbled back, their legs all but giving out. "Violet's...dead?"

"I'm so sorry."

"What happened? No, don't tell me. Just watch TV or something." They stormed off into their bedroom, slamming the door before pounding on it with their fist. They hit the white-painted wood until they cracked it, scraping their knuckles. They screamed, tears flooding their eyes and spilling down their reddened cheeks. They picked up a book and threw it into the wall, then another, and another. The world was collapsing in around them and there was nothing they could do to stop it.

"Are you okay?" Adia called from the other side of the door. "Do you need anything? What can I do?"

"Go away!" they shouted, covering their ears and dropping to the floor, curling up in a corner, knees to chest, even the sound of the bird chirping outside the window overwhelmingly loud. "Just leave me alone!"

"Hey," Adia said, opening the door. "I just wanted to--"

"*I said go away!*"

"I know, but..." She looked around the room, noticing the noise-canceling headphones and fidgets on the nightstand. "Oh," She quieted her voice. "Okay, I'm sorry." She stepped tentatively into the room, closing the shades to block out the streetlight and taking the headphones and fidgets from their place. She set the items softly on the floor next to them and backed out, closing the door as quietly as she could.

"Why?" they cried into their hands. "*Why?*"

It was nearly midnight by the time Rue got to the hunters' apartment in Philadelphia, the last location on Adia's list. Standing in the hall, she listened at the door, hearing four distinct heartbeats inside. All were between forty and fifty beats per minute so she was sure all of the men in the apartment were asleep. To maintain the element of surprise, she refrained from kicking the door in as had been her plan. Instead, she turned the doorknob hard, breaking the lock. Once inside, she pulled the door closed as softly as she could, hoping to avoid any neighborly interference.

The living room was stark with only four lawn chairs and a folding table for furniture. The exposed brick wall to her left was bare and to her right was a galley kitchen next to the hallway. There were no pictures on the walls, no artwork or decoration of any kind. It looked as though the hunters were squatting there instead of paying rent which was the case, for all she knew. Did these men really live there or were they nomads, stopping in one city to kill as many of her kind as they could before moving on to the next? *Who gives a fuck?* she thought, shaking the curiosity from her brain. *They deserve to die and that's all that matters.*

There were two bedrooms and a bathroom down the hall, two men per bedroom. The sound of one of them snoring was enough to trigger her annoyance so she decided that he should die first. She crept into the room, her footsteps silent on the ratty carpet covered in stains and discarded cigarette butts. She leered at the hunters, their unshaven faces and body odor adding to her disdain. They took no care of themselves or their presumably temporary home. It seemed to her that the only thing these cretins cared about was murdering vampires as evidenced by the stockpile of weapons she could see poking out from under their folding cots that sat on either side of the room's only window. *Definitely squatting.*

She knelt next to the snoring man, glancing back through the dark to make sure his roommate was still asleep. Then, without hesitation or remorse, she covered her victim's nose and mouth with one hand, sank her fangs into his stubble-covered neck, and drank. He startled awake, his muffled screams waking the man across the room. By the time the second man was on his feet, the first was dead, his blood dribbling from one corner of her mouth. The second man pulled a handgun from under his pillow and pointed it at her, shooting her in the head. Her body crumpled to the floor, the sound of the blast bringing the other two men into the room. One carried a rifle while the other brandished a water gun filled with Holy water. The three stood over the downed vampire, pointing their weapons at her.

"Is it dead?" one of them asked.

"Looks like," another responded, kicking her in the side.

"How'd it know we were here?"

The others shrugged, the occupant of the room turning on the overhead light.

"Should we stake it to be sure?"

"Trust me, it's fucking dead."

But, as they stared in horror, the bullet was pushed out, her skull and tissue healing underneath until the tiny piece of wood was fully expelled, falling to the carpet in a bloody mess.

"Guess again," she said, kicking their legs out from underneath them and knocking them on their asses. Shots rang out as she snapped one man's neck and bashed another's head into the brick wall. She was getting hit, she knew, but she didn't care. She didn't feel the pain. Rage filled her so completely, that no other sensation could be felt. The only thing that mattered was revenge and she would have it, no matter the consequences.

Only one hunter was left, the one whose bullet had torn through her brain. He was out of ammo and reaching for a crossbow under his cot when she yanked him up by the hair. She slammed him into the wall, holding him there by the throat, her fangs bared and her eyes black as coal.

CHAPTER 74

"Should I just kill you," she said through her teeth as he trembled in fear. "Or, should I make you the thing you hate? And, if I turned you, how long before your hunter pals come for you? Or, would you despise what you've become so much that you end it yourself?"

He gripped her wrist, trying and failing to break her hold on him. "Wha--what are you?"

She tilted her head in confusion. "You don't know? Are you new?"

"You're no vampire."

He said it with such conviction, she thought she'd giving him brain damage. "How hard did you hit your head on this wall?"

"I shot you in the head with a wooden bullet marked with a cross and blessed by a priest. We've used them to kill stragoi for years. You should be dead."

"Guess I'm just lucky." She dug her nails into his skin, slowly enough that he had time to panic. "I'm bored of you." She clenched her fingers around his trachea and ripped it out, blood splattering on her face and shirt. His lifeless body dropped to the floor with a thud as she backed away, relief washing over her.

Her senses returned, she felt a strange burning sensation in her chest. She looked down at herself and saw her shirt riddled with holes. She was soaked in blood, some of it hers, and as she gasped at the odd, stinging pain, five wooden bullets fell from under her tee shirt. She knelt to pick one up and sure enough, it was marked by a cross. She pulled her shirt away to look at her skin underneath and it was somehow healed.

"Well, that's new," she said to herself, standing and looking around at the room. Four bodies with nowhere to go. There was no incinerator and she couldn't burn them there without potentially harming innocent people in the building. Her DNA would give a lab an 'inconclusive' result, her fingerprints weren't in any database, and she had no connection to these men that an investigator would know to look for. She was safe from being discovered but leaving bodies was a bad practice, especially when what looked to be an animal attack was combined with a broken lock and no animal DNA. Vampires could leave corpses in the woods without issue but in an apartment? Police would have no explanation and it would just take one cop with a disdain for unsolved cases to poke around and stumble upon something they have no business knowing. "What to do with you bitches?"

As she tried to decide between risking innocent lives by burning them or using their guns to shoot off the parts she'd bitten and torn apart, loud banging echoed through the apartment. "Police, open up!" a man shouted.

"Fuck me," she breathed, hurrying to the window and opening it. She looked down at the sidewalk three stories down and sighed. "Well, this is gonna fucking suck." She hopped out, plummeting to the ground. Her feet hit the cement hard, sending vibrating pain shooting up her legs and back. Ignoring her discomfort, she took off around the corner where she'd parked. She got into her car, turned the ignition, and slammed on the gas, squealing away, her only concern getting back to Iman. She needed him more than ever, her grief hitting her like a punch to the gut. "Just a couple of hours," she told herself as she made the drive back to the city, tears forming in her eyes. But, her mission of revenge wasn't over, not by a long shot, and while she needed to let herself grieve, she knew she couldn't do it for long. There was still work to be done.

"Hey," Adia said as Lennon emerged from their room, their face red and puffy from hours of crying. They didn't acknowledge her, instead following their nose to the kitchen. "I made you some mac and cheese. It's on the stove. I assumed the box was yours since everyone else that lives here is on an all-liquid diet."

"Thanks," they said quietly, taking a fork from the drawer, removing the lid, and eating straight from the pot.

"Welcome." She turned off the reality show she'd been watching and crossed her legs, resting her elbow on the sofa arm.

"How'd you know what to do, with the blinds and everything?"

"I had some autistic friends in high school before my mom pulled me out to focus on the craft."

"Craft?"

"Magic."

"Oh."

"I'm really sorry about your friend."

"She was *your* sister. I should probably be the one making *you* feel better."

"Sister, yeah, but I only knew her for like, a day. She seemed nice, though."

"She was...occasionally."

"Maybe you could tell me about her sometime, when you're ready."

They nodded, eyes still on their food.

"She really loved you. She told me you were the best friend she ever had."

Again, they nodded, their bottom lip starting to quiver.

"Is your dinner okay? It's been sitting there for a while."

"It's good, thank you. So, you and Violet got along?"

"Yeah, she helped me get through my transition. Then, she saved me from hunters. She's a hero."

They looked up, their green eyes shining with fresh tears. "Thank you for saying that."

She shrugged. "It's the truth."

They swallowed another bite, leaning on the kitchen counter. "I'm glad you liked her. Most people didn't."

"Maybe most people just didn't get to see her kind side."

"I think you're right about that. So, you liked *her*. What do you think about Rue?"

Her eyes widened. "Oh, she scares the hell out of me."

Chapter 75

"What happened?" Iman asked, rushing to meet Rue as she locked the door to the apartment. He cupped her face and looked her over, his eyes wild with worry. He poked his fingers through the bullet holes in her shirt, pulling them wide to inspect her skin. His voice was low as he tucked her hair behind her ears to get a better look at her face. "Who did this to you?"

"No one still breathing," she said, fighting back tears.

"You shouldn't have gone off on your own. I know you can handle yourself but--"

"I'm fine. Apparently, I can't die, so you don't have to worry."

"What?"

"I don't know." She wiped away a tear, her hands shaking. "Listen, I want you and Ophelia to go stay at Dylan's for a few days. Me and Kenton are working on a list of witches and hunters to fuck up and--"

"Rue, look at me."

She took a breath and looked up at him.

"What's going on?"

She swallowed, realizing how dry her throat was. "I just want you to be somewhere safe in case more hunters show up here."

"Okay, but I can help. I'm--"

She shook her head. "No. You're too new. Besides, I," She paused, choking back a sob. "I want to shield you from this. Killing people, even when they deserve it, it's a burden. The guilt eats at you. Breaks you down."

"You don't have to protect me."

"I do. I do because there has to be someone left when this is all over. Someone I love has to be okay." Her tears now fell freely, streaking down her cheeks in waterfalls of mascara and pain.

He held her face, wiping her tears with his thumbs. "What happened?"

She shook her head, her face scrunching with grief.

"Baby, tell me."

"They found us, the hunters. Last night. They came to the house and," She covered her mouth, afraid to say the words. After a few seconds, she took her hand away and told him, "They killed Violet and my dad."

His eyes widened with shock. "Oh, God," he whispered, sliding his hands under her arms and hoisting her up, her arms and legs wrapping around him as he held her close. "I'm so sorry." He kissed the side of her head while she cried into his shoulder. "God, baby, I'm so sorry."

"They were after Adia. They would've gotten her if Violet hadn't gotten her out of there. They had wooden bullets and--"

"Shh," He kissed her head again. "You don't have to talk about it now." He squeezed her tighter, the pressure of his arms on her back making her feel safe for the first time in days.

"There's more," she said, hopping down and wiping her face. "Adia, Ophelia's witch friend..."

"Yeah,"

"She's my sister."

"She's what? How?"

"Turns out her adopted family, Marley's bunch, kidnapped my mom when she was pregnant with her. They did some freaky mojo on her that made the baby human, killed my mom, cut Adia out of her, and raised her as a witch."

"Holy shit."

"There's more. The other covens decided Adia's blood is the key to curing vampirism so they killed her to get it but her death triggered her dormant vamp genes so now she's one of us and when the covens find out, they're gonna be pissed. Kenton's out with the first of our kind hacking witches to bits and I was just out doing the same thing when all of a sudden, not shit can kill me. Oh, and Ophelia's a witch now, I might've forgotten to mention. She's not the vampire-hating kind or anything, just wanting to feel like she can defend herself. I think that's everything."

"That's...a lot to process."

She nodded in agreement. "The me not being able to die thing isn't for sure. There were just these special wooden bullets that popped out of me like some kind of morbid confetti. The hunter bro was rattled, said I should be dead. Plus, I'm like, ninety percent sure I got staked back at the house so that's weird. I don't know, I'll figure it out, eventually. In the meantime, just please go to Dylan's. I can't take the thought of something happening to you."

"Okay," He kissed her forehead. "I will. But, first, what do you need? Anything, just name it."

"Right now, I need to meet up with Kenton and fuck up some witches. After that, probably four days of hysterical crying followed by two nights of heavy drinking and smoking. The bar will be closed for a while. A week, I think. Oh, also, Lou was a fucking hunter! Can you believe that shit? I'm gonna have to hire a new cook."

"Yeah, I saw his head when you kicked it across the bar, then again when I tossed it in the incinerator."

She cleared her throat, regaining her composure. "Hey, can you tell Ophelia about Violet?"

"Sure but are you sure you don't want to? She's your best friend, I'm sure she'd--"

"I have to get going, besides, if I do it and see relief on her face, I might break her nose."

"Hey, man. What's up?" Dylan said, leaning on the door frame.

"You knocked?" Ophelia asked, walking up behind her boyfriend to address Iman who stood hung back in the hall. "Weird."

"Iman shrugged. "I don't live here anymore, so..."

"Also weird."

He turned his focus to Dylan, hushing his tone just a bit. "Can you give us a minute? We'll meet you at your place."

CHAPTER 75

Dylan turned to Ophelia who nodded. "Sure, man. See you in a few." He kissed Ophelia's cheek and as he walked out, Iman walked in, closing the door and folding his arms, his chin lowered as he looked at the floor.

"What's wrong?"

He tilted his face up to look at her, his eyes dark.

She gulped, her heart rate quickening. "Rue?"

"No. Rue's fine. Well, not *fine*, but dealing...in her way."

Her stomach dropped as the realization hit her, her voice no more than a whisper. "Violet."

He dropped his chin again. "And her dad."

"Holy shit." Her legs went to jelly, barely keeping her upright as her mind raced. "What happened?"

"Hunters showed up at the house."

"Fuck. Rue must be a wreck."

"She's off with Kenton killing witches so, yeah, she's not great. I'm not a hundred percent on how she made it out of there but--"

"What about Adia? Is she okay or is she..." Her throat went dry before she could finish her sentence. Adia was a vampire now and probably still salty with her about not telling her who she really was sooner but she was still her mentor and more importantly, her friend.

"She's okay. Rue took her to hide out at Kenton's place until it's safe."

She blinked. "She, what?"

"She took her to--"

"I heard you, I was just hoping you were kidding."

"Why would I joke now?"

"Because that's the dumbest shit I've ever heard. She threw a brand new vamp, unsupervised, into an apartment with a human so she could take off on her revenge fantasy shit?"

"I guess, but she's not thinking clearly. Her whole family is *dead*."

"Oh, God." She froze for a second, her blood like ice in her veins. "Does Lennon know about Violet?"

"I don't know. Why?"

"Jesus Christ." She grabbed her purse and flung open the door, pushing past him and marching across the hall into his apartment.

"What are you doing?" he asked, following her.

She opened the fridge and snatched two blood bags from it, throwing them into her bag and storming out. "Damage control."

Lennon paced the living room, hugging their arms. Eating had calmed them for a few minutes but they were now in a frenzied state, not knowing what to do or how to cope. They hadn't felt this out of control in years and as their eyes fell to the butcher block on the counter, they remembered how they used to handle feeling this overwhelmed. They pivoted to the kitchen, their steps fast and their arms dropping.

"What are you doing?" Adia asked from the sofa, looking up from her phone for the first time in over an hour.

"Not your concern." They grabbed a knife and pulled it from its place in the wood holder.

Adia stood. "No, what the fuck are you doing?"

"Don't worry, I'm not gonna hurt you."

"I'm not worried about *me*. Come on, put it down."

"Relax, I'm not gonna kill myself." They held the blade to their forearm and took a deep breath.

"No!" Adia rushed toward her but it was too late. They slashed open their skin, just deep enough to allow a small amount of blood to seep from the wound. Adia stopped, her eyes, now black fixed on the seeping fluid. Her chest heaved as her fangs slowly descended, Lennon so caught up in their sense of relief, that they hadn't noticed her face changing. Before they knew what was happening, she'd again lurched forward, fangs bared, a strange hissing sound emanating from her throat.

CHAPTER 75

"Abite!" Ophelia barked, bursting into the apartment, and sending Adia flying back into the living room. She glared at Lennon, still holding the knife. She pointed to it and shook her head, reprimanding them as if they were a badly behaved child. "No." Adia got to her feet and flew toward them, halted by Ophelia's command of, "Subsisto!" She froze in place, Lennon spared from her violent hunger.

"Get back," they demanded. "I know what I'm doing."

"You don't know shit." She waved her hand, the knife dropping to the floor and skidding across the room. As Lennon stood motionless, eyes wide in disbelief, Ophelia took a small container of healing salve from her purse. She opened the little jar, scooped some out with her fingers, and smeared it on Lennon's wound. "Sana." Within seconds, they were healed. "You are not doing this shit again, you hear me?"

Tears gathered in their eyes as they watched her use a dish towel to wipe their arm clean. "Violet's gone."

"I know. But, *I'm* not. I know I'm not your favorite person but I *am* your friend, like it or not. No matter what."

"Oh, God. I'm so sorry," Adia said, her fangs retreating and her eyes going back to normal. I don't know what happened. I lost control. I saw the blood and I just…"

"Went fangs out," Ophelia said, shaking her head. "Solvo."

Adia's body relaxed, released from the spell. She backed to the couch and sat, catching the blood bag Ophelia tossed her. She slurped it down, closing her eyes, her shoulders lowering.

"I figured you'd do something dumb when you heard about V," she said to Lennon, pointing at their arm. "I don't have to give you a lecture about how this was a step back and you need to make an appointment with your therapist, do I?"

Lennon shook their head, crossing their arms.

"All right. In the meantime," She looked to Adia and back and them. "Since neither of you can be trusted and this is the safest place in town, I guess I'm on babysitting duty."

"I'm eighteen!" Adia piped at the same time that Lennon said, "I'm not a child."

Ophelia sighed. "And, I'm not a fucking nanny but here we are."

Chapter 76

Kenton surveyed the room, remnants of witches littering the floor. Fueled by adrenaline and despair and doused in blood, he lumbered through the house, desperate for one more kill.

"Yo," Rue said, plodding down the winding staircase of the Massachusetts coven's mansion. She dropped the heart she'd taken from the Priestess a moment before. "Any left?"

"Just one," he said pointing to the ceiling. "Won't take but a tick." He leaped up, punching through the drywall, grabbing the witch by the ankle, and wrenching her through. She screamed, crashing to the floor in a pile of plaster and hardwood. He gripped her by the throat and lifted her to her feet, his eyes boring into her, their grey-blue hue exaggerated by their bloodshot sclera.

As he fumed, she choked out, "Dimittunt me." He flew back as if by a gust of wind, his leather captain's boots skidding across the floor as he was pushed to the front door. The witch ran in the opposite direction, presumably to flee out the back but Rue was fast, snatching her by the hair and yanking her head from her body.

"Well done, sister," Kenton said, strolling toward her, the witch's spell broken. "Apologies, *Rue*."

"Sister's fine," she told him, offering a weak smile and patting his shoulder. "So, where's Grandpa? I thought he'd want in on this."

He shook his head. "Pressing matters. Admittedly, I was only half listening. Something about ending this once and for all. He's very dramatic."

"Mm," She checked her phone, a disappointed frown turning down her lips. "That's every coven on the list."

"Haven't had your fill of exterminating witches?"

"Not really."

CHAPTER 76

"Neither have I." His phone chimed in his pocket and as he read the text, a twinkle came to his eye.

"What is it?"

"Florin." He put the phone away to look at her. "Fancy a trip?"

The sky glowed an Adriatic blue with pre-sunrise, the vibrant shade filling Adia's bedroom with calming ambiance. Florin stood over her, watching intently as she slept. She was as beautiful a creature as he'd ever seen, and if he had more time, he might indulge in an early morning tryst. As it was, he had little time for pleasure, the war between his kind and witches coming to a head. Perhaps when the battle was over, assuming he'd win, he'd take her for his next bride. He laughed to himself, such thoughts ridiculous even when not spoken aloud. While she fascinated him, half witch, half vampire, and stunning, the two had nothing in common, he was sure. What could come from such a match? Passion, of course. Unbridled ecstasy, no doubt. But, was that enough? Was a physical intimacy all he could continue to hope for? After centuries of one fruitless romance after the next, was he finally ready for something more, and if so, was this girl, barely no longer a child, the person to give it to him? As he pondered this, she began to stir, rolling from her side to her back, exposing a taut nipple peeking out from an ill-fitting cami. He sucked air through his teeth as his eyes went black in arousal. He took a step back, suddenly very aware of his invasion of her personal space. He was behaving inappropriately, and though what he needed to discuss with her was urgent, it would have been far more polite to knock on her door rather than to hover over her bedside like a would-be rapist. But, even as he lectured himself in his mind, he couldn't help but draw closer, his legs against the mattress before he'd realized he'd moved. He bent down, his pale fingers brushing her long hair away from her chest, revealing more of her ample breast. His fangs ached in his gums, begging to descend as his manhood stiffened in his brown leather pants. He wanted to touch her, wanted to taste her. He wanted to sink himself into her, feel her around him, and bury himself deep within her. He wanted to feel only her. He wanted to give her everything and take her for his.

Her eyes fluttered open, his hand brushing her cheek. "Is this a dream?"

"Does it feel like a dream?"

She nodded, her eyes closing.

"This," he said, tracing down her throat and clavicle to the neck of the cami and pulling it down to expose both breasts. "Is whatever you want it to be."

Her lips parted, a ragged breath escaping them as his hand moved down her body, underneath the covers, and into her satin shorts. She spread her legs, inviting him in, his middle and ring fingers wasting no time in penetrating her silken folds. He gently stroked her, her hips moving in the rhythm he'd set. He leaned in closer, running his tongue over her impossibly hard nipples, her light moans of pleasure causing his erection to jump. She bent her knees, drawing her legs up as he plunged his fingers into her, caressing her G spot and taking her left nipple into his mouth.

"Oh, shit," she whispered as she came, her arms stretching over her head. "*Oh, fuck.*" She quaked in his hand, her muscles clenching around his fingers, so wet she was nearly dripping. "Is this real? Is this really happening?"

He didn't answer. Instead, he continued to knead her, faster and with more pressure until her entire body trembled, a howl of pleasure escaping her throat and a flood spilling into his palm. When her body relaxed, he pulled away, his desire pounding in his pants.

She opened her eyes, adjusting her top as she stared up at him. "I've never done that before."

He sucked her from his fingers. "Never come or never felt the touch of a man?"

"Neither." She sat up, cringing at the wetness in her shorts.

"Oh," He cleared his throat, excitement and a bit of shame dancing in his stomach. "Should I not have…"

"No, it was…awesome."

"Oh, good. I'm glad you're pleased."

Her sparkling eyes fell to the front of his slacks where his arousal had made itself exceedingly evident. "I've never actually…I mean, I've seen it in videos but I haven't…" She drew the blanket away and swung her legs over the side of the bed to face him. "I could," She tentatively unbuckled his belt. "Reciprocate."

CHAPTER 76

"That's not necessary," he told her, wanting to be a gentleman but praying she'd ignore his words.

"Maybe not." She untied the thin leather straps of his pants and pulled them down followed by his underwear. Her eyes widened at the sight of his nude form which he took as a compliment. "But, I'd like to give it a shot."

"As you wish."

His eyes rolled back as she licked up the underside of his shaft and teased the head. Soon, he felt the warmth of her wet mouth engulf him, her hand gently massaging his testes. It was hard to believe she'd never done this before as she was sucking and stroking like an expert. His legs shook as he struggled to stay standing, his hands now in her hair as he began to thrust involuntarily. Shocks of pleasure like electricity snapped throughout his body, tingling up his spine and giving him goosebumps. He grew even harder, looking down to see her eyes looking up at him. He drew in a sharp breath and grunted, coming directly into her throat, which seized around him as she swallowed. He staggered back, holding himself up on the nightstand and catching his breath.

"Was that okay?" she asked, wiping the corners of her lips.

He got dressed and flashed her a sly smile. "That couldn't have been any more perfect."

"Did you hear something?" Lennon asked, barging into Kenton's bedroom that Ophelia now occupied.

"What?" she said, sitting up and rubbing her eyes. "No. Go back to bed."

"What do you mean, *back*? It's not even six."

"You're still up? I thought you went to sleep at four."

They shook their head, hovering in the doorway.

"Okay," She got out of bed and turned them around, walking them to the kitchen. "I'll make you some tea."

"I don't need tea."

"Yes, you do."

Florin sat next to Adia on the bed, turning his body to face her. "That was lovely and I do hope for more rendezvous like it but--"

"*But?*"

"It wasn't what I came here for."

"Oh."

"I've come to request your assistance. By now, Kenton has removed the threat to my people in the Americas but the covens of Europe assemble as we speak, led by a witch from New York with immeasurable power. My spies tell me this witch teleported her entire coven to Romania where they're planning a siege on my home."

"Where it all started," she said, causing him to raise an eyebrow. "I've heard the story."

"Yes, well, if they destroy my home, they'll be emboldened. They'll spread across the continent like a plague, massacring every vampire in their path. It'll only be a matter of time before they're back here, putting you and your sister in harm's way yet again. I must stop them in Romania, while they're all in one place. I have an army, of course, but I'd feel more confident with a witch by my side."

She thought for a moment then nodded. "Then, you'll have one."

"Make that two," Ophelia said from the now open doorway.

"Another witch that fights on the side of the vampires?" Florin said, getting to his feet. "And, this one human?"

"As fucked up as it feels to say, vamps have been better to me than any human. Rue's like a sister to me and Adia's my friend and sister witch so, I'm in."

He tilted his head, creeping toward her. "You're no ordinary witch, are you?" She hugged her arms and took a step back as he sniffed the air around her and grinned. "Le Fay."

"How did you know that?" she asked, squeezing her arms tighter.

"You smell like her, underneath the sweet perfume and stench of wolf."

"Her?"

"I met your ancestor once. She hid me from a horde of townspeople. She protected me. Now, it seems, you'll do the same."

She dropped her shoulders. "You knew her?"

"Only briefly. She was preoccupied with her brother's affairs. But, she was tender-hearted and took pity on me when I was alone and in need of sanctuary. I wasn't in a position to repay her kindness but perhaps there's something I can do for *you*."

She clicked her tongue, looking at Adia and back at him. "Maybe there's one thing."

"Name it."

"Rue and Adia make it out of this alive. I don't care what happens or what it takes, they live."

He smiled again. "Noble, loyal, and fiercely protective. You are Morgan's descendant, all right."

"So?"

"I will defend them with my last breath, Miss le Fay."

"That's not my last name."

"Pity. From where I'm standing, it absolutely should be."

Chapter 77

With Lennon finally asleep and Irie standing guard in case they tried to hurt themselves again, Ophelia made a quick stop at the loft before joining Adia and Florin at the airport. She knew Lennon would hate having another stranger in their apartment, but she couldn't risk leaving them alone and she had to help Rue win this war. She owed her for all the times she'd helped her out and with Violet and Booth gone, it was her turn to be there for her for a change.

She headed straight to her bedroom closet where she took the forbidden spell book from its spot in the closet. Florin had a jet on standby so there was no chance of being late but time was of the essence. She could never memorize the whole book in just a few minutes but she wanted to have every weapon possible at her disposal so she used a spell she'd seen online and hoped it would work. Holding the book in her hands and closing her eyes, she recited the incantation, "Sorbeo cognitio intus."

The book flew open, its pages turning on their own. She watched in awe as the words slid from the paper to her hands and up her arms, covering her skin and inching toward her face. She screamed as every page, every spell burrowed into her brain, downloading like a computer virus. Her head throbbed as her mind was overloaded with new information. It was all with her now, ready to be accessed whenever she needed it. Every spell, hex, potion ingredient list, and curse. She repeated the process with every spell book she had, including Adia's family's grimoire. Armed with this plethora of knowledge, she was confident she'd be an asset in the coming battle and that she and her friends would come out of it in one piece, even if Florin didn't keep his word.

CHAPTER 77

"Ophelia's going to help in 'Florin's war', whatever that means," Dylan told Iman, sitting on the dingy sofa and dropping his phone onto the cushion between them. "She says we should hide out here until it's over."

"Rue said pretty much the same thing." Iman flashed his cell's screen to his friend and put it back in his pocket.

"How concerned should I be about this?"

He shrugged. "A witch and a vampire fighting with the strongest vamps ever, including the first? They'll probably be fine."

"I guess but shouldn't we be helping? We're not exactly useless."

"If they needed us, they'd ask. Besides, I thought you had a no-kill policy after what happened at the bar."

"I'm trying but..."

"But, what?"

"I don't think there are words to explain how crazy protective I feel sometimes. Like, psychotically protective. Not long after I got to town, I looked in on you at the bar with your girl. Not sure what was going on but it seemed tense. It took everything I had not to break through the glass and rip her throat out just for making you look a little sad. Soulmate thing, I guess."

"That's fucked up."

"I know."

"I'm glad you didn't. I would've hated to have to eat you."

They both laughed.

He shook his head, his voice turning somber. "After I killed the thing that made me like this, I was so terrified of becoming like him, I swore I'd never kill again. But, the second I thought Ophelia was threatened, I pulled the wolf out of my back pocket like pepper spray."

Iman slapped his back lightly and turned to face him. "If those hunters had gotten past you, they would've killed us all. Or, tried to, at least. You did the right thing."

Dylan took a swig of beer and placed the bottle back on the coffee table. "No, I know. I'm not saying they didn't deserve what came to them. I'm just saying," He paused leaning back on the couch and sighing. "There's no escaping what I am."

He pat him on the shoulder before taking a sip of his own beer. "Yeah, I get it, the guilt. While I was transitioning, two witches came looking for the one that killed me. They were threatening Rue. One of them had her hands on her. She could've handled them on her own but I was all instinct. I ripped those women apart like I was opening presents."

"Damn."

"After that, I went to stay with Rue's dad for a while. I didn't trust myself. Thought I'd turn into some kind of monster serial killer. Mr. Witcomb was like a vampire mentor to me. He was the smartest guy I've ever met so I'll tell you what he told me."

"Let's hear it."

"You are who you've always been. You're just this now, too. You have *enhancements* and with them comes responsibilities. You have to be careful, of course, but no physiological alteration can change one's heart."

After a brief moment of silence, they burst into laughter.

Iman took another drink. "It sounded more profound with the accent."

Dylan pat him on the back and clinked his bottle to his friend's. "To Mr. Witcomb."

"To Mr. Witcomb." He finished his bottle. "I'm gonna miss that guy."

Chapter 78

"Not much to look at," Rue said, her studded-toed ankle boots sinking into the soft ground at the base of the cave's entrance. Even with slip-resistant soles, she'd almost slipped twice climbing the rotted-wood steps to the mouth of the cave which opened under a thirty-foot high hill. Overgrown shrubbery and moss covered everything but the entrance, an opening just tall enough for Kenton to walk through without ducking his head. Inside was a cool fifty-degrees, stalagmites and stalactites making it difficult to navigate, and somewhere in the distance she could hear the sound of water dripping.

"You were expecting a mansion?" Kenton asked, chuckling softly. "Or, a castle, perhaps?"

"Kind of."

"He has one, connected to these caves by a tunnel ending in the underground dungeon where he used to keep...snacks."

"Lovely."

"Hunters have already made an attempt on his life there. We presume that's where they'll make their final stand but this is his real home, the place he was reborn."

They made their way down a few hundred feet of slopes and walkways to a series of tunnels, each one leading deeper and deeper into the pitch. Finally, they came upon a steel door with a combination lock. Kenton entered the code and the door opened to a remarkably modern apartment complete with electricity and running water.

"He's upgraded it over the centuries."

"I can see that," she said, looking over the dimly lit room, a kitchenette on her left, a living room with an electric fireplace and sofa on her right, and at the center back wall, a king-size platform bed with drawers underneath draped in royal purple, its sheets satin and its blanket crushed velvet.

"This is where you'll retreat to if you get badly injured or if things get to be overwhelming."

"I can handle a fight," she told him, not appreciating his lack of confidence.

"I'm aware of your capabilities. My intention is not to insult you but this isn't a dozen or so hunters or a handful of witches. This is war. Trust me when I tell you, you've never seen a battle like what's coming. We'll be vastly outnumbered and I don't need to remind you that our enemy wields Holy water and magic. It's very likely most of us, if not all won't come out of this alive."

"Grim but all right."

"If you find yourself in mortal danger, you *will* withdraw here until it's safe."

She cast him a defiant glare, knowing full well that no matter what happened on the battlefield, she would never back down. Hiding while others fought her battles was *not* her style.

"Swear it. I've already lost my wife. I will not allow her sister to perish as well. Do you understand?"

"Fine," she reluctantly agreed.

"There you are," Florin greeted, ushering Ophelia and Adia into the four-hundred-square-foot space. "I was just coming to show the witches the safe-house. Ladies, my home is your home, should you require it." He placed a hand on Kenton's back and walked him to the door. "Let's rally the troops, shall we?"

He nodded and they left, neither man noticing the livid scowl now on Rue's face. She closed the door, her evident rage causing the two women to take several steps back.

"What in the drunk monkey fuck are you two imbeciles doing here?"

"Um," Ophelia stammered. "Fire with fire?"

"I should lock your dumbass in here with her and cross my fingers she doesn't eat you."

Ophelia flicked her wrist, the door opening and then closing behind an indignant Rue.

"For fuck's sake." She pinched the bridge of her nose. "Fine, but if you get yourself killed, I'm kicking Dylan's ass from Manhattan to Hoboken."

"What? Why?"

"Spite."

"I'll be fine," Ophelia said. "I downloaded every spell I could find directly to my brain. I have easy access to all the magic in the world. You don't have to worry about me."

Adia blinked. "You did *what*?"

"I'm a human in a cave full of vampires, not to mention a witch fighting her own kind. If the target on my back was any more obvious, I'd be a big box store. Of course, I'm gonna come with everything I've got. I'd be stupid not to."

"Being here at all is stupid as shit," Rue lectured.

"Rue," Ophelia put her hands on her friend's shoulders and looked her in the eye. "I love you for caring about me but I promise, I can take care of myself. You don't have to protect me anymore."

"I'm serious about kicking Dylan's ass."

She giggled, hugging her and rubbing her shoulder. "I know."

"I won't kill him...probably. Iman would be salty as fuck."

"He would be." She pulled away. "And, I know he's your favorite."

"And, you," Rue said, giving her new sister an annoyed stare. "Are you sure you're up to this?"

"I'm a witchpire," Adia said. "Vampitch? I'll work on the terminology. Point is, I'm as badass as they come. Besides, Florin practically begged me to join him here."

"No, he didn't," Ophelia said, giving her a puzzled glance.

"Um, he kind of did."

"No."

"Yes, he did."

"There was not one morsel of begging. Not a single crumb."

"Girl, let me have this."

Ophelia shrugged. "Okay."

Rue sucked her teeth, looking from one woman to the other. "Okay, what the fuck is this now?"

"I think she's got a crush," Ophelia blurted.

"I do not have a *crush*," Adia defended. "We have a connection."

"Ew." Rue grimaced. "He's like, a million years old."

"Sure, but you've seen him, right?"

"Yeah, I have. He looks like he's dying of iron deficiency and pretension."

"He's *beautiful* and nice, and he's got the softest hands..."

"Nope," she waved her hands in front of her face. "I can't hear this right now. It's too disturbing. Let's just join the damn vampire army and get this battle over with. I'll give you a lesson on grooming when we're done."

"He's not grooming me. I'm an adult."

She rolled her eyes. "Yeah, okay."

"All right," Ophelia said as they piled out the door. "But, can you guys turn on your phone's flashlights? I almost fell eight times getting down here."

"Just use an illumination spell," Adia condescended.

"I don't know a...wait, yes, I do! Alumbrar." In her hand, a sparkling ball of white manifested. It lit up the cave walls in a fifty-foot radius around them making it easier for all of them to see where they were going, though the vampires could see well enough without it.

"Is that Spanish?" Rue asked, trying to remember her eighth-grade Spanish class.

Ophelia marveled at the shining globe in her palm. "I have no idea."

After a mile-long trek and several texts to Kenton for directions, the women came to a tunnel so narrow, they could barely squeeze themselves through it. On the other side was an open area lit by two dozen torches along the walls. There stood the army of vampires, hundreds of them, armed to the teeth with swords, axes, and guns. They were packed like sardines in the too-small space, their expressions varying from resolved to excited to terrified. Kenton assessed the crowd, taking note of how many weapons of each style were present and making a note of who there seemed unfit to fight. They were all capable warriors, each one having copious kills under their belts. Some, though, looked positively skittish, no doubt having tangled with witches in the past. They would have to be the first line of defense, a stall to the witches' assault. Essentially, cannon fodder. "Poor bastards," he whispered. But, it was a worthwhile strategy, the logic being that they would tire out the witches and hunters they couldn't kill, giving the less daunted vampires more time to plan targeted attacks.

"Kenton," Alexander said, moving through the crowd to meet him, pistol on his hip and scythe in his hand.

He laughed, the first real bit of levity he'd allowed himself in days. "A little ostentatious, don't you think?"

"It's a skosh over-the-top but it promises to put fear in the hearts of those that would do me harm."

"If you say so."

A few yards away, Rue watched a woman wind effortlessly through the horde, her gold dress shimmering in the firelight, its slits up both sides revealing long, slender legs. Her ink-black hair was up in a tight bun, not a hair out of place as she moved. She looked like a movie star with plump, crimson lips and charcoal eyeliner arched at the top and bottom. Rue could tell by the way she walked that she was old, ancient, even. She looked completely out of place and carried no weapons that she could see. What was she doing there? And why was she coming toward her?

"You're Rue," the woman said, more an accusation than a question.

"I am," she said, suddenly feeling under-dressed.

She eyed her necklace, a twinge of jealousy in her eyes. "Your mother wouldn't want you to be here."

"Yeah, well, what's she gonna do? Haunt me? Give me a lecture from the grave?"

The woman smiled, seeming to be amused. "Knowing her, she just might."

"You knew my mom?"

"For a time. My cousin didn't check in much once she joined Shabaka."

"Sh-what-a? Did you say, cousin?"

"Yes. When I heard she'd married and moved to the States, I'd hoped she'd left her old life behind. I was naive. I should have known that a commitment to Shabaka is a commitment for life, even one as long as ours."

"Oh," Rue said, realizing what she must be talking about. "The spy thing?"

She nodded, slipping two fingers between the amulet and Rue's skin, admiring it for a moment before holding her hands behind her back. "Still, she loved you more than herself. Let that be a comfort to you, little cousin." She touched her arm then sauntered away, leaving Rue with a flurry of questions and not a single answer.

"Eshe," Florin said as the woman approached him. "How long has it been?"

"Since you abandoned our people and left my parents to be slaughtered? Three thousand years, give or take."

"You know why I couldn't stay."

"And, yet, here you are."

"This is my home."

"You have many homes. What makes this one any more special than the rest?"

"It's symbolic. You know how witches are with symbolism."

"I am aware but that doesn't answer my question. Why would you risk being here knowing what the consequences could be?"

"I must take a stand. If they destroy the place our kind was created, they'll never stop coming for us."

"And, if you die here--"

"My general won't allow that to happen." He pointed to Kenton, still speaking with Alexander several feet away.

"Him? He can't be more than five hundred."

"Four, actually. I found him on a battlefield in Spain, one breath away from death and still taunting his assailants."

"Mockery isn't strength and it certainly isn't loyalty."

"He killed more men that day than anyone else on that field. He showed no mercy, no hesitation. He put himself between his commander and a borage of enemy soldiers. He's proven himself repeatedly since. He will not fail me, now or ever."

Chapter 79

"They're here!" the lookout shouted, speeding through the tunnel leading to the castle's dungeon and into the space the rest of the vampires occupied.

"Positions!" Kenton ordered, his voice echoing throughout the cavern. The warriors divided into three groups, the first of which lining up at the mouth of the tunnel. "Remember, they're expecting Florin to be alone in the castle. We have the element of surprise on our side, so use it to your advantage. Strike hard and *don't hesitate*."

"Yes, sir!" the crowd chimed.

"On my mark." He raised his arm, silence falling over the vampire army. Rue stood next to him at the front of the second group, noticing Eshe from the corner of her eye slinking into the shadows. He lowered his voice, leaning in to speak into her ear. "Are you ready?"

She nodded, eyes forward as she smoothed a wisp of hair that had unraveled from her braided faux hawk when she'd struggled to squeeze through the final tunnel on her way to the meeting place.

"First wave," he commanded, throwing his arm down at his side. "Attack!"

The group charged into the tunnel, weapons in hand, the only sound their shoes on stone. After a few moments, a ghastly chorus of screams and gunshots echoed in the distance. Ophelia and Adia, who stood at the back of the third group, instinctively grasped each other's hands.

"Don't be afraid," Alexander told them. "Kenton knows what he's doing."

"You sure?" Ophelia asked. "Because that sounds straight-up terrifying."

"He's been through worse, believe me. I've fought at his side on a number of occasions and each time, we've prevailed. He tells me you were a friend of his wife's."

"I don't know if I'd say *friend* but--"

"And, you," he said, averting his gaze to Adia. "Are important to Florin."

"I told you," she said, tapping Ophelia on the arm who fought the urge to roll her eyes.

"As such, you'll both be under my protection. Stay behind me. The vampire/witch will be safe among us but you," He gestured to Ophelia with his scythe. "If you get hurt and start to bleed, *flee.*"

She gulped, nodding, very aware of the fact that she was in a lion's den of bloodthirsty monsters that were one scraped knee away from ripping her throat out with their teeth. She was confident in her abilities but accidents happen. She could trip on a slippery rock in the dark and end up some vamp's lunch. Maybe Rue had been right to worry.

As the screams of witches and vampires in the castle above faded, the second group stood at the ready. Kenton raised his arm but before he could give the order to charge ahead, he was distracted by the clink of metal on stone. He looked down in time to see a canister hit the toe of his boot. Nine more canisters rolled in from the tunnel, all releasing a fog of vapor. It filled the cavern like a low-hanging cloud and by the time anyone realized what it was, it was too late. The vampires choked, coughing as their eyes swelled, tears of blood leaking from the corners.

"What's happening?!" Ophelia asked.

Alexander grabbed his throat, half-hunched over. "Holy water."

"Oh, shit."

"Turn around!" Kenton wheezed at the highest volume he could. The other vampires complied. "Go outside. They don't think we can survive the light of day. We'll march to the castle and catch them by surprise."

One by one, the vampires squeezed through the too-tight tunnel that led to the mouth of the cave. All, but one. Eshe stayed hidden in the shadows, her hand over her nose and mouth.

Ophelia saw the panic on the vampires' faces as they tried to escape the poison air, Adia looking like she might pass out any second. She closed her eyes, searching her mind for a spell that would help. Finally, she found one and called out the word with as much base as her voice would give. "Evaporo!" The fog began to dissipate, clearing out entirely by the time Rue's group made it to the tunnel.

"Nice work," she said as she walked past, giving Ophelia a sense of accomplishment she assumed a child would feel when their parents tell them they've made them proud. Filled with newfound confidence, she stood against the cave wall, letting the vampire army pass into the crevice ahead of her, every ounce of fear draining from her body.

There were a little more than a hundred vampires still in the cavern when dozens of hunters brandishing semi-automatic weapons flooded in. They sprayed the crowd with wooden bullets, injuring many and killing more than twenty.

"Get out," Ophelia told Adia, pushing her toward the crevice.

"I can help," she argued.

"Not if you're dead." She shoved her into the tunnel and turned back just in time to see Eshe emerge from the shadows, using her fingernails to slit the throats of hunters as they entered. She watched in amazement as the woman in the golden gown zipped around the cave, moving so fast it was as if she was teleporting from one man's neck to the next. Bullets whizzed past Ophelia's head, shaking her from her trance. It was time for her to step up. She waved her hand at a cluster of hunters heading for the tunnel she now guarded. They flew back, crashing into the wall, their black camo sleeves catching fire on the torches lighting the space. She didn't want to kill them. She wasn't a murderer. She just wanted to give the vampires a head start. But, while the men were distracted trying to put out their burning comrades, Eshe pounced, snapping necks at lightning speed. By the time the last vampire made it out, the hunters were all dead.

"You're the witch," Eshe said, stepping through the carnage to meet her, not a hair out of place.

"Y-yes."

"I've been told you're a friend of my cousin's."

"Your cousin?"

"Rue."

"Oh. Yes."

"In that case, I'll do my best to keep you alive," She looked her up and down. "Not that you need my protection."

The two shuffled through the tunnel, Ophelia again using her illumination spell to see in the pitch-dark cave system. "Can I ask you a question?"

"Certainly," Eshe said.

"I mean, you do you but why are you wearing that? It's getting filthy."

"Superstition."

"What do you mean?"

"It's been said that the garments you die in are what you'll wear in the afterlife. On the chance that happens to be true, I'd like to live out eternity looking my best."

"You think you'll die here?"

"I think I could die anywhere, at any time. Best to be prepared."

They exited the cave to see a battle in progress; vampires tearing limbs and heads from hunters' bodies, hunters shooting vampires with wooden bullets and Holy water, and witches casting targeted spells at vampires, some causing their hearts to stop and others forcing their blood out through every orifice.

"What the fu--" Ophelia started, but Eshe was already gone, moving like a freight train into the sea of blood and gore, shoving a manicured hand into the chest cavity of a hunter whose Kevlar had been removed by another vampire a few moments before.

"We've been ambushed," Alexander said as he ran up to her, blood spilling down his temple. "They knew we were in the caves. They flushed us out into the day. They knew the sun wouldn't kill us. They were ready. I don't know how they knew."

"Even I didn't know that before I turned. No witch knows that." Adia moved from behind Alexander to stand before Ophelia who breathed a sigh of relief at the sight of her friend alive. "They must have a vamp-insider. A familiar or a vampire themselves. Maybe a really strong psychic? They know we're weaker in the daytime."

"You two stay here, near the cave," he told them. "Use your skills how you can but don't run out into the fight." He turned his back to them, bolting off in a blur.

Ophelia scanned the field below, just fourteen feet down, panic bubbling in her stomach as she searched the crowd for Rue.

"Rue's okay," Adia told her, sensing her fear. She pointed her out at the right edge of the skirmish, using an ax she'd taken from a beheaded vampire to hack into the abdomen of a witch before slicing off a hunter's legs. "She's so badass. Is it weird that she's kind of my new role model?"

"Nah, I look up to her, too...in some ways."

CHAPTER 79

"Where are my witches?!" they heard Kenton shout from somewhere in the distance.

"They're weak in the sun," Adia said. "What can we do to help?"

She thought for a second then took her friend's hand. "Solaris umbra on three."

"Yes!"

"One, two, three."

"Solaris umbra," they said in unison. Overhead, the noonday sun was slowly covered, a false eclipse blocking out most of its radiation.

On the field, Kenton's lip turned up in a menacing grin as his, along with the rest of the vampire's strength returned. He and the others fought now at full force, shredding the torsos of witches and beating hunters with their own rifles. The battle had turned in their favor, the hunters' numbers dwindling and the witches scrambling.

"There!" a hunter shouted, pointing up to where Ophelia and Adia stood. "Kill them and their spell ends!" He and two others raced toward the wooden steps, their guns trained on the women.

"Not on my watch," Alexander said, stepping in front of them, lopping off two of their heads in one clean swoop of his scythe. The third hunter stopped, his face going ghost-white. He turned and ran in the opposite direction.

"You were right about that weapon, after all," Kenton said, walking with Florin to meet him and slapping him on the back.

"You doubted my logic?"

"I'll never make that mistake again."

"Can't let him get away." Alexander took his pistol from its holster and pointed it at the back of the fleeing man's head, pulling the trigger, and shooting him dead.

"Good work, boys," Florin said.

"Thank you, sir," they responded.

"I beg you," Kenton said, looking his sire in the eye. "Stay with your witches. They can shield you."

"I spent centuries hiding. I can't leave you all to fight my war for me."

"Benedictio sanguinis!" a woman called, slinking through the crowd, her eyes fixed on the first vampire as she made the sign of the cross. She wore a black tunic dress and a massive silver crucifix. Her eyes flared with the lunacy of religious fervor, a terrifying sight to anyone with a shred of sanity.

"What did she s--" Kenton started, forgetting his words as he saw Florin's skin flush. "What is it, sire?"

The elder vampire froze, then began to convulse, falling to the muddy ground. His veins swelled, showing thick and red through his nearly translucent skin.

"Sire!"

Alexander flew to the woman, snapping her neck and returning within seconds.

Kenton listened as his sire's heart beat faster, then slowed. "Halfling!" he screamed, getting Adia's attention.

She looked down, away from Rue whom she'd been watching, her priority having been keeping her sister alive. "Oh, God." She hurried down the steps, dropping to her knees next to Florin whose eyes had glossed over.

"What have they done?" Kenton asked, terror tinging his voice.

She looked Florin over, touching his forehead and yanking her hand away. He was boiling hot. "Did you hear the spell? What did she say?"

"Benedictio something."

"*Oh, shit.*"

"What?!"

"She blessed his blood."

"She...*what?*"

"Whoever did this wasn't a witch. She was ordained."

"What are you saying?"

"She...she made his blood...Holy."

"*What?*" Alexander blurted.

"Can you heal him?" Kenton begged.

"I can try, but--"

"There can be no 'buts'," he scolded. "You must heal him, quickly."

"I don't know if--"

"*You have to.* He is the first. If he dies, we all die!"

Alexander's eyes widened. "Is that true?"

"Yes, it's true! He told me not long ago. That's why he went underground, keeping his distance from us all these years. He knew if the witches found him--"

CHAPTER 79

"Okay," Adia said, getting to her feet. "I'll do my best." She pulled Florin up by his arm and flung him over her shoulder. "Vamp strength," she said. "Dope."

"Get to the safe-house and spell the door. Someone will come for you when the battle is won. Stay there until they do and for God's sake, *fix him*."

She dipped her head in half-hearted agreement, unsure if she could do what he wanted. As she climbed the stairs back to the cave, Florin groaned, the sound so quiet, even she had a hard time hearing it. "I've got you," she told him, entering the darkness of the cave. "I've got you."

Chapter 80

"*Vis ager!*" Adia said, throwing her hand up at the door of the safe house as it closed and locked, the air in front of it shimmering with her newly formed force field. She carried Florin to the bed and dropped him there, his eyes rolling back as he convulsed. She could hear his heart barely beating as hers raced, panic making it impossible for her to think. What spell did she need? Was there one at all? She paced for a few seconds and whispered to herself, "How do you reverse sanctification?" She'd never been taught a spell that could do it but he was dying. She had no choice but to make one up.

She stood over him, tearing his shirt open and placing her hands on his chest. His skin was so hot, she instinctively pulled back before trying again, clenching her jaw as she fought through the pain. He writhed under her palms, the bed shaking along with him. "Here we go," she told herself, psyching herself up. "You can do this." She blew out a calming breath and said the words she hoped would save him, "*Facio impious.*"

Tears of blood sprang from his eyes as the tremors grew more violent. She repeated her spell five times, telling herself that she could do this. She didn't need her coven, her sister, or anyone else. No matter what Marley had thought of her, she knew she was powerful enough, blood-born witch or not. *She was enough.*

Suddenly, Florin's body went limp, his pale skin slick with sweat. His veins, once bulging and beet-red, returned to normal and his temperature lowered. His eyes fluttered open, a soft smile turning up his lips when he saw her hovering over him.

She whipped her hands away, her brows stitching together as fear and worry were replaced with agitation. "If you die, we all die?! What the hell were you doing out there?"

CHAPTER 80

He laughed with a cough as he tried and failed to sit up. "Not thinking things through, it would seem."

She rolled her eyes. "I fixed your blood but I think the herbs it would take to heal the damage to your organs would either make you sick or kill you and since everyone's life, including mine depends on you not kicking it, you'll just have to wait for your vampy self-healing to do its thing."

He laughed again. "Thank you. I'll be fine in a few moments, for a time, anyhow."

"What do you mean, 'for a time'?"

"I was cursed. Every time I take a life, a part of me dies. Several of my organs have failed already. Nothing I can't live without but it won't be long before my heart goes and when it does, so do we all."

Her breath caught in her throat. "And, you didn't think that was pertinent information?"

"One problem at a time."

Hands on her hips, she mulled it over. "You can't just, like *not* kill people?"

"Of course. For two hundred years I avoided it, drinking only what I needed from lovers or volunteers. But, when the witches sent their hunters, I was given no choice."

"Fuck," she whispered.

"My hope is that this day will end the witch threat and I can return to my quiet life of pacifism."

"That's sweet but delusional."

"Excuse me?"

"They'll never stop coming for you," she told him. "Even if we manage to kill every witch and hunter here, there will always be more. Covens are bloodlines, information, and spells passing down from one generation to the next. You don't think the witches here have daughters and nieces that know about you? Sons and nephews being trained as we speak to be the next generation of hunters? Elders too old and frail to be here teaching those kids? Not to mention the pregnant witches. I'm sure there are hundreds of *them*. Winning this war won't solve the bigger problem. It'll only kick the can and we'll be having this same conversation in twenty years."

He arched a brow, looking impressed. *He thinks I'm smart*, she thought, butterflies in her stomach distracting her for a second. She shook it off. "So, two things need to happen. First, we need to lift that curse. Without the witch that did the spell, there's no real way to remove it but I *could* transfer it to something else. It'd have to be alive, though." She looked around the room, hoping to find a rat or something but the place was clean of vermin. "Ostende te." On her words, a cave spider skittered out from under the sofa, its champagne color making it stand out against the gray of the stone floor. "That'll do." She scooped up the creature, holding it between her hands so it couldn't escape, and recited the spell: "Ab hoc vir huic aranea movet hoc maledictio."

"What are you--" But before he could finish his sentence, a cloud of shimmering darkness seeped out of his chest, floating over him and away, covering Adia's fingers and sinking between them. She opened her hands to see the cloud settling around the spider and absorbing into it, the curse successfully moved.

She put it down and it scurried away, unaware that its next meal would be its last. "And, the second thing--"

"You've lifted my curse," he asked, propping himself up on pillows. "That easily?"

"Yeah, but that wasn't the hard part. Like I was saying, the second thing that needs to happen is we have to break this you-die-we-all-die nonsense. If the witches know about that, eventually they *will* find a way to kill you, and no offense but that's not a ship I want me and my sister going down on. The problem is, the spell requires the blood of the demon that created you and I have no idea how to get that."

"The witch," Florin said. "The le Fay. She can summon demons, as her ancestor did. She only needs to learn how. Perhaps when this is all over."

"Okay," she said, feeling relieved. "So, we'll back-burner this until the fighting's over. She's needed out there and I can't leave you alone in case someone figures out where you are. The shield should hold but a skilled enough witch *could* get it down. Better to hide and live than go out there and risk the end of all vamp-kind."

"You're right, of course. We should stay." His smoky eyes twinkled in the dim light as he stared her down, some color returning to his cheeks. "Thank you, Adia, for saving my life."

The way he said her name sent sparks flying in her chest, warmth spreading from her chest to her lower abdomen. "Y-you're welcome," she said, her voice husky with arousal.

"Would you like to sit?" He patted the spot next to him on the bed. "We could...talk."

"Talk?" Her throat went dry, having a conversation with him being the last thing on her mind. He was gorgeous, even after having almost died. His long curls hanging to his shoulders, his exposed torso, thin but muscular, his lips wet and inviting. Memories of the night before flooded her mind as lust flooded her panties. His kisses on her neck. His mouth on her breasts. His hands on her body. It was the worst time for this, she knew. The enemy could find them any second. But, if they'd be dead by the end of the day, anyway, waiting was just a waste of time.

"If you'd like."

"I don't want to talk."

"All right."

"You like me, right?"

He sat up as much as he could, leaning in a reclined position against his pillows. "Very much."

"Why? You don't even know me."

"When you've been alive as long as I have, you learn to read people. I knew from the moment we met that you were kind, gentle, and ferociously powerful. Your loyalty to a sister you've only just discovered shows incredible character. Your beauty is unparalleled but your intelligence and bravery are what keep me captivated. My affection for you grows with every second spent in your presence. I only hope that I'm not alone in my adoration."

"You're not," she said, unzipping her jeans and pulling them down. She stepped out of them and her underwear, her sage green blouse falling just over her hips.

His pupils dilated. "Are you sure this is what you want? I don't want you to feel pressured."

"I don't."

"The battle continues above us. It would be understandable if you felt a sense of urgency but there is no rush. And, in my current state, I'm afraid I won't be much of a lover."

"That's fine." She slinked out of her top and unhooked her bra, tossing it to the floor. "I'd rather be in control right now, anyway. And, I don't feel rushed. Just frisky."

His fangs descended and retracted as his erection bulged. She pulled off his pants and underwear exposing nine inches of manhood. His breathing quickened as she positioned herself on top of him, letting only the tip of his pulsing cock touch her inner folds.

"Adia," he said, his voice low, almost a growl. "You must be sure."

"I am." She leaned down, brushing her open lips against his, her tongue flicking the roof of his mouth. He ran his hands up her thighs as she slid up and down his shaft, stopping for a brief moment when his head met her clit, circling one over the other. She sat up, leaning back, gliding herself down to his balls and up again, using her fingertips to hold him in place. Her skin flushed, warming as tingles of pleasure coursed through her body. His hands moved up her legs to her backside, gripping the cheeks and pulling them slightly apart, opening her up. She shivered with delight, bending to kiss him again, deeply and slowly, running her fingers through his ebony locks. She continued to tease, pressing his throbbing cock against his stomach as she moved, letting him in just a little before sliding herself back down, her clit kissing his balls.

"You torture me," he groaned, kissing her neck and squeezing her ass, pulling the cheeks farther apart, his fingertips brushing her outer lips. "Don't stop."

She grazed the stubble on his jaw with her teeth, pressing her breasts against his chest, persisting in her movements until her pussy ached with longing. She suckled at his neck as she allowed him inside, little by little, stopping with every inch before sinking him further, her opening stretching to fit his abundant girth. When he was fully inside, she gasped, so full it was almost painful.

"Are you all right?" he breathed in her ear.

She nodded, unable to speak, her inner walls palpitating around him. When she got her bearings, she tentatively lifted herself until only his tip was left inside. She sighed with relief before dropping back down, plunging him deep within her. After a few seconds, the pain began to fade, leaving only pleasure more intense than anything she could have dreamed of. Her instincts took over, her hips rocking as she found her rhythm, her skin tingling as he wrapped his arms around her. He buried his face in her neck as she sped up her movements, her arms around his shoulders, holding tight to him as she began to come.

"Oh, my God," she panted, this orgasm twice as intense as the one from the night before.

"I assure you," he said, tangling his fingers in her hair and pulling her head back. "He had nothing to do with this."

She moaned as he sank his fangs into the side of her neck. Waves of rapture rippled through her as she came again, her walls clenching around him as he drank. She'd never felt anything like it, the sheer euphoria of bliss meeting bite. For a split second, she wondered if he would take too much. Would she die? But, she didn't care. Whatever the consequences, whatever the price, they didn't matter. Nothing mattered. Not the war, not her life. All there was was him.

Chapter 81

Ophelia watched the battle from her spot on the hill where she felt safe, shouting "Expungo incantamentum!" to cancel witches' spells before they could take effect, giving the vampires time to defend themselves and each other. From where she stood, it looked as if the vampires were winning, with more of them left alive than witches and hunters. Hours had passed since the start of the fight, the sun now beginning to fade from the sky, the eclipse spell no longer necessary. She began to feel a sense of relief, thinking it would all be over soon and that she'd be on a plane back to Dylan in no time. But, just as the sun dipped from view and the sky went from orange to deep blue, a shrill voice echoed up to her.

"Traitor!" the blond witch shrieked, running toward the entrance of the cave.

Before Ophelia could think, she was off her feet, floating inches off the ground, unable to breathe. *Is this bitch force-choking me?* she thought, more surprised than afraid.

From below, the woman called to her, "You side with *them*?! You're a disgrace to your kind!"

Her vision faded as red and blue sparks filled her periphery. She was losing oxygen fast. She had to do something and soon. "Aperta," she managed to choke out, the ground behind the witch opening up in a jagged chasm. The witch stumbled as the ground shook and with one telekinetic push, she fell back, dropping into the massive hole.

"Claudere," Ophelia said, waving her hand in the direction of the trench, closing it up as she lowered back to the ground, the witch's spell broken.

Meanwhile, a group of hunters had Rue surrounded. As she fought one off, another shot her in the back. "Shit!" she cried, holding the wound. "That stings like a motherfucker!"

"Wait until you feel *this*," a third hunter said, pointing his rifle at her head.

"I don't think so, mate," Kenton said from behind, snapping the man's neck. The hunters turned their guns on him but he and Rue made fast work of disarming and disemboweling them.

"Thanks for the save," Rue said, catching her breath.

"Don't mention it." He looked over what was left of the crowd. "How many of them are left would you say?"

She took a quick headcount. "Three hundred or so, give or take."

"More than double our numbers. All right. Let's--" He stopped, noticing six hunters, armed to the teeth, heading toward the cave.

"He's in there!" One of them called to the rest.

"They're going after Florin," Kenton said. "I must stop them." He darted off in a blur, Rue following. He sped to cut them off, blocking them from the entrance. "Tsk, tsk, tsk." He folded his arms. "This place is not for you."

"He's right," Rue told them, parking herself behind them, causing them to turn. "No douches allowed."

Without a word, the men opened fire, spraying wooden bullets into Rue's abdomen before she could make a move against them. She raced around them, snapping necks and using hunters' bodies as shields on her way to the cave. Kenton, too fought the men, bashing one of their heads into the ground until his skull shattered and throwing another into a nearby tree. When the men were all dead, Rue wiped blood from her forehead with the back of her hand.

"Not chatty, were they?"

"No, not particularly."

"What's wrong?" Rue asked, noticing how pale he'd become.

"Nothing, really," he said, taking his hand away from his chest to reveal four bullet wounds. "Just dying is all." He dropped to his knees, then lay himself on his back, a single tear trickling from the corner of his eye and blood trickling from his mouth.

"Oh, shit," she said, kneeling next to him. She examined his wounds, knowing just by looking at them that his heart was shredded. "Ophelia!"

"It's all right, love," he wheezed, holding her hand, his face serene, almost happy. "I'm going to find my wife." His eyes rolled back and closed with his final breath as Rue covered her mouth, tears slipping down her cheeks.

Ophelia flew down to meet her, placing a hand on her shoulder. "Holy shit. I'm so sorry."

She opened her mouth to speak but nothing came out as a voice in the distance rang out, "Cor!" She went white, falling face-first into her brother-in-law's chest.

"The fuck?!" Ophelia yelped, seeing the gaping hole in Rue's back, an empty cavity where her heart used to be. She screamed, the earth quaking beneath her. She trembled, rage and heartbreak filling every cell in her body. Rue was her friend, her family, and, the witches took her away from her. She felt like she might throw up or explode. Lost in her anger and grief, she didn't notice the birds fleeing from the trees or the sky changing from near-night blue to blood red. She didn't see the leaves and twigs floating from the ground and she didn't hear the gasps from the crowd or the screams. Pulse racing and eyes wild, she spun around to see the witch that cast the spell holding the dripping organ, her flaming hair mussed, her makeup smeared.

"What are you doing?" the murderer asked, dropping the heart.

She glared as more witches stepped forward, the fighting coming to a halt as witches, hunters, and vampires alike lost their footing in the magnitude seven earthquake. She seethed, growling through gritted teeth, "Lamia supernatet to salus."

On her word, the remaining vampires floated from the ground, hovering high above the rest of the crowd and drifting to the hill above the cave. There they stayed, exchanging looks of confusion as they watched.

"Why do you protect them?" the red-haired witch asked. "You're a witch. You should be fighting with us, not against."

"She made her choice," another witch said, stepping in front of her. "Sanguis coquere."

Ophelia began to feel hot, her blood heating up in her veins. Sweat beaded at her temples but she maintained her stance and her stare. "Finis." Her temperature returned to normal but her rage remained. "Abjice." The witch flew back, knocking people over as she was flung through the horde, past the clearing, and into the woods.

The red-haired witch approached her, desperation in her sapphire eyes. "It doesn't make sense. Why would you turn on your own kind? What do you want?"

A muscle twitched in her jaw, her heart shattering in her chest as she said the words, "I want my friend back, you bitch. *Ardeat.*"

One by one, the witches went up in flames, their flesh sizzling away as they screamed. Hunters, too burned, their grenades as well as the gunpowder in their weapons booming in a symphony of explosions. Blood and gore sprayed in all directions, bits of men crackling in the blaze like meat fallen in a campfire. She watched her enemies burn in the inferno she'd created without a shred of remorse, too angry to feel guilty. When she was satisfied they were all dead, she called out, "Subsisto," ending the earthquake and returning the sky to its original color. From above, she heard the vampires cheering, their merriment signaling to her that the fight was over...finally.

When the bodies of the burned were nothing more than charred bones, she looked to the now visible stars and took a deep breath, almost coughing from the smoke. "Goddess of the West," She took another breath, suddenly feeling how exhausted she'd become. "You know what I want. So mote it be." She spit on the grass in front of her, disappointed that it didn't reach the murderer's corpse. Clouds filled the sky and with one resounding clap of thunder, a torrent of rain fell, extinguishing the flames. More cheers from the vampires as they skidded down the hill, Ophelia muttering, "Finis" to stop the rain.

Alexander dropped his scythe at the sight of Kenton, tears filling his eyes.

"I'm sorry about your friend," she said, patting his shoulder.

"And, I yours."

She nodded, tears of her own welling as he patted her hand.

"I was quite sure this was going to end with *me* on the ground in a puddle of my own blood. I never thought it'd be him." He turned his face to her, wiping away his tears. "Thank you for standing with us. We owe you a great debt."

Her breath caught in her throat before she could respond, her eyes saucering.

"What is it?"

She couldn't speak. She couldn't breathe. All she could do was point.

He followed her gaze to see the wound in Rue's back...healing. "Bloody hell."

"Fucking shit," Rue said, coughing as she got up on her knees.

"What the…"

She stood, turning around to see them staring at her, eyes wide and mouths agape. She looked over their shoulders to see the blackened battlefield, brows furrowed in confusion. "How long was I out?"

Ophelia grabbed her by the shoulders, pressing her ear to her heart, shocked by the sound of it beating. "How the fuck?!"

Rue gently pushed her away. "What's with you?"

She threw her arms around her, crying tears of joy and relief into her shoulder.

"Okay, this is an unreasonable amount of affection during a witch war."

She laughed, pulling away and stepping aside to give her a clear view of the field. "It's over. You should rest. Let's get you to the safe house."

"I'm fine. How…did *you* do this?"

"She did," Alexander told her. "She saved us all."

Ophelia smiled. "Fried 'em like wings on game day. How are you alive?"

"Um, I'm a vampire?"

"Girl, I watched your heart get yanked clean out."

"She grew a new one," Eshe said, walking to meet them.

Rue glared at her. "What?"

"Your mother's amulet. It belonged to Sekhmet, enchanted with rejuvenation magic. The wearer is made immortal regardless of injury. It's been passed down from mother to daughter for millennia."

She touched her fingertips to the necklace. "You're telling me if my mother hadn't given it to me, she'd still be alive?"

"Perhaps, but if the coven that murdered her had been unable to do so, they may have come for you." She touched her cheek, a glimmer of affection in her eyes. "Your mother protected you, and continues to do so." She walked off, leaving Rue reeling.

"No," Florin whispered as he and Adia exited the cave. Standing over Kenton's body, gray eyes shining with tears, he looked to Alexander for an explanation.

"I don't know how this happened," he told him, fresh tears pooling.

"Hunters," Rue said. "Six of them stormed the cave, looking for you. He blocked them, we fought them. We killed them but not before they shot us."

"And, you were saved by the scarab, yes, I see."

"You know about that?"

"Of course. Who do you think commissioned the witch to create it?"

"I'm sorry, *what*?"

"Once upon a time, I loved your ancestor, Sekhmet. When the hordes came for her, I did what I could to save her."

"If only you'd loved your wife so," a voice called from the field. It was the High Priestess, back from the forest where Ophelia had flung her.

"You're not dead?" Ophelia asked.

"I can change that," Alexander said, picking up his scythe.

"You'll do no such thing," Florin said, pulling him back, his eyes fixed on the approaching witch.

"She's one of them, sire."

"Yes, I know."

"What's happening now?" Rue asked.

Florin stared as the woman got closer, waving his hand to signal the others to get behind him. They did so, exchanging bewildered glances.

"Florin," the High Priestess said. "How long has it been?"

"S--Silviana?"

"*What*?!" Alexander exclaimed.

"Who's Silviana?" Adia asked.

"His wife."

"His *what*?"

"She died thousands of years ago...I thought."

"No," the High Priestess told him. "Not Silviana. I'm just," She ran her hands over her chest. "Living in her."

Rue crossed her arms. "Okay, I'm confused."

"Explain yourself, witch," Florin demanded.

"*Witch*." She laughed, tossing her dark curls over her shoulder. "Not even close." She held her hand in front of her, making a fist in the air. Florin went down, dropping to his knees and clutching his chest. "*Your wife* was a witch. I'm something else entirely."

"Procul!" Ophelia shouted to no effect.

She laughed again. "I'm ready for you this time, witch. I've warded myself from your magic. And yours," she said, addressing Adia. "You're his new plaything. I hope you're not too terribly disappointed when I rip him apart. If I'm remembering correctly, he *is* an excellent lover."

"Get away from him!" Adia ordered, but she ignored her, turning her attention back to the first vampire.

"Who are you?" Florin wheezed, blood dribbling from his nose.

"You know, I've been stuck in this body for so long, I can't seem to remember."

"Why are you possessing my wife?"

"Possessing?! You think I wanted this?" She dropped her fist and smacked him across the cheek, bloodying his lip. "It was your precious wife that did this to *me*."

"What are you talking about?"

"Oh, I know the story she told you. I was here," She poked herself in the temple four times. "Listening, watching. She convinced you that she freed me. That I was so grateful I did her a favor by raising you, turning you into *this*, this abominable creature. That I did so voluntarily. *She lied.*"

"She wouldn't lie to me. She was--"

"A monster! Worse than you know. She didn't request that I bring you back from the depths. *She forced me.* Trapped and subjugated me. Invited me into her then *locked me in*. Even when she died and her soul fled, I remained."

He shook his head. "That's not true."

"How do you think you were able to have children? A vampire and a human can't procreate. Not unless, of course, the human is harboring something *other*."

"Holy shit," Rue muttered.

"Not quite."

Florin tried to stand but she waved her hand in his direction, forcing him back to his knees. "It wasn't all bad, for a time, once the bitch was gone. I sewed seeds of chaos, watched as witches attacked vampires and vice versa. I enjoyed the torture and the killing. I was thrilled when the humans took it to the next level, creating hunters the way governments create armies. Running experiments. The depravity! It was glorious."

Alexander gripped his weapon. "You've been watching us all suffer for entertainment?"

"You would judge *me*, vampire?! What of the humans?" She began counting on her fingers. "Sports, reality television, poisoned air and water, *war*. What they do to themselves and to one another is-- no. I will not justify myself to the likes of you."

"To be clear," Ophelia interjected. "You're a *demon*?"

"I thought that was obvious."

Her lip turned up in a half-grin, her hands falling to her sides, palms up. "I'm a le Fay. I can control demons."

She scoffed. "Are you stupid or just hard of hearing? I said I warded myself against your magic."

"Oh, I know. But, *they* didn't." She closed her eyes, reciting her ancestor's spell. "Gythreuliaid dod allan." Thunder rang out above them, clouds covering the stars as the ground once again trembled.

"What the fuck?" Rue said, holding onto her sister for stability.

"Yes, child!" Florin shouted over the rumbling of the earth. He looked up at the demon and smirked. "Never underestimate a le Fay witch."

"Gwnewch fel y gorchymynaf."

A chasm appeared behind the demon, the ground tearing itself open, the stench of sulfur making the vampires gag.

"What have you done?!" the demon screeched.

Ophelia waved her hand in front of her nose to dissipate the smell. "Call it a family reunion."

Dozens of disfigured creatures clawed their way to the surface, body parts falling off and black slime pouring from their noses and mouths.

"Holy fucking shit," Rue said, covering her nose with her shirt.

"Cymryd hi!" Ophelia ordered.

"No!" the High Priestess begged. "I won't go back! Stop!" But, the demons came for her, grasping at her legs and climbing up her body, knocking her to the ground under their weight.

"Wait!" Adia said, pushing past the others. Braving the demon horde, she made her way to the High Priestess, grabbed her by the hair, and bit into her neck, sucking out a mouthful of blood. She hurried away, hiding behind Ophelia.

"Cymryd hi!" she repeated. The demons did as the witch commanded, dragging the demon, and Silviana's body along with it, into the abyss. When the creatures had all slithered into the fissure and they could no longer hear the High Priestess crying for help, she waved her hand at the ground and said, "Claudere." The ground closed and stopped shaking and Florin regained control of his body. Ophelia brushed her hands together and sighed. "You're welcome."

"*Damn, bitch*," Rue said, clapping her on the back. "Remind me never to mess with you."

"I don't think I'll have to."

They both laughed and they all breathed sighs of relief. It was finally, actually over.

Adia frantically dug in her pockets, then in Ophelia's.

"What are you doing?"

She pointed to her puffed cheeks.

"I believe she needs a vessel," Florin explained.

She nodded emphatically.

"Uh, okay," Ophelia said, reaching into her back pocket and pulling out a plastic bag of healing salve. She dumped out the contents and handed the bag to her friend.

She spit the demon's blood into the bag and sealed it shut.

"What was that about?"

"I'll tell you later *if* the spell works."

"What now?" Rue asked.

Florin led the group to Kenton's body, his eyes mournful as he looked him over. "Now, we bury our dead."

Chapter 82

The remaining vampires pulverized the dead witches' bones, scattering the dust in the wind for fear of their residual magic. They buried their fellow warriors in the forest surrounding the cave, each plot marked with a simple stone. They were buried as heroes in the place their kind was created; all but one.

Ophelia, Adia, Rue, Alexander, and Florin brought Kenton back to Connecticut to be laid to rest next to his wife in the place she'd called home. While Ophelia filled Dylan and Lennon in on what had transpired that day via text, Adia tried her best to comfort her bereaved sister. They stood several yards away as Florin and Alexander said their goodbyes, both men stone-faced and quiet as they stood over their fallen friend's fresh grave.

"He was my fiercest warrior," Florin said, hands clenched in front of him, white knuckles showing the sorrow he didn't allow his face to. "Certainly the strongest, bravest, and most loyal soldier I've ever known." He turned his head to look at his progeny who'd let two wayward tears slip from his bloodshot eyes. "If it's any consolation, he died saving my life and thereby the lives of us all. He was a hero and will forever be remembered as such."

"Thank you, sire," Alexander said, not lifting his head, letting the salty streaks of grief remain on his cheeks. "He was a true friend."

"And, as honorable as they come." He wrapped his arm around his shoulders and the two stood in silence, allowing the melancholy to enrobe them in its icy darkness.

"We'll have to bring Lennon to say goodbye to Violet," Rue said, wiping her red, puffy eyes.

"When they're ready," Ophelia agreed, putting her phone in her pocket.

"Are they okay?"

"No, but Iman is with them, helping pack up their stuff to move back in with me. They don't actually like me all that much but I'm familiar, so..."

Rue caught a glimpse of Adia staring at Florin across the garden, unable to stifle an exasperated sigh.

"What?" Adia said, feigning innocence.

"I can't believe you're banging Grandpa."

"Will you stop this, already? He's like, twenty."

"He's a billion years old and you're barely out of diapers."

"I'm eighteen."

"Yeah, eigh*teen*. *A kid*. And, full offense, he's a relic."

Adia looked to Ophelia for backup. "Is she always this judgmental?"

She smacked her lips. "Yup."

"Oh, my God, it's not that big of a deal. I mean, come on, Rue. How old was the first guy *you* hooked up with?"

"Age appropriate."

Ophelia choked on her own spit. "He was your first?!"

"Are you judging me, too?"

She threw her hands up and shook her head.

"Listen," Rue said, sniffing. "Do what you want. It's your life."

"Thank you."

"It's just fucking me up that I can't kill him when he screws you over."

"That's dark. And, pessimistic. You don't know," Adia defended, glancing at Florin's backside. "He could be the one."

"Yeah, okay," she mocked.

"You can't *kill* him," Ophelia inserted. "But, I *could* magic his balls into a volcano."

"I like this idea."

"Or, make his dick rot like expired meat until falls off."

"Even better."

Adia was horrified. "Jesus Christ, guys."

Rue's eyes lifted with an idea. "Could you conjure up some human food in his intestines so he'd have crippling diarrhea? Oh, or do a spell that makes his eyes explode in his head every time he looks at another girl? Like, they'd grow back but every damn day, *splat*!"

Ophelia thought for a second. "Both sound doable."

"Okay, okay," Adia said. "After I get some sleep, I'll do the separation spell. If he turns out to be a dirtbag, you have my permission to kill him. Just none of that other stuff. It's gross."

Rue gave her a wink. "That's my girl."

"You realize I *can* hear you," Florin called to them.

"You realize I don't give a fuck," Rue called back. "Be on your best behavior with my sister or we *will* have words."

He placed a hand on his chest. "On my honor."

"Mm, hmm." She turned her attention back to Adia. "It's getting early. We should get you home."

"Actually, I was thinking about staying here for a while. This is where my family, my *real* family comes from. I'd like to get to know the place. Plus, I feel...safe here. If that's okay."

"Of course, it's okay." She pulled her in for a hug. "Just don't do anything smutty in my childhood bedroom. I don't want to have to bleach my mattress."

She let a soft laugh escape her lips. "I promise."

Ophelia walked into the loft to find Iman standing over the dining table breaking down boxes.

"Rue?" he asked, not attempting to hide his worry.

"She's okay," she told him, closing the door behind her. "She's downstairs calling the beer guy. Said she wants to open back up next weekend."

"Probably needs the distraction."

"She cried the whole way back from Romania and the whole car ride back here. I think she's gotten it out of her system."

"Her entire family was murdered. I don't think 'out of her system' is a thing."

"Probably not but you know how she is; tough as nails even when she's falling apart."

"I do."

"Lennon in their room?"

He nodded. "They're not doing well. I tried to give them a hug but you know how they don't like being touched by anyone but…"

"Yeah. I'm gonna go check on them. You should head downstairs."

"Already on my way," he said, putting the box cutter in its place in the kitchen drawer. "What about you? Are *you* okay? I don't see any cuts or bruises."

"Yeah, I got out of there more or less unscathed. I thought I'd feel guilty about killing all those witches but I'm fine. Guess it just hasn't hit me, yet."

"If it does and you need to talk, you know where I'll be."

She nodded, watching him walk out the door. When it was closed, she locked it and headed down the hall to Lennon's room, tapping three times on the door before pushing it ajar. "Hey," she said.

"Hey," they said, taking a hoodie from a box and putting it in their dresser. "It's over?"

She nodded.

"You okay? Rue?"

"Yeah, we're good. Or, as good as can be expected."

"Kenton?"

She shook her head.

They dipped their head, still not making eye contact.

"How are you feeling?"

"Shitty. But, I'm done with the knives."

She arched a brow.

They looked over at her, eyes fixed on her mouth. "Promise."

"Good."

They stopped unpacking, hugging their arms and chewing on their bottom lip. "I know I don't make it easy but I *do* appreciate you caring about me."

"I know. And, you never have to apologize to me for being who you are. I'm kind of a dick, too sometimes."

"That's facts."

She offered a small smile. "Did you eat today?"

They shook their head.

"Okay, I'll order that pizza you like."

They raised their brows. "Extra breadsticks?"

"Of course, what, did we just meet?" She turned to go.

"Ophelia, wait."

"Yeah?"

"Thanks."

She flattened her lips, making eye contact with them for the first time since Violet's death. "You're welcome."

Iman got to the bar just as Rue was ending the call with her supplier. Still in her blood-stained clothes, she turned to face him, the streaks of old tears through dirt and gore on her cheeks breaking his heart. He sped toward her, scooping her up, her limbs wrapping around him as she rested her head on his shoulder.

"What do you need?" he asked, squeezing her tighter.

"This," she said, sniffing back fresh tears. "Just this."

When they'd finished eating, Lennon returned to their room to finish unpacking and Ophelia brushed her teeth, showered, and did her full hair routine. She then rifled through her closet, finding a black handkerchief dress and black leather lace-up knee-high boots. She got dressed and applied her eyeliner and two-toned lipstick, black with a deep red center. She gave herself a once-over before heading to the door, exhausted but too excited to see Dylan to sleep. To her surprise, when she opened the door, he was already there.

"I was just leaving to come see you," she said, letting him in and closing and locking the door.

"I got your text. Glad to see you in one piece. And, what a piece it is."

She giggled, doing a twirl. "You like?"

"I love."

"The outfit or me?"

"Why not both?" He gave her a peck on the lips. "So, how'd it go?"

"I basically saved the day, so."

"Did you?"

"You doubted me?"

"Never."

"Were you worried?"

"Out of my mind."

"Well, I'm fine, as you can see."

"Yes, I can," he said, looking her up and down. "So, what happened? You give those evil witches what for?"

"I absolutely did. Won the vamps their war, got their king kissing my ass. I don't know if I'd say I'm proud of what I did but I'm definitely proud of who I am."

"As you should be." He kissed her again.

"Speaking of who I am, I've made a decision. Tomorrow, I'm going down to County Court to officially change my name."

"Really? Why?"

"My dad was a piece of shit abuser and it's always kind of bothered me every time I have to write it down or someone calls me by that last name. It feels like a burden I've had to carry. But, no more. From here on out, I'll be known as Ophelia Marie le Fay."

He nodded in approval, not that she needed it. "I like it."

She smiled, feeling more like herself than she ever had. She pulled him close, sliding her hands down his body and giving his ass a gentle squeeze. "So…"

"So, what?" he asked, eyes twinkling.

She tilted her head and rubbed her body against his. "Wanna make out?"
The End

About Author

Leslie Swartz is an American urban fantasy, dark romance, and horror author. An ex-poet, her writing influences include Shakespeare, Poe, Dickens, Don McLean, and Freddy Mercury. Her works include Betrayal of Blood and award-winning, The Seventh Day Series. When she's not writing, she enjoys reading, spending time with her family and dog, Tilly, and listening to music.

Connect with Leslie
@leslieswartz333
on
Tiktok
Facebook
IG
Lemon8
Clapper
And X

Also By

The Seventh Day Series – Complete
Read Now on KU
Seraphim
Nephilim
Elohim
Cain
Alukah
Coven
Sinclair

Printed in Great Britain
by Amazon

2fcf9756-dffb-41fd-b909-e07152b01dfaR01